AN AMISH LOVE

Three Amish Novellas

Kelly Long, Kathleen Fuller,

Beth Wiseman

THOMAS NELSON
Since 1798

Kelly: For my husband, Scott, the husband of my youth and now, still, twenty-four years later, my love of all time

Kathy: To my daughter, Sydney, I love you!

Beth: To my sisters—Laurie, Valarie, Melody, and Dawn

* * *

© 2010 Kelly Long, Kathleen Fuller, and Beth Wiseman

All rights reserved. No portion of this book may be reproduced, stored in a retrieval system, or transmitted in any form or by any means—electronic, mechanical, photocopy, recording, scanning, or other—except for brief quotations in critical reviews or articles, without the prior written permission of the publisher.

Published in Nashville, Tennessee, by Thomas Nelson. Thomas Nelson is a registered trademark of HarperCollins Christian Publishing, Inc.

Thomas Nelson titles may be purchased in bulk for educational, business, fund-raising, or sales promotional use. For information, please e-mail SpecialMarkets@ThomasNelson.com.

Scripture quotations taken from the King James Version.

Publisher's Note: This novel is a work of fiction. Names, characters, places, and incidents are either products of the author's imagination or used fictitiously. All characters are fictional, and any similarity to people living or dead is purely coincidental.

ISBN 978-0-7180-9767-7 (Mass Market)

CIP data is available upon request.

Printed in the United States of America

17 18 19 20 21 QG 5 4 3 2 1

GLOSSARY

ab im kopp: off in the head, crazy
aenti: aunt
aldi: girlfriend
appeditlich: delicious
bruder: brother
bu: boy
daadi: grandfather
daag: day
daed: dad
danki: thanks
Derr Herr: God
dochder: daughter
dumm: dumb
dummkopf: dummy
Englisch: a non-Amish person
familye: family
frau: wife, Mrs.
freind: friend
geh: go
grosskinner: grandchildren
guder mariye: good morning

gut: good

hatt: hard

haus: house

kapp: prayer covering or cap

kinn, kinner: child, children

kumme: come

lieb: love

maed, maedel: girls, girl

mami, mamm: mom

mammi: grandmother

mann: man

mei: my

meiding: shunning

mutter: mother

narrisch: crazy

nee: no

nix: nothing

Ordnung: the written and unwritten rules of the Amish; the understood behavior by which the Amish are expected to live, passed down from generation to generation. Most Amish know the rules by heart.

Pennsylvania *Deitsch:* Pennsylvania German, the language most commonly used by the Amish

rumschpringe: running-around period when a teenager turns sixteen years old

schwester: sister

sehr gut: very good

sohn: son

vatter: father

ya: yes

Contents

A Marriage of
the Heart

Kelly Long

CHAPTER ONE

W hat did he do?"

Abigail Kauffman clutched her hands together and took a deep breath of the cool fall air that drifted in through the open kitchen window. Her father's repeated question and ominous tone had her doubting her actions. But once she began a plan, she usually stuck with it.

"I said . . . he . . . well . . . just made me feel a little uncomfortable with the way he was kissing me . . . and touching . . . and I . . ."

Her father's face turned beet red. "I–I will . . . have words with him."

He clenched and unclenched his heavy hands, and Abigail felt a surge of alarm and deeper indecision.

"Father . . . it was nothing, in truth."

"I will have words with the bishop and that—boy, and then he'll marry you."

Abigail's eyes widened, the swiftness of her impulsive plan ringing in her ears. "Marry me? But I don't love him!"

Her father regarded her with flashing eyes. "Love has nothing to do with marriage. We will go to the bishop and Dr. Knepp, and we will see this solved before morning." He drew a shaky breath. "When I think of that boy, just baptized today, just accepted into the community, and then . . . daring to trespass upon your honor . . . Go upstairs and dress in blue. I will bring the buggy round. Hurry!"

Abigail turned and fled up the steps. *"Dress in blue."* The color for marrying. She gained her small bedroom and slammed the door closed behind her, leaning upon its heavy wooden support. She saw herself in her bureau mirror, her cheeks flushed, her *kapp* askew upon her white-gold hair. She wondered for a strange moment what a mother might say right now, what her mother, whom she'd lost at age five, would say in this situation. Her heart pounded in her chest. This situation . . .

In truth, Joseph Lambert, with his lean, dark good looks and earnest eyes behind glasses, had done little more than speak to her . . . and annoy her. She'd just wanted to pay him back a bit for his casual dismissal of her usually touted beauty . . . and now she was going to have to face his mocking scorn. For she had no doubt he'd laugh outright at the suggestion of any impropriety between the two of them. They'd only been a few dozen feet from where everyone was gathered for the after-service meal, and it would be a bold young man indeed who'd risk anything, let alone steal intimate kisses . . .

But her father had believed her . . . or he'd believed the worst of Joseph Lambert, at any rate. She snatched a blue dress from a nail on the wall and changed with haste. She might as well get it over with, she thought with grim practicality. And yet there was one small part of her that wished things might be different, that wished she might truly be on her way to a marriage that would allow her to escape Solomon Kauffman's rule and cold distance.

She hurried back down the stairs and went outside to where the buggy waited. Her father started the horse before she barely had her seat, and as they gathered speed she tried to marshal her thoughts. She saw her life as it had been ever since she could remember . . . cold, lonely, devoid of love and even simple conversation. Somehow, the *Englisch* world outside seemed so much less austere and confining, so much less full of unspoken pain.

She let herself escape for a moment by imagining marriage to Joseph Lambert. Not only would it get her out from under her father's thumb, but she would be able to keep house, or not keep it, any way she pleased. They wouldn't have to live with her father—at the picnic she'd heard Dr. Knepp, the popular *Englisch* physician, say something about making his barn over into an apartment for Joseph. It would be just as easy to fit two as it would one. She didn't take up that much space. Her possessions were scant. She'd learned how to make two blouses last for a season and the secrets of turning out old dresses to look new again.

No, she'd be little bother to Joseph Lambert. She chewed a delicate fingertip in her nervousness. It might work out well, the more she thought about it . . .

. . .

Joseph Lambert eased a finger in between his suspender and white shirt and drew a breath of satisfaction at the comfort of the simple Amish clothing. He was tired, exhausted from the day and its happenings, but deeply happy. He glanced around the small barn that Dr. and Mrs. Knepp had done over for him and shook his head at the kindly generosity of the couple. To have a bed with clean sheets and a handmade quilt was more than he could have dreamed of in the past years—but to have his own space, his own home, was a gift from the Lord. He lay down in the bed and stared up at the wooden slat ceiling.

The faces of the people he'd been introduced and re-introduced to that day spun in a pleasant blur in his mind. Even the beautiful face of Abigail Kauffman was a delight to recall, though he knew he'd frustrated her—and deliberately so. She was too pretty for her own good, he thought with a smile, remembering their brief conversation near an old oak tree in the orange and red glory of early autumn. He'd had to thread his way through a throng of young admirers to reach the girl as she perched in the refuge of the tree, but the other boys had soon melted away under his penetrating look. But when he'd not shown the apparently expected verbal homage to her beauty, all of her pretense disappeared. He'd been thoroughly charmed by her indignation. But he knew that a girl like Abigail Kauffman was far beyond his reach, especially with a past like his . . .

He sighed and, dismissing the day from his mind, began to pray, thanking *Derr Herr* for all that he'd been given and asking for clarity of direction for the future.

He'd just fallen into the most restful sleep he'd had in days when a furious pounding on the barn door startled him awake. He grabbed for his glasses.

"Kumme!" he cried, scrambling to button his shirt, thinking it must be some urgent matter for the doctor. Instead, once he managed to focus, he saw Bishop Ebersol and another giant of a man crowd into his small living space, followed by the doctor and his wife.

The giant strode toward him, clenching and unclenching hamlike fists. "Scoundrel!" The huge man growled the word.

Who is he? Joseph frantically sifted through the identities of people he'd met that day.

"Now, now, Solomon. Let the boy have a breath." The bishop inserted himself between Joseph and the larger man.

"A breath? A breath is not what he wanted to have today—"

"Everybody ease off!" Dr. Knepp snapped, and there was a brief break in the tension.

"What's wrong?" Joseph asked.

The bishop cleared his throat. "Son, I just welcomed you back into the community this afternoon."

"Yes, sir."

"Well then, what were you doing dallying with Abigail Kauffman not half an hour later?"

"What? Dally—Abigail Kauffman?" Joseph suddenly recognized the strapping man as Abigail's irate father and took an automatic step backward.

"That's right . . . try and run!" Mr. Kauffman roared.

Dr. Knepp snorted. "Solomon, where exactly will

the boy go in two feet of space and his back to the wall?
Just let him explain."

Joseph knew by instinct that a simple denial of any
behavior was not going to satisfy Mr. Kauffman. He'd
had to defend himself enough in the past to recognize
that there were consequences at stake here, and he
didn't like to think where they might lead.

"We talked a little—that's all," he exclaimed.

Mr. Kauffman exploded. "At least be man enough
to admit that you dishonored her with your kisses and
your hands!"

Joseph's mind whirled. What had the girl been saying? And suddenly, a thought came to him—clear and
resonant. Here was a provision from the Lord to have
a girl like Abigail Kauffman in his life. It didn't matter
that she'd obviously lied; she was young. Perhaps her
father had forced her into it . . .

In any case, his impulsive nature took over. To deny
the claim would mean the scorn and possible dismissal
of his place in the community, something he'd worked
too long and too hard to reclaim. And even though the
little miss probably had a reputation for being wild,
a woman's word, her honor, would always be more
valuable than a newcomer's. To admit to the accusa-
tions might mean recompense as well, but perhaps not
as bad, not in the long run anyway. And he'd have the
beautiful Miss Kauffman eating out of his hand for
defending her honor.

He lifted his head and met Mr. Kauffman's blazing
eyes. "All right. I was wrong. I behaved . . . poorly with
Miss Kauffman. I apologize."

"There. He admits to it. I'll get Abigail from the buggy. You can perform the ceremony here."

"What?" Joseph and Mrs. Knepp spoke in unison.

Mr. Kauffman's lips quivered, and for an instant Joseph thought he might burst into tears. "The wedding ceremony. The bishop will do it here, now. When I think of what Abigail must have been feeling . . ." He swiped at his forehead with a rumpled handkerchief.

"Solomon, let Joseph explain," Mrs. Knepp urged.

"*Nee . . . nee* . . . I will see her done right by—" He broke off and tightened his massive jaw. "To think it's come to this for my girl." The big man turned and left the barn.

Joseph resisted the urge to speak. He hadn't expected a marriage . . . a courtship maybe, but a wedding? "Do I have a choice?" he finally asked the bishop.

"Not if you want to stay. *Nee*. Mr. Kauffman will go to the community to defend what he thinks is right."

Joseph nodded and ran his hands through his hair. Things could be worse; he could have been denied a chance to come back. A marriage seemed a worthy price for what he'd received that morning. "All right. Let's get this over with."

Dr. Knepp spoke with low urgency. "Joseph, I know you didn't touch her. You didn't have time, and you were in plain view. Tell the truth—the deacons will vote—"

"*Nee* . . . I'll not take the risk. It means everything to me to be back here, to find and keep a place, a home . . ."

Mr. Kauffman was sliding the barn door back open.

"Seth, do something," Mrs. Knepp begged in a whisper.

Dr. Knepp shrugged his shoulders. "The boy agrees."

"As well he might," Mr. Kauffman growled. He pulled Abigail into the room behind him. She was dressed in blue, and she kept her eyes downward.

Joseph considered the girl as the faces of the deacons flashed behind his eyes. He wondered for a moment how they would vote before he snapped back to awareness as the bishop joined his hands with Abigail's.

She wouldn't look at him. Maybe she was being driven to this. The thought gave him pause; she should have the right to choose.

"Do you want this?" Joseph asked, speaking to the top of her *kapp.*

She gazed up at him then. Her blue eyes were dead-steady calm. He'd seen eyes like those behind the wrong end of a gun, and now he wondered if she'd had a forceful hand in the matter herself.

"*Ya,*" she murmured, dropping her gaze once more.

Her hands were ice cold though, and he rubbed his thumbs around the outside of her fingers as he listened to the bishop speak in High German. It was like a dream, really. The light from the lamp Mrs. Knepp held high threw strange shadows across the corners of the room and made crouching things out of chairs and the table.

He was asked the simple, life-binding questions that would make Abigail Kauffman his wife, and his answers were steady—as were hers. And then it was over.

It seemed anticlimactic. There was no kiss or hug of goodwill between the couple. And once he saw his job done, Mr. Kauffman seemed to shrivel to a shell of a man whom the bishop had to pat on the back for reassurance.

Joseph let go of her hands and finished buttoning his shirt, ignoring the way Abigail's eyes strayed to his chest. He tensed his jaw and walked over to his new father-in-law.

"Mr. Kauffman—it's my plan to be a help and not a hindrance to you all of my days. I know you farm alone with some hired help. You won't need as much help anymore. I need the work, and I'm good at it. Abigail and I will take up living with you in the morning, with your permission, of course."

"*Ya*," the older man said, clearly surprised. "*Ya*, that would be *gut*; I would miss Abigail about."

Joseph nodded; it was done.

. . .

Abigail tried to regulate her breathing as she listened to her dreams of freedom being swept away like a house on a flood plain. It didn't matter at the moment that Joseph had defended her honor and married her out of hand. She opened and closed her mouth like a gasping fish as her father and the others filed out the door, leaving her alone with her new husband.

Joseph pulled an extra quilt and pillow from a shelf near the bed and knelt to lay them on the floor. She watched his strong, long-fingered hands ease each wrinkle until he looked up.

Then she said the first thing she could get out. "Are you *narrisch*?"

"What? For saving you from your lies? You can have a lifetime to thank me properly."

She strode to face him, stepping on his clean quilt. He gazed up at her.

"I don't care about the lies! Are you crazy to have told my father that we'll live with him? You didn't even consult me."

He choked out a laugh. "And you consulted me about this wedding, wife?"

He gave a swift tug to the hem of her skirt, and she lost her balance, landing beside him. He leaned very near to her, and she felt her heart pulse in a curious sensation.

"Just tell me your father forced you into this," he whispered, reaching to brush a stray tendril of white-gold hair behind her ear.

Abigail couldn't bring herself to lie again, not when she was feeling so strange and fluttery inside. She shook her head. "I cannot tell you that."

He ran a finger down her cheek. "I thought not; I just wanted to hear you say it. But why me? I'm genuinely curious."

She looked down at her hands, clenched in her lap. "I–I just thought that you were handsome, and I . . ."

"Please," he sighed, running a hand beneath his glasses and then studying her again. "Just tell me the truth."

"You came over," she burst out, "and then you just talked and mocked me. You treated me like a little girl, and then I thought that if you had to marry me, it might work out well for both of us. You're used to the *Englisch* ways, and I want the *Englisch* ways. We could live here and you could work for Dr. Knepp, and I could—"

"You could do exactly as you pleased, is that it? Without Daddy to interfere? With a husband who was on his knees this afternoon, begging for community, and not likely to make a fuss?" His voice was level but mocking.

"*Ya*," she whispered in misery.

"Well then, you got more than you bargained for, my sweet." He lifted her chin so that she was forced to meet his dark eyes. "I don't want the *Englisch* ways, Abigail Lambert—that's why I came back. And I will honor this marriage and the responsibilities it entails. And my expectation is for you to do the same."

He didn't wait for her to respond, but dropped his hand and lay down on the quilt, rolling over to his side and clutching the pillow to his middle.

She stared at his broad back.

She wanted to smack him a good one. Instead she sniffed and, with as much dignity as she could muster, rose to go and lie sleepless and chilled on the comfortable bed of her wedding night.

CHAPTER TWO

Abigail watched the sunlight break through the two small windows of the little barn and shifted in silence to stare down at her husband lying on the floor. The quilt was tangled about his lean hips, and one suspender had slipped down in his sleep. His hand was curled under his dark head, and he still held the pillow close to his middle, almost protectively. His glasses lay on the hardwood floor near the edge of the quilt. She let her appraising gaze trace down the fine bones of his face and the firm set of his jaw. He looked younger without his glasses, and she wondered how old he was, exactly. She herself had just turned twenty. She'd have to ask him.

She'd lain awake all night thinking, praying, and discarding plans as to how she might make him agree not to move back to her father's house. The best she could come up with was to try and get Dr. and Mrs. Knepp's support, since they'd gone to all the trouble of making up this place for him. She slipped like a wraith from the bed and tiptoed over Joseph, sliding open the well-oiled door and heading for the main house. She saw a light in the kitchen and knocked on the back screen door.

Mrs. Knepp appeared and cracked the door. "Good morning. Come in."

Abigail stood in the warm kitchen, her eyes tracing the neat shelves and the display of order that permeated the place.

"Are you hungry?"

"*Nee* . . . well, just a little."

"Seth's out on a call. I'll have something ready for you in a minute."

"*Danki.*" Abigail slid onto the bench at the table and watched the older woman's deft movements at the stove. She knew Mrs. Knepp did not especially like her but also knew that the doctor's wife would not be unkind. Abigail ran a small finger around the grain of a knothole on the table and bit her lip, for once unsure of what to say.

"How was your sleep?"

"*Ach*, fine. Just fine." Then she flushed as she realized that it was to have been her actual wedding night, and she sounded a bit too casual.

"Joseph's a good man; you're a very fortunate young lady." Mrs. Knepp placed a plate of scrambled eggs, bacon, grilled mushrooms and tomatoes, and toast in front of her.

Abigail's stomach rumbled and she bowed her head over the plate before beginning to eat with pleasure.

"*Ya*, a good man who deserves his own start in life. He's—much too kind to feel he's dishonoring my father by not going to the farm to live. But if we stayed here, he'd have so much more opportunity for independence."

Mrs. Knepp seated herself opposite with a cup of coffee in her hands. "Joseph's had all the independence he could ever want. What he needs now is a good family."

Abigail pursed her lips and wiped daintily at them with her cotton napkin. This wasn't going the way she wanted.

"Children too," Mrs. Knepp said in a casual tone. "They help give a man stability."

Abigail choked on her eggs and flushed scarlet.

"Oh, I'm too forward, I suppose, having been married so long . . . but you'll be more than a blessing to Joseph when you're carrying his baby."

There was a faint irony in the other woman's tone, and Abigail thought that she was being got at.

"I suppose you're right," she remarked airily, recovering her composure. "I'd love to give him twins."

"Now that would be a pleasant surprise," Joseph murmured from behind her, and she jumped.

He leaned close and pressed his mouth to the side of her neck, and she almost slapped him away. She caught herself just in time.

Mrs. Knepp laughed with seeming approval. "Ah, perhaps it is young love."

"Indeed," Joseph agreed, moving to sit next to his wife at the table. But when Abigail met his eyes, she saw the mockery in their dark depths.

"Are you hungry, my love? *Kumme*, share my plate," Abigail offered, pushing it between them and aiming an accurate sideways kick to his shin with one of her small, old-fashioned, hard-soled shoes.

He coughed.

"I do hope you're not unwell," she said with wifely concern.

"I'm fine. Just fine." He was forking up the remainder of her eggs with a set jaw. "Have you packed your things?" he asked. "But then, you had so very little with you last night."

Her pleasure melted away at his words, and she seethed in silence.

"This reminds me . . ." Mrs. Knepp rose. "I have a wedding gift for you." She bustled out of the room despite protests from both of them.

"Are you going to be angry at me for a very long time?" Abigail asked in a whisper.

"Very." He pushed the empty plate away.

"Well, fine. I will await your good grace; I have the gift of patience." She lifted her small, prim nose.

"You're going to need it." He reached a hand up and began to massage the back of her neck just as Mrs. Knepp reentered the room with her arms full.

Abigail tensed at his touch, but he didn't remove his hand. She struggled to concentrate on the beautiful quilt the older woman spread open before them.

"It's a double wedding ring pattern," she said with fond remembrance. "It was given to Seth and me from an Amish woman when we first started out, and I'd like it to be the first gift that you two receive as a married couple."

Abigail felt addled, between the woman's kindness and the warm hand at the nape of her neck. "It's lovely," she squeaked.

"More than that." Joseph dropped his hand and rose

to go around the table to embrace Mrs. Knepp, quilt and all. "It's a gift of the heart, and we'll cherish it. Won't we, Abby?"

Abigail blinked at the nickname she hadn't heard since childhood and nodded weakly. She felt sad for some reason. Her mother had called her Abby. To her father she was always the very formal Abigail. But here was her husband speaking to her with endearing words, though she knew he didn't mean a syllable of it. Probably he thought that the shortened version of her name would irritate her. Well, she wouldn't give him any satisfaction on that score.

She rose to help Mrs. Knepp fold the quilt and took it into her arms. *"Danki,"* she said and meant it.

Mrs. Knepp cleared her throat. "All will be well, you will both see."

They thanked her again for breakfast, then Joseph held the door as Abigail passed by him, carrying the quilt outside. She dreaded going back to the little barn where she had so hoped to escape to a new home.

"Best to hurry on," he said. "It will only take a few minutes to gather my things."

Abigail sat down at the little table and watched him pick up the quilt and pillow from the floor.

He raised an eyebrow. "How did you sleep?"

"Not well . . . I was thinking."

"I dread to imagine." He pulled a satchel from a shelf and stuffed a few Amish clothes inside.

"Where are your *Englisch* clothes?" she asked.

"Burned them last night, before I went to sleep—or I guess before I was awakened."

She nodded. Clearly Joseph was determined not to go back to his previous way of life. Well, that could change . . . even though she'd never found the courage within herself to leave the community.

"I'm ready," he announced, and she noticed for the first time the dark stubble on his face.

"Aren't you going to shave?"

He laughed. "I'm married, remember, little wife? It's my wedding ring I wear on my face now, and you'll just have to bear with the roughness on your tender skin until it grows in."

She lifted her chin a notch. "I do not think that it will be an issue."

"Oh no? Just wait until the details of our wedding get around . . . which should be happening right about now. We must present the loving couple to everyone, especially to your father. Although I know that Amish PDA is limited at times."

"PDA?"

He gave her a mocking smile. "Public displays of affection. We're not supposed to make out as obviously as the *Englisch* do, but Daddy is still going to expect to see something in the comfort of our own home."

She flushed at his use of the expression *make out*; she knew it from her secretive *Englisch* magazine reading. But she also realized that he was right. Her father would expect a normal happy couple, or he'd have more than something to say.

"So don't stiffen up like a schoolgirl every time I touch you."

"What else do you expect me to do?"

He leaned over the table and put his face very close to hers. He smelled clean, like fresh pine soap, and she couldn't help but look into his eyes.

"Relax," he murmured. "Just relax." He leaned closer still and she half closed her eyes, her heart beating in expectation of his kiss.

He laughed and lifted his satchel. "See, you can do it. Just pretend I'm one of those beaus of yours, surrounding you at the tree."

"Indeed," she said in a haughty voice and rose with her arms still full of the quilt.

He slid the barn door open to the full light of day, and she blinked at the sudden brightness.

"Well, Mrs. Lambert, let's go home."

CHAPTER THREE

Joseph turned his horse and buggy out of the Knepps' driveway and started down the highway. He glanced sideways at Abigail. She still held the quilt, clinging to it like a child. He hardened his heart at the thought. Although he'd chosen his own fate to be entangled with hers, it would still probably benefit him to remember that she was no child, but a very stubborn, manipulative woman, who was also his wife. He half smiled at the thought. He'd never imagined himself married to an Amish woman. When he'd lived as an *Englischer* he'd had girlfriends aplenty, and one in particular who was going to regret his leaving the outside world behind. But even Molly, with her riotous red curls and charming freckles, hadn't been enough to keep him from going home.

He glanced at Abigail's heavy white-blonde knot of hair hidden beneath her *kapp* and the thick tilt of her lashes as she appeared to study the passing road beneath the horse's hooves. She was indeed beautiful. But it was a beauty used as a device, and he told himself that it would be good to remember that as well. Still, he had to live with her somehow. He decided to try polite conversation.

"It's a fair day," he offered.

She nodded.

"The horse's name is Carl. Can you drive?"

She glanced at him with a wry twist to her soft lips. "Of course. Can't every Amish girl drive?"

They pulled into the Kauffmans' lane a few minutes later, and he noticed her chest heave with emotion against the outline of the quilt.

"Well, we're home."

"*Ya. My* home."

He pulled up close to the farmhouse and reached a hand to find hers beneath the pile of quilt. "Our home."

She pulled away. "You needn't pretend now; there's no one to see. Father will be in the fields."

"I wasn't pretending. It is our home—for life, as the Lord wills."

She didn't reply, and he jumped down to come around and hold his arms up to help her. She tossed him the folded quilt and leapt neatly down.

. . .

Abigail refused to give in to the tears that threatened as she entered the familiar bleak kitchen. There was none of the warmth and order of Mrs. Knepp's home here. Joseph Lambert had a rude awakening coming if he thought she kept house as well as other Amish women. She didn't, or felt that she couldn't, at any rate. No matter how many times she tried to cook or clean, things always ended up worse off somehow.

But Joseph merely glanced around and lifted his

satchel. "Where's our room? I'd better head out to the fields as soon as I can."

She blushed at the thought of letting him into her tiny girl's bedroom, but there was no choice. Father slept in the master bedroom, and the other bedrooms were not as well turned out as they might be. She led the way up a narrow staircase and entered the first door on the right. He followed her inside, and they both gazed at the narrow single bed, where her dress from yesterday's picnic lay in careless abandon. The remainder of her clothes hung in a neat row on the common nails beside the bed. The small window gave off a bit of light, illuminating her bureau and the clutter of hairpins and extra *kapps* that lay there.

There was barely enough room for him to lie on the floor beside the bed, she thought, ignoring his gaze. She moved to bundle up the dress and smooth the bright quilt beneath it.

Joseph set Mrs. Knepp's quilt at the foot of the bed. "Is it cold at night up here?"

"Very," she replied. "Look, I'm a lot of things, but I'm not completely selfish. We can take turns sleeping on the bed."

He gave her a wry grin. "Nice of you, but the floor is fine for me. I've slept in much worse places."

"Where?"

"Hmm?" He was unpacking his satchel. "Where? *Ach*, abandoned buildings, strange apartments full of people I didn't know, on the street . . . lots of pleasant memories."

"At least you had a choice."

"A choice? *Ya*, I guess I had a choice, to keep being a fool or to come home. You have that same choice."

She looked at him in alarm. "What do you mean?"

"You know exactly what I mean . . . when do you plan to stop being a fool and come home?"

"You told me yesterday at the tree that this place was never your home—until now. Well, it's never been mine either."

"Fair enough. All right . . . no more chatter. I need to put on work clothes. Do you want to stay?" He reached for the buttons on his shirt, and she glared at him before making for the door and closing it with a slam.

She went down the stairs, feeling breathless and unsure why. She wandered into the kitchen and thought of the endless rounds of meals that were to come. Now she'd have to try harder at cooking, she supposed, and frowned at the thought.

A quick knock on the back screen door broke into her thoughts, and she went to open it. It was Katie Stahley, one of her school friends, who'd already been married for over a year. She carried a covered dish and had an air of suppressed excitement that let Abigail know the wedding news was out.

"Please, *kumme* in, Katie."

Katie glanced around the kitchen, then gave an urgent whisper. "Is it true, Abigail?"

"*Ya*." Better to have it out and over with.

"*Ach*, I knew it. He was looking at you after worship service yesterday. I mean . . . well . . . here. I made bread pudding, extra raisins."

Abigail took it gratefully, thinking that it would

help supplement lunch. She heard Joseph's footsteps on the stairs.

Katie giggled.

Abigail rolled her eyes as Joseph entered the kitchen. He came to her and put his arm around her waist, giving her a quick squeeze. "Guests already?" He arched a handsome dark brow, and Katie giggled again.

Honestly, Abigail thought, *the girl has been married for a year already*.

"This is Katie—a friend from school days."

Joseph shook her hand, then turned Abigail to face him. He kissed her full on the mouth, once and hard. "Got to get out to the fields with Father, my love. Katie, a pleasure . . ."

He was out the door, leaving Abigail's cheeks and mouth burning. She bit her soft bottom lip, resisting the urge to touch it. She'd only ever had a beau steal a kiss on her cheek, never full on her mouth. She felt a queer sensation in her knees and turned a fuzzy smile on Katie.

"*Ach*, Abigail, he's so handsome and still so *Englisch*. I don't think Matthew's ever kissed me like that in front of anyone. Joseph Lambert must really love you."

The fuzziness drifted away, and Abigail almost denied the other girl's words before she realized how bad that would seem. Fortunately, though, her flushed cheeks must have satisfied Katie, because her friend left with a smile on her face.

Abigail took the cover off the bread pudding and poked a childlike forefinger into the top crusty layer. Delicious. Now if only she could come up with something to complement its goodness. She sighed and went to the back door and out into the sparse kitchen garden.

. . .

Joseph walked past the small herd of grazing dairy cows to where his father-in-law was mending a stone fence. Even from a distance the man looked mammoth as he lifted and balanced the heavy stones. Joseph wished he had work gloves, but there was nothing to be done about that now. He picked up a rock and wordlessly handed it to Mr. Kauffman. The older man accepted it and hefted it into place while Joseph got the next one ready.

"How is Abigail?" Mr. Kauffman grunted.

"Well, sir." Joseph wasn't sure what else to say. He supposed the old man was referring to the wedding night, and he could not offer any more details without lying.

"Looks like her mother, she does."

"I'm sorry that you lost your wife. I remember that time . . . I must have been ten or so."

Mr. Kauffman stared at him a moment, then spoke slowly. "*Ya*, I lost her, in more ways than one . . . But she would have done right by Abigail—the child needed a woman's touch."

The two men lifted and placed the rocks in a steady rhythm as Joseph pondered the words of his father-in-law.

"Can I ask why you never remarried?"

"*Nee.*"

Joseph grinned and nodded. "Sorry."

"No apologies needed."

"You've got a nice operation here. You must work sunup to sundown."

"*Danki.* I . . . appreciate your help. I've not had anyone about the place but Abigail and the hired help since Rachel . . . well, since Rachel's been gone."

The way he said his wife's name was odd, almost as if he feared it somehow, but Joseph decided not to press any more questions.

"You're more than welcome."

They continued to repair the wall in relative companionable silence until Joseph's stomach grumbled, and he noticed that the sun was high overhead.

"You are hungry?" Mr. Kauffman asked.

"*Ya.*"

His father-in-law sighed. "We'll go for lunch, then. Hopefully Abigail will have it prepared." But there was something in his tone that suggested the possibility was doubtful.

Joseph shrugged off the thought and walked in silence beside the older man back to the house.

CHAPTER FOUR

An amazing abundance of well-wishers dropped by with both curiosity and casseroles, and Abigail had her choice of the very best of the community's cookery to set up for lunch. She surveyed the table with satisfaction, admiring the clutch of wildflowers that resided in the center next to the steaming chicken and dumplings and the broccoli-and-cauliflower cheese bake. Potato salad, plum preserves, and peach jelly sat on heavy plates next to a fresh loaf of bread. A mayonnaise cake with white icing piled high completed the ensemble.

The scrape of heavy footsteps on the back porch broke her reverie, and she swept the kitchen with a hasty eye to double-check that all unfamiliar dishes were out of the way. For once she wanted her father to think that she was succeeding at something domestic. That she didn't want to appear a fool in front of Joseph was not something she'd readily admit, but it wouldn't hurt to give him one less thing to be annoyed over.

Perhaps during the next few days she could take a lesson or two in cooking from some older woman. Maybe Mrs. Knepp might help or even Tillie Smoker, a friend who worked at Yoder's Pantry in town. Abigail's father had never permitted such a thing as cooking instruction before, although she had no idea why. But now she needed to satisfy her husband, and she was sure a few secret lessons might go a long way toward making his stomach happy.

The men entered, and she tried to appear nonchalant as her father stopped and stared at the table. Joseph sniffed the air with appreciation, then moved to brush his mouth across her cheek before turning away to the pump. She stiffened under his touch but remembered her father. She swallowed when she glanced at Joseph's broad back; he smelled like sunshine and sweat, all mixed in a way that caused her pulse to race. She was glad when her father had washed and they all turned to the table.

She sat down at the foot of the table, her father at the head, and Joseph took a space to her right. The table had always been too large for just two people, but they kept it for when it was their turn to host worship service.

Mr. Kauffman bowed his head for a silent grace and Abigail followed, peeking to see that Joseph did as well. She snapped her gaze down when she caught the dark gleam of his eyes, mocking her for looking.

Her father cleared his throat, and they all looked up together.

"Please, Father," Abigail urged. "Help yourself."

Mr. Kauffman took a tentative scoop of some chicken and dumplings, then breathed a deep sigh of satisfaction when he held the plate close to his large nose.

"I see that I am truly blessed—a beautiful wife and an excellent cook," Joseph announced, savoring a bite of the fresh bread and preserves.

Abigail held her breath, wondering if her father would contradict, but he was too busy enjoying the food.

"*Danki.*" She smiled at Joseph, then noticed his palm as he reached for the potato salad. "What happened to your hand?"

"Moving rocks. I forgot that I don't have work gloves yet. I'll have to pick some up in town."

Abigail was surprised at her fleeting feeling of protectiveness. She stared down at her plate in confusion.

"Plenty of gloves in the barn. Help yourself." Mr. Kauffman spoke between bites. "Should have thought of it earlier."

"Thanks." Joseph smiled, helping himself to a large slice of cake. "Mmm-mmm. Abigail Lambert, what a treasure you are."

He grinned at her, and for once she could sense no mockery in his gaze. *Just wait*, she thought ruefully.

He stretched out his work-worn hand across the table to her, palm up, and she placed her hand in his, not wanting to irritate the blisters. But he squeezed her hand with goodwill, and Abigail glanced down the table to where her father watched as he sipped at his coffee.

She knew the hand-holding was a show and not for her, and something about that sparked irritation in her blue eyes. Joseph must have seen the warning signs, because he withdrew his hand before she might do any damage. She rose to take her plate to the sink.

"I think I'll go get those gloves. Abby, will you show me where in the barn?"

"The barn is the barn. They're hanging up by one of the stalls," she said, a tightness around her mouth.

"Abigail, go along as your husband asks. I've a mind to read *The Budget* and digest a bit before we go back out."

"*Ya*, Father," she replied out of habit, but inside she was contemplating everything from pushing Joseph into the feed trough to dousing him with the sow's water. She stepped out onto the porch and took a deep breath.

"You sure do get riled," he whispered behind her, catching her around the waist and placing a quick kiss on her cheek.

"Let me go," she hissed, starting to struggle.

"I bet Papa's watching," he reminded her and she stilled, her breath coming out in a huff.

"That's better, my dutiful wife. Tell me, how have you lived so long with a man who does not speak more than two words in a whole morning's work?" He slid a stray wisp of gold from her hair covering, and the gentleness brought tears in her throat.

"It's been lonely," she admitted, amazed that someone else might understand how it was to live with her father.

Joseph squeezed her arms in response. "I bet. I see why you want to run, but it's not worth it. Believe me."

He let her go, and she blindly went down the steps toward the barn. She'd never met a man who so had her churning in her emotions from one moment to the next. She eased open the barn door and blinked in the dim interior.

Joseph shut the door behind them, and she whirled around.

"Will you relax?" he asked. "Look, we might rub along better together if we get some things straight."

"Like what?"

"Like, I'm not going to force you to exert any wifely duties, all right?"

"Never?" she asked in surprise.

He sighed aloud. "Never is a long time. Let's just leave it at . . . you decide when you're ready."

"That will be never."

"Are you sure?" He took a step toward her, holding her captive with a certain intensity in his dark eyes that made her think absurdly of warm maple syrup and lazing in the sunshine in the heat of a summer's day.

"No . . . I mean, *ya* . . ." She frowned as she tried to recollect her point.

He laughed. "When was the last time you played, Abigail Lambert?"

"Played . . . Wh–what do you mean?"

He reached down to stroke her cheek and cup it in his large hand. "Played. I don't mean with boys' hearts or people's futures, but just played—for fun."

She tried hard to think of an answer. Play always seemed like a stolen thing to her. Something that she'd had to do away from her father's sight and the endless chores. She was good at getting out of a job, but she always felt guilty about it. To play was an odd notion.

"No idea, right?"

She shook her head.

"Well, in order to improve our—marital relations—we're going to play."

"I don't know what you're talking about."

He gave her a swift swat on her bottom. "Tag! You're it. Now catch me." He darted away while she gasped in outrage.

"How dare you!"

"Catch me, and you can have your own price back." He posed behind a bale of hay. "Come on, Abby. You're not that out of shape, are you?"

"What?" She whirled on him as he danced within hand's reach.

She made an angry grab toward him and almost fell over when she missed. She turned to find him laughing at her and leaning against the gentle family *milch* cow, Rose.

"You need some work, sweet. You couldn't catch a cat."

She lunged for him then, something about his teasing sending tiny electric shocks down her spine. She told herself that she was furious.

She chased him across the hay-strewn floor, stirring up dust motes in a narrow stream of sunlight from the upper window, and then took off up the ladder at his heels to the haymow above. She almost had him at the top and laughed aloud with sudden pleasure.

"What was that? A real laugh . . . oh my!" He was hopping backward and didn't see the pile of feed bags behind him; he went over into the hay, and she grabbed his ankle with a vengeance.

"I got you," she gasped.

He was laughing, the full, rich sound making her shiver. "That you did." He lay in the hay, smiling up at her, his glasses slightly askew. "Now name your price."

She sank to her knees beside him breathlessly. "I want to make you pay."

He folded his arms behind his head, his lean stomach stretched out in easy repose. He wasn't even winded. "Go ahead."

Her blue eyes narrowed like a cat's, and she knew by sudden instinct how to make him pay. "I name a kiss."

"A kiss?"

"*Ya*, and you must keep perfectly still."

"All right." He looked a little bored, and she lowered her gaze to his firm mouth.

Not for nothing had she practiced kissing in the cracked bureau mirror since she was about twelve. She leaned over him and blew softly on his lips as if to awaken them, then she closed her eyes and pretended he was the mirror. She took her time, fitting her lips to the line and contours of his own, until she sensed a tensing in his chest. She drew back and found him staring up at her.

"Done?" he asked in a casual voice, though his tone didn't match the heightened color in his cheeks or his intense gaze.

"*Ya*," she said primly, gathering up her skirts and rising in some confusion. She couldn't tell if he'd been affected or not, and it made her annoyed and . . . hurt somehow. Perhaps the mirror wasn't really a good way to practice. She slipped down the ladder and out of the barn without saying anything more.

. . .

Joseph lay in the hay, trying to regulate his breathing. The kiss had thrown him, turned him upside down, in fact. Where had she learned how to kiss like that? He shifted in the hay when he thought of the boys gathered around her at the oak tree, yet he couldn't explain her innocent tenseness at his every touch or look. It was just him, he thought with a sigh. She'd got herself into the marriage with a leap and no look, and if she ever found out the truth about his past, she'd probably despise him.

He got to his feet, brushing himself down from the hay, and spied a pair of work gloves near the feed bags. He grabbed them and headed down the ladder before his new father-in-law could come looking for him.

He walked across the open field, listening to the stray, gentle mooing of the cows and the busy chirps of sparrows as they sought seed from the autumn's bounty. He resisted the urge to stretch his arms wide and lift his head in praise of *Derr Herr* for such a day. No matter the bonds of his marriage, he felt free. The grass beneath his feet did not seek to hold him, nor did the tree line of pine and oak condemn his every move. The Lord's nature was new and clean and healing, and it was what he remembered most from his time away.

He'd been a fool; he knew that. He'd tried in desperation to fill the void of emptiness with a multitude of the world's things. But nothing had worked, at least nothing that was life-sustaining. But here, even on the borrowed ground of his father-in-law, he felt the potential for peace, and he savored it to his very core.

The unmistakable high-pitched cry of a cat in distress cut into his thoughts. He turned his head to listen again. Then he walked with quick steps across the field to the ribbon of highway that bordered the farm.

CHAPTER FIVE

Abigail washed the last of the lunch dishes in a dreamy fashion. She still couldn't believe her boldness at taking a kiss from her husband. She half smiled at the thought, then frowned again when she wondered what he'd really been thinking. He'd probably kissed a hundred *Englisch* girls during his years away, and maybe she just didn't measure up. The teasing thought that practice makes perfect drifted through her mind, and she snapped the dishcloth to get her thoughts back in focus.

She'd have warm-ups for dinner and bring out a few of the desserts she'd held back, and then she'd worry about tomorrow, tomorrow. She left the kitchen and wandered over to the quilt frame that was permanently set up with the sheet-covered, un-finished quilt her mother had been working on when she died. The quilt pattern was called Abby's Wish, but only fifteen of the eighteen stars had been completed. Abigail often tried to imagine what was in her mother's mind when she'd been quilting and what her wish might have been for the young daughter she left behind.

Father allowed her to dust the frame, but finishing

the quilt or packing it away was always out of the question for some reason. And since the frame was "in use," or occupied anyway, Abigail could quilt no new work in her own home. Not that she really knew how.

She sat down in the rocking chair by the front window and gazed out at the sunny day, wondering how Joseph was getting along. Normally at this hour she would sneak upstairs to look at her hidden magazines of the *Englisch* world, but she didn't feel like it today. She longed for the visitors of the morning, even with their gentle nosiness. The house was too quiet, as usual.

Suddenly heavy footsteps sounded from the back porch and Joseph entered, his arms and shirt splattered with blood. Abigail jumped to her feet.

"What happened?"

"It's not me. An old mother cat got hit by a car up by the highway. I tried to do what I could for her, but it didn't make any difference. She was carrying a kitten in her mouth. I can't tell if it's hurt much or not."

He extended his hands, and Abigail took the tiny animal. It, too, was splattered in blood and meowed in pathetic cries. Its eyes were open, but it couldn't have been more than a few weeks old, judging by the slightness of its weight. She took it to the kitchen counter and got a damp cloth and began to swipe at its fur with gentle hands.

The blood came off, revealing no major injuries. "I think she's okay," Abigail said, peering at the animal.

"*Gut.* Well, you can keep her for company, then, if you want."

"My *daed*'s never allowed pets." Her voice was

wistful, but then she frowned, not wanting to appear weak in front of him.

Joseph shrugged. "We'll tell him it's a wedding gift, from me to you. There's not a whole lot he can say about that now, is there?"

She gave him a reluctant smile.

"All right. So do you think you can get the blood out of this shirt?"

He started to unbutton his shirt, and Abigail turned her full attention to the kitten, wrapping it in a towel and setting it in a wooden box she pulled from beneath the counter. She wanted to watch Joseph, but she didn't want to give him the satisfaction of knowing her interest.

"*Ya*, I can try to clean it," she said.

"Thanks—I only have this and one other, plus my one for church, so I'd like it to last." He held out the shirt to her, and she took it, darting a quick look at his muscle-toned chest. He turned away and headed for the stairs.

"I'll just grab my other shirt," he called.

She stared down at the shirt in her hands, still warm from his body, and wondered how on earth to get bloodstains out of fabric. She decided she'd better look efficient before he came back, and hurried to pump some water into a basin. Opening the spice cabinet, she stared at its contents. Some of the spice jars were older than she was. She grabbed baking soda and a stray bottle of alcohol and dumped both liberally on top of the shirt. She began scrubbing in haste just as he jogged back down the steps.

He patted her shoulder as he passed by on his way back outside. *"Danki,"* he said, and she heard him walk off the porch.

She frowned and leaned her hip against the counter. The casual touch on her shoulder when no one else was about teased her consciousness with a warm tingle. She supposed he had touched her just to irritate her. It worked. Maybe she should give him a little of his own back. A small smile grew on her lips as she resumed scrubbing, plotting her next move.

CHAPTER SIX

They mounted the dark steps to their room together while her father rocked in his after-dinner chair next to the fireplace. Abigail lit the lamp on the bedside table and set the kitten in its box on the floor next to the bed. Then she went down the hall to raid a cedar chest for some extra quilts and a pillow. She returned to find Joseph standing, staring out the dark window with his back to her. She closed the door, then laid the quilts on the floor.

"Will you—will you stay turned, please, while I put on my nightdress?"

"*Ya.*"

She hurried despite his answer, wondering if his idea of "playing" might be to sneak a peek. And despite her resolve of the afternoon to get a little of her own back in teasing him, she found that she couldn't quite bring herself to anything so bold at the moment. So she wriggled into her gown, then grabbed her hairbrush from the bureau and jumped into the bed, pulling the quilt up to her neck and unpinning her *kapp*.

"You may turn."

"*Danki,*" he said with slight irony. He dropped to his knees and started to make his bed, then he reached for the buttons on his shirt. "Only my shirt, dear wife. Do you mind?"

"Of course not," she said, turning her gaze away and concentrating on releasing her braid. She ignored the nagging, innate curiosity that wanted to watch him and ran her fingernails through her scalp. She loved the moment each night when she might take down her hair. It was one of the things that she envied most about *Englisch* girls—their freedom of hairstyle. She had no choice but to let hers grow, as it had done from childhood, and never might she even so much as take shears to create bangs across her fair forehead. Her hair hung past her waist, and now it spilled over the side of the bed as she brushed it with long, even strokes.

A small sound made her turn and glance down at Joseph. He was kneeling on the quilt, shirt off, suspenders around his waist, and he appeared frozen as his dark eyes followed the movement of the brush. Her hand stilled.

"Don't stop."

"Why?"

"It's like a waterfall of gold, all shimmer and shine."

She blushed then, knowing it was only her husband who might view her hair unbound. It seemed he was claiming his right. She finished the remaining count of strokes, then laid the brush before her on the quilt. "There."

He seemed to shake himself as if from a dream and dropped to his back on the floor. She watched him stare up at the wooden slat ceiling as she had so often done herself and wondered if she should say something.

"There're thirty-seven," she remarked. "Boards, I mean—up there."

"Thirty-eight, if you count the half board at the end."

"I never count by halves."

He laughed. "*Nee* . . . for you, it's all or nothing."

"Well, there's nothing wrong with that."

"Maybe not, but it leaves little room for negotiation."

"You mean our marriage, don't you?"

He rolled over and propped his head up on one elbow, reaching to rub a tendril of her hair between his thumb and forefinger. "It's true; there was no room for negotiation. But there's always time."

She felt skittish at his touch and longed to pull her hair free.

"But," he went on, "I'd wager it's you who's been caught in your own web more so than me."

She lifted her chin. "I'm not caught."

"Aren't you?" He wound the white-gold strands around his hand.

She chose to ignore his game, but he only smiled, the dark growth of his beard making him look like a pirate, except for the glasses.

"Abby Lambert—now that's a name I never expected to hear. Time was you probably wouldn't have even looked at a Lambert. My family wasn't the best regarded in the community before we left."

A sudden, pressing thought intruded on her consciousness as she studied his handsome face and flash of white teeth. "Well, what name did you expect to hear?"

"Hmm?"

She rolled over, inadvertently giving him better access to her hair. "You know what I mean."

He looked up at her. "*Ach*, you mean another girl?"

"*Ya.*"

He wound and unwound the golden strands. "There was no one."

"You're lying!" she declared, yanking on her hair.

"How would you know that?"

"Because you looked down and not at me."

He shrugged his bare shoulders. "So?"

She felt her temper rise at the thought of some unknown *Englisch* girl, though she couldn't understand why. "Let me go."

She pulled free, leaving him with several long strands of hair entwined in his fingers.

"That must have hurt."

"It did not. Now tell me about the girl."

He gathered the hair together and slipped it under his pillow, took off his glasses, and buried his face in the quilted sham.

"No girl," he mumbled, muffled by the pillow.

She watched the lamplight play on the golden muscles of his shoulders and back, and pursed her lips. "Was she very pretty?"

"I'm going to sleep."

"Not until you tell me the truth, you're not."

"You'd be amazed at what I can sleep through." He nestled against the pillow.

She grabbed her own pillow without thinking and threw it at his head as hard as she could.

He lifted his face with his hair standing a bit on end and arched one dark eyebrow at her. "So you want to have a pillow fight?"

She shrank back in the bed. "No," she squeaked.

There was a glimmer of mischief in his eyes. He sat up, the quilt sliding from him as he lifted his pillow.

She scrambled out of her bed toward the door. "My father will hear."

"That's *gut*, for your father to hear."

He stood up, and she leapt back onto the bed and then dived over the side, snatching up her pillow. She faced him, heart pounding and bare toes digging into the wooden floor.

"Ladies first." He bowed.

She raised the pillow.

"Wait," he said. "My glasses." He bent to retrieve the lenses, and she smacked him across the back of the head and then jumped back on the bed.

He set the glasses on the bureau and grinned up at her. "Mrs. Lambert, I believe that you don't quite fight fair."

She swung her pillow fiercely. "Tell me about the girl."

He dived at her feet, and she would have gone backward off the bed if he hadn't hoisted her over his broad shoulder.

"Let me go," she hissed, whacking the pillow against his lower back.

He dumped her without ceremony on the bed, then gave her a swift pat with the pillow.

She scrambled to rise and he sat on the edge of the bed, holding her down with one hand on her shoulder.

She realized she was trapped, so she sucked in a deep breath and regarded him through venomous blue eyes.

"If this is how far you're going to keep from telling me, I'll just have to imagine the worst." She closed her eyes, ignoring his nearness. "Green eyes . . . a fine figure, brown hair . . . no, maybe red . . ." She peeked up at him.

There was a sudden tenseness to his firm mouth that bothered her.

"I'm right, aren't I . . . red hair?"

He rose and pulled her quilt up around her, tucking it in at her shoulders. "Good night, Mrs. Lambert," he said in a sober tone.

She watched him pick up his pillow and return to the bed on the floor. She felt lost somehow, adrift, and she admonished herself for the feelings. Of course there was another girl, an *Englisch* girl. Perhaps he'd been in love even, and she had stolen all of that with her careless plotting.

But then, he had been the one to rejoin the community and end any possibility of a life outside. Still, she swallowed and grasped a handful of her own hair. How completely opposite it was to red—he must despise her. She stifled a sniff and turned over, refusing to allow any tears to fall as she drifted into a fitful sleep.

CHAPTER SEVEN

He was dreaming. He knew it and didn't really want to wake. Molly was smiling down at him, her hands on his chest. They were sprawled on a picnic blanket in the summer sun in the middle of a park. He felt happy, sated. She bent to kiss him, and he could count the freckles on the bridge of her nose. He returned the kiss with ease, his hands threading through her wild red curls. But suddenly everything was being swept away by rushing water. He tried to hang on to Molly, but she was gone from him and he was drowning. He finally caught hold of a stand of honey wheat protruding from a creek bank and held on until the water slowed, then drifted to a lazy trickle. Shivering, he pulled himself up against the wheat and it turned into long blonde hair that wrapped around him with an intense warmth, making his chest feel tight. He clung to the hair and breathed in its sweet fragrance, like melting mint, and smiled as he buried his face in the hot strands.

He awoke with an uncomfortable gasp, hiking up to a sitting position and glancing over in the near morning light to the lump of covers that was his wife in her little-girl's bed. He stretched his fingers to touch her hair, which still spilled over the mattress and to the floor. Then he half laughed at himself for the dream; he was clearly a fool when it came to women and their wiles. He let her hair go and hugged the quilt against his chest, realizing that he was cold. He considered rising before the sun came up to start the chores when Abby rolled over and sat straight up in the bed.

"Wh–what are you doing here?" She was still half asleep.

He put his glasses on and smiled at her. "Just me, Abby—your husband, remember?" He watched her curl up.

"*Ya*," she murmured. "I did that to you."

"Did what?"

"The marriage . . . sorry," she murmured, still half asleep.

"Now, now—no time for regrets. Why don't you go start breakfast?"

She opened her eyes then, peering down at him with an annoyed look in the half-light. "Joseph?"

He was feeling for his shirt. "Mmm-hmm?"

"I might as well tell you something, a secret. It's really bad."

His hands stilled. With Abby, he should be prepared for anything: She only married him to make another man jealous? She knew where a body was buried?

"I can't cook."

"What?"

"I can't cook," she whispered, her tone taut. "All that food yesterday—it was from neighbors who wanted to know about us. I can't cook."

"So you're a bad cook, so what?" He resumed looking for his shirt.

"You don't understand, but you will. I make a mess of everything that an Amish housewife is supposed to do."

"And what is an Amish housewife supposed to do?"

"Everything right," she mumbled with sarcasm.

"Sounds boring."

She let out a huff of frustration, then began braiding her hair. "You're going to see—I don't know what my father thought. It was probably the first time he wasn't disappointed in me. Now you're going to be disappointed, too, but it's just going to have to be the way it is, because I am not going to try and change for you."

He considered her words as he hitched up his suspenders and folded the quilts.

"I'll help you cook," he said.

"What?"

He'd taken his glasses off and was splashing water on his face from the bowl and pitcher on her bureau.

"I know how to cook. We'll just get up a little earlier every day and go down and do it together. I can give you tips for lunch and dinner too."

He dried his face on a towel that smelled like fresh mint and put it down with haste, recalling his dream. He turned to the bed.

She was staring at him, her fingers poised on her braid. "You'd help me? Why?"

He shrugged. "I'm your husband."

"*Ach . . .*" she whispered. She finished her braid

and rose from the bed, careless of her nightgown this morning.

He turned to look out the window. "Do you want me out of here so you can dress?"

"*Ya* . . . I mean . . . *nee*, it's all right. I guess I'll hurry up."

He felt the back of his neck grow warm as he listened to the various sounds behind him. The slide of her gown coming up her body, the pulling on of another. He closed his eyes against the wash of images going through his mind. His wife. She was his wife.

"All right," she said, snapping him out of his reverie. He turned, feeling awkward, to watch her adjust her *kapp*. "I'm ready."

He nodded. "Let's go, then."

He waited until she'd scooped up the kitten in its box, then followed her down the stairs to enter the still-dark rooms below. She went about turning up the lamps while he peered into cabinets in the kitchen. He found a frying pan but no spatula, then went to light the woodstove.

Lighting a woodstove was like riding a bicycle, he thought; you never forgot how to do it. There was always a firebox in the left-hand corner that contained shredded paper, wood chips, and small pieces of wood. He knew that the type and amount of fuel used were one of the easiest ways to control the heat. Good cooking required a low, slow burn and no raging fire. The woodstove also had two dampers, which he fooled around with for a minute to get them just right. The chimney damper controlled the amount of smoke moving out of the woodstove into the chimney, while the oven damper regulated the amount of heat moving between the firebox and the oven.

When he'd adjusted the dampers to his satisfaction, Joseph rose and put the frying pan on top of the stove. The entire surface of the stove could be used for cooking, but you had to spend some time getting to know a stove's quirks to get adept at moving pots and pans around to capitalize on the hot spots. When he was done, he turned back to Abby.

"All right. When you say you can't cook, how bad do you mean?"

She frowned. "I can't even scramble eggs without them being watery."

"Why?" he asked.

"What?"

"Why can't you cook—I mean, really?"

She scuffed her small shoe on the wooden floor. "My *mamm* died . . . you know that. Father never taught me anything . . . and there's never been other womenfolk around. He wouldn't allow it. So I've just tried to figure it out, and I haven't been very good at it."

"You mean to tell me that your father let you try and run this house from the time you were little?"

She nodded. "I know . . . I should have it figured out by now."

"No, that's not what I mean. You were a baby girl—five years old. You could have been badly injured in the kitchen or even filling the lamps."

"Well, I have been burned a few times." She absently rubbed at her left arm under its long sleeve. "But

Mamm taught me a few things before she died—how to peel vegetables, just not how to grow them . . . and how to make up the beds and do the laundry."

"You were five years old," he repeated, his heart aching for the image of a blonde, tumble-curled little girl trying to cook breakfast all alone.

"*Ya*, but I'm not anymore, and I . . ." She grimaced. "I thank you for helping me."

He looked carefully at her face, recalling the circumstances of their marriage, and hardened his heart; she could be lying even now. He turned to the stove, then glanced at her over his shoulder.

"I hope that you can at least gather eggs," he remarked with sarcasm, ignoring the sudden flash of hurt on her pretty face.

"*Ya*." She nodded. "It's the least that I can do."

She marched out the back door, leaving him alone in the cold kitchen.

CHAPTER EIGHT

She stomped to the henhouse, wiping with the back of her hand at the unbidden tears of frustration that stung her cheeks. He'd seemed so kind, yet she forced herself to admit that she knew next to nothing about him, really. And just because he'd been amiable the day before didn't mean that he was in any way over his anger about her deception in their forced marriage. She sighed as she felt for the eggs beneath the warm, feathered hens that clucked at her in disapproval. She had no right to expect anything from him except anger . . . but she'd had enough of that from her father.

Yet she had patience on her side. One of the few times she'd received positive affirmation from a female in the community had been from her seventh-grade teacher. Miss Stahley had noticed her persistent efforts at the more difficult math problems and had touched her shoulder. "I do believe that *Derr Herr* has gifted you with patience, Abigail. You'll wear down those sums yet."

It was funny how she'd kept that stray observation tucked away in her heart through the years, probably because such encouraging remarks were so few and far between in her young life. But as she gathered the last egg, she found herself praying that the gift of patience would continue to bless her as she puzzled out her new husband.

She returned to the house with the egg basket and a much refreshed attitude. Joseph had found the bacon and had a good portion frying in a pan. She always managed to either overcook it to charred crispness or leave part of it underdone.

He glanced up. "Abby . . . look . . . I'm sorry for snapping at you. I'm just as new as you to this idea of marriage."

She nodded, feeling a strange surge of relief in her chest. "*Ach*, that's all right. I'd want to snap, too, if I were you. Here are the eggs."

"All right, let me show you the perfect way to scramble them."

"How did you learn to cook?"

He was cracking the eggs into a blue mixing bowl with a large chip out of its rim. "Well, first when I was a kid, I guess. My mom and dad, after they left the community, drifted from here to there and kind of drank—a lot. It was either learn how to cook or go hungry. My kid sister needed me, too, so I suppose that helped."

"Your sister?" Abigail was surprised. She didn't recall a little sister.

"Yep. She's twenty now, five years younger than me. She got a full ride—a full scholarship—to NYU. That's New York University. She's going to be an artist." He laughed. "She'll really be surprised that I'm married. We write to each other a lot."

So he's twenty-five, she thought, ignoring his comment about his sister's surprise at their marriage. He looked younger, except when he was serious, like now.

"And your *mamm* and *daed*?"

He shrugged his broad shoulders. "Don't know. I ran away when I was about seventeen. I'd send money back to Angel, my sister. She stayed with an aunt of ours. But I haven't seen my folks in years."

"Don't you—want to?"

He whisked the eggs with a fork. "*Nee*, not really. I don't know if I'm ready for that yet. I guess the Lord will let it happen when it's time. Now here's the trick with the eggs—instead of a little milk, add some cold water, about three tablespoons for every six eggs. The water makes them fluffy and light without the runniness." He poured the bright yellow mixture into a sizzling pan. "And watch the heat after the first minute or so. Move the pan around so things don't burn." He plunked the perfectly done bacon onto a towel while Abigail watched his every move.

Just then they heard her father's footsteps on the stairs. Joseph thrust a spoon into her hand and quickly sat down at the table. She turned and began to shift the eggs back and forth, wondering anew at his quicksilver kindness.

"It smells good in here," her father remarked suspiciously as he took a seat at the table.

"*Ya*, so it does," Joseph agreed as Abigail turned her first perfectly scrambled eggs out onto a platter. She brought plates and tableware and served the bacon and eggs with the bread pudding left from yesterday. Once more she watched her father's face relax from disbelief to enjoyment as he forked up his food.

She felt a sudden rush of gratitude and looked at Joseph with a quick smile, surprised to find him return her gaze with a wink of his dark eyelashes. She felt good inside, like she had a secret friend. Her heart softened toward him, and she uttered a silent prayer of thanks to *Derr Herr* and began to eat her eggs.

. . .

Joseph watched her from the corner of his eye as he ate. How pretty she was with the slight flush of pleasure on her cheeks. He wanted to remind himself that she was manipulative, but he couldn't bring himself to do so at the moment. He just knew that he felt content. His belly was full, he had work to attend to, and he happened to be married to a very beautiful woman.

A sudden mewing sound broke the silence in the kitchen.

Mr. Kauffman looked up. "What's that, then?" he asked.

Joseph smiled. "A wedding gift from me to your daughter, sir. A kitten to keep her company. Do you want to see it?"

Mr. Kauffman frowned. "*Nee*, I've work to be about. As do you, if you've a mind to." The older man pushed back his chair and rose from the table. "I've got a small harvest of corn to get in."

"Do you can it?" Joseph asked, then realized his mistake when he saw his father-in-law's frown deepen.

Obviously Abby didn't know how to can. "I mean, we'll can some of it, *ya*? I've missed canned sweet corn."

"I've just been storing it for stock feed the past years."

Abigail spoke up. "Well, this year, Father, please bring a few bushels to the house. I–I'll can it up right."

She glanced at Joseph, and he felt pleasure in giving her a faint nod. Maybe he could work in a late-night canning session. The tendrils of hair at her temples might curl in the steam, and her cheeks would be flushed . . .

He drew himself up sharply when he realized Mr. Kauffman had repeated himself.

"*Ya*, I'm coming now." Joseph rose, then bent to brush his lips across her temple before depositing his plate in the sink. He followed his silent father-in-law out the door and left Abby alone with the kitten.

CHAPTER NINE

Abigail decided the moment they'd left the kitchen that she would surprise Joseph with at least a basic knowledge of canning. It was the least she could do to return his kindness about the cooking. She ignored the warm rush of feeling that she had when she thought about her new husband.

She would need basic supplies, like canning jars. She'd go into town and get some information first, from the best source she knew, Yoder's Pantry. Tillie might be able to help. She saw to the kitten's small needs, then she raced upstairs to change her blouse, thinking how funny it was that she was getting so excited over something domestic.

Still, she considered, as she left the house a few minutes later to hitch Carl up to the buggy, her interest truly lay in surprising her husband and in wanting to see his face light up with pride. It was a curious sensation for her, this desire to please someone besides herself. If she'd felt it with her father, it had long ago been squashed by too many failed attempts.

Joseph was different. Although he could be angry and cutting, he was also infinitely kind—like with the kitten. He'd wrangled her father into a pet without so much as a cross word, something she had never been able to do. And he was willing to talk about his past and his family, willing to be open with her when most people kept their distance. *And probably for good reason,* she thought ruefully as she navigated the buggy into town. She had always been one to gossip, especially about other girls, and she didn't feel particularly good when she considered this aspect of her personality. Could it be that a few simple days of marriage were revealing her most intimate characteristics to herself? She wasn't too sure she liked the idea.

As she climbed down from the buggy to hitch up in front of Yoder's, a passing pair of *Englisch* girls caught her eye, and the old, familiar pull of interest in the outside world made her stand still on the sidewalk. She admired their clothes, the bright colors and cut of their skirts, as well as their free-flowing hair. But it was more than that. She felt like they walked unencumbered by the social boundaries so imposed by her own people—the role of women and the expectations of their duties in life. She mentally shook herself. For someone who had so longed after the *Englisch* way of life, it was a funny thing to be seeking out the best way to can sweet corn.

She entered the restaurant, enjoying the rush of air-conditioned coolness that met her arrival. Her friend Tillie was waitressing, just as she had hoped. She came over and greeted Abigail with a large menu.

"Abigail, I'm so glad to see you. We're still doing breakfast, if you like."

Abigail returned the smile. At one time she'd wanted to be a waitress. It would have allowed her a closer brush with the *Englisch*, but her father never permitted it. And now, her mind whispered, she had her own former *Englisch* man at home.

Tillie leaned close and spoke behind the menu. "How is it to be married to Joseph Lambert?"

Again Abigail smiled; it was nice to be the center of attention, even for a short time. And she found, to her surprise, that she could respond with honesty to the other girl's question.

"It's *gut*—really."

Tillie's eyes twinkled. "It should be. He's hot."

Abigail giggled at the use of the *Englisch* word, but she had to agree. Joseph was hot—the idea made her face flame.

Tillie laughed. "Come on, let me seat you."

Abigail caught her arm. "Tillie, wait . . . um . . . this may sound funny, but actually I came in today because I was hoping I could take a peek in the kitchen. Maybe talk to one of the cooks or to you for a few minutes— about canning."

Tillie looked at her blankly. "Canning?"

"*Ya* . . . you know, how to do it?"

"That's what you're thinking of during the first week of marriage?"

Abigail flushed. "Well, Joseph likes sweet corn, and I . . ."

"Just want to make him happy." Tillie beamed. "It must be true love if it brings *you* to the idea of canning corn. Come on in the back. I'll introduce you to Judith.

She's Amish and a great cook. And I happen to know that she's putting up carrots today and could probably use some help. You can learn firsthand."

Abigail followed her friend through a door into a large, modernized kitchen. She was amazed at the amount of stainless steel and all of the electric appliances and mysterious gadgets. She also recognized at once the precision and order of the busy place as four Amish women worked together to get orders met.

"We've got four wonderful cooks," Tillie explained. "Martha, Mary, Judith, and Ruth—this is Abigail. She wants to learn some canning tips; she just got married."

The older women laughed as Tillie continued. "Ruth mainly does desserts. Martha and Mary work the main dishes, and Judith processes all the produce that comes through. Judith, I told Abigail that you might be doing some canning of your own today."

The cheerful, round-faced woman nodded, her blue eyes twinkling. "*Ya*, and I could use a pair of young hands to help."

"Oh, *danki*," Abigail said, glad she'd changed into a spotless apron before she'd left home.

"I'll leave you to it, then." Tillie smiled and waved, leaving the kitchen.

"You need a hair net first, Abigail," Judith said, handing her a folded packet.

Abigail opened it awkwardly, withdrawing a white net and slipping it over her *kapp*.

"And plastic gloves. I think you'll take a small pair."

Abigail stood awkwardly but eagerly next to a shiny counter.

"It's *gut* for a young wife to have a cellar full of the colors of canning—the vegetables, fruits, and jellies, *ya*? Do you remember your *mamm's* pantry?"

Abigail shook her head and spoke low. "She died when I was five."

"*Ach*, I'm sorry." Judith regarded her with compassion. "So perhaps you've never had the chance to learn canning properly?"

Abigail shook her head.

"Well, I will teach you today, and someday you'll show your own daughter. Come, let's begin."

Abigail's mind caught on the image of a dark-haired, blue-eyed baby. Any daughter of Joseph's would be good-natured and beautiful, like her father . . . She snapped back to attention at Judith's brisk movements.

The older woman was lifting quart-sized glass jars from a sectioned box on the floor. Abigail bent to help her. Then she gathered up two parts of a brass lid for each jar: a flat lid and a screw band.

"To can fruits, vegetables, sauces, and the like, you use jars like these, with the wide mouths. The regular-size jars are better for jams and jellies."

Abigail nodded, almost feeling like she should be taking notes. But she was a quick study when she wanted to be, and she wanted to be now.

"What are you planning on canning?" Judith asked as she hefted a wooden box overflowing with carrots with green, leafy tops onto the counter.

"Sweet corn first, but we only have a small harvest."

"It doesn't matter; it's all provided by *Derr Herr* and is His bounty, *ya*?"

"Yes."

"All right. We're doing carrots today, but I'll write down the steps for sweet corn for you later. Much of the processing is the same. To begin, you wash your carrots very well, then you cut off the tops and peel them. There's a knack to peeling with a knife and getting it just right. You want to keep your peelings as thin as possible, so you've got to have a sharp knife and a steady hand." She gave an example, slicing fast and neat down a carrot. "Now you try."

Abigail took the knife and attempted to imitate the other woman, but ended up digging unevenly into the carrot.

Judith laughed good-naturedly. "You'll get better. In fact, you'll be an expert by the end of the day."

She was right. Abigail gained more confidence as her peelings began to resemble the neat piles that Judith made. And though she was slower, she became accurate and surprisingly interested in what she was learning.

"Carrots, like sweet corn, need to be cold-packed," Judith explained. "This means a lot of *gut* things for the cook. First, it is easy and doesn't require standing next to a hot stove for the whole day. And you can be fairly sure that all of the bacteria are killed with this method. There's nothing worse-smelling than a poorly canned jar of vegetables."

Abigail helped to blanch the peeled and sliced carrots, then she watched how Judith dipped the vegetables into cold water before beginning to pack them into clean, hot jars. She added a bit of hot water and some sugar to the top of each jar, and then she showed Abigail how to adjust the seals and lids before placing them into boiling water for a short amount of time.

"And that's it," she announced, removing the jars with long tongs. "Now we'll do the next batch, and you'll be more than ready to do your own canning—if you're not too tired."

Abigail laughed with the other women, feeling included and part of the group. It was an unusual sensation. There was more to this than just drudgery or the perfecting of a recipe, she could see. There was a legitimate science and method. She knew in that moment that *Englisch* or Amish, people had to cook to eat. She had a sudden desire to experiment in her kitchen, and she knew she would never be able to explain to Judith how much her friendly instruction had meant to her.

She settled for a quick thank-you and was surprised when Judith pressed a covered basket into her hands.

"Here're some of the carrots that you did and directions for the sweet corn. And there's something else so you needn't worry over supper. I also put in a *gut* box of Amish recipe cards. You can be a good cook, Abigail, if you'll have the patience for it."

"I will. *Danki*." And she knew it was a promise that she meant to keep.

CHAPTER TEN

The sun was beginning to set, framing the gentle curves of the landscape with pink and amber light when Joseph left the fields, tired but fulfilled. He walked back toward the house alone; his father in law had waved him on ahead. He was hot enough from the warm September weather that a good long soak in a tub sounded like heaven. But since he knew that Abby would probably be unnerved by the whole process, he decided instead to jump into the rather secluded creek that ran through the Kauffmans' property.

Ducking through some overgrowth, he eyed a fairly deep spot in the moving water and stripped down with pleasure, tossing his clothes over a bush. The water was icy cold but felt wonderful, and he wished that he had a bar of soap. He scooped up a handful of sand from the creek bottom instead and scrubbed with abrasive enthusiasm. Then he sat down on a convenient, flat, underwater rock and let the current swirl past his chest while his mind drifted into pleasant abeyance.

. . .

Abigail was hot and tired by the time she pulled the buggy up to the hitch at home. She knew that she should have been there a lot sooner to get supper ready, but she just felt like she had to get the canning supplies to apply her newfound knowledge. And, she admitted to herself, to make Joseph proud.

When she entered the house, she found everything quiet as usual except for the kitten, which wanted to be fed. She washed her hands, then poured a saucer of milk for the small creature and set it inside the box, blowing at the hair that clung damply to her forehead. She glanced around the kitchen with one eye on the setting sun. Joseph and her father were apparently working late in the fields. She decided she'd indulge in one of her favorite secret pursuits before attempting supper. Besides *Englisch* magazines, she loved dipping her feet in the local stream.

She stole out the back door and skirted the property to the creek that cut through the area. She slipped off her heavy black shoes and thick kneesocks, then she caught up her skirt above her ankles and went to perch on her favorite log, dangling her toes in the refreshing water.

"I see we're of a similar mind today."

Joseph's cheerful voice almost made her tilt backward off the log as she glanced down the creek and saw him sitting no more than ten feet away. Her gaze skittered to his clothes on the bush and then back to his bare chest. He grinned at her.

She said the first thing that came to mind. "Where are your glasses?"

"Safe on the bank." He started to tread water with

his arms, as if preparing to come closer, and she jumped to her feet, her bare toes digging into the rough bark of the log.

"Uh . . . just stay there, please . . . I've got to go back and start supper."

"Nervous, Mrs. Lambert?" he asked.

"*Nee,*" she snapped, though her face flushed.

He laughed aloud, the sound causing chills to run in delicious tingles across the back of her neck and down her spine. She pushed the intriguing sensations away and lifted her chin.

"Maybe you're the one who's nervous."

His smile deepened, and he held her captive with the intensity of his dark eyes. "Maybe. This is all new to me, too—having a wife share my bath."

She stuttered on her reply. "I am not sharing your bath. And why aren't you bathing at home in the hip bath, like everyone else?"

He splashed at a stray dragonfly. "I don't know. I guess I thought I'd preserve your maidenly dignity."

Another thought crossed her mind and caused her to frown in irritation. "You do realize that anyone could come along here and see you?"

"*Ach.* You mean another girl, right?"

She nodded in spite of herself. "That is exactly what I mean."

"Well then, I'd best get out, don't you think?" He moved as if to rise and she turned and fled barefoot, his laughter ringing in her ears.

. . .

Joseph brought her shoes and socks to her while her father looked on askance.

Abigail stood next to the stove, heating up the bean and bacon soup Judith had given her so she didn't have to worry about supper.

"You seem to have forgotten something," Joseph teased in a low tone.

Abigail ducked her head, then lifted it again, only to wish she hadn't when she caught the clean, masculine scent of him. His hair was damp, too, and clung to his neck overlong in places.

"You need a haircut."

"Can I trust you with a pair of scissors?"

"I cut Father's hair," she replied in an injured tone.

They both turned to look at Solomon Kauffman's hair, which was actually layered neatly and fell with some style to complement his long beard.

"What is it?" he asked, frowning at them.

"Just debating the merits of a haircut at home," Joseph answered.

"*Ach*, well, Abigail is a fair hand with the shears."

"Well, *gut*, then."

After supper Joseph found himself seated on the back porch. A large white sheet was draped around his neck and flowed down over his chest and arms. Abigail stood considering him while he chafed under her perusal.

"Just cut it already."

"Take off your glasses. I need to see the true shape of your face."

"Honestly, Abby, there's no style with the Amish— just saw away."

He knew she was ignoring him and he closed his eyes, holding his glasses under the sheet. When she first touched the back of his neck, he started with a little jump.

"You are nervous, Mr. Lambert," she teased.

He laughed. "Again, maybe—this is new to me too."

She ran her fingers through his hair, sending exquisite chills down his back. When was the last time someone had touched him with such gentleness? Her delicate, tentative fingers were playing havoc with his insides, and all she was doing was cutting his hair. He blew out a breath of disgust. Still, there was something to be said for being attracted to one's own wife, no matter the circumstances of the marriage.

She diligently combed and cut, and he began to relax beneath her touch. She had the persistence of an artist, and he knew no one had ever taken so much time with his hair. He let his hands rest on his knees and almost dropped his glasses when she spoke.

"There!" she said with satisfaction. She held up a small hand mirror. "Father always wants to see the back. What do you think?"

He slipped his glasses back on and peered at the mirror behind his shoulder. His dark hair fell neat and even, and she'd done something to make it curl at his nape.

"It's great, Abby. Thank you."

She trailed the mirror around to his front and he poked self-consciously beneath her gaze at his bangs. "Really great."

She smiled at him, clearly pleased, but there was also

an air of suppressed excitement about her that made him just a little nervous.

"What?" he asked.

She clutched the mirror to her chest. "I learned how to can today . . . carrots and sweet corn. For you."

He smiled up at her. "Where did you go?"

"In town, to Yoder's Pantry. Do you remember? It's a restaurant—one of the cooks was really nice and taught me about canning. I helped all morning and afternoon."

He felt a funny feeling in his stomach as he watched her. A surge of protectiveness and caring for her fragile excitement. For him. She said she'd learned for him. It humbled his heart somehow in the way that a hundred other gifts might not have done. He reached his hand out from beneath the sheet and caught her own smaller one in his palm.

"Thank you, Abby. I think that's one of the nicest things anyone's ever done for me."

She blushed, and he had to suppress the urge to rise and take her in his arms. It was one thing to tease, but quite another to kiss her with intent. And the way he was feeling at the moment didn't allow for any casual contact.

"I'd better go in and clean up the dishes. Will you— bring me some corn tomorrow from the field?"

"First thing, I promise."

"*Danki.*" She gathered up the scissors and the mirror and whisked the sheet from around his neck with one hand, shaking the dark clippings out onto the ground.

"The birds like the hair to feather their nests for winter."

He nodded. "I remember."

"All right, well, *gut.*"

She went in through the screen door, leaving him sitting in the falling darkness, alone with his thoughts.

CHAPTER ELEVEN

In the two weeks following the haircut, an uneasy tenseness settled on Abigail whenever Joseph was around. When she'd been touching him, she had felt overwhelmed by the feelings of tenderness and attraction that had caused her heart to race and her hands to be not quite as steady as she would have liked.

She tried to evaluate her feelings objectively as she lay on her bed one afternoon, snatching a few minutes of time for herself. Was he handsome? *Hot*, as Tillie had said? Yes. Was he intelligent, kind to the kitten and to her father as well as to herself? Yes.

But so what? There were plenty of kind, handsome men about. Why should she find herself becoming entangled with the man she'd married out of convenience? She turned over and thumped her pillow, groaning aloud. She hated now what she'd done to him, how she'd trapped him, but he never seemed to give her an opportunity to talk about it. And half the time, she had no idea what he was thinking behind those deep, dark eyes of his.

She laid her head down on her pillow for a moment, then she reached her hand down between the mattress and bedspring, sliding out one of the teen magazines she hadn't looked at in a while. Today the glossy *Englisch* girls and boys annoyed her with their perfect smiles and posed looks. Somehow they'd lost their appeal, and she wasn't sure exactly how it had happened. She sighed and was about to thrust the magazine back into its hiding place when the door opened and Joseph walked in.

"Hey, what are you doing?" He smiled, then caught sight of the magazine.

Abigail flushed and ignored the urge to stuff it under her belly.

"Just relaxing for a minute," she replied with as much casualness as she could muster. "What are you doing?"

"I need a clean shirt. I have to run into town to get a blade for the harvester for your father. What are you reading?"

He came close and sank down on the edge of the bed. She tried to ignore the pull of his handsomeness and the smell of the outdoors that clung to his skin and sweat-dampened hair.

"Nothing—it's just silly, really."

"Let me see."

"No, I'd rather not." She moved the magazine to her far hand and turned her head away from him. He reached across her back and snatched it from her, as she'd expected he would. She waited for his recriminations to fall on her head.

She heard the pages turning, and her face burned when she thought about all of the feminine details contained within. Then she felt a light tap on the back of her cap.

"Hmm . . . here you are. I've got to get moving or your *daed* will have a fit. Do you want to come?"

She rolled over and looked up at him, taking the magazine back with suspicion. "That's it?"

"What?" He paused in easing down his suspenders.

"The magazine? You're not going to say anything?"

"What do you want me to say?"

She bounced upward to sit, unsure of why she was irritated. "I don't know—something."

He laughed as he grabbed his extra shirt. "I will never understand women."

"What do you mean, *women*? Shouldn't you say *woman*? I am your only wife, right?"

"Look, do you want to go or not?"

"No," she pouted, feeling foolish.

"Suit yourself."

He whistled as he buttoned the shirt, and she glared at him. For some reason she wanted to fight, to break his easy calm. Even as she thought it, though, her heart convicted her. He was her husband. She'd made him sweet corn, cut his hair, and thought about him more than she ever had any other man . . . so what was wrong with her?

He had his hand on the doorknob when she cried out, "Wait!"

"What?"

"I'll go."

"Great, let's move."

Abigail slipped off the bed and grabbed up her

change purse, where she kept the household money her father gave her each month. She followed Joseph down the steps, pleased that she could go with him without worrying about supper. She'd been using the valuable recipe cards from Judith to a distinct advantage and had made great strides in the kitchen. She'd also found that she enjoyed both her own endeavors and the smiles of pleasure on Joseph's face when he tried something new. Today she left ham and green beans and a fresh huckleberry pie warming on the stovetop as she hurried out the door.

Joseph brought Carl around, and she climbed into the buggy without assistance. They set off at a good trot.

"I've got to get that blade back to your *daed*, but I think we can squeeze in a bit of lunch if you'd like." He slanted her a glance from his dark eyes, and she nodded in agreement.

It would be the first time they'd gone out together anywhere but church, and she thought it was both ironic and sad that they were having their first date weeks into their marriage. But she refused to be glum and set about chattering in the way she was used to doing to entertain a man. When she'd covered everything from the crops to the weather, Joseph laughed out loud and held up a placating hand.

"Whoa . . . please, Abby . . . you don't have to talk just to entertain me."

"I wasn't," she snapped, feeling embarrassed.

"Okay . . . let's just say that I like your normal way of talking."

"Which is what?"

"To the point."

She huffed aloud. "I should not have come."

He reached out a large hand and covered her own where they rested in her lap. "I'm sorry. I just want you to feel comfortable around me."

"I do," she lied, then thought better of it. "At least—sometimes I do."

He laughed, squeezing her hands, then letting go. "That's better. I can see that we're going to have to do more courting and playing until you feel more comfortable."

"Well," she admitted, "I do like to go out for lunch."

"And where should we go?"

"Yoder's Pantry," she answered promptly.

"All right. Yoder's it is." He clucked to Carl to pick up the pace.

Abigail tried to avoid glancing in his direction and looked at the passing farms instead. The land was alive with the harvest; crops coming in, butchering time, work from sunup till sundown. But soon it would be over, and the time for the county fair would come around. She wondered if Joseph would take her and realized that it was the first time she'd have a canned vegetable to enter. The thought made her smile to herself, and the day suddenly became more than promising.

. . .

Joseph caught the smell of fresh mint that drifted to him from her hair and tried to concentrate on his driving. In truth, he knew that her father wouldn't like it if he'd known Joseph was planning to spend lunch in town. But time with one's wife somehow outweighed a blade for the harvester, and he decided it was worth the possible irritation on the part of his father-in-law.

"So, you're looking well today. That wine-colored blouse is becoming." He sounded like a stilted old man, he thought ruefully. Why was he being so formal? She'd kept him at an effective distance of late, and he made a sudden decision to change that over lunch.

"Thank you," she murmured. "You look well too."

"Fresh from the field?"

"Well . . ." She turned appraising blue eyes upon him. "*Ya.*"

It was something, he considered.

They arrived in town in good time, and Joseph hitched Carl to the post outside Yoder's. He came around and made a point to help Abby down, letting her slide against the warmth of his body for a brief moment. He was pleased to see a blush on her cheeks and caught her hand with goodwill as they entered the restaurant. Joseph noticed that there seemed to be some secret between his wife and the waitress who greeted them, as they both smiled and looked at him appraisingly.

"Joseph," Abby said. "This is Tillie, a *gut* friend of mine. She helped get me my canning lessons."

Joseph smiled. "Then I hope that you will be a good friend of mine too. I really appreciate your helping Abby. Her sweet corn was great."

Tillie nodded with a happy smile and led them to a table near the window looking out onto the street.

"What would you like to drink?" she asked.

Joseph darted a look at Abby and thought how funny it was that he was having an actual first date with his wife. In his old life, the situation would have called for champagne, but he was more than happy to ask for hot tea. Abby did the same.

"So, this is a nice place," Joseph remarked.

"*Ya.*" Abby giggled. "Father had many a meal here before you came along."

Joseph gave her his best smile. "Your cooking has really improved."

"Thanks to you."

"It's been my pleasure," he said, reaching across the table to catch her slender fingers in his hand. "It's funny," he said. "I forgot that the Amish don't wear wedding bands or jewelry. I'd have liked to have given you an engagement ring."

"For our very short engagement?"

"Why don't we try to let that go?" he suggested. "You know, you've never considered that I might have been interested in marriage . . . and in you."

"Really?" She blinked wide blue eyes.

"Really. Now let's just concentrate on tea. Here it is."

"What will you have?" Tillie asked. "The specials today are potato soup, stuffed peppers, and Ruth's own sour cherry pie."

"That all sounds good to me," Joseph said, closing the menu, which he had yet to even glance at. He ignored Abby's startled look. "I'm hungry," he confessed.

"I'll just have the soup and the pie."

"Great. I'll get that right out to you two newlyweds."

Joseph saw Abby shoot a surprised look at her friend and smiled to himself. He lifted her fingertips to his lips and felt her try to pull away.

"Joseph! We're in a public place, and my father is not around. You don't have to pretend."

He smiled at her. "I think we're past pretending, Abby, don't you?" He let her go, and she tucked her hands into the safety of her lap.

"I don't know what you mean."

He took a long sip of his tea and watched her until she looked away out the window. Their food soon arrived, and he took pleasure in everything, but especially in watching Abby wriggle under his obvious attentions. It occurred to him that he'd never had such fun going out for lunch before.

CHAPTER TWELVE

It was mid-October and a bright, beautiful morning. But Abigail had seen the sun far too early for her liking, having been up half the night with a laboring sow. She had always felt more competent in working with the farm animals than she'd ever felt in the house, and the past night had been no exception.

The kitten, now a spry, streaking little thing that she'd named George, had kept her company while she'd let Joseph sleep. Now she came out of the barn, having finished tending to the mother and piglets. She wiped her filthy hands on her apron and blinked in the sunlight—then stopped dead, staring at the apparition of a low-slung blue convertible and a tousled red-haired *Englisch* girl with a devastating white smile. She was talking to Joseph, who leaned against the car door with familiarity, looking down into her face.

Abigail straightened her spine and walked toward her husband.

"Oh, here's Abby now. Abby, this is Molly, a—friend from the past."

Molly scooted her charming figure forward on the

front seat and leaned to extend a hand to Abigail. "Hi," she said with a bright smile.

"Hello," Abigail returned, catching Joseph's eye. "Joseph has mentioned you . . . your hair . . . It's lovely."

Molly giggled and looked at Joseph. "Thanks. It was always his favorite, but I guess he went and chose a blonde anyway. I can't believe you're married."

Abigail was working herself up to a boil, and Joseph must have sensed it, because he straightened from the car and looped an arm around her waist.

"Married as can be," he said with cheerful vigor.

"Well, I just was out this way and asked around for you. I'm staying at a bed-and-breakfast in town. I thought I'd stop for a few minutes," Molly offered, clearly wanting an invitation to stay and visit.

Abigail tried to ignore the girl's desire for hospitality, but her heart convicted her. "Would . . . you like to come in, then?" She felt Joseph's surprise.

Molly smiled. "Of course. Thanks." She reached out her slender arms to Joseph, who moved away from Abigail to swing her out of the car.

"I'll just go on in and change my apron and leave you two—friends—alone for a moment," Abigail said sweetly, though her heart was pounding. She marched past them and entered the kitchen, where she stood frozen for a moment. Then she found herself beginning to pray. "Please, Lord, give me patience, an extra measure, in this situation. Please bless this girl, Molly. Oh, Lord, please guard Joseph's heart. Help him not to remember too much of his time with her."

She realized that they were on the porch and rushed

to change her apron. She was slicing apple bread when they came in and was grateful for something to focus on.

"Mmm . . . a real Amish kitchen . . ." Molly looked around her like she was in a museum. "I'd like to paint it, Joseph."

"We like the light blue," Abigail said.

Molly laughed. "No, I mean paint it . . . like a scene, honey. I'm an artist."

"Oh." Abigail blushed, feeling foolish. "Would you like a drink?"

"What do you have?"

She was about to reply when Joseph interrupted, for some reason in a dry tone. "Lemonade, tea, or spring-water, Molly."

The girl laughed again, tossing her curls. "Things sure have changed, haven't they? I'll have tea, honey. If it's cold . . ."

Abigail nodded. "Of course. Please sit down. Joseph, what would you like?"

She kept her expression placid, though she felt furious with him for some reason. After all, he had no idea that the girl was going to come looking for him . . . did he?

"*Nee*, you sit. I'll get the drinks. Do you want lemon-ade?" Joseph asked.

Abigail could tell that something was bothering him by the tense set of his jaw, but she wasn't sure whether she was the cause, or Molly. After all, her conscience pricked her, she was the interloper here in a way. She'd forced this marriage upon him when maybe he'd been wanting to marry this beautiful *Englisch* girl instead.

But if that were so, why had he come back? She stopped trying to puzzle it out when she realized Molly had asked her a question.

"I'm sorry. I was thinking . . . Please, what did you say?"

"I asked how long you've been married . . . It can't be long. I was seeing Joseph as recently as a year ago."

Abigail flushed and met her husband's eye. He returned her gaze with an expressionless face. She pursed her lips, then smiled with sweetness, moving to slide an arm around Joseph's lean waist.

"Actually," she murmured, batting her eyelashes with a coy effect, "we're still newlyweds. Isn't that right, my love?"

Joseph half turned toward her body and stared down into her eyes. "Indeed. And I hope that we'll always feel like newlyweds, even when we're old and gray."

Abigail flushed beneath his intense eyes and at his unexpected words. She also noticed that Molly looked none too pleased with his response.

"Well," their visitor said with a toss of her curls, "I suppose that's nice, but what is it that they say—'Young marriages are the most fragile'?"

"I've never heard that saying," Joseph remarked. "Now let's finish our drinks. I've got work to get back to, as does Abby."

Molly quickly recovered her composure. Indeed, if Abigail didn't know any better, she would have believed the girl's sincerity and goodwill. But to someone who'd led boys on in the past herself, it was obvious to Abigail just exactly what Molly was up to.

She sighed within herself, kept up a silent running stream of petition to the Lord, and was glad when Joseph finally escorted the girl to the back porch and out of their lives for good.

CHAPTER THIRTEEN

Joseph watched the car drive away and felt the pull of desire so badly that he could taste it. As she said good-bye, Molly had offered him a bottle of pain pills with the same nonchalance that she always had. He'd wanted to say no, had heard himself say no in his head, but everything that was flesh in him was crying out yes. And he'd taken them. His eyes burned as he thought about the good feeling, the elation the pills had always given him. He'd felt more confident, productive, and kind. He'd asked himself a million times when he was with the *Englisch* why painkillers couldn't just be legal for everyone—especially when he'd believed they made people not just feel better but *be* better people. He was amazed now that he ever could have thought like that, but that was part of true addiction. And so was the fact that he now clutched the white-capped bottle until it imprinted his palm.

He swallowed hard and shivered as he looked at the dust rising from the lane as Molly's car turned onto the highway. He started to pray, just as he'd done the first time he'd said no, when it had nearly killed him to do so. Withdrawal, done alone in an empty apartment, with no support or food, had been a nightmare. He hadn't emerged victorious, just alive, and barely at that. God had been the only One with him, and it was then that he first felt the incredible desire to return home to his Amish roots. So then why had he taken the bottle? He stared down at it in his hand. Was he crazy? He had peace, freedom, a new way of life, and he was standing there willing to throw it all away.

The creak of the screen door brought him to his senses, and he turned to face Abby, who stood uncertainly on the porch.

"So that was Molly—the redhead," she said in a small voice.

He thrust the bottle into the pocket of his pants, mounted the wooden steps, and caught her unyielding figure in his arms.

"What are you doing?" she asked.

"Holding you."

"Why?" She tried to shrug him off.

"Because I need to right now. Hold me back, Abby—please." He rubbed his hands up and down her back and nuzzled his chin against her soft neck.

"I will not," she snapped. "Not when you're just pretending that I'm her."

He pulled away from her then and stared down into her hurt blue eyes. "Don't think that. It's not true."

"Then why do you want me?"

The question hung in the air between them.

He moved to thumb her delicate jaw. "You're my wife," he whispered. "Not her."

He ignored the sudden parting of her lips, the

yielding of her thick eyelashes against the cream of her cheeks, and began to feather kisses along her temple and down her jaw. He felt rather than heard the small sigh escape her as the tension unwound in her body, and she lifted her chin to give him better access to the line of her throat. He made a choked sound of pleasure and let his mouth trail along her sweet-smelling skin. He stopped and stared down at her; her hair was coming undone, and a few hairpins pattered to the porch below.

He gently lowered his mouth to hers, and she began to kiss him back. He closed his eyes against the wash of sensation, drowning in the honeybee-light touch of her lips. She lifted her hands to touch each side of his face and rub the soft lay of his beard.

"I'll hold you," she breathed. She lifted her slender arms and encircled his shoulders, and he gave in to the gentle touch, rocking his weight forward.

His eyes filled with tears as the thought came to him that perhaps the Lord Himself had had His hand in their marriage.

A sudden clearing of a masculine throat startled him and he pulled back, glancing over his shoulder. His father-in-law stood on the steps of the porch.

"It's lunchtime," Mr. Kauffman announced in a gruff voice.

"Right," Joseph agreed, turning fully to shield Abby's disheveled appearance. He felt her press against his back.

"I've a few chores to take care of in the barn. I'll be in directly." He stomped down the steps and walked away while Joseph turned back to his wife.

"Thank you," he murmured.

She nodded, clearly flustered, and bent to retrieve her hairpins. He stooped to help her at the same time and they knocked heads.

"I'm sorry." He laughed. "Are you all right?"

"*Ya,*" she said, smiling. "I'm fine."

He handed her the pins and she rose to hurry inside, her hands at her hair, leaving him to stare after her.

CHAPTER FOURTEEN

The bottle of pills stood among the casual clutter on Abby's bureau with deceptive innocence. Part of the everyday landscape to someone else, the bottle screamed to him with a chilling audibleness that reached to the edge of the bed where he sat and into his very soul. Abby was downstairs, cleaning up after supper, and he was wrestling a demon he thought he'd defeated. He rose and walked to the window, staring out at the moonlit fields. But out of the corner of his eye, the bottle called. Maybe just one . . . just one and he'd feel beyond good. He might even get up enough nerve to press Abby into a few kisses . . .

He shook his head, amazed at the pulse of addiction that riveted through his veins. Then he thought of Molly. She'd been the one to first introduce him to the drug, to drugs in general, but specifically to the pain pills. And he'd been in pain when he'd first met her, hurting deep inside for want of a family, a future. Now he had those very things, but he was still willing to pick up the drug.

He touched the lid with his fingertips, then gave the bottle an experimental shake. He clenched his jaw and unscrewed the lid, automatically doing a visual count of the white pills inside. A good twenty or so. He hadn't had anything in over a year, so just one would probably be enough to produce the familiar feeling. At the end, before, he'd had to take four at a time to get there. He spilled a single pill out into his hand, and a roaring like wind in a train tunnel filled his ears. His eyes watered; his mouth burned. But then it came to him—peace. The peace of *Derr Herr*. It crept softly in on the breeze of the dark air, swirling around him, touching his fevered head and heart. He drew a shaky breath and put the pill back in the bottle. He knew for sure that he could lean on the Lord, that Christ in him could defeat this unholy desire over and over again, if need be.

As he moved to replace the lid on the bottle, the door opened and Abby walked in. He started and spilled the bottle, the pills falling in a splatter on the hardwood floor. She stared at him, confusion on her pretty brow.

"Joseph, are you ill? Have you been to the doctor?"

He wet his lips, uncertain of what to say. But then his heart convicted him, and he began to speak in measured tones. "No, Abby—I–I'm not sick, at least not in the way you're thinking."

"What do you mean?" she asked, bending to pick up a pill.

"Don't . . ." He broke off, and she rose to her feet, extending her hand to him. He shook his head. "Abby, when I came back here, I told you, or the community, only part of my story."

She dropped her arm and walked into the room,

closing the door behind her. She sat down on the bed and looked up at him.

"Well then, tell me the whole story."

He gave her a wry smile. "You'll hate it—and maybe me. You won't understand."

Her bosom heaved indignantly. "You can try at least—does Molly know the whole story?"

He sank to the floor, his back against the wall. "Here." He stretched out a long arm. "Read the prescription on the bottle."

She leaned forward and took it from him, and he watched her face as she processed the name.

"Molly Harding? Why do you have her medicine?"

He waited while she clutched the bottle against her apron.

"I took it from her."

"You—stole it?"

"*Nee* . . . She offered, and I took it."

Abby shook her head in confusion. "What are you trying to say?"

"I'm a drug addict, Abby. Those are pain pills. I used to take them all the time, just to feel good."

She bowed her head, staring at the bottle in her hand. "You say 'used to.' Do you still?"

"No. But I wanted to—tonight, today. And I'll probably want to again. But for now, right before you came in, I felt like *Derr Herr* was with me, and I was able to stop. I believe that as long as I cling to Him, hide in Him, that I'll be able to stop."

She took a deep breath. "And Molly. Are you— addicted to her?"

He frowned, not understanding her trail of thought. "Molly . . . No, she means nothing to me." It was true, he realized, deep inside. There wasn't anything left for Molly.

"So whatever you had with her, with the pills—it's over?"

"Yes."

"Do you want it to be?" She looked him square in the eye. "I mean . . . You know what I did, we both know—how I got you to marry me."

"We're a *gut* pair, aren't we? Both of us thinking we're not worth the other . . . but maybe the Lord has a plan in all of this."

She placed her heavy shoe lightly atop a pill beneath her foot and pressed. "I want these pills gone. I want her gone. Will you let me help you?"

It was not what he had expected—her calmness, her steadiness. Where was the petulant, demanding girl who'd had the boys dangling after her barely two months ago?

"Well?"

"What?"

"Will you let me help you—do something, anything?"

Anything. The word echoed across his mind. When had someone last offered selflessly to do anything for him?

"Pray for me," he choked finally.

"I'll pray for you, for us."

"Me too."

"Gut." She pressed her foot fully to the floor, leveling the pill into fine powder. "I'll get rid of the pills?"

It was a question. He nodded in agreement, then spoke the truth.

"But it would be easy for me to get more."

"From Molly?"

"Not just her. Anywhere, really . . ."

"Are you going to get more?"

"I can only promise you moment by moment, day by day, Abby. If I say no forever and then fall, I'd be lying to you, and I don't want that. Not for you. Not for us."

It was the closest he'd come to admitting his feelings for her, but as he watched her beautiful face, he knew she was already on to another thought.

"Dr. Knepp . . . and his wife . . . they know about all of this, don't they?" She gestured with the pill bottle.

"*Ya.*"

"How?"

He sighed deeply. "Dr. Knepp was at a conference in Philadelphia. He—found me, on the streets. I had pneumonia and was out of it with a fever. I was speaking Pennsylvania *Deitsch*. He heard it and brought me back to the home of some friends there. He and Mrs. Knepp nursed me back to health, then they asked if I wanted to come here. It was the Lord who made it coincidence that he practiced in the same community where I was born."

"So he got you to stop the pills, then?"

"*Nee*, I did that alone . . . or with *Derr Herr*, I should say. It was before I got sick. I left Molly, all of our so-called friends, and went to an empty apartment and battled it out. But then I had no money, no food. I got sick—but I told Dr. Knepp the truth. He said—he said that he believed in second chances and persuaded me to come back, so I did."

"But, Joseph, how could you let Molly here then today? How could you even have her around?" Her voice rose in confusion, in accusation.

He hung his head. "How could I take the pills then too? I can't explain it to you . . ."

"Then you kissed me like that, on the back porch . . ." Her voice trailed off. "I thought—I thought that you . . ."

He looked at her. "I meant that kiss, Abby, every second of it."

"I don't know if you did or if you didn't, Joseph." Her shoulders sagged then straightened. "Please go, leave the room. I want to deal with these pills."

He slid back up the wall, needing to touch her, but he felt the barrier of her hurt, her confusion. Yet what did he want? It was enough that she'd said she'd pray—he didn't expect her to love him.

CHAPTER FIFTEEN

Abigail methodically began to gather up the pills from the floor. She got down on her hands and knees, looking under the bed and peering beneath the bureau. Then she realized that she could look at the bottle and tell how many were supposed to be there—if no one had taken any, that was. If Joseph hadn't . . .

She pulled her mind and heart together in support of him. He said he hadn't, so he hadn't.

But her mind whirled when she thought about his revelation. She had read things in her magazines about teenage addiction and drugs, but it all seemed so far away from her way of everyday life. Yet it was real, very real, and it threatened the one person who had gone out of his way to help her, despite how she had treated him in the beginning.

She sat back on her heels, deep in thought. And what of Molly? Abigail clutched a white pill in her hand and wished she could bring back the scene, turn away the red-haired girl who'd mocked her in her own house and brought this turmoil back into Joseph's life. Yet he had said it was a choice.

Still, she rose with determination. She may not be

able to keep him from other drugs in the future, but she could keep one girl from her husband; she was sure of it.

She grabbed up a dark cloak and put the last of the pills into the bottle. Then she slipped down the stairs and out the front door before anyone could see her. Her father had gone to bed, and Joseph must have gone into the living room. She moved steadily in the dark, going into the barn. Once there, she emptied the pills out onto her father's workbench, took a mallet, and pulverized them into a pile of white powder. Then she scraped the stuff back into the bottle, being careful to wipe the bench clean of every trace of whiteness. She peeled off the label on the bottle and tore it to tiny shreds, adding it to the bottle, then left the barn, moving into the cold night air. Whispering a prayer, she stood behind the barn, where she opened and tilted the medicine bottle, holding her hand aloft. An autumn wind caught the contents and sent them blowing away into nothingness. She drew a deep breath of peace. She walked calmly back to the house and threw the bottle into the garbage, being careful to press it down under several items.

"That was the easy part," she murmured aloud as she made her way back outside. "Now for the true battle."

She prayed as she hitched up Carl to the buggy. She felt as though she was driving to meet not just another woman, but a direct threat to her marriage and way of life. If Molly so carelessly thought to hurt Joseph, what else might she do if she stayed in town for a few days? And though she believed him when he said the girl didn't matter, she wasn't sure where Molly stood, especially since she'd gone to the trouble to find him.

She caught a firmer grip on the reins as a car whizzed past, honking at the buggy. She didn't especially like to drive at night, but it was something she'd learned to do well nonetheless. And Carl was a steady horse.

She soon gained the town, and though there were numerous bed-and-breakfasts throughout the streets and outlying areas, she'd prayed that she might be able to recognize Molly's blue convertible easily from the street. And sure enough, by the time she'd come to the third business, Bender's Bed-and-Breakfast, she saw the metallic gleam of the blue convertible reflected in the streetlamps. She pulled Carl in and slipped out of the buggy to hitch him up to the convenient post. The place was Amish owned and run; she knew the Benders vaguely, though they attended a different service.

She saw that lights still burned in the downstairs windows, and she marched up the steps and knocked. Her heart pounded, but she still prayed beneath her breath. *Derr Herr* would give her the words that she needed to say. The door opened, and Mrs. Bender peered out into the relative dark of the porch.

"*Ya?*"

"Mrs. Bender, it's Abigail—Kauffman. But I've recently married. I'm Abigail Lambert now."

Mrs. Bender smiled and the door widened. "*Kumme* in out of the chilly night."

Abigail stepped inside and darted a look into the adjoining sitting room. She was relieved to see only Mr.

Bender, reading *The Budget*. He nodded to her, then went back to his paper.

"I'm sorry for the late hour, Mrs. Bender." In truth, Abigail wasn't entirely certain of the time.

"It doesn't matter. Do you want some tea? What can I do for you?"

"Tea would be nice."

Abigail followed her into the kitchen and sat down at the wooden table. She glanced around at the beautifully carved wooden cupboards with their intricate scrolling.

Mrs. Bender followed her gaze. "My Luke does cabinetry on the side," she said with pride.

"It's beautiful."

"*Danki.* And your husband?"

"He works with my father."

"*Gut.* It's good to keep work in the family."

Abigail nodded, unsure how to broach the subject she'd come about.

"So you're Abigail Lambert now, hmm? It seems your husband is a bit popular around here lately."

Abigail lifted her gaze to Mrs. Bender's twinkling eyes.

"*Ach* . . . that's what I've come about."

"I'm sorry, my dear, for telling the *Englisch* girl that I knew of him."

"That's all right. And I . . . I don't want to disturb your guests, but . . ."

"You need to talk with her?"

"*Ya.*"

"Second door on the right at the top of the steps. I'll keep your tea warm for you."

Abigail got to her feet. "*Danki*, Mrs. Bender. I won't be long."

She went out of the kitchen and up the carved staircase, sliding her hand along the patina of the balustrade. She continued to pray beneath her breath until she came to the door. She knocked on the wood, and a moment later Molly stood in the doorway, considering her with an insolent smile.

"I think I rather expected you, little Amish wife. Or maybe not. Aren't your kind supposed to avoid confrontation?"

Abigail spoke in a quiet voice, though her ire was pricked by the other girl's words. "May I come in, please?"

"Sure, honey."

Abigail entered the room and closed the door behind her. She noted the heavy smell of perfume and the abundance of clothes thrown about. A half-painted scene of the countryside stood on an easel near the window, and fresh paint stained a palette. The bed was unmade, and a cigarette smoldered in an ashtray on the nightstand. It was a room of chaos for Abigail's senses despite the beautiful carved furniture and rumpled Nine Patch quilt, and for a moment she felt out of her depth. But then she remembered why she'd come.

Molly lounged with her denim-clad hip against a bureau while Abigail collected her thoughts.

"I can't believe that Joseph's got a girl fighting his battles for him."

"I'm his wife."

"Are you? I've heard it nosed about that yours was

a rather hasty marriage. Maybe you're not as pure as you'd like to present—all lemonade and apple spice . . . But then, Joseph is a very persuasive man."

Abigail smiled. "It might interest you to know that my character is exactly as you say, but his is not. You see, despite the Amish dress, I think I've been like you in some ways. So I understand what's in your heart."

Molly snorted and crossed her arms. "You're a child, for all you know of the real world."

"Maybe . . . but maybe not. Maybe you came looking for Joseph because you saw that potential for good in him and you hungered for it. Or perhaps you wanted to destroy it, because it's something you can't truly understand."

"Oh, I understand a lot more about Joseph than you ever will."

Abigail lifted her chin. "And I understand that you're hurt and lonely and despise who and what you are deep inside."

"Shut up," Molly hissed. "Do you think that I'm going to stand here and take this from some little girl? Some stupid, isolated, insular little girl. So you know about the drugs, hmm? But do you know everything?"

"I know what my husband told me, that's enough."

Molly laughed as she turned her back and picked up a paintbrush. She gave the canvas a few experimental strokes, then looked over her shoulder.

"Do you know that you can never trust a drug addict? That they lie, out of habit. Do you know that it's a fact that 'once an addict, always an addict'?" She stepped back to consider the painting, then began to walk around Abigail. "Do you know how easily he took those pills from me, at the very beginning of his so-called new life? What do you think he's going to do when things get hard? When boredom sets in? And it will. Joseph is too smart to be occupied by cows and bonnets for very long. How are you ever going to trust him fully? Can you answer that?"

Abigail felt as though it was a hungry wolf that prowled around her . . . but then a word of Scripture came to her mind. *"No weapon that is formed against thee shall prosper."* This girl was using all she had because she was intimidated, scared inside, and so very, very lost.

"I can't answer that, and that answer doesn't belong to you anyway. It belongs to Joseph. So listen well to what I say . . ."

Molly stood still and cocked one hip. "Go ahead, honey."

"If you come near my husband again, in any way, it will not go well with you."

"Aren't the Amish against violence?" Molly reached and flicked at one of Abigail's *kapp* strings.

"Yes, but you see, I'm not very good at being Amish . . . so remember what I say."

She stared with intent into the other girl's eyes until Molly looked away. It was enough for Abigail.

She turned and left the room without looking back.

CHAPTER SIXTEEN

Joseph paced the tiny bedroom. It was after ten o'clock, and Abby was nowhere to be found on the property. He hadn't told her father, but he'd found Carl and the buggy gone. He also knew, without a doubt, where she had gone. One aspect of his masculine pride was affronted at letting it seem like he'd sent his wife to fight his battles. But another part of him was touched to the depths that she would so want to defend him.

It was not that he couldn't go after her; there were three other horses in the barn. Yet something held him in check, some instinct or feeling from the Lord that he should wait.

But he wasn't good at waiting.

Finally he heard the sound of hoofbeats on the lane. He resisted the urge to run down and help her unhitch. Maybe she needed some time alone. But soon enough he heard her quiet movements as she entered the house and came up the stairs. He leaned against the window-sill, trying not to appear anxious when she walked in.

The first thing he noticed was that she looked very pale and distracted. She barely seemed aware that he was there as she slipped off her dark cape and missed the nail as she went to hang it up. She sat down on the edge of the bed, and he saw that her hands were shaking.

"Abby?" he said, coming to kneel in front of her. "What's wrong?" He caught her hands together in his own and felt their icy coldness.

She looked at him. "I saw Molly."

He nodded. "I thought that's where you were. You didn't have to do that."

"I know . . . and I felt all right when I was there, but then—coming home, I just started to shake."

He put his arms around her, rocking her forward until he felt her hands slide up tentatively along his shoulders.

"It's all right, Abby. I'm here, and you need never again deal with Molly. I promise." He felt her stiffen and drew back to study her face. "What is it?"

She wet her lips, and he was hard-pressed not to be distracted by the motion of her tongue, but he dragged his gaze back up to her blue eyes.

"It's—nothing. I'm all right now, just tired. I think I'll go to bed."

He didn't let her go. "Abby—I know you. At least, I think I do. What did she say?"

Abby wouldn't meet his eyes. "You said—you promised. And she said . . ."

"That you can never trust the word of a drug addict?" She nodded.

He slid his hands back to rest on his thighs and looked at her. "Well, maybe she's right. That's up to you to decide. But I've been honest with you this far. It's my plan to keep on telling the truth, inasmuch as I know it about myself. But I can't spend a lifetime trying to prove something to you; that would be cheating both of us."

"I don't want to hurt you."

"You haven't. At least, the truth may hurt, but it's a clean cut. I'm fine." He paused, then touched her hand once more. "How are you?"

"Better."

"*Gut,*" he whispered.

He rose up on his knees and bent forward to press his lips against her own. *Light,* he told himself. *Keep it light. A good-night kiss . . . that's all . . .*

But she was suddenly kissing him back with a fervor, her arms around him, her hands doing small things with the back of his hair that made him catch his breath.

"Abby . . ." he managed. "What are you—"

"I just want to forget tonight. Help me forget, Joseph, please."

It would have been easy just then to give in to the pull of her words, to help her forget, but he caught an iron grip on his emotions and pushed her gently away from him. He didn't want her responsiveness when it was based on fear or worry. He shook his head, swallowing hard.

"Abby, no . . . I can't . . . not like this. You'd resent it later."

"But you're my husband." Her voice took on a shrill note.

"I know, but . . ."

"Never mind. I'm going to bed." She yanked herself away from him.

"Abby, please . . ."

"Good night!" She climbed into bed, not bothering to change into a nightdress, and yanked the quilt up and over her shoulder.

Joseph slid in misery to his own cold place on the floor.

. . .

Abigail felt so confused and angry, she could spit. She tried to regulate her breathing beneath the cocoon of the quilt and to ignore Joseph's rustlings on the floor. She couldn't believe that she'd just been kissing him like that and he'd rejected her! She squirmed in embarrassment. And then that awful girl and her poisonous words . . . Why did she, his wife, repeat them to Joseph? She'd been so confident at the bed-and-breakfast, but in the reality of her own room, things seemed less clear. Her mind swirled and her stomach churned as she finally fell into an uneasy sleep.

All too soon it was morning, and she dragged herself from bed, wanting to get downstairs ahead of Joseph. She felt like a mess after having slept in her clothes, but she didn't take time to repair her *kapp* and hair. She had no idea what to say to him. She had her hand on the doorknob when his voice halted her.

"Running away?"

She turned, staring at him in the half-light as he leaned up on one elbow.

"*Ya.*" It didn't occur to her to do anything but to tell the truth.

"Come here."

She shook her head, biting her lip. "*Nee*, I've had enough of—everything last night."

He got to his feet easily, his torso half in shadow as he reached for her brush from the bureau. "Come here, Abby. Please. Let me help you with your hair."

Just the thought of him touching her hair made her mind tingle with delight, but she clung with stubbornness to the doorknob.

"Why should I?"

He smiled. "Because I'm a fool. Because I don't deserve it. Because you want to."

She glared at him. Why did he have to be so right all the time? She took one step forward and he was across the floor to meet her, his bare feet moving in silence.

"Come on. Sit down on the bed."

Reluctantly she let herself be led to sit on the edge of the bed while Joseph moved to kneel behind her on the mattress. She felt him put the brush down. His clever fingers found the hairpins with no problem. He lifted her *kapp* off and set it somewhere behind her. Then he began to unwind the complicated braid.

He took his time, separating the long strands with his fingers, reaching up to massage her scalp tenderly. She felt a constant ripple of chills play up and down her arms. Then he began to brush her hair, starting at her scalp and then arching his body to reach the very ends. He was so gentle, so thorough. She found it difficult to sit still.

"You're beautiful," he murmured, and she responded to the husky pull of his voice, though she shook her head at his words. She wished he'd kiss her, touch her somehow beyond the brush, but he kept stroking. And she soon thought she'd die with the sensuous tension spinning sparks inside of her.

"There," he said finally, leaning down over her shoulder so that their eyes could meet. "How's that feel?"

"Wonderful," she breathed.

He smiled at her, a warm, rich smile that touched his eyes and made her think of sunshine and shadows and enchanting forest glens. *He is the one who is beautiful,* she thought. And then he bent his head, and she saw the dark fall of his hair while his mouth found the warmth of her shoulder through her blouse. And then he stopped. She nearly fell backward at the sudden withdrawal of his body from behind hers. He got off the bed, replaced the brush, and leaned his hip against the bureau.

"That's the best I can do. I can't braid."

She stared at him. "I can't braid."

He arched one dark eyebrow. "What?"

"Nothing . . . I mean, nothing. Of course I can braid." She reached shaking hands up to work at her plait while he pulled his shirt on. She had to turn her head to ignore the movements of his fingers, and once more felt torn between a restlessness and a desire to wring his neck.

He pulled on his glasses and dropped a quick kiss on her cheek. "All right, sweetheart. I'll see you downstairs. I'm really hungry this morning."

He was out the door before she could speak, and she wondered for the second time in as many days whether she was losing her mind—or her heart.

CHAPTER SEVENTEEN

It was a Saturday in late October and the first day of the county fair when Abigail awoke with the beginnings of a bad cold. She sneezed and sniffled and roused Joseph, who peered up at her from his bed on the floor.

"Are you sick?"

"*Nee.*"

"You're sick. You're staying home today." He rose to stand next to the bed, considering her with a frown as he adjusted his glasses.

She set her lips in a firm line. "I am not staying home. I want to go . . . with you."

He sat down on the edge of the bed and reached a firm hand to press against her forehead. "You've got a fever. You're staying home. I'll stay with you."

She flopped back against the pillows. "No, you can't do that. Father is expecting you to look at the stock with him. I just wanted to see how my sweet corn does."

And spend the day with you, she thought.

She loved the fair and the freedom it had always brought in the past. Her father had always been too involved in his own manly pursuits, so she'd been able to roam as she liked. And she liked the idea of tasting treats with Joseph, walking beside him, and maybe winning a prize. But she did feel like a day of rest would probably do her good, so she sighed aloud in frustration.

"I'll bring you a present, then. And the vegetable ribbons aren't until tomorrow anyway. I've read the schedule." His tone was cajoling.

She pouted.

"And if you're feeling better, you can go tomorrow. But if you're not, I'm having Dr. Knepp come round."

"For a cold?"

"*Ya* . . . you could have strep throat or something."

"My throat's fine." She scrunched down beneath the quilts and sneezed again.

He laughed and bent forward to kiss the tip of her nose. "All right, little mouse. But today you rest. And wish me a blue ribbon with that bull I've been fostering for your father. I've never seen such a huge animal."

She sighed. "A big hunk of meat on four legs."

"That's right." He grinned. "And some nice prize money in the bank."

His soft beard rubbed her chin as he kissed her good-bye, and she listened with a forlorn ear to his and her father's voices as they talked, then left the house.

She buried her head in the covers and fell back to sleep. She was awakened several hours later by heavy footsteps downstairs and hopped out of bed to yank her clothes on. Everyone should still be at the fair. She did her hair with haste, then tiptoed out of the room to the top of the stairs.

• • •

Joseph sat on the kitchen table and shook his head at Dr. Knepp. "No," he rasped, catching his breath. "No drugs."

"Son, you've got three broken ribs. I've got to set them. A touch of something to help ease things off won't send you back."

Joseph shook his head again, groaning faintly. "Just do it."

"All right, then. Put your hands on my shoulders."

Joseph focused everything he had on raising his arms, but he couldn't stifle the cry that came from his lips as he reached the goal.

"Good. Now I'll set them. It will hurt badly."

"I . . . understand."

The doctor sighed and ran his large hands experimentally down the rib cage. Joseph squeezed his eyes shut and bit his lip until the blood came. Dr. Knepp shifted the bones into relative position, and Joseph felt the room swim before his eyes.

"Scream if you want, son. It won't bother me."

Just then the squeak of the steps interrupted the doctor. Abby walked into the room.

"What's going on here?"

Joseph made a faint sound of distress, and the doctor turned his head.

"Wait outside, Abigail, if you please."

"In my own home? I will not. What are you doing on the kitchen table? Joseph, you're awfully pale and your mouth is bleeding. What happened?"

"Abigail, your husband's got three broken ribs. Setting them is about one of the most painful things I can do to a man. Now, please, step outside."

"Well . . . I'll help you, then," she said uncertainly.

"No," Joseph gasped.

Abigail's face fell and she turned dejectedly, easing out the front door.

"Women!" the doctor exclaimed, tightening a strip of linen with such intensity that Joseph nearly gave in to the pull that had been haunting him for the past minutes. He sagged forward, almost unconscious.

"Thank the good Lord," Dr. Knepp murmured, tying off the rest of the bandages.

"*Danki*," Joseph whispered as the doctor eased him back, full-length, onto the kitchen table.

· · ·

Abigail clenched and unclenched her hands in distress and kept a keen ear on the goings-on inside. When she heard Joseph cry out, she felt her stomach drop and tears come to her eyes. He'd been so adamant about her not staying; she couldn't understand why. Then a thought came to her mind, almost as though God had whispered it. The pain. He was in terrible pain, and based on what he'd revealed about the pills, she didn't think the doctor would be able to give him anything. Or perhaps he'd be tempted to ask for something, and it would start him off again down that long, dark road.

She straightened her spine. She could help him through the pain, if only she knew how. The screen door opened and Dr. Knepp walked out, drying his hands on a towel.

"He's unconscious."

"What happened?"

Dr. Knepp gave her a wry look. "He took it into his stubborn head to try and ride a wild horse to win some prize money. He fell off and took a good kick to the ribs."

"*Ach,*" she murmured weakly. "Will he . . . be all right?"

"He's going to need careful nursing for the next week or so. Will you do it?"

"Of course . . . I–I'm his wife."

"So you are, and you can do this, Abigail. Help him through this time."

She swallowed. "He wanted me to leave, but I think I understand."

"Of course he wanted you to leave. What man wants to appear weak in front of the woman he loves?"

"But . . ." She stopped as the doctor's words sank in. *The woman he loves?* But he couldn't—could he?

"I'll fetch your father; we'll put the boy downstairs in the master bedroom before he comes round completely."

The doctor stalked off the porch, and Abigail tiptoed inside.

Joseph lay sprawled and pale as death across the kitchen table. His shirt lay on the floor in ruins, and his rib cage was bandaged tightly. He seemed to rasp when he breathed. She drew closer, fearful of rousing him. His glasses were nowhere in sight, and blood still dripped from the corner of his mouth. She gently lifted a corner of her apron and pressed it against his lips, and he moaned in response. She stepped back, anxious now for the doctor to return.

Joseph turned his head and opened his eyes, peering up at her in an owl-like fashion.

"Ab-by?" Even the syllables were obviously painful for him to get out, and she hastened to shush him.

"Shh . . . yes, Joseph. It's Abby. I'm right here. Do you—want me to go?"

He shook his head. "*Nee* . . . promise . . . stay." He tried to cough, then half sobbed with the effort.

She caught up one of his dirt-stained hands and pressed it close to her cheek. "*Ach*, Joseph. I'll stay," she whispered. "I promise."

"*Gut*," he mumbled, then he slipped into unconsciousness.

She stared down at him, her husband, and the doctor's voice rang in her head. "*The woman he loves . . .*"

CHAPTER EIGHTEEN

Joseph awoke to the feeling of crushing pain in his chest and the realization that each breath tortured with jagged awareness. The overwhelming desire to beg for something to help ease the pain simmered at the back of his consciousness until he felt the cool press of a cloth on his damp forehead. He opened his eyes to see Abby peering anxiously down at him, her blonde hair hanging loose in a blurred shimmer.

"Glasses?" he whispered, surprised that he had to visualize the word before he could actually get it out.

She shook her head so that he felt the soft curtain of her hair brush the top of his bare chest and trail down to cover his shoulders in a languid fall.

"The pain, Joseph . . . it's really bad, isn't it?"

Yes, he wanted to scream, but doubted he'd get enough air in his lungs to do anything but squeak. He settled for nodding, not wanting her to know how much it hurt.

"I know," she soothed, her voice softer and more womanly than he ever remembered hearing it.

He stared up into the twin pools of her blue eyes, wanting to see her better.

"I know you want the medicine, Joseph . . . the pills. I want you to know that I'm going to help you instead . . . so that you don't want, so that it doesn't hurt as much."

She leaned close to his ear to whisper the last words, being careful not to put any weight on his chest. He closed his eyes when she pressed her gentle mouth to his ear and began to sing a traditional Amish lullaby.

"*Schlof, bubeli, schlof . . .*" Sleep, baby, sleep . . .

He half smiled at the sweet, long-forgotten words and wondered just how lengthy his convalescence could be. He felt the pain melting away as visions of her singing to their own child danced across his mind. *She would be a wonderful mother,* he thought. *Strong. Patient. Loving.* He sighed and gave in to his body's need for rest, falling asleep with her soft voice still bringing peace to his mind and spirit.

. . .

Abigail slipped from the bedroom and avoided her father's gaze. She knew it was night and that she should still probably have her *kapp* on. But at the moment she didn't really care. She knew that her cheeks were flushed fever bright, and she was amazed that *Derr Herr* had brought it to her mind to sing to Joseph. But she was his wife, and she was determined to do anything she could to help her husband.

"How is the boy, then?" her father questioned in a gruff tone.

She was surprised that he was still up and that he'd

asked, and she busied herself refilling the water pitcher before answering. "He is—in pain, but he fell asleep."

"Doc should have given him something for it. It's foolishness to me why he should suffer along when he doesn't have to."

Hot words surged forward on Abigail's lips, but she bit them back. How could she explain to this cold, unfeeling man what her husband was going through? He'd probably just judge Joseph and find him lacking. So she said nothing.

Her father cleared his throat. "It won't be the same—working without him, I mean. He's a *gut*, hard worker."

Abigail turned to face him. "*Ya*, he is." She lifted her chin and uttered a silent prayer. It was time for her *daed* to know.

"Father . . . Joseph never did anything that day at the picnic. It was all me. I made it up because I wanted to get even with him for not being as interested in me as I would have liked. I betrayed him, and he still stood up for me. I don't expect your forgiveness or your understanding, but I want you to know. *Derr Herr* has prompted my heart many times to tell you, but I've never had the courage." She swallowed hard. "I know that you've never approved of me even when I was a child. I don't know why, nor does it matter really. Joseph has taught me a lot about the kind of person I had become, and it's not been a pretty thing to look upon. But I've changed, I think. Or at least, I'm trying to. I just wanted you to know so you'd stop blaming him for something he never did."

She turned back to the water pitcher, her heart

pounding in her chest. But she was amazed at how good it felt to finally speak the truth. The Bible verse "And the truth shall make you free" drifted across her mind, and she knew that it was true. No matter what her father's reaction might be, she had told the truth before the Lord and she felt more clean inside than she ever had before.

She jumped when she felt a light touch on her arm and turned to see her father standing close. She gazed up at him and was amazed to see his bleary blue eyes awash with tears.

"Abigail . . . I . . . I, too, have much to confess. I knew that Joseph did nothing that day."

"What?"

"I . . . was watching you both. I saw him turn from you. I saw him walk away."

"I don't understand. Then why would you . . ."

Her father took out his hankie and swiped at his eyes with his head bowed. "I worried for you. I—always have. I wanted to keep you safe. I thought if you were married, perhaps you'd stop wanting to go away. I also used the boy—it was just too easy an opportunity to pass by."

Her mind whirled, but one thing struck her especially. "But, Father, how did you know that I wanted to go away?"

He gave a heaving sob, and she instinctively laid a hand on his brawny forearm.

"Because . . . she . . . went away."

"She?"

He caught his breath. "Your *mamm* . . . I've always

told you she died in a buggy accident. That much was true. But she was driving that buggy to leave the community, to leave the Amish and me . . . and you."

Abigail dropped her hand and sagged back against the counter. All of the idealized images she'd nursed of her mother over the years swirled in her brain until she thought she might pass out, but then a thought struck her.

"Why should I believe you?" she asked. She had to ask. He'd been so cold, so unfeeling for years. Perhaps, even now, he was telling her this to hold her somehow.

He nodded. "You've a right to ask that. Come with me."

She followed him as he walked to the master bedroom door, then eased it open. He entered the room soft-footed, and she glanced at the bed. Joseph was still asleep.

Her father went to a small cedar chest that sat on his bureau. Abigail knew it held important papers and various letters from relatives, but she was surprised when he turned the chest over. He felt the bottom of the wood, and then she watched as he slid back a hidden panel, revealing a secret compartment carved into the depth of the wood.

In the dim light of the single kerosene lamp she'd left burning, she caught the shimmer of a silver thimble as it fell into her father's large palm. Then he pulled out a piece of paper, crumpled and yellowed with age. He slid the bottom back into place and set the chest back. Then he turned and reached out his hand to Abigail.

"Take these," he whispered.

She obeyed, not wanting Joseph to wake, and left the room with her father following as the press of the small thimble burned in her palm.

CHAPTER NINETEEN

My dearest Solomon, my little Abby,

Someday I hope that you can both forgive me for what I am doing, but I cannot go on any longer as things are. I've tried. The Lord knows how hard I've tried. First, I believed that marrying would ease the restlessness in my soul. Then I hoped that the precious golden-haired baby would make a way for me. But there is nothing that has been able to take away this desire, no, this knowledge that I do not belong with the Amish. It doesn't matter how I was raised or how loving and kind the community is to me. I never belonged. I've known that since I was a child and wanted to throw apple peels at my mother when she insisted it was my duty to help with the autumn canning. I've known it since the day I married. I knew it on the day you were born, Abby. I just want out. I want another way of life that doesn't involve the terrible confining pressure of being an Amish woman.

Solomon, there is no one else—I say this because I know that you will think it. There is no one else but myself. If I stay I will poison our daughter, her thoughts, her heart until she, too, senses my desire to run and then wants to run as well. I will not leave that legacy to her. I know that you will do right by her and cherish her as you always have.

Abby, someday, if you are reading this, I want you to know that I started a quilt when you were two years old. Even now, when you are five and deeply asleep, the quilt is not finished. I doubt that you will ever see it, but the pattern is called "Abby's Wish," I could not finish it because I cannot bear the wish that I have for you, that you, too, could be free. But it is not fair to take you from your father, from your home. Please forgive me someday, my dearest daughter. I love you.

Solomon, I love you as well. Please know this, for always. Tell everyone the truth, that I abandoned you and my child. It doesn't matter. Please go on with your life. Marry a good Amish woman, someone who will be kind to Abby, but keep living. I am not worth your giving up or closing up as I know you might do.

It is late now, and I must go. I will leave the horse and buggy in town. I have learned to drive and will be away before sunrise. Please do not try to find me. I love you both.

Rachel

Abigail pressed the silver thimble into the palm of her hand with such force that she thought for a moment that she could still feel the warmth of her mother's finger within its hold. But she knew now that there was nothing but the truth. She lifted her eyes to her father's as he sat still and quiet across from her at the kitchen table.

Her eyes filled with tears. "I have felt like this, like her—before Joseph."

"I know."

She impulsively reached to him. "But, Father, since Joseph and I . . . Well, the feeling's gone away. I am content to be his wife. I want to have a life with him. And we want to share that with you."

Her father gave a giant sniff. "I don't deserve that. I've treated you harshly all these years, because I was afraid and I was angry at her. But you were just a little thing who needed a *daed*. I haven't been one to you."

She drew a deep breath, her thoughts teetering between childhood expectation and the reality of life as she'd come to know it.

"*Nee*, you weren't the perfect father, but you did the best you could. And I accept that. I wouldn't change a thing if I could." And she realized that it was true. She wouldn't have become as strong-willed and resourceful if she'd been raised a different way. And it was *Derr Herr* who put people together in families, and it was He who allowed her to have the father that she did.

Then she did something she had not ever been able to do. She rose and came near to where her father sat. Stretching out her slender arms, she bent and embraced his broad shoulders, laying her face against the back of his neck. She felt him shake, then sob, and then he turned and hugged her tightly to his chest.

"My daughter, my child." He wept.

"My *daed*," she returned, her tears falling freely.

A sudden low moan from the adjoining bedroom broke the moment, and they both sniffed. Then her father dried her tears with his handkerchief, and Abigail gave him a brilliant smile.

"Go on, now. Tend to your husband. You're a good wife, Abby."

She nodded and moved toward the bedroom door.

· · ·

On the second day, Joseph developed a fever, which made Dr. Knepp frown with concern while Abigail anxiously watched the examination.

"I suppose a bit of a fever is to be expected, but I don't want him getting an infection. I'll leave these antibiotics for him. See that he takes them three times a day—morning, noon, and night. How's his pain?"

The doctor avoided her eyes, and she whispered her reply in a steady voice. "I know about the drugs, Dr. Knepp, and why he can't have the pain medicine. He told me. I–I've been trying to—distract him—as best as I can when he's awake."

The doctor cleared his throat. "I see. Well then, keep up the good medicine." He patted her shoulder.

She would help Joseph get well. But as the doctor left and she was alone with only the quiet sound of her husband's breathing, she realized that getting him well was the least of what she wanted. She wasn't sure how or when, but somehow she had fallen in love with him. Deeply in love. And there was an honesty in admitting it that liberated her thinking and drove out all shame about how their marriage began. If the doctor was right, if Joseph loved her and she loved him, then

Joseph might be right that the Lord had a plan in all of this. She was only too happy to follow along.

. . .

Joseph awoke by slow degrees, his pain half swallowed by tangled, warm dreams of Abby and her singing. But now something was tickling his nose, and he opened his eyes. He stared up at her, realizing that it was broad daylight and that she was properly *kapped* and dressed. But his nose still itched. He peered sideways and she laughed, a melodic, charming sound that he'd not heard often enough.

"You need to go into town as soon as you're able and get new glasses. The last ones were trampled by the horse. But in the meantime, two tokens from the fair . . ." She stopped twitching his nose and pulled away two prize ribbons, one blue, one red.

"What . . ."

"Your big, nasty bull took the blue ribbon, and my sweet corn took second place with the red. Aren't you happy?"

He gave her a lopsided smile. "Very . . . but my ribs still hurt quite a bit."

"I'm sorry. Is there anything that I can do?" she murmured, bending over him.

"*Ach*, I don't know . . . It seems that while I've been ill, some wondrous nurse has visited my bedside. Might she still be about?"

Even without his glasses, he recognized her flush and enjoyed it. She bit her lip and giggled, then she straightened to adjust his pillows. Her arm brushed against his face and he caught the sweet scent of her and wished he wasn't an invalid and could act like a man with his new bride. But for now he'd settle for her closeness.

"Dr. Knepp says that you're to sit up today, and if you're very, very good, you can sit in a chair tomorrow."

He grimaced. "I hate being down."

She laughed. "But I plan to keep you properly entertained, so you needn't worry about that." She pulled back and lifted a tray from the bedside table to settle on his lap.

"Really?" he asked. "How? Maybe just telling me will make me feel good."

"Well, I thought first of all that I'd help feed you."

He frowned. "I'm not a babe."

"No," she whispered in a husky voice that sent shivers down his spine. "I can see that. But there's something very intimate about letting someone else give you—sustenance." She drew out the word suggestively, and he decided right then and there that he'd eat anything from gruel to noodles from her hand.

She took her time adjusting the cotton napkin around his neck, letting it trail up his chest above the bandages, then leaning close while she fooled overlong with the knot. He felt himself growing increasingly warm and not with fever this time. At least, he thought wryly, not the ill kind of fever anyway.

But as it turned out, Abby's sliding one delicious spoonful of vegetable soup after another into his willing mouth was more than satisfying.

CHAPTER TWENTY

The full moon of an early November night cast its luminescent beams in shadowy play across the master bedroom. Abigail shifted in the rocking chair where she'd slept for the past weeks of Joseph's recovery and cringed when it squeaked. She nearly jumped, though, when he spoke from the shadows.

"It's foolishness, Abby, you know?"

"Are you dreaming, Joseph? What's foolishness? Do you have a fever again?"

He rose up on one elbow on the bed, and she could see the moonlight stray across his chest. Dr. Knepp had removed the bandages yesterday and had said that Joseph might resume light daily activities.

"What's foolishness?" she asked again, reaching to massage her neck where it rested against the hard wood of the chair.

"It's foolishness that one of us has to sleep either on the floor or in the chair. This bed is big enough for two people, and the weather is getting colder. Your father told me yesterday that he's quite comfortable upstairs in the spare bedroom, so why don't you get out of that miserable chair and come over here and lie down?"

There was a long pause.

He sighed aloud. "No, Abby, I'm not asking for anything except that you stop being uncomfortable. It makes me uncomfortable even to look at that chair. I'll tell you what. I will roll up our lovely double wedding ring quilt and put it like a fat, happy sausage down the middle of the bed. And you can stay on your side, and I'll stay on mine."

She considered further. "I might roll over, though, and re-injure your ribs."

"Oh, Abby, come on. Grow up just a little bit."

"What does that mean?"

"Okay. I have said what I'm going to say on the matter. If you want to freeze and contort yourself in that torture chair, it's entirely up to you. Good night."

Abigail listened to the sheets rustle as he made himself comfortable. It would be lovely to stretch out fully, but her pride was nicked by his words, and she kept her stubborn seat.

I'll wait until he falls asleep, she thought. *Then maybe I'll do as he suggests.*

So she waited, and the idea of being close to Joseph grew more and more appealing. When she thought he was finally asleep, she rose to tiptoe across the room, nearly tripping over George the cat as she moved toward the bed. She settled as gingerly as she could on the edge opposite Joseph and felt for the reassuring bulk of the "sausage," as he called it. She lay down on her back and adjusted her hair, staring up at the ceiling.

"Are you scared of sharing the bed with me?" a soft voice asked.

"No," she lied.

"I used to be scared of storms when I was a kid, especially when I was living on the streets and had no shelter. The whole idea of home or just having a home was so unfamiliar and seemed so out of reach to me then. It's just wonderful to be able to lie here with you and know that we're safe."

"I've never thought about what life must be like for a homeless person."

"The homeless face the brutal elements of the weather, but they also battle physical and emotional and spiritual storms."

She turned slightly, interested now in what he was saying. "Can you tell me about your time on the streets without it bothering you too much?"

"There's not a whole lot to say except that I met a lot of people who were hurt and in need of the Lord's help, but in some cases, they had never even heard of His name."

She played with the pattern of the quilt with a fingertip and shook her head. "I guess I never thought of what it would be like to really leave here. I had this idea that it would be easier somehow or more fulfilling, but I realize that life is just as hard, just as challenging no matter where you are."

"Yes, but having a community of people behind you makes it so much easier. You know the rules. You know what to expect. You know how to fit in. For some people, I guess all of that would be pretty boring, but I've had my taste and my fill of a life with no rules."

She stretched her open palm across the lump of a

quilt in between them and felt his hand enclose hers. She fell asleep with a smile on her lips.

. . .

Joseph awoke to the double sensation of warm sunshine on his face and an even warmer Abby next to his side. Somehow she had leapt the quilt barrier and was nestled against him as comfortably as if she'd always slept there. He kept his breathing shallow and even for fear of waking her and breaking the moment. It was enough just to hold her and smell the fresh mint of her hair and that delicate scent of Abby that was something between a storm and the sea. Soon enough, though, she opened her eyes and jumped like a scalded cat.

"What are you doing?" she asked, outrage in her voice.

"What am *I* doing?"

"You are supposed to stay on your side of the quilt."

"I'm sorry. I may need new glasses, but it's you who appears to have forgotten about the barrier."

He watched her gaze around the bed, and a bright blush stained her cheeks as she realized he was right. She started to pull away, but he caught her back. "Just a minute. Where are you going?"

"To my side of the quilt."

He laughed and then groaned lightly as the pain in his ribs stabbed him.

"Now see what you've done," she admonished. "Let me go."

He reached beneath her arm with unerring fingers

and began to tickle her. "When was the last time you played, Abigail Lambert?" he teased.

She squealed and, in her attempt to get away, accidentally knocked him aside the head.

"Oh, I'm so sorry, but—I'm really not." She laughed as she got away. "And maybe it's me who should remind you of what real play is like."

He rubbed his head as he considered her words. "I would be glad to see anything that you have to offer in the line of play."

She danced around the room in her nightdress, her hair a golden cloud, and picked up her clothes and small toiletries here and there. Then she caught up a towel from the back of a chair. "Unfortunately, it's time for my bath, Mr. Lambert, and you will have no play in that." She turned on her heel with her nose in the air and left him smiling on the bed.

He wondered how often she would continue to move in the dance between girlhood and womanhood. He would always find her entertaining, but he longed for a more mature relationship with his wife. She had told him once that she was patient, but he knew deep inside that he was just as patient. And, he thought with a grin, maybe just a bit more plotting than she was.

. . .

With a light heart, Abigail dragged the hip bath out near the woodstove. Her father greeted her with a smile and rose from his rocker to leave the room. She thought how wonderful it would have been to have had his smiles all her life, but she knew that it was never too late to have something put right. So she dropped a light kiss on his cheek and put a kettle of water on the stove to heat.

"There's one thing more that I wanted to talk to you about, Abby," her *daed* said. "I've been wrong also all these years about keeping that quilt up in its frame. I want you to have your own quilting and to make a wedding quilt for you and Joseph."

Abigail paused as she watched slow bubbles begin to form in the bottom of the kettle. Her father's words were a balm to her spirit, but she was struck with inspiration at the same time.

"You know, Father, I've been thinking, too, about the quilt and *Mamm's* letter. I wondered if you'd mind my finishing the Abby's Wish quilt?"

He gazed at her across the kitchen. "Why would you want that?"

She thought hard and examined her heart. "Because part of accepting who I am in the Lord is accepting who my mother was. I want to finish that quilt with some joyful women who will remind me that this life is more than worth living, even if the people we love don't always turn out the way we hope they will. I wanted a mother for years, but I've come to realize that I can be mothered in other ways, by other women and friends. The quilt would be a celebration of all of that."

For a moment she thought he might cry again, but he simply nodded.

"That's good enough for me, and very wise for such a young woman as yourself to realize."

"Thank you, Father."

He cleared his throat. "Well, I'll just take the sheet and cedar off of the quilt, then, and tighten the rolls of the frame up a bit so that it can be ready for you. When do you want to have your quilting party?"

Abigail considered. If she were through with her housework and Joseph remained well in the afternoon, she might be able to take Carl around and deliver individual invitations to a quilting for Saturday. That gave her three days to prepare. She glanced around the rather dim kitchen with some doubt but decided that true friends would accept her home in any condition.

"Saturday," she told her *daed*.

"Fair enough. I'll take Joseph somewhere that day to get away from all the female fussing."

"I'm sure he'll enjoy that."

Her father nodded again, then he left the room, going out the back door. Abigail pulled the screen around the tub and emptied the kettle full of hot water into the bath. She filled yet another and dropped a bar of homemade mint soap into the tub. She played dreamily with her hair as she thought about waking up in her husband's arms. He was so strong and so handsome, but he was also smart and funny. She realized that she liked the edges of his humor and that it was a fair complement to her own.

When the rest of the water was heated, she slipped into the tub and began a leisurely wash. A thumping noise, followed by the opening creak of the master bedroom door, drew her upright in the tub, and she squeaked in surprise. "Who's there?"

"No one," Joseph answered, and she could hear the smile in his voice.

"You get back in that bed and stay outside of this screen."

"I just wanted to get some milk. I had no intentions of playing in your bath. Is that all right?"

"Just get the milk and go." She hugged her chest to her bended knees and longed for the towel or her dress, which hung out of reach atop the screen. She would not give him the satisfaction of seeing even so much as a silhouette of her form, which he could probably do by the light of the stove and the thinness of the screen.

She heard Joseph moving about the kitchen.

"Father will be back soon."

"Well then, you'd better get out of that tub, hadn't you?"

She fumed at his good humor and decided to concentrate on finishing her bath. She caught up the soft mint soap and squished it between her fingers, enjoying the feel and the smell. She made haste to scrub her arms and shoulders and decided she'd wash her hair at a more convenient and private time. Suddenly the towel, which had hung out of reach, was flipped down atop her head, and she blinked in surprise.

"Thought I'd help you out a little bit," he said, very near the screen.

She clutched the towel. "I don't need any help, and I really think that you're overdoing things and should just lie down."

"Well . . ." And then her skirt fell on the floor beside the tub. "You didn't mind my help last night when that chair was so uncomfortable. I thought we were making some progress toward understanding each other better."

He flicked her blouse off its perch to land next to the skirt, and she stared with fury at the outline of his body on the other side of the screen.

"Oh, I understand you perfectly," she replied. "And I am going to catch pneumonia if I don't get out of this tub soon."

Her apron landed atop the other clothes.

"We can't have that, can we? All right, I'll leave the lady to her bath and me to my milk."

With great relief she heard the master bedroom door creak, but then he called out in a loud voice, "Do you know, it's an interesting fact that ladies used to actually take baths in milk. It softened their skin."

She couldn't reply, and hoped for a wild second that he would trip on the way back to his bed.

CHAPTER TWENTY-ONE

Joseph was well enough that afternoon for them to make a trip toF town to get him fitted for new glasses. Abigail bundled up in a warm cloak, as the weather had changed and winter was truly upon the area. It had even begun to snow a little.

She had to drive Carl, as Joseph couldn't see two feet in front of him, and she thought it funny that her husband was nervous about her handling the horse. She decided to pull on Carl's reins and make him break trot just to tease Joseph.

"Do you need me to drive?" he asked in a gruff tone.

"No," she replied sweetly. "I'm quite capable."

"Then you're either as blind as I am or you are deliberately baiting me. Which is it?"

"I'd go for the baiting."

He was silent for a moment. "So you're actually playing with me, your husband, right?"

She turned to smile at him. "*Ya.* You need more play in your life."

He rolled his eyes.

They passed the rest of the ride in companionable

silence and arrived at the office of the *Englisch* optometrist, Dr. Stokes.

Abigail came around to Joseph's side of the buggy.
"Do you need help down?" she asked.

He jumped beside her with ease and caught her
close in a hugging embrace. "Yes, you can hold me and
help me up the steps so that I don't break my neck."

She pushed him away and they both laughed. He
then caught her arm, and they walked together up the
steps to the office door.

Abigail was struck by how modern the room was
with its glossy magazines and the well-dressed recep-
tionist who greeted them with a smile. A few months
ago, her first impulse would have been to dive for the
magazines and catch a glimpse of the outside world. She
now knew that the man giving his name at the recep-
tion window was her world, and the thought thrilled
her to her core. She took a seat on one of the comfortable
leather couches, and Joseph soon joined her.

"Look," he said, "do you want to go and get some
shopping done while I'm here? It might take a bit to
get an exam and pick out some glasses. Although"—he
laughed—"I know there's not much potential for style
in Amish glasses, so I'll just have to do the best I can."

"You'd look good in anything," she said in a matter-
of-fact voice, and he leaned forward to brush his lips
against hers.

"Thank you, Abby. That's quite a compliment coming from the most beautiful girl I know."

He left her to go with the nurse, and Abigail decided
to begin offering invitations to her quilting while she

had the chance. She crossed the busy street and made her way to Yoder's. She was glad to see Tillie, who gave her a bright smile.

"And where's that handsome husband of yours?"

"He's getting new eyeglasses. I came over to invite you and the other ladies from the kitchen to come to my house this Saturday for a quilting. It'll be my wedding quilt since I never really had the chance to do one before we married."

She felt no shame in bringing up the hurriedness of her marriage. It all seemed like part of what was supposed to happen, now that she thought of it.

Tillie agreed at once. "I know I can be there, and I'm sure Judith and the other ladies would love it. What time should we come?"

Abigail settled on ten o'clock, knowing that there was actually only a small part of the quilt to finish. Normally a quilting would begin very early and last the whole of the day.

"I have an idea," Tillie said. "Why don't we make it a quilting and kitchen frolic too. We can help stock your pantry, eat some good food, and do our quilting."

"That sounds wonderful," Abigail said with a smile. "But I don't want to impose on anyone. I'll just be glad to have you all there."

Tillie waved away her words. "It's no imposition. I'll tell the other women, and I know that they'll be so glad to help. Food is easy for us around here, and so is friendship."

Abigail blinked back tears at Tillie's spontaneous generosity and kindness. It was almost as if the Lord was revealing to her that, by being patient, by waiting for Him to work, she would see Him bring forth an abundance in her life. An overflowing cup . . . or an overflowing pantry. Both were wonderful, but the friendship was especially something to be treasured.

Abigail left the restaurant feeling a deep contentment in her spirit, which increased when she saw Joseph coming down the street toward her.

"Well, how did it go?" she asked, staring up at his handsome face.

"Great. My new glasses will be ready in about an hour, so we have some time to ourselves," he said. "Abby, your father has paid me well these last months, and I'd like to buy my bride a gift. What would be your heart's desire, madam?"

Abigail thought hard. She couldn't remember the last time someone had bought her something just for pleasure.

"You got me George as a wedding gift," she pointed out.

Joseph frowned. "I like the cat, but that is not a true wedding gift. You deserve something beautiful."

She was aware of people passing them in the street as they stood together, but it didn't matter. She felt like the very world could go by and she'd be content just to stand with Joseph forever.

"George is beautiful to me. And . . . so are you." She whispered the last words shyly, and he reached down and caught her hand.

"You continue to amaze me, Abby." His voice was hoarse. "You've got me coming and going, and I never know which end is up with you. It feels so good that I want . . . I want . . ."

The sudden appearance of an *Englisch* woman with bright red curls broke the moment. For a moment Abigail's heart dropped to her stomach, then she realized that it was not Molly. But she recognized in that moment that she still felt vulnerable and a little insecure, especially toward these tender new feelings for her husband.

"Did you see that redhead?" she asked in a small voice.

"Yep."

"So . . . do you . . . think of Molly?"

"No. I think about how much time I wasted in foolishness and pursuit of the things and people who I thought would make me happy. The truth is that I've never felt more content than to be here with you, in the middle of a little country town, while the rest of the world goes by in a blur of colors and all I can truly see is your beautiful face."

She blushed. "You need those glasses."

He laughed aloud. "All right, Abby Lambert. Now tell me what you want for a wedding gift, or I'll buy you chocolate in a cardboard box and write you a bad card."

She couldn't bring to mind anything that she actually needed. It seemed that the Lord had supplied her with all that a heart could want, but then an idea came to her. "All right," she said, smiling. "Let's go to Stolfus's Dry Goods."

"Dry goods? That doesn't sound very romantic."

"Oh, you'd be surprised."

They walked along the sidewalk together, and Abigail noticed how many Amish people mixed with the *Englisch*, and how many women, both *Englisch* and Amish, threw interested glances in Joseph's direction.

She put her hand in his and squeezed, and they walked up the broad wooden steps to Stolfus's together. They entered to the familiar scent of spices, soaps, and a myriad of good things, but it was the fabric that drew Abigail's eye.

She had taken Joseph's measurements for a new shirt when he was ill and figured she might make him a new one in a color besides white. But knowing his stubbornness, she knew he wouldn't want to buy the fabric if he realized it was for him. So she pretended a great interest in a sky blue material that she said would be just right for something personal that she had in mind.

As she turned away from the counter after giving her order for the dry goods, she accidentally bumped into a small display of soaps and sachets. Catching a rose sachet in her outstretched hand, she lifted the pouch to her nose and breathed in deeply.

"Mmm, this is lovely." She held it up for him to try.

He shook his head. "No. I have a particular preference for mint, especially soap."

She blushed and put the sachet down, and then he was serious.

"Abby, do you like that perfumy thing? If you want it, I'll be glad to get it for you."

She shook her head as Mrs. Stolfus handed her the fabric across the counter. She couldn't help but notice the more than curious glances the woman cast in their direction, but she ignored them and turned back to Joseph, who was studying the sachets with an indifferent eye.

"Joseph, I've got everything I need except some thread and needles. I better get some extra needles for the quilting too. And I was thinking about making teaberry cookies for Saturday. I need some dried teaberries."

She led him back to the dried spices and found the small red berries. Soon they had checked out and were headed back to the optometrist's. She clutched her brown-paper-wrapped fabric and thread with secret pleasure, trying to decide when she'd get a chance to sew for him.

At Dr. Stokes's office, Abigail thought Joseph looked even more handsome in his new circular frames and lenses than he had in his old pair.

"Now you're Amish," she declared, and Dr. Stokes laughed.

Joseph smiled, and she thought how endearing he was to her heart, even though he could drive her to temper sometimes. She decided that they made for a good stew together, like one of Judith's best recipes. A little spice mixed with the taste of love could make for a sumptuous life.

They were soon back behind Carl and headed out of town when it occurred to Abigail to invite both Katie Stahley and Mrs. Knepp to the quilting.

"Do you mind making a few more stops?" she asked him.

"Not at all. Where are we going?"

Soon they turned down the Stahleys' narrow lane, and Abigail hopped out to give a quick invitation for Katie through her husband. She was back in the buggy within moments.

"Is she coming?" Joseph asked.

"I don't know. Her husband is kind of shy. He wouldn't even look me in the eye when I was giving him the invitation."

"Blinded by beauty," Joseph declared.

"Ha."

"And where else do we have to go?"

"Just to Dr. and Mrs. Knepp's, and that's all."

"Maybe we can stay and visit with them for a while, if you wouldn't mind," Joseph suggested.

"That would be nice. I'd like to thank Mrs. Knepp once more for the quilt."

"Ahhh. You mean the sausage roll."

"Yes," she agreed. "The sausage roll."

CHAPTER TWENTY-TWO

Joseph felt good about going to visit the Knepps. He would always be very grateful for the role that they had played in his past. They were good, kindhearted people, but more than that, he knew that they lived out the love that was preached about in Amish meetings. He also wanted Abby to have the chance to get to know Mrs. Knepp better, perhaps as a mother figure or someone to turn to.

The Knepps' farmhouse came into sight, and Joseph was glad to see the doctor's truck out front.

"Joseph," Abby murmured under her breath, "I don't think Mrs. Knepp likes me very much."

"What?"

"No, I'm serious. Even though she gave us the quilt and wished us well, I bet she still remembers the time I was a little girl and pulled all of her tulips up by their roots when they were just blooming."

He laughed and turned his head with interest. "Why would you do that?"

"I thought I was saving them from being cut, so I took them home and put them in water—dirt, roots, and all. My father was so mad at me. And Mrs. Knepp's face was as red as a beet when she found out it was me."

"What did the doctor say?" he asked.

"He laughed, as usual," Abby answered.

Joseph smiled. "I'm sure she's forgiven you." He took Abby's hand and helped her down, and they both went to the door.

Joseph knocked on the door, and Mrs. Knepp opened it. Abby ducked her head as if she were still carrying tulip stains on her cloak, but the older woman greeted them both with a broad smile.

"Come in, come in. I'm so glad to see you both. It's chilly out today, and I've got a fresh baking of gingerbread that I just took out of the oven. The doctor is here too. He just returned from delivering twins and is a bit testy from being up half the night."

"Oh," Abby said. "Maybe we should come back another time."

Mrs. Knepp shook her head. "There is no 'better time' in a doctor's life, my dear. Just come right in and make yourselves at home."

With Abby at his heels, Joseph followed the smell of gingerbread, and they soon were sitting around the kitchen table sharing coffee and gingerbread with fresh whipped cream.

The doctor talked with Joseph about crops and the weather, then Mrs. Knepp invited Abby to come into the sitting room for their own conversation.

Joseph noticed that Abby was hesitant to leave him, but Mrs. Knepp pressed a kind hand on his shoulder.

"No, no," she said. "You menfolk stay here while Abigail and I have a woman-to-woman talk."

The doctor laughed. "You go on. Joseph and I will have seconds on the gingerbread."

. . .

Abigail followed Mrs. Knepp into the comfortable sitting room. A fire burned with cheerful vigor at the hearth, while comfortable chairs covered with bright afghans and quilts dotted the room. It was not the room of a rich man, as Abigail knew the doctor most certainly could be, but rather the room of a true home.

"I'd like my house to look like this," Abigail said.

Mrs. Knepp smiled. "Yes, I've always found that comfortable and neat does just as well as fancy and frilly. But, please, let's sit down and talk. I'd like you to tell me the truth, and I give you my word that it won't be repeated to anyone else. How is it going with you two? The doctor told me that Joseph had shared his past with you. That's a big thing for a new wife to swallow. Are you all right?"

Abigail nodded. "*Ya*. We really have spent time talking about it and how both of us need to lean on the Lord for support to get through life. I don't mean just looking ahead long-term, but day-to-day living. Or maybe hour-to-hour living."

Mrs. Knepp gave Abigail a warm smile. She reached out and patted Abigail's hand. "I still remember the tulips, you know."

Abigail blushed. "I just told Joseph about that on the way here. I wish I could take that back. They were so beautiful."

"You were so impulsive, but I wish that I could take back my anger at a little girl who just thought she was doing the right thing. I want you to know that I sense a change in you . . . a calmness of spirit and peace that was not there before. I also want to tell you that I've prayed for you often."

Abigail bit her lip. "Thank you so much. You don't know what it means to me to have the praise of another woman, especially one that I admire." She smiled. "I actually came today to invite you to attend my wedding quilting. I've only asked a few women. The truth is that I haven't spent much time trying to make friends with the women of our community."

Mrs. Knepp smiled. "But you have all the time in the world to do that now."

"I know. I just wish I'd known it sooner."

As they said their good-byes, Mrs. Knepp pressed a small package into her hands. "Just a little something, my dear, to help with Saturday."

Abigail climbed into the buggy and started to unwrap the gift.

"What is it?" Joseph asked.

Abigail sat and stared at the contents of the package. It was a beautiful case of quilting needles, some with golden eyes, and a bright silver needle threader. "Oh, they're so beautiful."

Joseph cast an eye over the small gift. "If you say so. They look sharp to me, and I can just see one of the ladies pricking her finger and getting blood all over the quilt."

"Do you have to be so positive?" Abigail asked.

Joseph laughed. "Well, I try."

She sighed. "On a more serious note, there is one more woman I would like to invite to the quilting, but I don't have time to deliver a personal invitation."

"Who is it? We still have half the afternoon."

"Your sister," she said in a quiet voice. "But I know she's too far away."

"Oh . . . that's really nice. She'd love it. I told you that she is an artist, and she'd think quilting with a bunch of Amish women would be just the height of modern art." He pressed her hand. "Thank you for thinking of her."

Abigail nodded and held her new needles in a tight grasp.

CHAPTER TWENTY-THREE

Joseph took Abby's hope of inviting his sister to heart and stole away in the dark of night to put a call in to New York. Angel said she'd be on a plane Friday night.

"But I don't have any way to pick you up at the airport. The horse just will not do."

She'd laughed, his own laugh, many gentle tones lighter. "You forget that I'm a New Yorker and pretty resourceful, Joe. I'll be there, but don't tell her. Okay?"

He'd agreed and was glad he'd made it back to the master bedroom in time for a cuddle with Abby. It was gradually becoming a regular thing, this touching of her skin to his. One hand against him here, one knee drawn up in sleeper's balance, her cheek resting against his shoulder. It was enough to both lull his sensibilities and make him want to scream at the same time.

. . .

The morning of the quilting dawned bright and clear but ice cold. A fine frost covered the fields, making enchanted things of the barren trees and the stray bent plants. Abigail was excited as she looked out the window.

She'd never been the hostess of a social gathering before and wasn't entirely sure of what was expected of her, but she would make a good try at it. Joseph and her father had already left, the buggy tracks on the driveway proof of their eagerness to get away before any of the invited females showed up.

Joseph had kissed her, though, and wished her well. "I'll pray for you," he'd whispered. "That you will have a fulfilling and peaceful time with your friends."

She clung to that prayer as the first buggy arrived and she saw the ladies from Yoder's all pile out in a ridiculous number from behind one horse. She wondered how they had managed to fit, especially when they came bearing baskets and boxes and bags bulging with supplies. She opened the door, and George the cat skittered outside.

Judith was the first to enter and gave Abigail a big hug. "Thank you, Abby, for having us. It's a good, cold day to stay warm and happy inside."

Abigail tried to help the older woman with her packages, but Judith waved her away. "No, honey. You just go on ahead and greet your guests. I'll take care of all our stuff."

Abigail hugged each woman from Yoder's in turn, ending with Tillie, who had a broad smile on her face.

"We brought just about everything you could think of for your pantry, Abby. And we'll have your quilt finished in no time."

Abigail wanted to cry, but laughed instead. She felt so overwhelmed by the generosity and love that filled the room. She watched as Judith and Ruth made short work of filling the shelves of her pantry and was amazed at the canning jars full of bright colors. Yellow peaches and corn and squash, red tomatoes and jellies and preserves, green beans and peas and bread-and-butter pickles . . . The baskets kept producing. Soon she had a more than an adequately stuffed provision of stores for the coming winter.

"There," Judith said with a smile. "Next year we'll come again at canning time and help you do all of this work, so you can know what you're about."

Ruth interjected, "I say we come in the spring when it's time to order seeds, so she'll know what to plant in the kitchen garden."

A knock interrupted the conversation, and Abigail went to greet Katie and Mrs. Knepp. They both bore baskets, which turned out to be full of spices of every kind.

"You'll have the best-stocked medicine closet in the district, next to the doctor's," Mrs. Knepp declared once she'd finished putting up her gifts. "And you'll need it, if Joseph keeps insisting on trying to ride wild horses!"

They all laughed together, and Abigail felt the warm camaraderie and power of what a group of women could accomplish together if they set their minds to it. A year ago, stocking a pantry would have been something she would have disdained. Now she saw it as the result of tremendous work and an accomplishment to protect and provide for those you love.

The ladies had just settled around the quilting frame when the sound of a motor vehicle barreling down the lane reached them inside.

"What in the world?" Abigail asked as she rose from her place and hurried to look out the window. Her first thought was that Joseph had been hurt again somehow, but then she saw a slender *Englisch* girl hop out from the passenger side and wave the driver away. The girl began walking toward the porch, a bright patchwork bag swinging jauntily over her shoulder and her long black hair blowing in the wind. Abigail's heart caught, and her eyes filled with tears. There was no mistaking her identity; she was so much a delicate version of her husband.

Abigail ran to the door and flung it wide just as the girl had the screen door open to knock.

"Abby?"

"*Ya*, I mean, yes . . . and you're . . ."

"Angel, Joe's sister. I hope it's all right . . . He called me the other night and said that you wanted—"

Abigail half sobbed and threw her arms about the girl. All of the usual reserve and uncertainty were gone as she hugged her new sister-in-law, who returned the embrace with enthusiasm.

"Come in," Abigail sniffed. "Please come in I'm sorry I'm so emotional . . . It's just that you look so much like Joseph."

Angel rolled her dark eyes. "I know. It's always been that way. And I have to say that Joe was right—you are one beautiful girl!"

Abigail smiled and caught her hand. "Come and meet my friends. Everyone, this is Joseph's sister, Angel, from New York. She came just for the quilting. She's an art student."

Judith moved over a space and patted the empty chair beside her. "Sit down here, honey, and tell us about yourself. Your brother's become a hero around these parts lately."

Angel smiled. "He's never been one to look before he leaps . . . except, I bet, when he married Abby . . . I bet he did a whole lot of looking then."

They all laughed, and Abigail thanked God that here was someone new and wonderful who was willing to love her and her family. It was almost more than she could bear.

And later, when the remaining three stars had been quilted, the women stopped to admire each other's handiwork. The stitches were marvelous in their uniformity and precision, and Abigail felt a warm glow inside as she surveyed them. She'd used her mother's thimble throughout the quilting and knew a rippling sense of peace that the woman lost to her long ago had still been a part of the day.

Then she served the teaberry cookies and hot tea. They all talked and laughed, and Angel fit right in, sharing stories from New York and listening with obvious, deep interest to the life tales of the women around her. And Abigail felt encircled by love and laughter that melted away all the vestiges of uncertainty in her heart about herself as a person and becoming a wife in truth.

. . .

Joseph tilted his root beer bottle back and let the rich sweetness slide down his throat. He was playing checkers with his father-in-law in a little country store, and they'd attracted quite an interest from the Amish men looking on. Joseph was an expert at checkers but decided early on in the game that it wouldn't be quite right to beat this particular opponent, so he let himself slip on a last move.

"Aha!" Solomon cheered, taking his king. And the other men murmured in approval. Soon Joseph and Solomon were back in the buggy, shivering a bit against the cold.

"You think we can go back now?" Joseph asked and was surprised when the usually taciturn man laughed out loud.

He still found it hard to match the renewed good humor of his father-in-law with the stoic man he'd worked with all fall.

"*Ya*, we can go back, in time for a cookie or two. I bet they're about finished now except for the talking, and that will never be finished."

Joseph chuckled. "I think I like your sense of humor."

"And I like yours, son. I like yours."

CHAPTER TWENTY-FOUR

It was late on the night of the quilting. Angel was ensconced upstairs in Abigail's old room, and the house was quiet except for the gentle brush of Abigail's nightdress as she puttered about the master bedroom putting things away and taking overlong to brush her hair. A single kerosene lamp burned on the bedside table, and Joseph sat up against the pillows watching her. She knew that she was dallying, but she wasn't quite sure how to broach the subject that had been on her mind since that afternoon.

"So, the quilt is beautiful," he remarked, and she turned to watch him run his hand over the pattern of multicolored stars. "Abby's Wish, hmm?"

She nodded. "When your sister found out the pattern name, she actually went around the table and had everyone make a wish for me."

He smiled. "That's nice. When are you coming to bed?"

She bit her lip. "Don't you want to know the wishes?"

"I know what I wish." His voice was husky, and she turned on her bare feet to face him, leaning against the bureau for support.

"What?" she whispered.

He laid aside his glasses and closed his eyes, and his thick lashes fanned against the flush of his cheeks. He began to speak in a dreamy tone that made her curl her toes into the wooden floorboards.

"I wish that you'd put down the hairbrush and that you'd walk toward me and that you'd smile your beautiful smile and that your eyes would shine. Then I wish you'd look at me the way you did when I was sick and whisper that you'd do anything to help me, because I need help, Abby. I need you, and I . . ." He broke off and opened his eyes, and she stared into their warm, dark depths, almost as if she could see herself reflected there.

And she could see herself as he'd described, coming to him . . . *just as she was meant to do as his wife.* The thought simmered across her consciousness, and she took one small step forward. She saw him swallow and watched as a pulse beat strongly in the bare line of his throat.

"Abby . . ."

She smiled and let the love she felt for him show in her eyes. She could hear him breathing, short, deep intakes of breath as if he'd run a long way and now was finding rest.

She came until she was within hand's reach of him, but he still didn't move. She wet her lips and gazed down at him, all of the love she felt for him heating her heart and her mind. She bent forward from the waist, letting her hair enclose them like a curtain, and then she kissed him.

"Joseph," she murmured.

He opened his eyes. "Is this real?" he asked in wonder. "Do you . . . Are you . . . ?"

Her lips found his once more, and then he reached strong arms up to pull her to him. He pressed hot kisses along the line of her throat and through the cotton fabric of the shoulder of her gown.

"And what do you wish for, Abby Lambert?" he whispered in a breathless sigh, drawing the quilt over their heads.

She stared up at him, then pulled his eager mouth down to meet her own once more. "That's easy," she said between kisses. "As the Lord wills, I wish for a lifetime of joy, and children, and peace, with the husband of my heart."

He smiled. "Well then, Mrs. Lambert, I'll give it my earnest attention to make sure that your every wish comes very . . . very true."

WHAT THE HEART SEES

KATHLEEN FULLER

CHAPTER ONE

Ellie Chupp sat straight up in bed, her nightgown soaked with sweat and sticking against her clammy skin. Her chest heaved as she fought for breath. After a year's reprieve, the nightmare had returned with a vengeance. Her fingers curled around her quilt as the vivid memory finally faded—the sound of metal scraping against metal, the car flipping over, the scent of burning rubber, Caroline's scream—

She gripped both sides of her head, willing her heart to slow and the images to slide away. She fell back against the bed. Darkness surrounded her. Why had the dream returned now? Five years should be long enough to heal. Long enough to forget.

But the nightmare proved she would never forget.

She tried to fall back asleep, but remnants of emotion kept her awake. Pain. Fear. Anger. Regret. All of them mixed in her mind and soul as she tossed and turned.

Finally she reached for the watch on her nightstand and read the time. Four thirty. Might as well get up. She slipped on her dress, then she put her white apron over it and quickly pinned up her hair before fastening her white prayer *kapp*. She made her way downstairs to the kitchen and put on a pot of coffee, knowing her father would want a cup when he got up.

With the coffee percolating, Ellie sat at the table, bowed her head, and began her morning prayer time with the Lord. But the dream still haunted her.

Please, Lord, take these memories away. Help me face life with the courage only You can give. Guide my heart, my thoughts . . . and my dreams.

As she finished praying, she heard the heavy tread of her father's footsteps down the hallway. Ellie rose and poured him a cup of coffee as he entered the kitchen. A moment later the hiss of the gas lamp filled the room.

"*Danki*, Ellie." He took the cup from her hands and slurped. "*Sehr gut.* Just what I needed this morning. Your *mamm* was up half the night making lists about what she needed to do to help your *aenti* with Isaiah's wedding."

Ellie smiled, found the chair next to him, and sat down. In a couple of weeks her cousin Isaiah would marry one of her dearest friends, Sarah Lynne Miller. Her mother was consumed with the preparations. "That sounds like her."

The cup hit the table with a soft thump. "You'd think we were marrying off one of our own the way she's carrying on."

Ellie's smile faded a tiny bit.

Her father suddenly cleared his throat. "Ah, what's for breakfast, *dochder*?"

"Eggs, bacon, and toast."

"Sounds *gut*." He rose from the chair, the legs scraping against the wood floor. "I'll be back after I tend to the animals."

Ellie's smile slid completely from her face. *Daed* had meant no harm, yet his unspoken message hurt. Still, she accepted the reality of her situation. An Amish man needed a healthy wife. A whole wife, one who could take care of the home and the children without impediment. Ellie couldn't be that wife to anyone. Because the accident that still haunted her hadn't just taken the life of her best friend, Caroline. It had also taken Ellie's sight.

. . .

Christopher Miller looked at the packed duffel bag on his bed and ground his teeth. He could still change his mind about going to Paradise. He'd done it before, many times. But he couldn't keep running away from the past. He'd spent the last five years ignoring God's prodding. Like Jonah avoiding Ninevah. But Chris couldn't keep ignoring God's will, no matter how much he tried.

He sat on the bed and withdrew his mother's latest letter from his pocket. He'd been in the *bann* for five years, since Caroline's death, and she had written him almost every month during those years, telling him that life wasn't the same since he left. But it was the last paragraph that had stirred him the most.

If you could just come home, *mei sohn*, we would all be grateful. We all miss you, Christopher, including your *daed*. I pray for you every single day . . .

Chris shot up from the bed and shoved the letter back into his pocket. Her words echoed in his brain, and he could almost hear her soft voice, as if she stood right there in his one-bedroom apartment in Apple Creek, Ohio, looking at him, pleading not only with her words but with her light gray eyes. But she wasn't. She, along with everything he loved, was back in Paradise.

Pacing the length of the room, he fought with himself. More than once he had packed up his few belongings, jumped in his used car, and headed for Pennsylvania. But every time the memories stopped him. The pain of losing Caroline had sent him in a downward spiral that ended with his being shunned and leaving his family. One act could reinstate him in the church and reunite him with his parents, his brothers, and his sister, Sarah Lynne. But he couldn't do it. Not when they were wrong and he was right.

A knock sounded on the door, yanking him from his thoughts. He opened it, and his landlord, Mr. Russell, walked in. The stout man's red-and-black-plaid shirt stretched over his rotund belly, barely covering it.

"I was just about to turn in the keys," Chris said, stepping to the side.

"Thought I'd save you the trip." Russell strolled around the apartment, his eyes narrowing beneath overgrown graying eyebrows. "Didn't do much with the place while you were here, did ya?"

Chris shook his head. Even living as one of the *Englisch*, he'd maintained a sparse existence the past five years. His furniture was minimal: a lumpy couch, an old recliner, a small kitchen table, and his bed, all secondhand. Living alone, he hadn't needed much. What he had was enough. Or so he thought.

Russell faced Chris and gestured to the furniture. "Sure you don't want to take any of this with you?"

"Like I said, get whatever you can for the stuff. I don't need it anymore."

Russell glanced around the room. "I'll probably just dump it. Won't get more than a few bucks anyway. Hardly worth the effort."

Chris shrugged. "Whatever you want to do."

"Sorry to see you go. You're a good tenant. Paid your rent on time and never caused me no trouble. Can't say the same for all the renters I got here. Sure wish you were sticking around." He held out his hand.

Chris put the two apartment keys in Russell's beefy palm. It would be easy for him to stay. But lately he'd been thinking more and more about home, about the Amish faith he'd turned his back on but was still entwined with every fiber of his soul. He'd lived an *Englisch* life since the day he'd been shunned, cutting his hair, buying *Englisch* clothes, even getting his driver's license and purchasing a beat-up car. Shortly after arriving in Apple Creek, he found a job with a construction company, building houses all over Knox and Holmes counties. Before long he was making more than enough money to afford an apartment and a better car. He even joined a Mennonite church. On the outside, he'd made a successful transition from Amish life.

On the inside, it was anything but.

He snatched up a faded brown baseball cap and

plopped it on his head, then he slung his duffel bag over his shoulder. "Thanks for that, but I've got to get going."

Russell nodded. "Good luck."

Chris left the apartment and went to his car. He felt freer than he had in a long time, but doubts plagued him. He stopped in front of his car and looked up at the cloudless sky, questions and doubts battering him. Had he made the right decision? Could he reconcile with his family and the church? Could he forgive the person who'd ruined his life? Could he ask the community to forgive his transgressions?

He wasn't sure if he could. But he had to try.

. . .

Sarah Lynne carefully aligned the simple label on the jar of strawberry jelly, then smoothed it against the glass. *Ellie's Jellies* it said in black print, with a small picture of a cluster of grapes above the name. She breathed in the sweet scent of cooking fruit and sugar wafting throughout Ellie's kitchen as the next batch of jelly simmered on the gas stove. Her lips curved into a smile. "Did I tell you it smells *gut* in here?"

"About a dozen times," Ellie said.

Ellie's light blue eyes were directed just beyond Sarah's shoulder. They held no expression, but from the twitch of Ellie's lips, Sarah Lynne could see the compliment pleased her friend. "Here's another jar." She placed it in Ellie's outstretched hands.

Ellie gripped the jar with her left hand, then guided it into one of the six square openings inside the box.

"It's nice of you to take the time to give me a hand. I know how busy you are with wedding preparations."

"I'm happy to do it. Especially since I know I can get all the free samples I want."

Ellie chuckled. "Does Isaiah know what a sweet tooth you have?"

"*Ya*. He quickly learned the way to my heart and has been keeping me supplied with treats ever since."

"He's a *gut mann*, your Isaiah." Ellie rose from her chair, turned, and made her way to the gas stove a few steps from the round kitchen table. She picked up a wooden spoon from beside the stove and stirred the pot of strawberries and sugar.

"He is, *ya*." Sarah Lynne watched her friend move about the kitchen with ease. Ellie never ceased to amaze her. Completely blind from a car accident five years before, she didn't let her disability stop her from creating her own line of jams and jellies, which she sold at Yoder's Pantry. Before losing her sight she had been a cook at the restaurant, a job she had loved.

Last year she had announced her new venture to her former employers. Sarah Lynne worked as a waitress at the Pantry, and she clearly remembered the scrumptious samples Ellie had brought with her that day. One taste and everyone was sold.

Sarah Lynne put her elbow on the table and leaned her chin on her hand. So much had happened over the past year, not the least of which was her falling in love with Ellie's cousin Isaiah. She'd known him forever and had never had a romantic thought toward him for most of her life. But then she'd been without a ride home from a Sunday singing, and he offered to take her. She was drawn to his shy manner and strong faith, and soon they were dating. Now she couldn't imagine spending the rest of her life with anyone else.

"You've gotten quiet over there." Ellie tapped the handle against the lip of the pot, letting the residual ruby-colored jelly slide off the spoon. She placed the spoon on the rest by the stove and sat down again. "Anything you want to talk about?"

Sarah Lynne looked at her friend's eyes. They were so beautiful, like tiny ovals of blue glass, with round black pupils that never changed size. The accident hadn't damaged her eyes, nor had it left any physical scars. Her blindness was due to blunt force trauma, damaging her optic nerve. From a glance one would think Ellie Chupp absolutely perfect, with her pale blonde hair, slender figure, and those gorgeous eyes. Sarah Lynne looked away, feeling guilty even though she knew Ellie had no idea she was staring at her.

"Are you worried about the wedding?" Ellie folded her hands on her lap. Her posture, as always, was perfect.

"*Nee*. Well, maybe a little." She dropped her hand from her chin and leaned forward. "*Mamm*'s been writing to Chris. I don't think *Daed* knows. If he did, he might be upset. He's very strict about the *bann*."

"Do you agree with him?"

"*Nee*. But we're not going to argue with him about it."

Ellie leaned forward. "I don't understand that. How can we possibly bring our loved ones back to the faith if we send them away? If we don't let them know how fervently we pray for them?"

"I wouldn't let Bishop Ebersol hear you say that."

"Don't worry, I won't." Ellie sighed. "It's not like I'll ever have to worry about that."

"Being in the *bann*?" Sarah Lynne smiled at the thought of her friend doing something worthy of shunning.

"*Nee.*" Ellie lowered her voice to an almost inaudible level. "Having a *kinn* to worry about."

Sarah Lynne's eyebrows lifted. She'd rarely heard a self—pitying word cross Ellie's lips. "Ellie, you can't say that."

"*Ya*, I can. I've accepted that I may not ever have a husband. God has helped me to see that I can find fulfillment in other ways."

"Like your business. We can't keep your jelly in stock at the Pantry."

"That's *gut* to hear. I'm glad the customers are enjoying it."

"Enjoying?" Sarah chuckled. "They're devouring it."

Ellie smiled. "Then I'll have to keep making more." She leaned forward and searched for Sarah Lynne's hand. When she found it, she gripped it. "But we're not talking about me. We're talking about you. And about Chris. Did your *mutter* mention the wedding in any of her letters?"

"I don't know. We don't talk about what she writes. But I would be surprised if she did." Having Chris here for the wedding would be a complete disaster. Yet Sarah Lynne wished her brother would come home. She missed him.

"I can understand why she wouldn't say anything."

Ellie paused. "But your family has wholeheartedly accepted Isaiah into their fold. Perhaps Chris can find it in his heart to do the same."

"Someday, perhaps." Knowing the history between the two men, Sarah Lynne doubted it. In fact, her brother's complicated relationship with Isaiah had kept her from accepting Isaiah's first marriage proposal. But when he asked her a second time, she knew she couldn't put her happiness on hold waiting for her brother to come around. "I'm not counting on it. And it doesn't matter, really. If *Mamm* told him about the wedding and he decides to come, then we'll deal with it. And if he doesn't, we'll still have a *gut* time." This was her wedding, her time to celebrate. She wouldn't let Chris ruin that.

Ellie squeezed her hand and let it go. "How is Chris faring in Ohio?"

"I guess he's doing fine. *Mamm*'s the only one who has contact with him, and like I said, she doesn't tell me anything." She sighed. "It would be wonderful if Chris would realize how wrong he's been. *Mamm* hasn't been the same since he left."

"I'm sure it's been hard. On all of you. I'll pray he comes back and reconciles with your family and the church."

"*Danki*, Ellie. We've all been praying for that as well. Especially Isaiah." A lump formed in her throat. "He's still carrying around so much guilt."

Ellie gripped the table, her light brows furrowing. "He shouldn't."

Her forceful reply surprised Sarah Lynne. "That's what I keep telling him—"

"Because we've all put the past behind us, *ya*?"

"*Ya*. Ellie, is something wrong?"

Ellie released the edge of the table, the lines of strain fading from her face. "*Nee*," she said, putting her hands in her lap. "Isaiah shouldn't punish himself after all this time. What's done is done, and it can't be changed."

"I know that. He knows that. But . . ." She couldn't bring herself to say the words out loud. Her future husband would never be at peace as long as Chris stayed away. She looked at Ellie. "It seems to me the only person who should be angry with Isaiah is you."

"Me?" Her mouth tugged down in a frown. "Sarah Lynne, I could never be angry with Isaiah. Look at what a wonderful *mann* he's become. He's so strong in our faith—everyone knows that. And whenever there's a need in our community, he's there, not only providing help with his hands, but with his time and his money. There isn't a more generous *mann*."

Hearing about her fiancé's qualities made Sarah Lynne's heart swell with love. His image came to mind. The smoky gray eyes that were always filled with kindness, the soft, low tone of his voice, the mop of curly, sandy blond hair that could never be fully tamed into the bowl-shaped Amish haircut.

Ellie was right. Isaiah shouldn't carry so much guilt. It wasn't fair, not when the one person who should really resent him had forgiven him long ago. Sarah Lynne couldn't wait to be his wife, and if her brother couldn't give him the peace he needed, she'd spend the rest of their lives making up for it.

CHAPTER TWO

After Sarah Lynne left, Ellie wiped off the counter-tops in case any jelly had spilled. Then she rinsed the rag and hung it on the divider between the double sink. The window above the sink was cracked open a bit to let out some of the heat that had built up in the kitchen. But now that she had finished canning the jelly, the late October air brought a chill into the room. She groped for the sash, then closed the window.

She lifted the plastic lid on her Braille watch—something Bishop Ebersol had given her special permission to wear—and checked the time. Nearly five o'clock. Her parents would be home soon, her father from his construction job and her mother from visiting her older brother Wally's children, who lived a few miles down the road. Ellie usually accompanied her mother on her visits—she adored her nieces and nephews—but she had to finish up the jelly. God had seen fit to bless her small venture, keeping her plenty busy. She needed to be busy. She needed to be *needed*. And this new business met that need.

For now.

She shoved the thought away. Ellie didn't like thinking of the future, not anymore. Before the accident thoughts of the future consumed her—a future with John Beachy. When would they marry? How many children would they have? Would they have all boys, all girls, or a mix of both? She'd even wondered how many grandchildren she might have.

But in an instant all those hopes had been dashed, forcing her to live in the present, taking each day as the blessing it was. She'd spent years adapting to a life without sight, relearning the simplest tasks, things she used to do automatically. To pin up her hair, she needed to place the hairpins in the same spot every day. If she put them somewhere else, or if someone moved them, she might never find them, and then she would have to depend on someone else to locate them. The day John left, she decided she would never depend on anyone. She didn't want people's pity. She spent enough time pitying herself.

Ellie turned from the window. That was all behind her now. Her future was in God's hands. Her sole focus was today, and at the moment, on what she would make for supper.

Twenty minutes later she had a fragrant beef stew bubbling on the stove, filled with potatoes and carrots from the root cellar and canned meat from the cow her parents had butchered last month. She pulled a loaf of bread she'd baked that morning from the breadbox on the counter and was slicing it when her mother walked into the kitchen.

"That smells great, *dochder.*" *Mami's* soft footsteps

sounded against the wooden floor in the kitchen as she moved to stand next to Ellie. "Did you use homemade broth?"

"Of course."

"And are those barley pearls I see?"

"Absolutely." Ellie smiled as she placed the palm of her left hand on the loaf of bread, using the tip of her finger to find the edge. She moved her fingertip back about an inch, then she placed the knife close to it before slicing off a big piece of soft bread. Laying that on the plate nearby, she repeated the process again as she tilted her head in the direction of her mother's voice. "I'm using the restaurant's recipe tonight."

"Your specialty? Mmm, I can't wait to taste it. You have a gift for cooking, Ellie. You always have."

Ellie was grateful she hadn't lost her ability to work in the kitchen. It had taken months and months to acquire the new skills and techniques until she had mastered again what she had once taken for granted. More than once she had felt the slip of the knife blade into her finger as she learned how to slice bread, and the splash of hot water from the kettle as she practiced pouring. Yet she'd never had a major accident and had almost regained her former confidence in the kitchen. But the satisfaction of cooking at home would never replace what she had permanently lost.

She would never have her job back at Yoder's Pantry, a job she loved. She'd never know the pleasure of cooking for the customers again, both Amish and *Englisch*, and seeing them enjoy the food she prepared. The compliments hadn't stoked her pride;

they only spurred her on to become a better cook. She loved inventing tiny twists on common Amish meals, such as adding a touch more thyme to the chicken and noodles or a bit of orange zest to the cherry pie filling. She loved it when customers asked what was in the recipes, trying to identify that one flavor they just couldn't pinpoint.

Now she had to be content with pleasing her parents and occasionally families in the church when she brought a meal to potluck.

Her father arrived, and after he cleaned up from work they all sat down at the table. After saying a silent prayer, they started to eat.

"I see you got your jelly jars finished today." Her mother's voice broke the silence that had settled over them once they dug into the meal.

"*Ya*, Sarah Lynne came over and helped me." Ellie found the lip of the bowl with her left hand and guided her spoon into the stew. From the temperature of the bowl she knew the stew was still pretty hot. She gently blew on the spoon before putting it in her mouth. The flavors exploded on her tongue, and the beef chunks were so tender they almost melted before she could chew them.

"That reminds me, I need to visit her *mamm* and find out how the wedding preparations are going. Did she mention anything to you?"

Ellie turned her head in the direction of her mother's voice. She'd learned in rehabilitation the importance of looking at the person speaking. She'd been amazed how quickly she had stopped doing that after the accident.

Now it had become natural again. "They're going well. Sarah Lynne asked if I'd make a couple of desserts."

"Brownies."

She directed her sightless gaze to her father's deep voice at her left. "Brownies?"

"You should take your brownies, the cream cheese ones. Best dessert I ever had."

She warmed at the compliment, which she knew her father didn't give lightly. "*Danki, Daed*. I'll do that. And I'll make an extra pan just for you."

"That'll do."

Ellie could imagine the small smile twitching on her father's face, the crinkles forming in the corners of his eyes. As she usually did, she tried to imagine what he looked like now, at age fifty-five. Was his beard close to full gray? Did he still wear his hat at a slight left angle? Did he have more wrinkles? She'd never know, as she would never ask him such strange questions, nor would she ask her mother. What were looks anyway? She'd never thought about them too much when she had her sight, knowing that God saw the inside of a person, not the outer shell. Character was the important thing. But she had to remind herself of that, instead of being curious about what her family and friends looked like.

"I wonder if Chris knows about the wedding," her father said before taking another slurp of his stew. "If he does, maybe he'll come back."

"I certainly hope not," her mother responded. "At least not before he repents of his sin."

Ellie could sense her mother shaking her head, as she always did when she became indignant.

"He's in the *bann*. He must be willing to make things right with God and the church."

"I don't think you should judge him so harshly, *Mami*," Ellie said. "He lost someone very important to him."

"And you losing your sight wasn't important?" Her tone held an edge. "He would do well to follow your example, *dochder*. You were able to do as God calls. You were able to forgive. That *bu* has done nothing but cause pain for his family. His poor *mutter*." She clucked her tongue. "At least he should think of her. It breaks my heart to see the sadness in her eyes, even after all this time."

Ellie reached for her bread, which was on a small plate to the left of her bowl. She tried to set her place as consistently as possible, using a mental clock face as a guide. Her plate was the center, her water glass at one o'clock, her bread plate at eleven, and her fork and knife situated close to the plate on the right and the left.

Her mother had always been strict about her faith, even more than her father. She'd never been shy about expressing her support of *meiding*, even when others, including herself, in the community were less sure about the fairness of the practice. Her mother had balked about her father having a cell phone in the small appliance repair shop that he used to run before he started to work in construction, but even Bishop Ebersol approved of having the phone for business purposes.

"Maybe he is thinking of her," Ellie said, putting her bread back down on her plate.

"What?" her mother asked.

"Maybe Chris is thinking about his mother. If he's not ready to repent, then staying away is the right thing to do. Being close by would be even more painful for her, *ya*? Besides, who's to say what's in his heart? People forgive in their own time. Or rather, in the Lord's time, I like to think."

"Humph. It's been five years, Ellie." She felt her mother's hand on her arm. "You have such a gentle heart, *dochder*. You see the *gut* in everyone. But sometimes people aren't *gut*, even Amish people."

Ellie pulled her arm away. She hated when her mother spoke to her like she wasn't smart enough to figure things out. She was blind, not stupid, and it was on the tip of her tongue to say so, but she held the words in. "I just like to give everyone the benefit of the doubt. That's all."

"And that's very admirable." Her mother took another quiet bite of the stew.

As usual, her father remained silent. She heard him slide his chair from the table.

"*Sehr gut*, Ellie. As always." His knees creaked as he rose and walked out of the room.

Ellie had expected to hear the heavy thud of his work shoes on the wooden floor, but he must have removed them before supper because she barely sensed his soft footsteps as he left.

She and her mother ate the rest of the meal in silence. She finished off the stew, dipping the last few bites of her bread into the rich broth.

After praying at the end of the meal, her mother

spoke. "I'll get the dishes." The clink of silverware against the plates filled the kitchen as her mother started to clear the table. "Oh, and I brought another book from the library. I think you'll like it."

"Is it about the Amish?"

"*Ya.*" She leaned close to Ellie, her voice lowered to a whisper. "And it's a *romance.*"

Ellie tamped down a giggle. Her mother sounded like she was smuggling something illegal into the house. Before the accident she had expressed disdain over Ellie's choice of reading material. Her mother had always preferred Bible reading, or a few non-fiction books. She claimed to never have time for "that non-sense." But Ellie was glad that her mother had softened and brought home books she knew Ellie would enjoy.

"*Danki,*" Ellie said. "I can't wait to read it. Are you sure you don't need any help?"

"*Nee.* You just go on, I'll take care of this. It's the least I can do in return for such an *appeditlich* meal."

Ellie nodded, then stood from the table and made her way to the living room, which was through a small hallway just off the kitchen. She didn't use her white cane at home. Her parents had kept everything the same for years, even before the accident. That made navigating through the house a lot easier.

As she walked into the room, she breathed in deeply and smiled. Her father had started a fire in the wood-stove in the corner. She loved the rich smell of smoke and went to sit in the chair near the newly crack-ling fire.

Her father tossed another log in the fire, then eased

himself into the chair on the opposite side of the fire-place. The soothing warmth covered her body, seeping through the thin fabric of her pale green dress. She leaned back in the comfortable chair and closed her eyes, enjoying the peace. She heard the soft rustle of her father opening the daily newspaper.

"Any news worth mentioning?" she asked.

"Not too much." He turned a page. "Sure are a lot of jelly jars on the counter in the kitchen. Looks like your business is doing well."

"It is, *Daed*. Even I'm surprised." She angled her body toward his voice, the heat from the fire warming her legs through her dark blue knee socks. "I thought a few people might want to buy a jar of jelly every once in a while, but I can barely keep up. Every day I have to *geh* to the grocer's to get more fruit."

"You using frozen?"

"I have to. Fresh is so expensive right now and will be until next summer. I can tell a difference in the quality of the jelly, but Sarah Lynne says the customers can't. A few have asked if they can buy it by the case."

Her father lowered his voice. "Now that your *mutter*'s out of sight, I can say this. I know I'm not supposed to have a speck of pride in my bones, but I can't help it when it comes to you. You've done real well for yourself, Ellie. You let that *Englisch* woman come here. The one that taught you Braille and how to use your cane and stuff. What was her name?" He snapped his finger.

"Mrs. Neeley." Ellie smiled at the thought of her rehabilitation teacher. They hadn't always gotten along, especially in the beginning. She'd been a stubborn student at first, still struggling to accept her blindness and John's increasing retreat from her life. But the woman never lost patience with her. Ellie owed her much more than she could ever repay.

"*Ya*, that's her. And you stuck with it. And never once did I see you feel sorry for yourself."

Ellie tilted her chin down. He may not have seen her piteous moments, but she'd had plenty over the years.

His voice started to quaver. "Now you've got your thriving business. And you've done it on your own."

"Not exactly on my own, *Daed*." She'd been raised to deflect any praise, but hearing the emotion in her father's voice brought tears to her eyes. She fought to keep them from sliding down her cheeks. "The printer in town gives me a *gut* discount on the labels. Sarah Lynne helps me with the packaging. *Mami* drives me to the store when I can't get a taxi and takes me to the Pantry when she can. I've had lots of help."

"I reckon you're gonna need more if things keep going like this." He cleared his throat. "You've done *gut*, *dochder*. You've done *gut*."

Ellie took a deep breath. If her mother came in and saw her crying, even happy tears, she'd pepper her with endless questions. And Ellie didn't want to reveal what her father had told her. She loved her mother, but Ellie's personality meshed more with her father's, and she'd always felt closest to him. Knowing that he thought well of her meant everything.

"Dishes are all done." Her mother entered the room and huffed. "Goodness, Ephraim, you're going to roast us in here. Turn down the damper!"

A moment later the damper squeaked closed.

"There. That's much better. Here you are, Ellie." Her mother handed her the portable CD player. "The librarian said if you enjoy this one she can order the other two in the series."

"*Danki*. I'm sure I'll enjoy it." She was glad Bishop Ebersol had given her special permission to listen to books on her battery—operated CD player. If not, she would have to depend on her mother or father to read to her, and they would never read a romance out loud, even a Christian one. Her father would probably die of embarrassment if she even hinted at it.

Her mother had slipped the CD in the player for her already. But as the story floated through the speakers of her headphones, she could barely focus on the words. She had made her father proud. She would carry his praise with her for a long time.

CHAPTER THREE

"Two weeks is a long time."

Sarah Lynne peered around Isaiah's shoulder as they sat on the swing on the front porch of her parents' house. Satisfied that no one was peeking through the window, she threaded her fingers through Isaiah's, her palm pressing against his large, calloused hand. The air had a bit of a chill in it, but she didn't care. Not only did her jacket keep her warm, but so did the man sitting next to her. "It's a long time to me too."

"I wish we had scheduled the wedding for the first of November." He leaned back in the swing, pushing against the wooden porch with the toe of his work boot.

"Patience is a virtue."

"*Ya*, but it's hard to be patient when I'm about to marry the best *maedel* in Paradise." He turned to her. "Make that the world."

The sun had dipped past the horizon, but there was enough daylight to see the redness of his cheeks and his slightly crooked teeth as he smiled. He was handsome and kind. He was also so shy that they hadn't even shared a kiss on the cheek since they'd started courting. She squeezed his hand. Isaiah wasn't the only impatient one.

She tore her gaze away before her thoughts got her in trouble. "We should focus on the wedding preparations. And who we'll be visiting afterward."

"Your parents, of course. Then mine."

"There's also my cousin. Although she has seven *kinner* and is expecting another one, so she may not notice we're even there."

They continued to talk about visiting various friends and relatives after their wedding. They both had large extended families, so there would be plenty of visiting going on before they were settled in their own house, which Isaiah had just purchased a few weeks ago. Located down the street from his family, it was a modest house, but with plenty of room for a growing family.

"I thought maybe next week we could go shopping for furniture." He started the swing moving again. "We'll need a couch, a table for the kitchen, a bed . . ." His voice trailed off and he averted his gaze.

Laughing, she lightly tapped his arm with her hand. "You're the shyest *mann* I know." She sighed. "I wouldn't have you any other way."

Out of the corner of her eye, she saw the headlights of a car coming down the long, winding dirt driveway. Her parents' house was at least a half mile from the road, and rarely did cars venture here, except the occasional taxi when necessary. She released Isaiah's hand and stood up. "Wonder who that is."

"Are you expecting anyone?"

She shook her head. "Not tonight."

"Maybe your parents are?"

As the car neared she said, "They didn't say anything to me about it."

The dark blue two-door car pulled up near the house. When the door opened, a tall, slender man with short black hair stepped out, then reached back inside the car to pull out a big duffel bag. Finally he turned around.

Sarah Lynne gasped. Was the dim light playing tricks on her? "Christopher?"

Then the man grinned, and her heart tripped. Even with his short hair and *Englisch* jeans and leather jacket, she knew him. "Christopher!" She ran toward him, her arms outstretched, then stopped short. She couldn't hug him, not while he was still shunned.

She hadn't seen him since she was fifteen years old. Suddenly she didn't care that he was in the *bann*. Her brother was here, and that was all that mattered. She reached out to him, and he held her tight.

They finally separated and she looked up at him. He tweaked her nose. "Can't hardly call you my little *schwester* anymore, can I? You're all grown up."

"And you've become *Englisch*, I see."

He immediately sobered. "Not completely, Sarah Lynne. In my heart, I'm still Amish."

Her breath caught in her throat. "Does that mean you're coming back to the church?"

He didn't say anything, just looked past her shoulder to Isaiah, who was standing several feet away. She glanced over to see that he had put on his hat, pulling it low over his forehead.

Just at that moment she saw Chris lock eyes with him, and her stomach twisted like a metal spring. Her pulse thrummed as the two men stared at each other.

"What's he doing here?" Chris sounded like he'd just chewed a mouthful of glass.

"We should go inside. *Mami* and *Daed* will want to see you—"

"I want him to answer me first." Chris directed the question to Sarah Lynne but kept his eyes on Isaiah.

Sarah Lynne stepped to the side, her gaze shifting from one man to the other. Isaiah kept his eyes on the ground. His broad shoulders slumped, like the confidence had whooshed out of him. Even as Chris strode toward him, he didn't look up. Then she realized why. He wouldn't engage her brother. He couldn't and still adhere to the Amish tenant of nonviolence. And with the anger coiling off Christopher right now, Isaiah had clearly made the right decision.

"Christopher!" Sarah Lynne grabbed the crook of his elbow and pulled him to the side. She lowered her voice, not wanting Isaiah to hear. "Why are you here?"

Chris pulled his gaze from Isaiah. "I came back to . . . to . . ." He shot another look at Isaiah. "Why won't anyone tell me why he's here?"

Sarah Lynne put her hand on her brother's shoulder, steeling herself for his reaction. "Things have changed since you left." The knot in her stomach suddenly unwound as a sudden peace fell over her. She loved her brother, and always would, but her place was beside Isaiah. "A lot of things."

Chris looked at her, then back at Isaiah, who lifted

his head to gaze at Chris directly but without confrontation. Chris focused on her again. "What are you talking about?"

She took a deep breath. "Chris, Isaiah and I are engaged."

. . .

Chris froze for a moment, then he turned around and walked a few steps to his car. He kicked the tire, then whirled to face them. "You're marrying him? After what he did to our family?"

The front door opened, and Chris saw his father, closely followed by his mother, come out to the porch.

"What's going on here?" His father, still nimble for a man in his midfifties, hurried down the steps. "Christopher?"

Mamm came down the stairs, the white strands of her *kapp* flying behind her shoulders. She passed by her husband, Isaiah, and Sarah Lynne, and rushed straight to Chris. "*Sohn?*" Her voice was thick with tears. "Is it really you?"

Chris's posture softened as he looked down at his mother. "*Ya, Mami.*"

She reached up to embrace him, only to freeze at her husband's approach.

"Melvin—," his mother said, moving to stand in front of him. But when he waved her to the side, she stepped back.

"Are you here to ask forgiveness? Are you ready to come back to us?"

Chris's gaze darted from his father to his mother and finally to Sarah Lynne. He had thought he was ready to let go of the past and repent, but how could he do that now? "I'm not sure."

A muscle in his *daed's* cheek twitched. "Then why are you here?"

"I . . . I don't know."

His father turned to their mother. "*Geh* in the *haus*."

"But, Melvin—"

"I said . . . *geh* in the *haus*." He didn't raise his voice or even change the tone. Just spoke the words slowly as he moved closer to her.

Without another protest, his mother turned around. But Chris saw her wipe at her nose with the back of her hand before disappearing inside.

His father turned toward Sarah Lynne and Isaiah. "Isaiah, it's time you head home. Sarah Lynne, *geh* inside with your *mamm*."

Chris's stomach turned as he saw Isaiah and Sarah Lynne gaze at each other for a long moment. Even in the dim light of approaching night he could see the emotion in their eyes.

Isaiah turned and headed behind the house. He must have parked his buggy near the barn, probably in the same spot Chris used to keep his buggy . . . the one he'd bought to surprise Caroline on their wedding day. The twist in his gut tightened.

Sarah Lynne took one more look at Chris before running into the house. He hoped she could comfort their mother. It didn't seem he'd have the chance.

Why hadn't his mother told him Sarah Lynne was

marrying Isaiah? How could his parents approve of this? Why would they allow their daughter to marry a criminal? They had all betrayed him. Every last one.

Isaiah's buggy appeared from the opposite side of the house. Long ago Chris's father had formed a crude but effective circular dirt driveway that made parking the buggy easy. It also made for a quick getaway for Isaiah. He didn't have to directly pass by either of them to get to the road.

Chris's *daed* kept his back to him, watching Isaiah. When Isaiah turned his buggy on to the main road, his *daed* faced Chris again. "You may stay here tonight. But we will follow the rules of *meiding*. Understand?"

Chris shook his head. He couldn't stay here, not after what he had learned. "*Danki*, but I made other arrangements." He hadn't, but his father didn't need to know that.

His *daed*'s nod was almost imperceptible. Then he turned around and went back in the house.

The wind suddenly picked up, and Chris drew his black leather jacket closer to his body as he leaned against his car. His gaze drifted to the large picture window, focusing on the soft, yellowish glow cast by a gas lamp. A few seconds later the light was extinguished, leaving him in darkness.

He grabbed his duffel and tossed it inside the car, then he hurled himself into the driver's seat and yanked the door shut. But instead of turning on the engine, he leaned his forehead against the steering wheel, trying to make sense of his feelings. He should head back to Apple Creek. He had a good life there. No lies. No betrayal.

No family. No faith. No real connection to God.

A heavy sigh escaped him. He had no idea what to do, but he knew he couldn't stay in his parents' driveway. He lifted his head and reached for his keys in the pocket of his coat. A knock sounded on the window, making him jump. He turned and saw Sarah Lynne tapping on the glass.

He turned on the ignition and pressed the button for the automatic window. Even though he was furious with her, he couldn't turn her away. "What?"

She leaned forward, hugging her shoulders with her hands. "*Mamm*'s upset, Christopher. And so am I."

"*You're* angry?"

"*Ya*, I am. For starters, I don't appreciate the way you treated Isaiah."

He gaped. "I treated him the way he deserves."

"*Nee*. You didn't. You're acting like a little *kinn*, Christopher. Just like you did when you left Paradise."

"I didn't have a choice. I'm in the *bann*, remember."

"That's your own doing."

"Look, I don't know how this became about me, but—"

"It's always about you, Christopher. You saw *Mami* tonight." She paused. He couldn't see her expression clearly, but he heard resentment creeping into her voice. "And now *Daed*'s all upset. Do you have any idea how hard this has been on him? You're his only *sohn*."

Her words pierced his heart, but he wouldn't let her see it. Instead he focused on the real offense. "How can you marry him, Sarah? After what he did to Caroline?"

"Because I love him," she said without hesitation. "And he loves me. There's no finer man in Paradise."

"I find that hard to believe."

"Believe it."

He slumped against the seat. The exhaust from the engine reached his nostrils, and Sarah Lynne had started to shiver. "I don't want to argue with you," he said. "Not now."

"I don't either."

"Then you should *geh* back inside."

"I will. I just came out here to find out where you're staying."

"Staying?"

"*Ya. Daed* said you were staying somewhere else. Don't be thick, Christopher."

"I'm not being thick, and I'm not staying." If he had waffled before about leaving for Ohio, he had just made up his mind. His family had chosen sides. There was no point in hanging around here any longer.

"But you can't leave." Distress colored her tone. "You saw how excited *Mami* was to see you. She couldn't take it if you left now."

Alarm shot through him. "Is there something wrong? Is she sick?"

"Sick? *Nee*, she's not sick. Unless you count heart-sick. *Daed* is too. I know he won't talk to you, but I'm sure *Mamm* will. So where are you staying? She can meet you there tomorrow. I'll call the taxi myself."

Chris paused. He wanted to see his mother one last time before he went back to Apple Creek. "I'm not sure."

"Let me know in the morning. I'll be at the Pantry

starting at seven. My shift ends at three, so don't wait too long to come by."

She stepped away from the car. "There's a bed-and-breakfast near the restaurant that has a vacancy. They're rarely busy during the week."

He nodded, then rolled up his window and watched her shadowy form run back to the house. So much for leaving Paradise tonight.

CHAPTER FOUR

Ellie slid into a booth near the front window of the Pantry. She folded up her cane and laid it beside her on the bench seat. She really didn't need it. She had worked there for over four years, from the time she was sixteen, and she knew the restaurant inside and out. But she carried the cane anyway, more as a way to alert others that she was blind.

She checked her watch. Two o'clock. She couldn't believe a couple of hours had passed since the taxi had brought her here to drop off the jelly jars. She'd gotten sidetracked visiting. Her stomach rumbled. Definitely time for some lunch.

She ran her hand across the smooth tabletop. It was white, and she could see the entire layout of the restaurant in her mind. Yoder's Pantry hadn't changed its décor in years.

Ellie heard footsteps approach. Probably the waitress to take her order. She always got the same thing—a grilled chicken salad with a wedge of Swiss cheese on the side and a cup of chicken noodle soup. Sometimes she would splurge on vanilla ice cream for dessert, but not often, and not today.

"I hope you don't mind me bothering you."

Her eyebrows lifted. It wasn't the waitress she'd been expecting, but Levina Lapp, one of her mother's friends. "*Nee, Frau* Lapp. You're not bothering me at all."

"I'll only be a minute. I just wanted to tell you that your jellies are the best I've ever tasted. I've bought too many jars to count lately."

Ellie smiled. "*Danki*. I appreciate that."

"I wondered if you ever took special orders."

"I can. Is there a particular flavor you want?"

"I was actually thinking more of amounts. I'd like to purchase a couple cases of all the different flavors, if that's all right."

Ellie's jaw dropped. "Cases?"

"At least four. I think they'll make lovely Christmas presents for my family in Indiana. I've been raving to them about your jellies."

Ellie was still trying to wrap her head around such a large order. "When would you need them?"

"Mid-November should be fine."

"Then you shall have them mid-November."

Levina touched Ellie's shoulder. "*Danki*, Ellie. You have a fine day, now. And we'll be in touch."

As Levina walked away, Ellie tried to calculate how much fruit she would need to prepare four cases of jelly. She still couldn't believe she'd made such a large sale. Levina's order alone would ensure she could stay in business for the next several months, even if she didn't sell another jar.

Footsteps approached. This time it had to be her waitress. But she was wrong again when she heard someone slide into the seat across from her, then let out a big sigh, one she immediately recognized.

"Doesn't sound like you're having a *gut* day, Sarah Lynne."

"I'm not." Another sigh.

Ellie put thoughts about Levina's order out of her mind and focused on her friend. "What's wrong? Please tell me you and Isaiah aren't fighting."

"I'm fighting with someone, but not him."

Ellie waited for Sarah Lynne to elaborate, but her friend remained silent. Not wanting to pry, she changed the subject. "I thought Brandy might be coming over here to take my order."

Sarah Lynne gasped. "Oh, I'm sorry. You must be starving. It's well past lunchtime."

"I'm not starving, exactly—"

"I don't know where Brandy is, but I'll make sure you get some bread right away, fresh from the oven. I'll be right back."

When Sarah Lynne left, Ellie smiled and turned her face toward the window. The sun warmed her skin as it streamed through the glass. The sounds of the restaurant filled her ears—the low hum of conversations, the clinking of silverware against dishes, the faint ding of the cash register bell up front. From what she could tell, there weren't too many customers at the moment. Then again, it was after two on a Wednesday afternoon.

Ellie waited awhile longer, letting the sun shine in her face and warm her through. As the minutes ticked by she wondered where Sarah Lynne had gone. It wasn't like her to forget.

Her stomach growled again, spurring her into action. Scooting herself out of the booth, she started toward the front of the restaurant. She walked along the narrow aisle that separated the booths from the tables, which were situated in the center of the large room.

Suddenly something hit her in the face. Hard. She sank to the ground.

. . .

Chris didn't need any more reasons to leave Paradise. However, he'd just found another one. He knelt beside the young woman he'd knocked to the floor as he'd entered the restaurant. The door had hit her square in the face.

"Are you okay?" He looked down at the woman. Her arms were propping her up, but her eyes were still closed. Then they opened.

His sister rushed up to them, kneeling down on the opposite side of the woman. "Chris, what did you do?"

"It was an accident, okay?"

The woman still seemed dazed, her eyes unfocused. A small bump had already formed on her forehead. What if he'd given her a concussion?

Sarah Lynne shot him an irritated look as she tried to help the woman to her feet. Chris ignored it and assisted on the other side, putting his arm around her slim waist. When she got to a standing position, he let go, marveling at how petite she was. The top of her head, covered in a white prayer *kapp*, barely reached his shoulder.

But the weird thing was how she didn't look at him. In fact, there was no expression in her eyes at all.

"I'm really sorry." He moved closer to her, wondering why she didn't glance in his direction. Was she that angry? Not that he would blame her.

"Nothing to be sorry about," she said. Finally she turned toward him, but stared at his chest instead of his face. "I forgot my cane."

Cane? Why would a young woman like her need a cane?

"You should sit down." Sarah Lynne put her arm around the woman's shoulders and guided her to one of the booths near the back of the restaurant. Chris followed, trying to ignore the stares of the other patrons. The woman was doing a good job of that herself, keeping her attention focused directly in front of her.

Sarah Lynne guided her into the booth. "Do you need some water? Ice?"

She shook her head. "I could use some bread. I'm starving." She smiled, looking, yet not looking, directly at Sarah.

But Chris had stopped paying attention to her gaze. Instead he was transfixed by her smile. Wow. It was wide and genuine. Then he paid attention to the rest of her face—the light dusting of freckles that gave her fair complexion a darker hue, the roundness of her cheeks, the upturn of her nose. She about snatched the breath right from his lungs.

"Oh, I meant to bring the bread to you."

Sarah Lynne touched the woman's shoulder, as she

often did when she spoke to people she knew. His sister had never been stingy with affection.

"When I went back to get the bread, a party of eight walked through the door and into my section. But I found Brandy, and she said she'd bring it over. I don't know what happened to her . . . You're late, by the way."

"I'm what?"

"Not you, Ellie. I was talking to Chris."

Ellie's face registered her surprise. "Your brother?"

"*Ya.* He was supposed to meet me this morning." Sarah Lynne's gaze shot through him like an arrow. "Remember?"

He nodded but kept his focus on the woman in front of him, wondering how she knew him. Then he suddenly realized who she was . . . and why she wasn't looking at his face. "Ellie Chupp?"

"*Ya.*" She tilted her head up, but not enough to look him square in the eye.

He couldn't help but stare at her eyes. They were a bright crystal blue that nearly matched the color of her long-sleeved dress. She had long, almost transparent lashes that brushed the tops of her cheeks when she blinked. How could he not have recognized Caroline's best friend? They had hung around together for years, ever since they were in school. But for some reason she looked so different to him. Except for those eyes. He'd noticed how striking they were, even back then.

"Ellie, I'm really sorry." Now he felt like a double heel. Not only had he hurt a woman, but a blind one at that. "I should have been paying attention."

"And I should have been using my cane. I left it here

in the booth. I wasn't even thinking." Her slender fingertips touched the bruise on her forehead. "Does it look bad?"

He shook his head. Then, realizing she couldn't see the motion, he added, "*Nee*. Just a little black and blue."

She smiled again. "I've been through worse."

Her words were like a knife twisting inside. In his grief over losing Caroline, he'd paid little attention to what happened to Ellie. He'd heard she'd been in the hospital for a long time.

Sarah Lynne interrupted his thoughts. "I'll be getting off soon. Is your car outside?"

"*Ya*." Without thinking he stole another glance at Ellie. Her gaze was focused straight ahead.

"*Gut*. I'll meet you there. I'm off in half an hour." Sarah Lynne laid her hand on Ellie's arm again. "I'll have someone bring you that bread. And take your order, which will be on the house for all your trouble."

"You don't have to do that."

"I know, but you deserve it after waiting all this time, then getting hit in the head." She fired another glare at Chris, who gave her a cool glance in response. "I'm sure the boss will okay it," she continued, looking back to Ellie. "He loves your jelly, too, you know."

As his sister sped away to take care of her customers, Chris turned his attention back to Ellie. He tried to pinpoint why she looked so different. Or maybe she hadn't changed as much as he thought? He hadn't noticed her too much when they were growing up, not when his attention was always on Caroline.

He sure was noticing her now.

. . .

Ellie's forehead ached, but the pain didn't compare with the ache of embarrassment she felt. She kept her hands underneath the table and fiddled with the hem of her white apron. She felt like an idiot, allowing herself to get smacked like that. She knew better than to walk so close to the door. Chris probably thought she was completely helpless, not to mention stupid.

He didn't speak, but he didn't move away either. Why didn't he leave? Questions swirled in her mind, but she couldn't ask him a single one.

Finally he spoke. "I'm really sorry about hitting you with the door, Ellie."

His deep voice flowed over her. Had his voice always been so rich and appealing? She didn't know—maybe it had. But since she lost her sight, she noticed the quality of voices much more than before.

"It's all right," she said. "It was more my fault, really."

"*Nee*, it wasn't. I'm the one who messed up."

He paused for a moment, and she wondered what he was doing. Not being able to see facial expressions or body movements was one of the hardest things for her to deal with, especially when no one said anything. She only had her imagination to fill in the blanks.

He finally spoke. "I'll leave you alone now." She heard him move, and his voice sounded closer. "There are a couple of older *fraus* looking at us. They've already started whispering to each other."

"Maybe they're discussing the weather. Or the Pantry's apple pie recipe."

"I don't think so. Not by the dark looks they're giving me. And here . . ."

His hand suddenly touched hers, and she jumped.

"I'm sorry."

She knew why he was apologizing. According to the *bann*, they were forbidden to touch.

"I just wanted to let you know, lunch is on me. The restaurant shouldn't have to pay for my mistake."

She swiveled toward him, forgetting everyone else in the restaurant. "You don't have to do that. I should have been paying better attention."

"How could you? You can't even see." He drew in a sharp breath. "There I *geh* again, putting *mei* foot into *mei* mouth."

She chuckled. "Now that's something I wish I could see!"

To her surprise he let out a quiet laugh. "I'm putting the money on the table. Please take it. It would make me feel a lot better."

"All right, if you insist." Ellie folded the open bills and placed them on the table near the window. She expected to hear him walk away, but he remained in place. "Chris? Did you need something else?"

He paused before answering. "Um . . . just wondering if the pretzels are still *gut*."

"*Ya*, they're delicious."

"Then I guess I'll get one of those before I leave. Haven't had one since . . ." He cleared his throat. "*Gut* seeing you, Ellie."

She angled her face toward him. "*Gut* seeing you, too, Chris."

Then he left.

Her heart pinched at the sadness she'd heard in his voice. Clearly he still wasn't over Caroline's death. She also had moments when she missed Caroline terribly. Her infectious laugh and her excitement about the future were just two aspects of Caroline's bright personality that had touched everyone.

She heard the jangle of Brandy's trademark thin, silver bangles as the *Englisch* waitress approached. "Here you go." Brandy sounded rushed as she placed a basket of bread on the table. "I'm sorry, Ellie, I meant to get this to you earlier. We had a bit of a catastrophe back in the kitchen."

Ellie tilted her head up. "Is everything okay?"

"It is now." Her tinkling laugh sounded above the restaurant's din. "Thought we might have to call the fire department."

"That doesn't sound *gut*."

"Hey, it's all good. So . . ." Brandy slid into the seat across from Ellie. "Who was your *friend*? Haven't seen him around here before."

Brandy's not-so-subtle connotation made Ellie look away for a moment. "He's Sarah Lynne's brother, Chris. And he's not my *friend*. Not like that anyway."

"Well, that's too bad, because he's really cute."

"He is?" The words were out of her mouth before she could stop them.

Chris had been nice looking, if a little gangly, when they were younger. She wondered how much he'd changed over the years. She wished she could find out for herself.

"Yup. Although I didn't know Sarah Lynne had a brother who wasn't Amish."

"What do you mean?"

Brandy's bracelets chimed together again. "His hair's cut short in the back and on the sides."

"Is it still black?" Why couldn't she keep her questions to herself? Her curiosity had taken control of her common sense.

"Yes, it's still black." Brandy's voice had a sly sound to it. "Black and straight. He has it parted to the side."

Ellie tried to picture Chris with an *Englisch* haircut, but she couldn't.

"He looks a lot like Sarah Lynne. They both have the black hair and greenish eyes. He's also got the most incredible mouth, with these full lips that are so cute—"

"Brandy!" Ellie blushed.

"What? You asked me to describe him."

"*Nee*, I didn't!"

"I can tell you're curious. I would be, too, if I were you. He's got a dreamy voice, but you probably already know that."

She did, but she wasn't about to admit it.

"Maybe *curious* isn't the right word. How about *interested*?"

"I'm not interested in Christopher Miller." Ellie lowered her voice.

"Why not?"

Ellie touched her teeth to her bottom lip. She couldn't reveal the reason. Talking about something this sensitive and private constituted gossip, and she wasn't about to spread it around to anyone. "I'm just not."

"Okay, I won't ask. But let me get back to describing that gorgeous guy to you."

"Brandy, you don't have to—"

"Oh yes, I do—this is the most fun I've had all day. Oh nuts, he's leaving. I didn't even get a chance to talk to him. Why isn't he dressed Amish, again?"

Striving for patience, Ellie said, "He's not Amish anymore." Just admitting that out loud saddened her.

"Oh. Hmm."

"What are you *hmm*-ing about?" Sarah Lynne suddenly appeared and touched Ellie's shoulder.

"Your brother." Brandy slid from the booth. "Where have you been hiding that hottie all this time? Is he available?"

"*Nee.*" Sarah Lynne's tone was firm. "Absolutely not."

"Now that's a shame." Brandy's voice dripped with disappointment.

"Brandy, why don't you *geh* check on Abby and Joseph Lambert?" Sarah Lynne said.

"I just gave them a refill on coffee."

"Well, maybe they want dessert or something." Impatience edged Sarah Lynne's tone.

"Humph," Brandy said. "I can take a hint, Sarah Lynne. Why don't you just say you need to talk to Ellie?"

"I need to talk to Ellie."

"Fine. Nice seeing you again, Ellie. Thanks for bringing the jelly. I've already put three jars in the back for myself."

"I can't believe she's interested in Chris," said Sarah Lynne after Brandy went back to work. She sat across from Ellie. "The nerve! She's not even Amish!"

WHAT THE HEART SEES

"Neither is he," Ellie said softly. But she had felt a tiny twinge in her chest when Brandy had asked Sarah Lynne about Chris. Which was ridiculous. He'd been engaged to her best friend. And she had no business thinking about any man, for that matter. She'd learned her lesson with John. To stray from that reality would only mean heartache, and she didn't need any more of that.

"Right now he isn't Amish. But why would he come back if he wasn't ready to forgive Isaiah? Although that might never happen now."

"Why? What happened?"

"He came to the house last night. While Isaiah was there."

Ellie said a quick silent prayer, then reached for a slice of bread. "That had to be a shock."

"Not as much as when I told him we were getting married. He was so angry, Ellie—like he was when Caroline died. He threatened to leave last night, but I persuaded him to stay and see *Mami* one more time before he left. But then what happens after that? How can someone hang on to all that anger for five years?"

So that's why Sarah Lynne had been out of sorts this morning. Ellie found the small bowl of peanut butter spread and put some on her bread. As she spread it with a knife she said, "How is your *mami* going to talk to him?"

"I said she'd meet him at the bed-and-breakfast. She and *Daed* are really upset. When *Daed* asked Chris if he was ready to ask forgiveness, Chris said *nee*."

Ellie took a bite of the bread, but it wasn't as tasty

as she'd anticipated. Hearing about Sarah Lynne's and Chris's problems had curbed her appetite. "I'm so sorry, Sarah Lynne. Not just for you and your parents, but for Chris too."

"I appreciate that, Ellie." She paused for a moment. "I've got to *geh*. Can you say a little prayer for me— actually for all of us? Isaiah feels really bad about all of this. I thought he might come by today and we could talk about it, but he never showed up."

"I will." Ellie nodded. "If there's anything I can do to help, let me know." It was an empty promise. This was Sarah Lynne and her family's problem, not hers. But she wanted to give Sarah Lynne her support.

"Actually, there might be something."

"What?"

"I don't know yet, but I may need your help." Sarah Lynne slid out of the booth. "*Ya*, you might be able to fix this after all."

"Wait a minute—"

"I'll let you know!" Sarah Lynne called out.

CHAPTER FIVE

I don't think there's anything else to say."

Sarah Lynne touched her fingertips to her forehead. Her brother was more stubborn than a thousand mules. And since Isaiah owned a couple, she knew what she was talking about. Why wouldn't Chris listen to reason? "All you have to do is say you forgive him. Why can't you do that?"

"Because it would be a lie, Sarah Lynne. And I can't get up in front of God and the church and lie."

"Then make it the truth. Forgive Isaiah, really forgive him. Then you can repent with a clear heart."

They were in the parking lot in the back of the Pantry, near the Dumpster. He had been pacing back and forth while they were talking, and she could tell he was battling something inside himself.

Finally he halted and faced her. "You're asking me to do the impossible."

"Then why did you come back here, if you weren't ready to forgive him?"

"I thought I was. But it's different now. You're marrying him. He's going to be my *bruder*." He spat out the last word. "That changes everything."

"It should change nothing." She clenched her fists at her sides, catching a slight rancid whiff of the garbage from the Dumpster.

A muscle twitched in his jaw. "Every time he's around I'll be reminded of what happened to Caroline."

"Haven't you spent every day of your life thinking about that?"

He didn't answer.

"Christopher, you have to let this *geh*. You have to let her *geh*."

He remained silent, his back toward her. She saw his shoulders slump, and for the moment she pitied him. But he had the power to change the situation, and it made her almost *ab im kopp* that he refused.

A horse and buggy clip-clopped past the restaurant, followed by three cars. They couldn't stand here all day at an impasse.

"Christopher?"

After a long moment he turned around, his expression haunted with grief. "What?"

Her heart went out to him. "Come home. Come back to the house and talk to *Mami*."

"I can't. You know how *Daed* feels."

"I don't mean right now. Come back tomorrow while *Daed*'s at work."

He rubbed his chin, but his expression was no less tortured. "I should just *geh*. It would be easier on everyone."

"Oh *ya*, you running off will make us all feel a lot better." She crossed her arms over her chest, bunching the front of her navy blue jacket. "Please, Chris. Can't you see how selfish you're being?"

. . .

Chris stared at his sister, her sharp words slicing through him. He shouldn't expect her to understand. But deep down he knew he was being selfish, at least where his mother was concerned. "All right. I'll come over tomorrow. But just for a little while. I can't promise more than that."

Sarah Lynne let out a long breath and hurled herself into his arms. "*Danki*, Chris. This will mean so much to *Mami*. And to me." She stepped back and looked at him, her smile dimming. "I'm not trying to make light of your pain over losing Caroline. If anything happened to Isaiah, I don't know what I'd do."

He ground his teeth at Isaiah's name. He'd spent the last five years trying to erase the memory of what that man had done to him and Caroline. And now he could see he had failed. Just seeing Isaiah again brought back all the resentment and anger he'd held inside for so long. And soon Isaiah would be his brother-in-law, and the father to his nieces and nephews, should God choose to bless them with children. Isaiah had taken Caroline's life, and now he would have what Chris had been denied—a wife and family. *How is that fair, God?*

He turned away. He couldn't be around Sarah Lynne anymore, not with the emotions wrenching inside him. "Tell *Mami* I'll see her tomorrow." He walked away.

"Christopher?"

He looked back at his sister, five years his junior. He had been her tormentor when they were little, her protector as they had gotten older. But he had failed at that too. Maybe if he hadn't left, he could have stopped Isaiah from insinuating himself into her life. "What?"

"I have to ask you one more thing." She went to him, her eyes wide and hopeful, the way she used to look when they were little and their parents promised them a special treat if they behaved in church. "I'm begging you. Give Isaiah a chance."

Chris felt the muscles tense in his cheek.

"He's not the same *mann* he was five years ago. The accident changed him, Christopher. And it still haunts him."

"*Gut.* He deserves to be haunted."

"How long should he have to pay for one mistake?" Her voice cracked.

"He *never* paid. Not the way he should have."

"That was your judgment. Not the community's. Not even the police agreed with you."

Chris knew that firsthand. After Caroline had died from her injuries, he went to the police to have charges filed against Isaiah. That started his downward spiral, resulting in his shunning.

"Everyone else has forgiven him, Christopher, including Caroline's family. Why can't you?" She whirled around and headed back into the restaurant.

He stood there for a moment, letting her question sink in. Why couldn't he forgive Isaiah? All it would take was a confession in front of the church. In front of God. But God knew his heart, saw the black spot of anger etched on it. He couldn't lie, not even to make his mother and his sister happy. God would know his confession wasn't sincere.

. . .

"Would you mind dropping me off at the cemetery?" Ellie held her folded white cane across her lap. "It's not far from my *haus*. I can walk home from there."

Trish Moore, the young woman Ellie paid for rides to and from Paradise, sucked in her breath. "I don't think that's a good idea, Ellie," she said from the front seat. "There are no sidewalks on your road. It's not safe."

"I don't walk on the side of the road. I cut across the fields between the cemetery and my *haus*."

"Aren't you afraid of tripping over something?"

"I've got my cane." Ellie held it up and smiled, leaning forward a little in the backseat. She set it down in her lap and said, "I promise, I'll be fine. I've done this before."

"I don't mind waiting for you," Trish said. "I've got a magazine to keep me occupied."

Ellie shook her head. "I don't want to keep you from your family, Trish. Your children will be getting home from school soon, *ya*?"

"They'll be all right by themselves for a little while. Trevor's thirteen—he can watch the other two."

Ellie could feel her patience slipping away. "I appreciate it, but I'd prefer if you dropped me off."

"Oh."

Ellie heard the small hint of hurt in Trish's voice. She wanted to apologize, but Trish might take that as agreement. A few minutes later she felt the car come to a stop. *"Danki,"* she said, opening the car door.

"Ellie, if something happens to you—"

"Don't worry, I won't hold you responsible. Please don't worry about me."

Trish sighed. "All right. As long as you're sure."

Ellie opened the door and stepped out of the car. She was perfectly capable of making her way home on her own. It wasn't that far, and she knew those fields as well as she knew the layouts of her house and the Pantry. When would everyone realize she could take care of herself?

Turning around, she opened her cane, which was three parts that telescoped into one long piece. The cemetery had been here since before Ellie's birth, and from memory she knew it had a narrow asphalt driveway that led to the entrance of the burial ground. She glided the tip of the cane in front of her, arcing it smoothly to detect any debris that might be in the way and to keep herself walking straight on the path. Before long she reached the short chain-link fence that surrounded the cemetery and swung open the unlocked gate.

After the accident she'd often come to visit Caroline's grave. At first it was out of grief over what she'd lost. Over the years, coming here had brought her comfort and peace. But since she started her jelly business, she had neglected her visits. Talking to Chris today had impelled her to come back.

She made her way around the perimeter of the graveyard, stopping at the upper west corner. Leaning down, she searched for the small, plain stone slab that marked her friend's grave. When she found it, she knelt down, placing her cane beside her.

"Christopher came back, Caroline." She ran her finger along the grassy edge of the site. "I pray it's for *gut*."

. . .

Christopher turned into the narrow gravel drive that led to the cemetery where Caroline was buried. He turned off the car engine and leaned his head back against the seat. He'd driven past the burial ground three times before finally summoning the courage to pull in. Closing his eyes, he searched for the will to step out of the car. He hadn't been here since the day Caroline was buried.

Taking a deep breath, he opened the door and stepped out, breathing in the crisp fall air. Orange, yellow, and brown leaves skittered across the drive and the fields of grass surrounding the cemetery. He looked up at the clear sky, the sun still shining bright, its heat seeping through his leather jacket. Growing up, he'd spent such autumn days outside as much as he could, helping his father with the chores or playing baseball and volleyball with his friends. When he and Caroline started courting, he took her for open-air buggy rides, something she had always loved.

Before him he saw the small cement markers identifying each grave, a stark contrast to the large headstones and statues in an *Englisch* cemetery. The chain-link fence reached his waist, and he opened the short gate. He scanned the small cemetery, which was less than an acre in size.

"Hello?"

The female voice came from the back corner of the burial ground. A woman suddenly rose to her feet, not looking in his direction. Ellie Chupp.

He should turn around and leave. He didn't want to intrude. Besides, he wasn't sure coming here was a great idea. He hadn't made too many smart decisions lately.

"Hello? Is someone here?"

He could simply walk away without speaking. She would never know. But he couldn't sneak off. That wouldn't be fair. "It's me. Christopher Miller."

"Oh, hello, Chris." She bent down to pick up something. When she stood, he could see it was her cane. "I was just leaving."

"You don't have to leave on my account. I'll *geh*."

She shook her head and walked toward him, moving the white cane in front of her at an angle. "Please. Stay. Caroline would be glad you were here."

Her words held him in place. "It's been a long time since I was here."

"I know." Ellie reached him, stopping a few feet in front of him. She tilted her chin up, gazing at him with those stunning blue eyes. "It's been awhile since I visited her too. I used to come here all the time after the accident. But lately I haven't had the chance."

"Is John picking you up?"

She frowned. "Why would he do that?"

"I thought . . . Didn't you two get married?"

Her frown turned into a bitter smile. "*Nee*. We decided we weren't . . . suited for each other."

Chris wanted to kick himself. That was the second

time he'd said something insensitive to her. But from what he remembered of Ellie and John, they were very much in love. Caroline had been certain they would soon get married. His gaze strayed to the corner of the cemetery, to Caroline's grave site.

"I'll get out of your way," Ellie said, moving her cane in front of her. It tapped his foot, and he stepped aside.

Suddenly he didn't want her to go. She was his last tangible link to Caroline. But he couldn't ask her to stay. "You're not in my way, Ellie."

"And you're still as polite as you used to be." She smiled. "I'm glad you came back. I know Sarah Lynne is."

"She's not too happy with me now."

"Maybe not, but I'm sure that will change."

"I don't know about that." He glanced down at her, taking in her cane, the way her gaze was off center. "How did you do it?"

"Do what?"

"Forgive Isaiah." The question had flown out of his mouth. But now that it was out there, he wanted an answer. "After what he did to you?"

Her lips pinched together. "Isaiah didn't make me blind. The accident did that."

"But it was his fault." Chris shoved a hand through his close-cropped hair and leaned against the fence. He rammed his hands into the pockets of his jeans. "He was driving the car."

"Which he wasn't supposed to be doing." Ellie's expression grew soft. "Chris, he was sixteen and trying the *Englisch* ways. We were all guilty of that before we joined the church."

"I never drove a car."

"You do now."

"That's different. Never mind." He started to move past her, but she held out her hand to stop him. When it landed on his waist, she jerked it back.

"Sorry." Her cheeks turned the color of a strawberry. "I didn't mean to upset you."

Without thinking he touched her on the shoulder. "It's all right."

CHAPTER SIX

Ellie felt the warmth of Chris's hand through her lightweight coat, and for a moment she was frozen in place. A shiver coursed through her body.

He let go of her shoulder. "You're cold."

She wasn't cold at all. From the tingling in her belly at his touch to the heat on her face, cold was the last thing she was feeling.

"I should let you get home," he said. "Some people might get the wrong idea if they see us together."

The cemetery was fairly secluded, situated in the middle of two fields, the houses far enough away that visitors could have privacy as they visited their loved ones. And it didn't matter if they were in an empty cemetery or in a crowded room, she couldn't ignore the pain in Chris's voice when he asked her about forgiving Isaiah. "I'm not worried about anyone seeing us."

"You should be. I'm in the *bann* for a *gut* reason. At least the church thinks it is."

"What do you think?" Ellie asked.

He didn't say anything for a moment. Neither did he move away. She wasn't quite sure how close they were to each other, but she detected the scent of his leather jacket, a smell she found appealing.

"I think they're right," he said.

"You do?"

"I went against the church. That I'll admit. But it doesn't mean I wasn't right about going to the police." His low voice cracked with emotion. "When they refused to press charges, I knew there wasn't any hope for justice."

"It's not our job to dispense justice. Only God can do that."

"You sound like Sarah Lynne."

Ellie heard the sound of his shoes against the pebbles littering the grass. When he spoke again he sounded farther away. "I can't believe she's marrying him."

"She loves him, and he loves her. My cousin is a *gut mann*, Chris. You can ask anyone in the community. He's changed—"

"I know, I know. I've heard it from Sarah Lynne. That doesn't change what he did to Caroline. What he did to you. How can you forget about that?"

"I haven't." She was surprised at the tremor in her voice. Since the accident she had said little about what happened. She had to be strong, not only for Isaiah's sake. The accident had plunged him into a deep depression, and her entire family had worried about him. She had never wanted to pile on more guilt. She also had to be strong for her parents. And for John, although in the end that didn't matter. Her blindness had doomed their relationship.

But there was another reason she rarely spoke of that day. One she couldn't tell a single soul.

"Ellie, I shouldn't have said that." He moved closer, enough that she could smell the spicy-sweet scent of the cinnamon gum he chewed. "Please don't be upset."

"I'm not upset." She fought for the inner strength she had relied on for so many years. The last thing she wanted was Chris's pity. "I can't forget about the accident. I'm reminded of it every day."

• • •

Chris looked down at Ellie, seeing the sorrow in her face. She was only inches from him, the ribbons of her prayer *kapp* trailing down the back of her short navy blue jacket.

Then she lifted her chin, her expression composed. "But I was able to put what happened in the past, where it should stay."

She did what he found impossible. "You're a better person than I am."

"That's not true." She turned her head away from him. "I'm not a saint, Chris. Don't make me out to be one." She moved her cane in front of her, angling it to the side. "I have to get back home."

"How are you getting there?"

"Walking." Ellie turned to the right and pointed. "I live across the field over there."

He looked where she was pointing. "The white house?"

She chuckled. "Aren't they all white?"

"*Ya*. I suppose they are." He grinned, his first smile since he'd arrived in Paradise. "You're going to walk that far by yourself?"

"I've done it before."

"I could give you a ride." He bit his lip, forgetting that he wasn't allowed to drive her anywhere.

"I'll be fine." She brushed past him, her steps faster than they had been moments before. "I can manage."

"All right." He watched as she hurried out the cemetery and made a sharp right turn. The brown grass reached her knees, but it didn't seem to bother her as she used her cane to guide her steps. He admired her determination and fearlessness. She really was different than he remembered. Back then she was more cautious and unsure of herself. No one could deny she had confidence now. But while she seemed capable of making her way home, it didn't seem right to let her go alone. He rushed after her, reaching her quickly and adjusting his long strides to match her shorter ones.

She kept her gaze straight ahead. "What are you doing?"

"Walking you home."

She sighed. "I told you I don't need any help."

"I didn't say I was *helping* you home, did I?"

She didn't answer right away. "I guess you didn't. But it's what you intend to do, right?"

"So you have a sixth sense or something?"

"What?"

"You know, like mind reading. Because that's the

only way you could know my intentions. You're amazing, but not supernatural."

He nearly tripped over his feet as the words slipped out. But it was true, she was amazing. The way she had forgiven Isaiah, how well she managed despite being blind, the fact that she had taken the time to talk to him even though he was in the *bann*. He just hadn't intended to say it out loud.

But his compliment seemed to irritate her further. "Don't patronize me, Chris."

"I didn't realize that's what I was doing."

"You are." She stared straight ahead again, her mouth set in a thin line. "You don't have to feel sorry for me either."

Now that remark hit home. He *did* feel sorry for her, at least he had a little while ago. But that feeling had gone away during their conversation. "I don't."

She didn't respond. Her cane hit a large stone, and she sidestepped it with ease.

"You don't believe me, do you?"

"*Nee.*" She quickened her pace, the sound of the grass brushing against her legs filling the air.

"Okay, I'll prove it to you." He stopped and watched as she walked away. She had gone a few feet before she stopped too. "Chris?"

"I'm back here."

She turned around, moving her cane in front of her. "Why?"

"I told you I don't feel sorry for you, so *geh* ahead and walk home by yourself."

Her mouth opened, then shut. For the second time that afternoon, he smiled.

"Okay," she said, suddenly sounding unsure. "Well, then I guess this is good-bye."

"I guess it is." He put his hands in the pockets of his jacket.

Then her expression softened. "I hope it's not forever, Chris. I mean it."

His smile faded as she turned and walked away. "I hope not either," he whispered.

. . .

Ellie didn't know what to think. In many ways Chris was exactly the same as he'd been five years ago—polite, caring, and a little self-deprecating. Yet she could hear the bitterness in his tone, hanging on the edges even when he was being nice. His grief over Caroline had thoroughly permeated him.

She was glad he had gone back to the cemetery. He had come there to visit Caroline, and if he had walked her home she would have taken up more of his time, which wasn't fair.

"You're amazing . . ."

Ellie's stomach fluttered. His words hadn't registered when he said them, because she'd been aggravated by his accompanying her. But now they hit her full force. He thought she was amazing? Her mouth tilted up in a smile.

And her foot landed in a shallow hole. Her ankle twisted, and she'd have gone down if it weren't for the support of her cane. She grimaced, regaining her balance. That's what she got for losing her concentration. But when she stepped forward, pain shot through her ankle and foot, making her bend over and nearly lose her balance again.

. . .

"Ellie!" Seeing her trip, Chris sprang into action. He sprinted toward her. "Ellie!"

She righted herself, hanging on to the white cane as she regained her balance. Thank goodness for that thing. He had just reached her side when he saw her step forward, then almost fall again.

"Are you all right?" he asked.

She stood up, nodding. "I'm fine. Just twisted my ankle."

He looked down at the ground. Although it was partially hidden by the tall grass, he saw the shallow hole she'd stepped into. His gaze went back to her face. "You're not fine."

"Ya, I am." She put her cane in front of her and hobbled forward two steps. "See," she said through gritted teeth.

"I bet you sprained your ankle." He went to her, putting his hand on her arm to make her stop. He didn't care that she couldn't accept a ride from him. There was no way she'd be able to walk home now. "Let me take you home."

"It's not that far to walk."

"Ellie, you're nowhere near your *haus*."

"I can make it." She tried to walk again and winced.

"And Sarah Lynne says *I'm* stubborn." He moved to block her path. "I'm taking you home."

She tilted her head up. Those eyes again. For a second he was lost in their beauty. It didn't matter that she wasn't looking exactly at him. He barely even noticed.

"If I can walk back to your car, I can make it home," she said.

"Who said anything about you walking?" He scooped her up in his arms and started toward his car.

"Chris, put me down!"

"I will when we get to my car."

Her face was inches from his, and something stirred inside him, emotions he hadn't come close to experiencing since Caroline's death. He nearly stumbled himself as he looked at her face, his gaze lingering on her lips, then traveling to her gorgeous eyes again.

"What if someone sees us?"

Her voice sounded small, and he felt her grip tighten around his neck, her cane lightly bouncing against the back of his shoulder as he walked. He wasn't supposed to touch her, much less carry her.

"I'll take full responsibility." And he would too. He wouldn't do anything to get her in trouble with the bishop or the church.

She relaxed in his arms, and he held her a little closer, partially out of not wanting to drop her, but mostly because he wanted to. He had no idea what had gotten into him this afternoon. He was saying and doing things that surprised him. But he was here for

Ellie when she needed him, and that was all that mattered right now.

When they reached his car, he stopped. "I'm putting you right next to the car. You can lean against it while I open the door." Gently he lowered her to the ground, not letting go until he was sure she had her balance. When she did, he opened the car door and moved to pick her up again.

"I can get in the car," she snapped, her expression stormy.

He took a step back and watched her hop on one foot as she got in the car. She collapsed her cane with jerky movements.

He braced his hands on either side of the door opening and leaned close. "Just so you know, I would have helped you whether you were blind or not." He shut the door and walked around to the other side.

CHAPTER SEVEN

Ellie flinched as the car door slammed. She felt like a fool. He had helped her, and she treated him badly for it. "I'm sorry," she said when he got in on his side.

"It's okay."

She heard him let out a long breath.

"I just wanted you to know I didn't help you because I feel sorry for you. I helped you because you needed it."

She nodded, breathing in the scent of the car's interior. It smelled like him—cinnamon gum and leather. She closed her eyes for a moment, savoring the scents. Then she heard him start the car.

Her eyes flew open, and she gripped the door handle.

"Ellie? Are you okay?"

"*Ya.*"

His concerned voice did little to soothe her. Irrational fear took hold, and for a moment she thought about getting out of the car. But her ankle throbbed, and he would chase her down again. Should she ask him if she could move to the backseat? But that was ridiculous. She was less than a mile from her house. She could sit in the front seat for five minutes.

"You don't sound okay." She heard him shift in his seat. When he spoke he sounded closer, as if he were leaning toward her. "You're pale."

Her breathing grew shallow as she tried to calm herself. The accident was five years ago. She shouldn't be acting like this now.

Images of the crash exploded in her mind. The car speeding toward her. Caroline's blood-chilling scream piercing the air. Her own body pitching forward, then jerking back as the car slammed into the side of Isaiah's vehicle, making them spin into the center of the intersection—

"Ellie, you're worrying me." Chris shut off the car. "Is it your ankle?"

"*Nee.*" She leaned forward. Darkness surrounded her as it always did. But this darkness was different. Suffocating. The memories continued to flash through her mind, accelerating her heartbeat. A panic attack. She'd had them before, especially soon after the accident. But time had diminished them. Until now.

She felt his hand cover hers. "It's okay, Ellie. Take a deep breath."

"I'm . . . trying." And she was, but her lungs wouldn't let the air in.

Then his fingers entwined with hers. "Lean back. That's it." His arm went around her shoulders, his free hand gripping her and gently guiding her back against the seat. "There you *geh.*"

His voice and touch were her anchors. Her heart slammed against her rib cage, but she was able to draw breath.

"It's all right, Ellie. You're okay." He kept talking, his low, rich voice providing a comforting cocoon, forcing the panic from her body. The images retreated. Her pulse slowed. Her breath evened out. But even then he held on to her hand and kept his arm around her.

"Ellie?" He squeezed her hand.

"I'm okay." She still sounded breathless, but the strangling sensation was gone. "I'm . . . okay."

"Thank God." He moved his arm from her shoulders but kept holding her hand. "Scared me for a minute. What happened?"

She dipped her head, embarrassed. It wasn't enough that she'd walked into a door and fallen into a hole, now she had to have a complete meltdown in front of him. How could she explain?

But she didn't have to.

"Is it the car? I didn't even think how that might affect you."

She shook her head. "It's not the car. Well, it is . . ." She shut her eyes against the humiliation. "I haven't been in the front seat in five years."

He squeezed her hand again. "That makes sense."

She opened her eyes. "It does?"

"*Ya.* You were in a horrible accident."

"Five years ago." She finally relaxed against the seat. "Long enough to get over it."

He didn't say anything for a moment, and she wanted to take back the words. He hadn't gotten over Caroline in five years. Anyone could see that.

"Ellie, don't be hard on yourself. We were talking about the accident. It probably triggered a memory."

He lowered his voice. "I'm sorry you had to *geh* through that."

His words moved her, touching her heart in a place she had shut away from the rest of the world. The light pressure of his palm against hers warmed her through.

"I could carry you to your *haus*," he added, a bit of humor entering his voice. "You don't weigh much."

She shook her head and removed her hand from his. She still felt the strength of his arms around her when he picked her up. Her hand had brushed against the back of his head, where she felt his short, soft hair. She had been shocked, then upset, when he picked her up. But those emotions had changed into something else by the time he set her down on the ground. She didn't think she could handle him holding her any more.

"You can drive me. I'm all right now."

"Would it be better if you sat in the back?"

"Nee." She took a deep breath. "I can do this. I *need* to do this. I learned a long time ago to face my fears. That's the only way I can overcome them." She fumbled for the seat belt, tamping down her frustration as she tried to locate it.

"Let me." Chris leaned over, his body close to hers as he reached for the seat belt.

Normally she'd insist on doing it herself, but she was too weary to argue. His leather jacket brushed against her shoulder, and she tried not to be obvious as she breathed him in. He brought the seat belt across her and snapped it in place.

"*Danki.*"

"No problem. I'm turning the car on now. You sure you're gonna be all right?"

"*Ya.*" And she would, even if she had to cling to the edge of her seat all the way home.

. . .

Chris studied Ellie for a moment before turning the key. She had given him a good scare, one he didn't care to repeat. But looking at her now, she appeared much calmer and her face had some of its peachy color back. He glanced at her hands, which gripped her cane. The knuckles were white, the only indication that she wasn't as confident as she claimed. But he had to get her home somehow. And while he would have made good on his offer to carry her home, it would have been tough. Not because she was heavy; she wasn't. But because he didn't think he could be that near to her again. Just leaning over her to get the seat belt had set his pulse racing.

He gripped the steering wheel, forcing his gaze from her. He turned the key and the engine roared to life. A quick glance told him she was still okay. Slowly he backed his car down the long driveway, turning it around at the wider portion at the end. "Talk to me, Ellie."

"I'm *gut.*" Her voice sounded as if it were being pushed through wire mesh.

"Tell me about your jelly."

"What?"

"Sarah Lynne said something about her boss loving your jelly." He had to get her mind off the drive. Jelly was the only thing he could come up with.

"You heard that?"

"*Ya.* Do you make it yourself? Or is it just your recipe?"

"Both." She sounded a little more relaxed. "I've had my own business for the past year. Ellie's Jellies."

He smiled. "Perfect." He looked to his left, making sure no cars were coming. "I'm going on the street now."

"*Danki* for telling me."

"What kind of jelly do you sell, Ellie?" He meant to make the rhyme, and he was glad to hear her tiny chuckle.

"All kinds. Name a fruit, and I make jelly out of it."

He turned onto the road, driving well below the speed limit. "Gooseberry."

"When they're in season, *ya.*"

"Orange?"

"I make a great orange marmalade. Or so I've been told."

He smiled at her humility. "What about kumquat?"

"Kum what?"

A horn blared behind him, making them both jump. Chris glared at the car as it whizzed by, the driver making a rude gesture. He looked at Ellie. She had the death grip on her cane again.

"What happened?" she asked, sounding nervous again.

"*Nix.* Just some bozo in a hurry. So you were telling me about kumquats."

"I don't even know what a kumquat is." She angled her head toward him. "Do you?"

"*Nee*. Just wanted to see if I could trip you up. Which one is your *haus*?"

"It's the one set back farthest from the road. There's an old swing set in the side yard. My *mamm* has been trying to get *Daed* to take it down, but he won't. Says the *grosskinner* still have fun with it."

Chris spotted the house several yards ahead. He glanced at the speedometer. Five miles per hour. A horse could go faster, but he didn't care. He'd never driven his car this slow in his life. "How many grandkids do they have?"

"Four. My sister has two and my brother has two with one on the way. Do you see *mei haus*?"

"Just about to turn in the driveway." He sneaked a look at Ellie. She appeared to be back to normal. He let out a breath as he maneuvered his car onto the drive. For the first time he noticed how low the sun was in the sky. It had almost dipped below the horizon. He had no idea so much time had passed.

He pulled his car to a stop near the house. It was a typical Amish home, painted white with no shutters or decoration of any kind. Two steps led up to the porch, which spanned the length of the front. Chris could see part of a white barn in the back.

"*Danki*, Chris." She opened the door and started to get out.

"Wait a sec." He jumped out of the car and met her on the other side. He put his hand under her elbow to help her up.

"I'm okay. It feels better actually."

But from the pained look on her face, he could tell it didn't. He looked down at her feet. "Your ankle is pretty swollen."

"I'll put some ice on it when I get inside." She had already opened up her cane and was leaning against it. For a second he wished she'd lean against him.

"Ellie?"

Chris looked up to see an older woman come out of the house. She had a white apron over her gray dress, and her graying hair peeked from beneath her white *kapp.* Her gaze narrowed as it landed on Chris. "Who are you?"

He didn't answer right away. He shouldn't be surprised that Ellie's mother didn't recognize him. He looked *Englisch*, drove a car, and had just brought her daughter home. He'd be suspicious too. It would be better for Ellie if he kept his identity hidden from her. But before he could come up with a fake name, Ellie spoke.

"It's Christopher Miller, *Mamm*." She hobbled around the car door, forcing him to take a few steps back. "I hurt my ankle and he brought me home."

"You did what?" Ellie's mother practically shoved Chris out of the way. She looked down at Ellie's ankle and scowled. "How did you do that?" She whirled around and glared at Chris. "Did you have something to do with this?"

Chris held his hands up. Since his *meiding* he was used to being ignored, not turned against.

"*Nee, Mamm*. He was only helping me home. I twisted my ankle all on my own."

Frau Chupp turned her back on him. Now that's what he'd expected.

"I thought Trish was bringing you home."

"She did, but I asked her to leave me at the cemetery."

Frau Chupp put her hands on her hips. "Why didn't she wait for you?"

Ellie's face was pinched. Chris could see she was in pain, and standing there leaning on a thin cane while her mother fired questions at her wasn't helping. "Ellie should *geh* inside. She needs to get her ankle up."

Frau Chupp didn't acknowledge Chris's statement. "Answer me, Ellie."

"I didn't want her to have to wait around. She has a family to take care of." Ellie gripped the cane and leaned against the car. "Besides, I've made that walk home several times."

"That was when you could see! What kind of person lets a blind *maedel* fend for herself?"

Ellie's bottom lip shook for a moment. Then she lifted her chin. "Can I *geh* inside now?"

"*Ya.*" Her mother took a step backward, giving her daughter room to walk. Ellie positioned her cane and started limping toward the house. She stopped in front of Chris and turned her face toward him. "*Danki,*" she said, her voice whisper-soft.

"Ellie Chupp! Inside, now." Her mother shot another glare at Chris.

Ellie's face contorted into a mix of pain and irritation. But she didn't say anything else. He watched as both women walked into the house, her mother finally lending a hand to Ellie when they reached the steps.

When the door closed behind them, Chris shut the passenger door, then got in on the other side. He started the car and reached for the gearshift on the steering column. He glanced at the empty seat next to him, remembering how tightly Ellie had held on to his hand when he offered it to her. He was glad he'd driven her home, despite her mother's treatment. Ellie was nothing like *Frau* Chupp. He was glad about that too.

He drove down the road toward the bed-and-breakfast, making sure he drove the speed limit this time. Only when he passed by the cemetery did he realize he hadn't visited Caroline's grave.

CHAPTER EIGHT

Sarah Lynne paced the length of her front porch, her fists opening and closing. Where was Isaiah? Since they had gotten officially engaged, he had stopped by after work every day except Sunday. Now it was nearly seven o'clock and almost dark.

She plopped down on the swing, letting the force of the movement push her back and forth. She wondered if Chris would keep his word about meeting with *Mamm* tomorrow. She was off work and would make sure her mother didn't go anywhere until Chris arrived. But what if he'd left Paradise already?

She couldn't believe her brother hadn't forgiven Isaiah after all this time. He could at least do it for *Mamm's* sake, if not his own. She had never thought Chris could be this selfish. He was clinging to his bitterness like it was his life raft.

At the sound of a horse's hooves, she looked out at the street and saw Isaiah's buggy coming down the driveway. She should have known he wouldn't let her down. She jumped out of the swing and rushed down the porch steps to meet him.

But when Isaiah got out of the vehicle, her relief disappeared. "Isaiah, what is it?"

He'd never looked so forlorn.

He stood next to the buggy, not moving toward her, his gaze fixed on the house behind her instead of her face. Finally he spoke. "I'm not sure we should do this."

"Do what?" She went to him and grabbed his hand, not caring if her parents saw. "Do what, Isaiah? Get married?"

His Adam's apple bobbed up and down as he looked at the ground. Then he met her eyes, tears shining in his. "*Ya*. Maybe we shouldn't get married. Not after what happened last night."

She gripped his hand. "I will not let my brother's selfishness stand in the way of our happiness. I love you, Isaiah. And I'll love you no matter what Chris does."

Isaiah ran the back of his hand over her cheek. She closed her eyes against his touch.

"I love you, too, Sarah Lynne. More than I thought possible. The thought of living without you . . ." His voice cracked. "But I can't stand to see you so upset, and you've been that way since your *bruder* came back. He's angry because of me."

"*Nee*, not because of you. And Chris will come around." But she couldn't be completely sure.

Isaiah gazed down at her, doubt alive in his eyes. "I want to marry you more than anything. But is our marriage worth tearing your *familye* apart?"

"Chris is doing that, not you!" She wished she could take away the pain she saw in his eyes. "Don't let him break us apart, Isaiah. I love my family, but I love you more. And if I have to choose between them . . . I will always choose you."

Without warning Isaiah pulled Sarah Lynne into his embrace. She leaned her cheek against his chest, her arms going around his waist. His heart thrummed against her temple, and she felt his hand splay across her back.

"You can't get rid of me, Isaiah Stolzfus," she said, her voice muffled against his chest. "So you might as well stop trying."

He held her from him, his blue eyes still filled with sorrow. "That's the last thing I want to do, Sarah Lynne. But—"

She reached up and touched the cleft in his chin, stopping his words. "Then don't."

"But what about Chris? Maybe if I talked to him about how much I love you and about how sorry I am about the accident, he could forgive me."

She considered his words, then shook her head. She doubted Chris would listen to him. Instead he'd probably be even more resentful. She didn't want Isaiah to deal with that. "I love you for offering, but we have to give this to God, Isaiah. There's nothing we can do to make him change his mind. Only the Lord can do that."

"I know. And I've tried to let this *geh*." He took a step back and rubbed the back of his neck, staring at the ground. "But I can't. I don't want to cause any more problems for you or your *familye*."

Sarah Lynne pressed her palm against his cheek, causing him to look at her. "What about me, Isaiah?" Her voice trembled. "You're breaking my heart."

He closed his eyes and pulled her against him. "I'm sorry," he said, his arms tightening around her. "I just thought—"

"You thought wrong." She looked up at him, willing him to understand that they couldn't sacrifice their happiness for Christopher. "I want my brother to find peace too. But only God knows if it's possible."

. . .

"Ellie Chupp, I can't believe you would disobey the church and allow that *mann* to drive you home." Ellie's mother balanced a kitchen towel filled with ice cubes on Ellie's ankle. "I don't know what's gotten into you."

Ellie winced as her mother adjusted the ice. She was sitting on the couch near the fireplace with her leg propped up on a pillow.

"I hurt my ankle, *Mamm*. He was nice enough to help me." She didn't mention that he had first carried her across the field.

"You shouldn't have been alone." Ellie heard her mother step back from the couch. "How many times have I told you that?"

More than I can count.

She understood her mother's worry. At first she had even appreciated it. But over the past year her *mamm's* admonishments had grated on Ellie's nerves, undermining her confidence. She didn't want to go back to the days when her mother hovered over her every move. "I can't have someone watching me every minute of the day," she blurted.

"You're blind. You need—"

"I know I'm blind!" She turned her head in the direction of her mother's voice. "I don't need you to tell me that. I live with it every day."

"There's no need to be snippy, *dochder*."

"I'm sorry." Ellie leaned back against the armrest of the couch and gave up. To argue with her mother further would be disrespectful, and it would earn not only her ire but Ellie's father's reprimand. Besides, her mother would never understand how much Ellie craved her independence.

Despair filled her at the thought of always living with her parents, of spending the rest of her life under her mother's thumb. But what other choice did she have?

"Christopher Miller has become *Englisch*," her mother said. "I see that he's fully embraced their ways now. He's turned his back on his family and on God. You are not to have any dealings with him, not until he has reconciled himself with God and the church. If he ever does."

Ellie clamped down on her lip to keep from arguing. She couldn't keep that promise. Chris deserved more than a whispered thank-you for what he'd done. She had no idea how to thank him, but she would figure out a way, hopefully before he left Paradise.

"I wonder if his *mutter* knows he's here. I can only imagine her heartbreak if she sees him, his hair cut off and driving a car. Clearly he's not here to ask forgiveness."

As her mother continued to speculate about Chris,

Ellie tuned her out. She didn't want to hear any more negative comments about him. She tried to ignore the pain in her ankle, too, but it throbbed. Her skin had felt tight and warm before she applied the ice.

"Is the ice helping?"

Her mother's sudden question intruded on Ellie's thoughts. "What?"

"The ice? Does your ankle feel any better?"

"It's fine. I'm sure I'll be able to walk on it soon."

"*Gut*. But I don't want you working in the kitchen or going anywhere for a couple of days." When Ellie started to protest, she cut her off. "I'm serious, *dochder*. You must let the ankle heal."

With a sigh Ellie nodded. She couldn't be independent, but at least she was needed. And since she had delivered a large supply of jellies and jams to Yoder's Pantry today, she wouldn't have to make any more for a few days. That would give her time to rest her ankle and catch up on her reading. She still had plenty of the audio book left to listen to.

"Will you be all right for a few minutes? I need to make supper."

"*Ya*." Ellie paused. "I'm sorry about this, *Mumm*. I just wanted to spend some time alone with Caroline. I still miss her."

"I know you do." Her mother's voice softened. "I only ask that you use common sense next time."

"I will."

Her mother left the room, and Ellie exhaled. Suddenly weary, she closed her eyes and tried to rest, but images crowded her mind. The panic she'd felt in

Chris's car sent quick warmth to her face. She recalled
the way Chris's hand felt on hers. The way his low, mel-
low voice soothed her overwrought fears. John would
never have acted that way. He would have grown angry,
told her to snap out of it. But Chris seemed to have
infinite patience, enough to drive slower than a buggy
to keep her panic at bay. Ellie's mouth formed a half
smile. Caroline had been a lucky woman to love and be
loved by a man like Christopher Miller.

. . .

Sarah Lynne lifted up the curtain in the living room
and peeked out the window. It was past noon and
Chris still hadn't shown up. She shouldn't be surprised.
All these years she'd tried to understand why he had
turned against the church and left the community and
his family behind. Especially since falling in love with
Isaiah, she could empathize with how Caroline's death
had devastated him so deeply. She didn't know what
she'd do if she lost Isaiah. But she had never thought
Chris a coward. Until now.

"Are you expecting someone?"

Sarah Lynne turned at the sound of her mother's
voice and joined her on the opposite end of the cush-
ioned couch. She picked up the scarf she had been
knitting and started working the needles again, avoiding the curious lift of her mother's graying eyebrow.
"*Nee.* Just thinking about taking a walk outside. It's a
nice afternoon."

"Oh. I thought . . ." Her mother's gaze dropped to her

husband's torn work shirt perched on her lap. She twisted the silver thimble protecting the tip of her middle finger. "You haven't heard from Christopher, have you?"

Sarah Lynne paused. She didn't want to lie to her mother, but getting her hopes up about Chris coming over wouldn't be fair to her either. She saw the sorrow in her mother's eyes, sorrow that had never completely disappeared since Chris's *meiding*.

Sarah Lynne shook her head. "*Nee*," she said, silently asking for forgiveness.

"Then I guess he went back to Apple Creek." Her mother's lower lip trembled, but her eyes remained dry. She picked up the shirt again and drew the white thread through one of the ripped buttonholes. She cleared her throat but didn't look up. "I'm going out myself, after I finish your *daed*'s shirt."

Sarah Lynne hid her surprise, which was quickly turning to panic. Until her father came home in a couple of hours there was still a chance Chris might show up. She didn't want her mother to be gone if he did. "Where are you going?"

"Bertha Chupp's. She's been a great help to me with the wedding plans. Ellie too. I hear she's making some of her famous brownies." Her mother shook her head, revealing a slight smile. "The things Ellie can do amazes me. She's a marvel, *ya*?"

"That she is."

"I just hope she can find happiness in her circumstances."

Sarah Lynne set down her knitting. "What do you mean?"

Her mother put the shirt down in her lap. "I always thought Ellie would marry John, you know? And then the accident happened and everything changed. So much loss." Her mother looked away again. "At least Ellie's mother still has her daughter."

"What time are you planning to leave?"

"Probably in an hour. I shouldn't be gone too long."

She nodded, giving up on Chris. She wouldn't try to stop her mother from leaving. "Don't worry about supper," Sarah Lynne said, fighting to keep an even tone. "I'll take care of it. Stay at *Frau* Chupp's as long as you like."

"*Danki.*" Her mother smiled, but as always since Chris left, her expression held a tinge of sadness.

A knock sounded at the door, and Sarah Lynn jumped up from the couch and ran to answer it. But when she opened it, Chris wasn't standing on the front porch.

"Ellie."

"I hope it is all right that I stopped by," Ellie said. "I won't stay too long." She frowned a little. "I can come back if this is a bad time."

Sarah Lynne tamped down her disappointment and smiled. Even though Ellie couldn't see the expression, Sarah Lynne knew her friend would hear it in her voice. "*Nee*, this is a great time. Come on in."

Ellie stepped inside, holding her cane. In her other hand she held a small basket. As she took a step forward, Sarah Lynne saw she was limping. She offered Ellie the back of her arm, as she usually did to help guide her. "Did something happen to your foot?"

Ellie gripped Sarah Lynne's arm right above the elbow and followed her lead. "I twisted it yesterday. I thought I might have sprained it, but it's better today."

"I'm glad to hear that."

As they walked into the living room, Sarah's mother looked up from her sewing. "Hello, Ellie. What brings you by today?"

"I came to talk to Sarah Lynne for a few minutes."

"*Gut*. I think she was getting restless this afternoon." Her mother tied off the thread and snipped it with a tiny pair of sewing scissors, then started folding the shirt. "I was just telling her I'm paying your *mutter* a visit in a short while."

Ellie turned her face toward *Frau* Miller. "She mentioned that to me. I wondered if I could catch a ride home with you when you leave? My *daed* just dropped me off. He's on his way to Paradise to run an errand for work."

"Of course." She lifted the folded shirt and stood. "I have a couple more things to do upstairs, then I'll be ready."

"All right. I'm not in a hurry."

When her mother left, Sarah Lynne led Ellie to the chair across from the couch, putting Chris out of her mind. "What did you want to talk about, Ellie?"

Ellie sat, setting her cane on the floor beside her. She touched the sides of the small basket in her lap. It was Amish made, with tightly woven straw-colored thin strips of wood, while the handle was one solid, curved piece. "Have you seen Chris today?"

"*Nee*." She sat down, unable to keep from frowning.

Then she glanced toward the staircase near the living room, making sure her mother wasn't close by. Still, she lowered her voice. "He was supposed to come by today to see *Mamm* before he went back to Apple Creek, but he hasn't shown up. I doubt he's coming."

Ellie's expression turned troubled. "So he's definitely not coming back to the community?"

"That's what it looks like." Sarah Lynne's heart ached. "I'm trying not to be angry with him, but I can't help it. I don't understand why he can't let this go."

Ellie sighed. "I'm not sure either. I saw him yesterday—"

"You did? Where?"

"At the cemetery. He came to see Caroline, and I was there visiting her." Ellie touched the handle of her basket. "That's why I stopped by here. He helped me with something yesterday, and I wanted to thank him. I didn't know where he was staying, so I thought you could give him this, if you see him again." She picked up the basket. "It's just a couple jars of jelly and some homemade bread. I don't have much else to offer him."

Sarah Lynne took the basket from her. "I'm sure he'll appreciate it. What did he help you with?"

Ellie's fair cheeks turned red. "He gave me a ride home when I twisted my ankle, that's all."

Sarah Lynne didn't know why Ellie was blushing. Maybe she was embarrassed about twisting her ankle. She knew how important it was to her that she be independent and capable.

"Well, it's *gut* to know that deep down he's got some redeeming value. Lately he hasn't shown it to us." She set the basket on the floor. "I'll keep this, but honestly, I don't know if I'll be able to give it to him. I'd go into town and look for him, but *Mamm*'s taking the buggy over to your *haus*." She sighed. "Maybe I should just forget about him. He's forgotten about us."

"I'm sure that's not true."

"Did he say anything about coming by here?"

Ellie shook her head. "I'm sorry, he didn't. But he's still struggling with what happened to Caroline, and finding out about you and Isaiah. Learning that you two are marrying shocked him."

"Well, if he'd been here all along, he wouldn't be shocked." Sarah Lynne grimaced at the look on Ellie's face. "Sorry. I'm frustrated. Chris isn't the only one upset about this. Can you believe Isaiah tried to call off the wedding last night?"

Ellie's brows went up. "Oh *nee!*"

"*Ya*. I think I convinced him not to, though."

"You think?"

"I don't know." Sarah Lynne curled her bottom lip. "I told him he's stuck with me, no matter what."

"And he's lucky he is."

Sarah Lynne tried to smile but couldn't. This was supposed to be an exciting, happy time for her and Isaiah. Instead they were both miserable. "He's not feeling lucky, and neither am I. He's filled with guilt." Sarah Lynne rubbed one of the ribbons of her prayer *kapp* between her thumb and forefinger. "I'm sorry to say this, but I wish Chris hadn't come back. He's upsetting everyone. *Mamm*'s sadder than usual. She just asked me about him, and I had to lie." She rubbed the ribbon harder. "I didn't want to get her hopes up that she would see him again."

Ellie nodded but didn't say anything.

"And *Daed* has been so quiet lately. It was hard on him to turn his back on Chris." She released the ribbon, her shoulders drooping. "I'm supposed to be focusing on my wedding. Instead I'm worried there might not be one."

Ellie reached in the air for Sarah Lynne's hand. Sarah Lynne grabbed it, comforted by her friend's touch. "I'm sorry. I'm so sorry about this."

Sarah Lynne squeezed Ellie's hand. "It's not your fault. Christopher's to blame for all of this."

Ellie suddenly released her hand. "*Nee*, he's not, not completely—"

At the knock on the door, she and Ellie looked up. Sarah Lynne walked to the door and opened it, her breath catching in her throat.

CHAPTER NINE

Chris shoved his hands into the pockets of his jeans and looked down at his little sister as she stood in the doorway, her mouth agape. He shouldn't blame her for being surprised; he had almost decided not to come. He still wasn't sure why he was here, other than he had to see his mother one last time before he went back to Apple Creek. He wished he could see his father, too, but judging from the way his *daed* had reacted the last time they were together, he knew that was impossible.

Sarah Lynne finally spoke. "You came."

He nodded, glancing away for a moment. He'd spent the first twenty years of his life here, playing on this front porch, learning how to break and ride a horse, helping his father and mother raise a garden and take care of the house and land. Yet never had he felt more like an outsider than he did at this moment.

He looked back at Sarah Lynne. "Can I come inside?"

She nodded and stepped away so he could walk in. As he strode into the living room, a mix of bittersweet memories flooded him. Everything was the same, including the way the old, plain furniture was arranged.

Then he saw Ellie Chupp sitting on the couch, reaching for her cane as she moved to stand. He started toward her. "How's that ankle?"

"Better, *danki*. I only twisted it." She lifted her face in his direction.

He stood there for a moment, an unfamiliar warm sensation spreading through his stomach as he looked at her. She was the last person he'd expected to see here, but for some reason her presence comforted him. "I didn't see another buggy outside. I hope you didn't walk here."

She shook her head. "My *daed* dropped me off."

At the sound of his sister clearing her throat, he turned around. She had an odd look on her face, a blend of surprise and bewilderment.

"What?"

"Ellie brought something for you." Sarah Lynne went to the easy chair near the couch and picked up a small basket. But instead of handing it to him, she put it in Ellie's hand. "I'll *geh* get *Mamm*," she said, hurrying out of the room.

Chris scratched his head. "What's wrong with her?"

Ellie shrugged, but the way she tilted her head away from him he knew something was up. "Ellie, what happened? Why is my sister acting strangely?"

Ellie hesitated. "She's upset, Chris. I probably shouldn't tell you this, but yesterday Isaiah tried to call off the wedding."

Chris's brows lifted. "He did? Why would he do that?"

"I don't know. Maybe because he doesn't want Sarah Lynne to be unhappy?"

"That's a weird way to show it. Anyone can see she's crazy about him. Unless he's just stringing her along. I wouldn't put it past him."

"Stop."

He snapped his mouth shut at Ellie's exclamation. Her light blonde brows pinched together, strain showing around her mouth. Even the color of her eyes had darkened with anger.

"Isaiah would never ruin Sarah Lynne's life. He loves her so much he was willing to give up his own happiness because he thought it might bring you back into the family." She moved toward him, stopping just short of stepping on his toes. "You don't know *mei* cousin. What he's sacrificed over the years. How he's had to live with . . . how the accident changed him."

"He doesn't seem to have suffered too much." Chris couldn't stop the bitter words from escaping.

"You have no idea."

Her voice trembled, touching Chris deep inside. She wobbled for a moment, and he remembered her ankle. "You should sit down." He put his arm around her shoulder, but she shrugged him off and walked past him.

"Your *schwester* is right. You are selfish. You would rather blame Isaiah for your bitterness than face the real reason for it." The tone of her voice suddenly grew thick, as if something clogged her throat. "It's not my cousin's fault you're unhappy. You've managed that all on your own." She turned and walked out the door.

Chris stood frozen, her words stinging him. What did she know about his unhappiness? If it hadn't been for Isaiah, he would be married right now, and probably a *vatter* too. He'd have his own house and wouldn't be at odds with the community. Isaiah had stripped him of all that and more. Most of all, he'd robbed him of his peace.

"Christopher."

He turned to see his mother standing in the living room, her lips pale. Had she heard what Ellie said?

Sarah Lynne appeared, standing behind their mother. The same deep green eyes and dark eyebrows. So alike, and yet his mother had aged over the years, more than he had expected her to. Frown lines rimmed her mouth, and her gaze didn't hold the same spark as Sarah Lynne's. Guilt dug at him, accusing him.

"Where's Ellie?" Sarah Lynne stepped around their mother.

"She left." He caught his mother's gaze, and he knew she had heard their conversation.

"And you let her *geh*?" Sarah Lynne exclaimed. "She's hurt and doesn't have a ride."

He'd been so distracted he hadn't thought about that. "I didn't have a choice. She walked out the door."

Sarah Lynne stormed over to him, her bare feet pounding on the wood floor. "There's always a choice, Christopher. Someday you'll learn to make the right one." She rushed outside, the screen door slamming behind her.

Without a word Chris's mother went and shut the inner door. Then she turned around and faced him. "Why are you here?"

Chris turned around, trying to get control of his

emotions. He couldn't even answer her simple question. Everything had been so clear a few days ago, and he thought he was following God's lead to return to Paradise. Now he didn't know what to do.

He felt his mother's hand on his arm. He turned and faced her, swallowing the lump that had appeared in his throat.

"It's all right, *sohn*." Tears welled in her eyes. "It's all right." She lifted her arms to him.

Overwhelmed with emotions he couldn't understand or define, he embraced his mother, holding her close for the first time in five long years.

. . .

"Ellie! Ellie!"

Ellie heard Sarah Lynne's footsteps hurrying down the few steps leading from the front porch to the yard. When her friend called her name again, she sounded farther away, as if she had headed toward the street.

"Over here." Ellie lifted her hand from where she sat. After leaving Chris, she had made her way to the end of the porch and sat down on one of the Millers' wicker chairs. Her ankle had started to throb shortly after she arrived at their home. Knowing she had no choice but to wait on *Frau* Miller to give her a ride home, she waited on their porch. For the first time in years her blindness angered her. If she had her sight, she would have driven a buggy over here. She wouldn't be stuck waiting for someone to give her a ride.

"Thank goodness." Sarah Lynne stood in front of

her, sounding breathless. "I thought you were trying to walk home."

Ellie shook her head. "Too far." She heard the edge in her own voice, but she couldn't help it. Chris had infuriated her with his stubbornness. She didn't blame Sarah Lynne for being upset with him. He didn't deserve her understanding.

Ellie heard Sarah Lynne plop into the other wicker chair next to her. "You didn't have to leave, you know. We're almost *familye*, and besides, you know everything about the situation with Chris."

"They needed their privacy." Which was true, even though it wasn't the reason she'd left. She couldn't bear to listen to him complain about Isaiah any longer.

"They have it now." Sarah Lynne sighed. "I hope *Mamm* can talk sense into him."

Ellie doubted it, but she remained quiet. Ellie didn't know what it would take for Chris to let go of the grudge he held against Isaiah. "Caroline wouldn't want him to do this," she said, thinking aloud.

"What?"

She turned to Sarah Lynne. "If Caroline were here right now, she'd be able to convince him to let *geh*. The last thing she'd want would be for him to live like this, separated from everyone, unable to move on with his life."

"Then maybe you should tell him that." Sarah Lynne's voice rose as she spoke.

"Me?" Ellie shook her head. "He's not going to listen to me."

"I think he will. Ellie, I hope this doesn't offend you,

but you didn't see the way my brother looked at you a few minutes ago."

"*Nee*, I'm not offended. But I am confused."

"Me, too, but I know what I saw. When he was talking to you about your ankle, it was like I wasn't even in the room. And when he offered you a ride and you refused, he got this hangdog look on his face that I haven't seen since . . ."

"Since when?

"Since Caroline." Sarah Lynne's voice softened. "*Mei bruder* looks at you like he used to look at Caroline."

. . .

Chris downed the iced tea his mother gave him, then set the glass on the kitchen table. He looked at her sitting directly across from him, her hands tightly clasped in front of her. The hug they exchanged gave him relief, as if she had somehow taken part of his burden as her own. Then again, she probably had carried his pain with her for the past five years. Once more he was reminded of what his choices had cost everyone else.

"I'm glad you came by," she said in her usual soft voice. "I prayed you would."

"I couldn't leave without seeing you."

Her eyes filled with sadness. "Then you're going back to Apple Creek for certain?"

He started to nod but stopped. Since he arrived in Paradise and learned about the wedding, all he could think about was going back to Ohio. But now he wasn't so sure. "I don't know."

"What is your life like there?" She leaned forward, her gaze seeking his.

"It's . . . all right. Fine, actually. I have a *gut* job, a nice apartment." He'd had those things but had given them up to come here. Still, he didn't think it would be too hard to get either back . . . if he needed to. Right now he didn't know what he needed.

"Freinds?" Worry creased her brow.

"Ya. I have *freinds."* They were more like acquaintances, but he wouldn't admit that.

"What about an *aldi?"*

He shook his head, frowning. Her questions were starting to irritate, but he couldn't blame her for wanting to know about his life. *"Nee.* I don't have a girlfriend."

She unclasped her hands and reached for his. "Are you happy, Christopher? Because if you're happy, then I can be happy for you too. It would set my mind at ease knowing you have made a new life for yourself, one that is pleasing and satisfying."

He gave her fingers a light squeeze and released her hand. Was his life in Apple Creek pleasing and satisfying? Far from it. *"Nee, Mamm.* I'm not happy."

She nodded. "I didn't think so."

"Am I that easy to read?"

She smiled, though it didn't reach her eyes. "You are my *sohn,* Christopher. How could I not know these things? But I thought . . . I hoped . . . when you came back it was because you had finally made peace with the past." She looked beyond him, her gaze un-utterably sad, making Chris's gut clench. "I see now that's not true."

He didn't answer right away, embarrassed to admit the truth. "If Sarah Lynne was marrying anyone else . . . Why does it have to be Isaiah?" He gripped the empty tea glass. "How can I find peace in that?"

She took his other hand. "By forgiving, Christopher." She squeezed his fingers. "By following the Lord's example. He sent His Son to forgive our sins. What makes us better than God?"

"I don't think I'm better than God. I don't think I'm even worth His mercy."

Her thin lips smiled. "None of us is. Yet He gives it to us freely if we but ask. Forgiveness leads to peace in our hearts. But peace and strife can't live together. That's the battle you're waging, and it's one you can't win, not unless you let your bitterness *geh*."

Chris shoved his hands through his hair. He looked around the kitchen. Like the living room, it hadn't changed since his childhood. The table and chairs were the same, the walls painted the same white color he remembered. And just as the house had remained the same, his mother was as wise as ever. He was pulled in different directions, his head pounding with indecision.

"When are you heading back?"

He looked at her. "Tonight. I was going to head out after I said good-bye to you and Sarah Lynne."

"Please. Stay one more *daag*." She took his hand again, this time holding it tightly in both of hers.

"What difference will a *daag* make?"

For the first time since she sat down, his mother looked unsure. "I don't know. I just know God wants me to say this to you. Don't leave until tomorrow night."

He took a deep breath, then blew it out. "All right. I'll stay." He squeezed her hand again. "For you."

CHAPTER TEN

Ellie gripped her cane, still unable to believe Sarah Lynne's words. "You're seeing things that aren't there."

"*Nee*, I'm seeing what is there. At first I couldn't believe it—"

"Then don't. Because it's not true."

Christopher Miller couldn't possibly have feelings for her. And not just because they'd only been around each other a short while. No, the reason Chris couldn't feel anything for her was the same reason John had left her, and why no other man had shown any interest in her. Her blindness robbed her of her independence, made her helpless. He had witnessed that firsthand.

"I'm sure he just feels sorry for me."

"*Nee. Nee!*" Sarah Lynne touched her shoulder, the pressure of her hand firm. "That's not what I meant at all. The only person my brother feels sorry for is himself. The reason I'm surprised is because he's been so wrapped up in his own issues he can't look beyond them. But leave it to you to reach through all that."

Ellie shook her head, even as the thought of Chris

showing interest in her sent a tiny thrill through her. She had spent most of a sleepless night trying to erase the sound of his rich voice, his woodsy scent, the way he touched her. He didn't make her feel foolish or weak for having a panic attack. If she hadn't twisted her ankle, she knew he would have let her walk home alone from the cemetery. He was one of the few people who seemed to understand how she wanted to be treated. Warmth and an attraction she could not deny tugged at her, but she tried to ignore it. Was she so starved for male attention? How pitiful she must seem.

"You have to talk to him, Ellie. You're right about Caroline, and as her best friend you're the only who can remind him that Caroline wouldn't want him to wallow in self-pity and give up his family."

"You can say the same thing." She didn't want to get involved with this. But even as the thought popped into her mind, she knew she was already involved.

"It's not the same. He's angry with me for marrying Isaiah. You're the only one who can reach him. Please, Ellie. Just talk to him. It could be his last chance."

She sighed. How could she stay mad at Chris, knowing his deep pain fed his stubbornness? Still, she didn't know how she could convince him of anything.

She heard the rusty squeak of the door hinge. Chris's heavy footsteps sounded on the porch floor, followed by the softer steps of his mother. Ellie stood and gripped her cane, conscious not to put too much weight on her sore ankle.

Sarah Lynne walked over to her mother and brother,

and Ellie tried not to listen to what they were saying. Even though she turned away and they lowered their voices, she could hear parts of their conversation.

"I'm glad you decided to stay a little longer," Sarah Lynne said, sounding relieved.

"*Ya*. I better get going."

He sounded agitated, and Ellie surmised his discussion with his mother hadn't gone well.

"It's too late for me to *geh* to the Chupps'," *Frau* Miller said. "Sarah Lynne, could you take Ellie home?"

"I can take her."

Ellie's brows lifted at the swiftness of Chris's offer—and that he'd offered at all.

"I think that's a great idea." Sarah Lynne's enthusiasm sounded a little too obvious. "Don't you, Ellie?"

And though she knew her friend had Chris's best interests in mind, she couldn't help but feel manipulated.

"*Nee*," *Frau* Miller said. "You should be the one to take her, Sarah Lynne."

Frau Miller didn't have to explain any further. Ellie knew she was thinking of how her mother would react if Chris dropped her off.

"But by the time I get the buggy hitched up, Chris could have her home."

Sarah Lynne was starting to sound desperate, and Ellie second—guessed her resolve to stay neutral. She needed to try to reach Chris one more time for Sarah Lynne's sake, and riding in the car with him would be the perfect opportunity. She'd explain it to her mother later.

"Sarah Lynne's right. If Chris doesn't mind, I'll *geh* with him."

"I don't mind at all."

The emotion in his tone sent a shiver through her. Could Sarah Lynne be right? Was Chris feeling more for her than friendship? Was that even possible?

Frau Miller didn't respond for a long moment. Then she sighed. "I can't stop you."

Ellie moved to the porch steps, trying not to limp too much on her sore ankle. The last thing she needed was for Chris to carry her to the car in front of his mother and sister. That would send Sarah Lynne's imagination running rampant.

Chris said his good-byes to them. She heard his heavy footsteps as he descended the stairs, and she was surprised he didn't offer to help her down them, as so many other people would have.

"The car's to your right," he said.

She lifted a brow, turning her head toward his voice. He'd known she'd need a verbal cue without her saying anything. She walked toward the direction of his voice. "*Danki.*"

"You can sit in the back if you want. I'll still *geh* slow."

"*Nee*, I need to sit up front. I can't let fear rule my life."

He didn't say anything to that, but she heard the car door open. Using her cane to find the passenger side door, she got inside and sat down, this time doing the seat belt herself.

"Wait!" Sarah Lynne came rushing toward them. "Ellie, you forgot this." She put the basket in Ellie's grasp then leaned forward. "Don't forget what we talked about. I will owe you forever if you persuade him to forgive Isaiah."

She might as well have asked Ellie to pluck the moon out of the sky and hand it over on a silver platter. But Ellie nodded anyway. "I'll see what I can do," she said, lowering her voice to match Sarah Lynne's.

Chris got into the car, and from the scent filling the interior, she realized he had his leather jacket on. She heard the vehicle roar to life.

"I'm surprised you agreed to this."

"Sarah Lynne was right. It's easier if you take me home."

The car jerked into reverse.

"Ready, Ellie?"

She gripped the basket, but her nerves were steady. "Ready."

"Like I said, I'll drive slow. I'm not in any hurry."

"You can drive normally." She didn't want him to be overly cautious on her account. "I think I'm over my anxiety."

"I think you are too. You haven't lost the color in your cheeks yet, and we're already on the road."

Ellie let her grip on the basket relax. Then, remembering why she had it in the first place, she said, "Oh. This is for you."

"What? The basket?"

"*Ya.* It's not much, but I wanted to thank you for taking me home the other day."

"You don't have to thank me," Chris said. "I'm glad I could be there. What's in it?"

"A loaf of homemade bread and some jelly."

"Ellie's jelly?"

His tone held a touch of humor, which put her at ease a bit. "*Ya*. My very own jelly. I'm afraid it's not kumquat, though."

"Well, that's disappointing. What's a *mann* got to do to get some kumquat jelly around here?"

"I don't know, but I hope you like strawberry."

"I do." His voice lowered. "It's my favorite. *Danki*, Ellie. That's the first gift I've gotten in a long time."

She felt sad for him. She didn't know what his life was like in Apple Creek, but she suspected he wasn't happy there. "Why are you leaving?"

"What?"

"Why are you leaving Paradise? Is there something, or someone, waiting for you there?"

He hesitated a long moment before replying. "*Nee*. There's not much for me back there."

"Then you should stay here."

The heaviness of his sigh filled the car. "You know it's not that simple, Ellie."

She heard the sound of him flipping on the turn signal and sensed the car moving to the right. "I never said it was simple. Often the most worthwhile things are hard." She curved her hand around the base of the basket. "Caroline wouldn't want this for you, Chris. You know that."

A low squeak sounded, like he was rubbing his palm back and forth on the steering wheel. "If she were here, I wouldn't be going through this."

"But she's not here. That's a fact, just like I'm never

going to see again and your sister is going to marry Isaiah."

"Ellie, I don't want to talk about this anymore." His good-humored tone turned curt. "I know how you and my mom and Sarah Lynne feel. And I'm sorry I'm hurting my *familye*. But why does everyone expect me to forgive Isaiah just like that?"

"It's not 'just like that.'" She couldn't keep the frustration out of her tone. "It's been five years. You've spent five years of your life hanging on to Caroline." She leaned back in her seat, her eyes growing wide. "That's it."

"What!"

She angled her face toward him, wishing she could see his expression. She was missing so much by only hearing his voice. "This isn't about Isaiah at all."

"*Ya*, it is. It's all about Isaiah."

She shook her head. "It's not, Christopher. You can't forgive Isaiah because you can't let *geh* of Caroline. And until you do . . . you'll never move on."

. . .

Chris gripped the steering wheel so hard his knuckles started to ache. Was Ellie right? Did his refusal to forgive Isaiah stem from his not wanting to let Caroline go? Maybe it was part of it. "But not all," he whispered.

"Not all what?"

He glanced at Ellie, not realizing he'd even spoken aloud. He pulled his gaze away, something he found difficult to do. She looked so pretty today. She was dressed the same as yesterday, except her dress was dark purple instead of blue and her blonde hair was pulled tightly from her face. He liked that nothing obscured the view of her amazing eyes that were so beautiful, yet unseeing. But he was learning fast that Ellie saw much more of him than anyone else. She saw his heart.

"Chris?"

Turning his gaze back to the road, he spoke. "I can't remember what she looked like. At least not completely. I can still see her smile sometimes, and every once in a while I hear her laugh." His jaw jerked. "At one time I thought I'd never forget her."

"And you haven't. Just because the physical memory has faded doesn't mean you don't carry her in your heart. A part of you always will."

"Like you with John?"

Her head dipped. "That's different. John is still here. He's married and has a family." Then she lifted her chin. "Which was for the best. His wife is a very nice *frau*. From all accounts he's happy."

Chris wished he hadn't brought John up. He could tell she was trying to put his marriage in a positive light, but there was a tinge of sadness to her voice. "I'm sorry. I shouldn't have mentioned him."

"*Nee*, it's fine. God has a way of working things out for the best."

"I'm not so sure about that. I can't see how Caroline's death was *gut* for anything."

"Sometimes we can't see God's plan while we're in the midst of it."

He looked at her again. "You really believe that, don't you?"

She turned to him again, a smile forming on her lips. "*Ya*. I really do. I pray that someday you will too."

They neared Ellie's house. He slowed down the car, not wanting his conversation with Ellie to end. He continued to be amazed by her capacity to forgive, to completely trust God and accept what happened to her.

"Are we at my *haus*?" she asked.

"*Ya*. We're nearly there."

"Could you do me one last favor? You know how *Mamm* is. I don't want her to see you dropping me off."

He nodded. He didn't want her getting into trouble with her mother on his account. "Where do you want me to drop you off?"

"Near the end of the drive will be fine. I can make my way to the *haus* from there."

He didn't like the idea of her walking the long length of the driveway on her sore ankle, but he didn't have a choice. He also didn't like the idea of parting company with her so soon. He pulled his car to the side of the road, then brought it to a stop. But before she could open the door, he blurted, "Can I see you again?"

She froze, and he wished he could take back the words, or at least say them in a less abrupt manner.

"I . . . don't know." Ellie turned to him, her delicate brows forming a V shape above her jewel-like eyes.

"Please?" He was practically begging her, but he couldn't help it. He had to see her once more before he left Paradise. She was the only one who came close to understanding him. He needed her to listen, needed the advice and wisdom she so easily offered. When she didn't reply, he couldn't help himself from reaching out and taking her hand. It was so soft, warm, and small in his palm. He clung to it like a lifeline. "I need to talk to you again."

"Chris, I . . ." Her head bent down as if she were looking at their hands clasped together. Then she pulled hers out of his grasp. She opened the door, and he sat back in the seat.

He should have known he was pushing it. Besides, she didn't owe him anything. Certainly not her time, especially at the risk of her mother's anger. That didn't stop the rush of regret flooding him as she left.

Her foot landed on the gravel, crunching beneath her black lace-up shoes. "Meet me at the cemetery tomorrow morning. Before eight." Then she handed him the basket, took her cane, and quickly exited the car.

His regret turned to surprise as he watched her unfold her cane and limp toward her *haus*. He stayed there until she walked inside. As he drove away, he glanced at the basket in the passenger seat before easing his car onto the road. He smiled. Eight o'clock couldn't come quickly enough.

• • •

"Something on your mind, Ellie?"

Ellie turned her head toward her father's voice. They were sitting in the living room again, the crackling fire warming the room. Her mother was in the kitchen cleaning up the supper dishes. On the surface, tonight seemed to be like every other night. But not for Ellie. She couldn't stop thinking about Chris and wondering if she'd made a mistake in agreeing to meet him. Yet she thought she had kept her inner strife to herself.

"How did you know?"

"I think I know you pretty well. Plus that player has been lying in your lap for the last half hour. Usually you're eager to listen to your book."

Ellie set the player to the side on the couch. She couldn't focus on her reading, especially a romance. Not when her thoughts were consumed with Chris. She let out a sigh, then heard the soft flutter of a newspaper page being turned.

"Anything you want to talk about?"

She started to shake her head but stopped. Maybe her father would have some insight into Chris. She certainly couldn't talk to her mother about him. Her *daed* was less stringent about the rules of *meiding* and might be more sympathetic to Chris and his plight. Then again—

"It's all right if you don't," her father said. "Never been too *gut* understanding women stuff anyway. Ask your mother."

Ellie chuckled. "You're not that bad, *Daed*. Besides, I think I need a *mann's* opinion about this anyway."

Her father shifted in his chair. "What about?"

She told him about her decision to meet Chris in the cemetery, explaining everything that had happened since Chris's return. When she finished, her father didn't say anything, and she wondered if she had made a mistake confiding in him.

"I see why you didn't want to talk to your *mamm* about this," he finally said. "She would be very upset if she found out you were meeting with him."

"Are you saying I shouldn't?"

"*Nee*, Ellie." He lowered his voice. "I think you should. Just be careful about it, that's all."

"I will." She appreciated her father's support. "But I don't know what else I can say to him. If his *mutter* and Sarah Lynne can't convince him to forgive Isaiah, how can I be expected to?"

He paused again, and she imagined him tugging on his beard, something he always did when he was deep in thought. "Maybe he doesn't need any more convincing. He might just need a *freind*."

Ellie nodded. Her father's words put things into perspective. Chris did need a friend. That had to be what Sarah Lynne was interpreting as romantic interest on his part. And she would be that friend to him when they talked tomorrow.

But she couldn't help but feel disappointed that there wasn't something more between them.

CHAPTER ELEVEN

The next morning dawned cool and crisp. An abundant array of leaves fluttered across the grassy field surrounding the cemetery. Chris got out of his car and shut the door, then he shoved his hands into his pockets and walked over to the small burial ground. The gate squeaked open as he stepped through. A strong breeze kicked up, making the colored leaves swirl and chilling the tops of his ears. He wished he had his wide-brimmed hat, but he'd given that up along with the other articles of Amish clothing he used to wear—the broadfall pants, home-made shirts, and suspenders—after being shunned. But since he'd returned to Paradise he longed for those simpler clothes.

He slowed his pace as he headed toward the corner of the graveyard where Caroline lay. He glanced around, looking for Ellie. He was a good fifteen minutes early, but still . . . it was in the back of his mind that she might not show up. He stood in front of his fiancée's grave and looked down at the small, plain concrete marker, the same shape and size as the rest of the headstones.

He knelt down beside the faded green grass that covered the grave and closed his eyes.

Memories of the funeral and burial flooded his mind. How he had balled up his grief that day, trying to keep himself from breaking down in front of family and friends as they viewed her casket in her parents' basement per Amish tradition. The hours before taking her casket to the graveyard had been excruciating, and the only way he had gotten through it was by plotting his revenge against Isaiah. He clearly remembered standing by Caroline's graveside and vowing that Isaiah would pay for her death, and pay dearly.

He opened his eyes and ran his palm along the grass. "I failed, Caroline." His voice was thick with the emotion he had allowed to fester for all these years. But even now he couldn't let the grief flow, not when faced with how he had let Caroline down. Isaiah had gotten off free from blame and consequences while the woman he had loved lay in the cold ground. How was he ever supposed to let that go?

"Christopher?"

He turned and stood at the sound of Ellie's voice. He hadn't heard her approach. She was standing just outside the gate, as if waiting for his permission to come in. He strode over to her and opened the gate for her. Her limp was less noticeable than it had been yesterday. "How did you get here?"

"*Daed* dropped me off on his way to work."

Chris was surprised; he hadn't even heard the buggy approach. "Didn't he see my car?"

She nodded.

"And he didn't care?"

"He's not as strict as *Mamm* is." She turned toward the sun and closed her eyes, allowing the warm beams to shine on her face.

He tried not to stare at her, but he couldn't help it. "I'm glad you came."

She turned toward him. "You thought I wasn't going to show up?"

"The thought did cross my mind."

Ellie shook her head. "I wouldn't do that to you, Chris."

And he believed her. Ellie kept her word. That was the type of woman she was. Strong. Filled with faith and forgiveness. She was perfect, while he was so flawed. He turned away, trying to fight his emotions, even though he knew she couldn't see his expression. Then he felt her touch his arm.

"Chris?"

He faced her again and, without thinking, moved closer. "I failed her, Ellie. I didn't realize it until this moment. I promised her that day that I would make Isaiah pay for the accident. He never did."

"You didn't fail her, Chris. That promise was given out of pain and grief. Believe me, Isaiah has paid dearly for what happened."

He let out a sigh. "I think we all have."

She nodded. "Why did you ask to see me again?"

Her blunt question caught him off guard. How could he admit he just wanted to be with her, to hear her voice, to listen to her say things that spoke to his heart? He couldn't tell her, not without scaring her off.

He was scared enough by the abruptness and intensity of his feelings. The thought of leaving her tomorrow was almost unbearable.

But she wasn't the only thing keeping him here. If he had really wanted to leave, he would have done it as soon as he heard about Sarah Lynne's engagement. Yet he didn't. Something else kept him from going back to Ohio. God had brought him back to Paradise, and He was telling Chris to stay.

"I think I'm ready," he said, taking her hand from his arm and holding it in his. Her touch warmed his soul much like the sun warmed him through the leather of his jacket.

Her brows shot up. "Ready to do what?"

"Ask for forgiveness and rejoin the church."

• • •

Ellie pulled her hand out of his grasp and stepped away, almost losing her balance. She used her cane for support, not only because she had almost tripped, but to contain her surprise. "You're ready to repent?"

"*Ya.*"

She heard him approach her again, and she moved away until she felt the fence against the small of her back.

"You're right," he said. "*Mamm*'s right. Even Sarah Lynne's right, although she'll never let me live it down." His chuckle held more mirth than she'd heard from him since his arrival in Paradise. "Just talking about letting this *geh* is freeing."

Ellie was speechless. It was what she and so many others were praying for. Yet it seemed so sudden. Yesterday he had still been filled with bitterness. Now he was ready to let go. Perhaps God had done the work in his heart that they had all longed for. And who was she to question God?

"Ellie?" His tone changed from happiness to trepidation. "Why aren't you saying anything? I thought you'd be happy."

"I am. It's just so . . . sudden."

"I don't call five years sudden."

"*Noo*, that's not what I mean." What did she mean? Doubt niggled at her head and heart. "I am glad, very glad that you've decided to ask for forgiveness."

"But?"

"There are no buts." She bit her tongue.

"*Gut*." He stepped away from her. "Now that I've made the decision, I don't know why I didn't make it before. I think it was because I was trying to hold on to Caroline, like you said. Her memory slipped away from me, and at least by being angry I felt *something*, instead of being dead inside. But you've shown me that I can't live my life like that anymore."

"I have?"

"*Ya*. You're the example of what I should have done all along. I should have left the past in the past. I shouldn't have put my family through all this."

He was saying all the right words, but she still wasn't sure. "What about Isaiah? Have you stopped blaming him for Caroline's death?" She held her breath while waiting to hear his answer.

"If that's what I need to do to get back with the church, then I will."

Her heart sank. It was what she feared. His forgiveness wasn't coming from his heart. It was a means to an end.

"Ellie, what's wrong?"

She felt him move closer. She was backed up against the fence and there was no place for her to go. Despite her disappointment that his repentance was less than genuine, she suddenly realized she didn't mind being this close to him. An attraction stronger than anything she'd ever felt before bloomed inside her.

"Ellie, I want this. I don't want to *geh* back to Apple Creek, to an empty apartment, to no *familye*, and to people I barely know being the only *freinds* I have. This is where I belong, I know that now." His voice lowered. "You showed it to me. I don't know how I can ever repay you for that."

"You don't owe me anything, Chris." She willed her pulse to slow, but it wouldn't. His rich voice, a tone she could listen to all day, flowed over her. He had on his leather jacket again, and his breath smelled sweet, as if he'd had flavored coffee for breakfast.

"Ellie, I . . ."

She heard him gulp, giving her the first indication that he might be nervous. But why? He cleared his throat but didn't step away.

"I'm going to see Bishop Ebersol today and ask him to take me out of the *bann*. When is the next church service?"

"This Sunday." Which was only two days away.

"*Gut.* I don't want to wait longer than that. And, Ellie, once I'm back in the church, I don't want us to stop seeing each other."

Ellie's belly swirled. "We won't," she said, fighting for an even tone. "We're *freinds*, Christopher. We were before the accident, and we always will be."

"That's not what I mean."

She drew in a sharp breath when she felt his palm cup her cheek, then release it quickly. The touch was light, nearly imperceptible, but enough to make her heart almost leap out of her chest. Sarah Lynne was right— Christopher did like her. Or at least he thought he did. One thing was for sure, he was a very mixed-up *mann*.

. . .

Ellie had Chris drop her off at the Pantry on his way to visit Bishop Ebersol. She hadn't answered him directly about what would happen between them after he was accepted back in the church, and he didn't press.

"Say good-bye to the car," he said as she was getting out. "I'm selling it after I see the bishop."

She paused. "You're serious about this."

"I'm serious about everything I said, Ellie. It's time for me to move on with my life. For the first time since Caroline died, I'm looking forward to it."

Ellie recalled his last words as she slipped into a booth in the back of the restaurant. She had told her mother she would be gone to Paradise for most of the day and asked to be picked up this afternoon at Stitches and Things in downtown Paradise. At least she didn't have to worry about dealing with her *mamm* for the rest of the day. She had enough things on her mind as it was.

"Hello, Ellie. How are you today?"

Ellie turned, recognizing the cheerful voice. Tillie always seemed to be in a good mood. "Hi, Tillie." She was grateful her tone sounded friendly and even. "How are you?"

"Doing great. We've got some delicious specials today. I've already snuck a few bites." She lowered her voice, giggling. "But don't tell anyone."

Ellie managed a smile. "I won't."

"Would you like a menu?"

"*Nee.* I'll just have a cup of coffee." She didn't even want that, but she couldn't sit in the booth taking up space without paying for something. "Is Sarah Lynne here?" She prayed she would be.

"*Ya.* She just came in an hour ago. I'll send her over with the coffee."

Ellie checked her watch as Tillie walked away, then she drummed her fingers against the hard plastic tabletop, her nerves strung taut.

"I'm so glad you're here!" Sarah Lynne set the coffee cup on the table and slid into the seat in front of her. "We're in between breakfast and lunch rush, so I have some time to talk. How did your ride home with Chris *geh* yesterday?"

"*Gut.* We talked—"

"Did you tell him about Caroline? Did you convince him to stay? Did he say anything about coming back to the community?"

Ellie held up her hand. "*Ya.* Sorta. *Ya.*"

"Wait a minute. So he's staying?"

"I don't know—"

"And he's going to forgive Isaiah?" Sarah Lynne grabbed her hand. "Ellie, you're amazing. Well, I've always thought you were amazing, but now you're double amazing. How did you do it?"

Ellie swallowed. This conversation wasn't going the way she planned—much like her last conversation with Chris. Events were spinning out of control, and she couldn't reel them back in.

"Sarah Lynne, I think your *bruder* is really confused right now. He says he wants to come back to the church. In fact, he went to see Bishop Ebersol after he dropped me off."

"He did? That's great. How is that confused? Sounds like he's finally making sense."

"He's doing the right thing, but I'm not sure it's for the right reason. I asked him if he forgave Isaiah. He said if that's what it took to get back to the church, then he would. Then he said something else."

"What?" Sarah Lynne gripped Ellie's hand tighter.

"I think he wants to court me after he's been accepted into the church."

"I knew it!" Sarah Lynne released Ellie's hand. "I told you he likes you. I love it when I'm right."

Ellie shook her head. Sarah Lynne was missing the point. "That's what I mean by him being confused. For one thing, he can't possibly like me."

"Why not?"

"You know why. Everyone knows why." Surely she didn't have to say it out loud.

"Because you're blind? Ellie, obviously that doesn't matter to him."

"It mattered to John."

"Because John was an idiot. I'm sorry, but he was. And Chris isn't like that. He's stubborn, but he isn't shallow."

Ellie shook her head. "It's not just that. His repentance doesn't come from the heart, Sarah Lynne."

"Did he say that to you?"

"*Nee*, but—"

"When Chris first came here and I asked him to forgive Isaiah, he said he could never get up in front of the church and say something that wasn't true. He wouldn't be doing this if he didn't really feel it deep in his heart." Ellie heard Sarah Lynne slide out of the seat. "I've got to run, but this is the best news! I can't wait to tell Isaiah. We'll all finally be happy."

As Sarah Lynne walked away, Ellie wondered if it would ever be possible. Especially when everyone learned the truth.

CHAPTER TWELVE

Ellie knocked on the door of her cousin's house, praying he would be home. She heard the taxi she'd hired drive away. After talking with Sarah Lynne, she knew she had to speak to Isaiah. He often worked from home, but sometimes he would go out into the community to work on various construction projects.

Her aunt Roberta opened the door. "Why, hello there, Ellie. What a lovely surprise. Did your mother come with you?"

"*Nee*. I came alone. I need to talk to Isaiah for a minute. Is he home?"

"*Ya*, he's out in the workshop. You want me to take you there?"

She shook her head. "I remember where it is."

"All right. I'll be out in a minute with some fresh iced tea."

What she had to say was for Isaiah's hearing alone. "That's all right, *Aenti*."

"Okay, but if you change your mind, let me know. I have a fresh pitcher, just made it a little while ago."

"*Danki*, I'll keep that in mind."

Ellie turned away from the house as her aunt shut the door. Although she and her mother were sisters, they weren't anything alike. Aunt Roberta hadn't changed the way she treated Ellie since the accident, and occasionally Ellie heard her aunt admonish *Mamm* for hovering so much, especially after the accident.

As Ellie made her way to the workshop behind the house, she could hear the sounds of the cows and pigs her cousin's family raised. She could smell them, too, and the scent helped her find her way to the workshop instead of the barn, which were right next to each other. The sound of the hydraulic-powered saw reached her ears. She waited a few moments for the whirring to stop, then with a firm fist she rapped on the door, hoping Isaiah heard her. She didn't dare walk into the shop, not knowing the layout of the building or where Isaiah kept his tools.

Soon she heard the muffled thud of footsteps coming toward the door. When it opened, she felt a slight breeze and inhaled the scent of fresh sawdust.

"Ellie." He sounded surprised to see her. "What are you doing here?"

"I need to talk to you. Now, and alone."

"All right. Let me tell *Daed*, and I'll be right out." Isaiah walked away, and she could hear him speaking with her uncle. Then Isaiah walked back to her. "Let's go behind the barn. That's a *gut* place to talk."

Ellie reached for Isaiah's arm, grasping it just above the elbow, letting him lead her to the back of the barn. A few moments later they stopped.

"There's a wood fence right in front of us," he said.

She reached out and touched the rough, splintered wood, holding her cane.

"I think I know why you're here," Isaiah said. "I also hope I'm wrong."

She leaned against the fence, as if its support would give her the strength to say what she should have said a long time ago. Over the years she had accepted what Isaiah had done. And up until Chris's return, she had seen no need to have this conversation with her cousin. But after hearing what Chris told her today, she knew she couldn't keep silent anymore. "We have to tell them, Isaiah. We have to tell everyone what really happened."

. . .

"And are you willing to fully repent of your sins? Of going against the church and trying to have your brother in Christ prosecuted?"

Chris looked at the bishop, who was peering at him over the rims of his spectacles. He fidgeted in his chair, gripping the mug of coffee the bishop's wife had offered him. The older man's steel-colored eyes made him feel like a child again, and perhaps that was the point. He had been acting childishly. He knew that now. Unfortunately, it had taken him far too long to realize it.

"*Ya*," he said, sitting up a little straighter in his chair. "I ask that you forgive my sin against Isaiah Stolzfus."

"It isn't I who needs to forgive you, Christopher. Forgiveness must come from the congregation, and ultimately from God."

Chris nodded, understanding. All the way over here he'd prayed, harder than he ever had before, asking God to heal his heart for good this time, to give him the strength he needed not only to stand up in front of the church on Sunday and admit his guilt, but also to face Isaiah, which would be much harder. At the forefront of everything was Ellie. He could almost hear her prodding him on, and he wished he had thought to ask her to come with him. But she would have refused, and rightly so. This was his battle, and he had to face his past on his own before he could let it go.

Bishop Ebersol stroked his long, graying beard. The man had been bishop of their district for as long as Chris could remember.

"I'll have to speak with the other ministers about it, but I don't think they would have any disagreement about you making your plea on Sunday. I believe they will think, as I do, that this has been long overdue. Your absence has been missed, Christopher, not only by your *familye*, but by all of us."

Chris hadn't expected the surge of emotion that ran through him. He blinked back the tears, swallowed the lump in his throat. *"Danki,"* he said, his voice cracking.

The bishop nodded, his expression still stern. He looked Chris up and down. "You'll have to give up your fancy clothes and car. You realize that, *yu*?"

Chris set the cup down on the coffee table in front of him. "They mean nothing to me." His car was a convenience, nothing more, and he had no attachment to the clothes. Everything of worth he had in his duffel bag, which he could easily give up. He would be coming back to the community with nothing, ready to fully embrace the Amish life again.

Bishop Ebersol steepled his fingers beneath his fuzzy beard and stared at Chris for a long moment, enough to make Chris squirm again. Finally the man spoke. "What made you come to this decision, Christopher? It's been five years. Your sister is marrying the man you tried to have sent to jail, the *mann* who was at fault for your fiancée's accident."

Chris rubbed his palms over his jean-clad thighs. Was the bishop trying to rile him up? He gripped the tops of his kneecaps. "I realize that."

"Then how have you found it in your heart, after all these years, to forgive Isaiah?"

He leaned back in the chair, suddenly serene. "Someone has changed my heart," he said, smiling. "Someone very special."

"So you are doing this because of a *maedel*?" The bishop's gaze narrowed, and he looked more stone-faced than ever. "Does your change of heart come from God . . . or from her?"

. . .

"I don't want to talk about this," Isaiah said. "What's done is done."

She could hear Isaiah's voice drifting away, indicating he was walking away from her. She took a tentative step toward him, using the fence as a guide. "Things have changed, Isaiah. We both know that. I should have said something before now—"

"Ellie, I said I don't want to talk about it. The past is past. Remember? It's what we say to each other when we forgive, *ya*?"

"Isaiah, please don't be angry."

"I'm . . . not." He sounded closer now, and she could tell he was facing her. "I'm not angry with you, Ellie. I'm still mad at myself. I should have never driven that car."

"Caroline and I got in there with you. We trusted you."

"And look what happened." Isaiah touched her shoulder. "You've suffered enough, Ellie."

She moved her head up. "As have you."

"Not as much as I deserve." He sighed, dropping his hand from her shoulder. The wood fence creaked as he leaned against it. "Why are you bringing this up now? Is it because of the wedding? Because of Chris?"

"Both. And because of my conscience."

"Your conscience should be clear."

"But it's not. I've been talking to Chris, Isaiah. He said he's ready to forgive you and come back to the church."

She heard him move.

"He did? That's great! Sarah Lynne will be so happy."

"She is. I just told her about it."

He let out a deep breath. "I prayed so hard for this, Ellie. Sarah Lynne has been so sad since Chris came back. I think it was worse with him being here than when he was in Apple Creek. I offered to call off the wedding, to spare Sarah Lynne's *familye* any more pain. I thought stepping aside might make Chris change his mind about me."

"Not one of your smarter decisions."

"I realize that now. But, Ellie, listen to me." He gripped both of her shoulders, almost hard enough to make her wince. "The decision we made five years ago was a *gut* one."

"You didn't give me much of a choice at the time. I was in the hospital, still hurt and confused."

"I did what needed to be done. At the time I didn't know what would happen. Caroline was dead, you were blind . . . I had no idea what would happen to either of us. That's why I did what I did. And I'd do it all over again." He released her, but he didn't step away. "Just drop it, Ellie. Chris is forgiving me. He's coming back to the church."

"But I don't think he's doing it for the right reason. I don't think he's forgiving you with his heart."

"Who are you to make that judgment? Ellie, please. Just leave it alone. After all this time, everything is finally getting back to normal. I have to get back to work." He brushed past her, then added, "Can you make your way back to the *haus*?"

She nodded, not wanting to press the matter further. Her cousin had made up his mind, and she wasn't about to change it. "I'm fine. You *geh* on."

Once Isaiah left she turned, feeling the fence pressing against her waist. She couldn't mistake the pleading in her cousin's voice, nor his admonishment about her judging Chris's heart. He was right about that; she had no right to assume what Chris was feeling. After five years he was practically a stranger to her. And she knew judging others was frowned upon, not only by other Amish, but by God. Why did she have a hard time letting this *geh*?

But she knew the answer to that. And even though her cousin wanted her to keep their secret, she wasn't sure she could do it anymore.

. . .

After his visit to Bishop Ebersol's, Chris drove his car back to the bed-and-breakfast in Paradise and checked out. He loaded his duffel bag into the back and put the basket Ellie had given him in the passenger seat. As he turned the key in the ignition, he realized this might be last time he would drive this car. He didn't have a single regret. Smiling, he headed to his parents' house, his nerves steady until he got a few feet from their driveway. He glanced at the clock on the dashboard. It read four thirty. His father usually arrived home before five.

He turned in the driveway, excited to see his mother's face. She had been right about staying one more day. Talking with Ellie had put things into perspective. She was a special woman, and once he rejoined the church, he hoped she would be willing to let him court her.

He pulled his car to a stop and hopped out, went to the front porch, and knocked on the door. A few moments later he knocked again. After a third time, he frowned. No one was home? His sister and father were probably still working, and his mother sometimes visited friends in the afternoon. But he didn't mind waiting for them to return.

Chris left the porch and went around to the backyard. He saw a couple of cows grazing in the pasture next to the barn. He strode toward the white wood fencing, then leaned against it, watching the cows nibble on the tender blades of grass. Peace filled him like he hadn't experienced in so long. Why had he fought so hard all this time? He could barely remember his reasons.

He wasn't sure how long he stood there, soaking in the afternoon sun and watching the cows in front of him. But when he heard the sound of a car in front of the house, he dashed around to find out who it was. He didn't recognize the car, but he knew the woman stepping out of it. Ellie. He went to her just as she was taking out her cane.

"Here, let me get that." He dug into his back pocket for his wallet so he could pay her taxi fare.

"Get what? Oh." Then she nodded. "*Nee*, I've already paid." She turned to the driver. "*Danki*, Mrs. Jones."

"You're welcome, Ellie."

Chris ducked to see an elderly woman behind the wheel of a car that seemed to swallow her whole.

"What time do you want me to pick you up?" Mrs. Jones asked.

"Half an hour will be fine," Ellie replied.

"You don't have to pick her up." Chris stepped beside her and leaned over, poking his head through the passenger doorway. "I can take her home."

"Are you sure?"

He heard Ellie say something behind him, but he didn't let her finish. "I'm positive. Thanks anyway."

"Okay."

Chris stood up and shut the car door. After Mrs. Jones started pulling away, he turned to Ellie. He opened his mouth to speak but shut it when he saw her stormy expression.

"I wanted Mrs. Jones to pick me up."

"I'm sorry. I thought I'd save her a trip and take you home. I should have asked."

"*Ya*, you should have. Just because I'm blind doesn't mean I can't take care of myself."

The strength of her irritation surprised him. "I never said that you couldn't. I didn't think you'd mind. It's not like I haven't driven you home twice before."

"You shouldn't assume anything about me, Chris. You don't know . . . You don't know the real me. And once you do . . ."

The break in Ellie's voice made Chris go to her. But when he touched her shoulder, she shrugged him off. "What's going on here, Ellie? I don't understand why you're upset with me."

"I'm not." She took in a deep breath. "But I need to talk to you. Privately."

"No one's home, so you have me all to yourself." That didn't come out exactly right, but at that moment he didn't care. He bit the inside of his cheek. Remembering her sore ankle, he said, "Let's sit on the front porch."

She nodded, and he followed her as she made her way to the porch. Even though she obviously knew the way, her steps were slow. A few moments later they were both seated in the wicker chairs. But she didn't speak. "What did you want to talk to me about, Ellie?"

"Did you see the bishop today?"

He nodded. "*Ya*. Everything is ready for Sunday. But I thought I'd go over to Isaiah's on Saturday and talk to him. I think a conversation is long overdue."

Her hands clutched the ends of the wicker chair. "Whatever he tells you about the accident, don't believe him."

He looked at Ellie and frowned. What was she talking about?

"Maybe Isaiah was right," she murmured. "Maybe I should leave this alone."

"Leave what alone?"

"But I have to tell the truth. I should have told the truth a long time ago."

Her words unnerved him. He leaned forward in the chair and reached for her hand, not caring if his mother and father showed up and saw them together. Soon everyone would know how much he cared for Ellie. But just as before, she shirked from his touch.

"Ellie, please, talk to me."

Her body started to shake before she turned toward him. "Chris, Isaiah isn't to blame for Caroline's death. I am."

CHAPTER THIRTEEN

Ellie couldn't stop shaking. Every bone in her body quaked. She pulled her light jacket closer to her body. She'd said the words aloud, the secret she had kept inside for five long years.

"What are you talking about?"

An edge had crept into his voice, which she had expected. Once he knew the full truth, he wouldn't want to see her again. She heard him get up and start to pace the front porch. Then he suddenly stopped.

"What happened? And start from the beginning."

"Caroline spent the night at my house the night before the accident. We both had to work the afternoon shift at the Pantry, and I was going to call a taxi when Isaiah showed up. He had borrowed one of his *Englisch* friends' fancy cars." She sighed. "I lost patience with him right away. We were trying to arrange a ride to work, and he kept bugging us to *geh* for a ride with him. Finally Caroline pointed out that we could make Isaiah happy and get to work on time if we would ride with him. 'It'll be fun, Ellie,' she said. With both of them trying to convince me, I gave in. She got in the back, and I got in the front.

"As he drove us, Isaiah told us it was the first time he'd ever driven a car. I panicked and held my breath. Neither he nor Caroline noticed how nervous I was; Caroline was enjoying the ride, telling him to go faster. The car had one of those sunroof things, and he opened it up and put one hand through it, leaving only one hand on the wheel. When we got to the intersection right before Paradise I saw a car coming at us. I grabbed his arm and squeezed, screaming for him to look out." She tilted her head downward. "He already had one hand off the wheel. When I grabbed him, he let go and lost control of the car. That's when he spun out of control and rammed into a tree. Caroline was thrown out and . . . you know the rest."

Chris didn't say anything for a long time. She hadn't expected him to. She thought by telling him about the accident, a burden would have lifted, but it didn't. Instead she felt worse. She had never admitted any of this to anyone else. Saying the words out loud made her feel ashamed.

"Why didn't Isaiah say anything?" he finally asked

"That was the way he wanted it. He came to see me in the hospital the day after the accident." She could still remember the sound of his crutches hitting the floor. He had broken his left leg and had just been released by the doctors. "They had given me some kind of drug for the pain, and I wasn't sure exactly what he was telling me, but it was something about not mentioning my part in the accident. At the time I didn't care—all I thought about was Caroline and my injuries. Later on I heard he had taken complete blame for the accident. I tried to talk to him about it after I came home from the hospital, but he wouldn't listen. He said no matter what, the accident was his fault. He was the one driving. He also said I had suffered enough."

She paused, waiting for him to speak. His silence drove her to distraction. She wished she could see his face, because then she could gauge his reaction. Now she could do nothing except sit there, waiting for him to tell her what she already knew. She was a coward and a liar.

But he didn't say either of those things. "Is that all?"

She angled her head toward his voice, which sounded like it was coming from the far end of the porch. She nodded, shame robbing her of her voice.

"Why are you telling me this now?" He approached her, his footsteps harsh against the wooden porch floor. "Why tell me at all?"

"I should have told you a long time ago. I should have admitted it to everyone, instead of letting Isaiah shoulder the blame on his own. I even talked to him about it today, but he still insisted on keeping the secret."

"Does Sarah Lynne know?"

"*Nee*. Only Isaiah and me. And now you." She took a deep breath. "You should have been angry at me as well all these years, Chris. I'm sorry about that. I'm sorry I was too weak to speak the truth. It was easier to let Isaiah carry it all. But if you're going to forgive him . . . you'll have to forgive me too."

In the distance she heard the clip-clop of the horse's hooves. She also heard Chris walking away, stepping down from the porch. She wanted to call out to him, but she couldn't. She wouldn't blame him if he never talked to her again. The sound of a buggy and horse traveling over gravel reached her ears, and she knew Sarah Lynne or her parents were home. Standing up, she reached for her cane and made her way down the porch steps. The buggy pulled to a stop, and she heard someone get out.

"Chris!" Sarah Lynne said, her tone exuberant.

. . .

Sarah Lynne rushed over to her brother. It had to be a good sign that he was at the house, knowing their father usually came home at this time. But instead of looking happy, he seemed miserable. Then she spied Ellie standing a couple feet away, her shoulders drooping and her head dipped.

Her mother came up behind her. "Chris?" she asked, moving toward him. "Christopher, is something wrong?"

He glanced at Ellie, his dark eyes narrowing, then shifted his gaze to his family.

"I came to see if I can stay here tonight. I checked out of the bed-and-breakfast earlier today."

Sarah Lynne heard her mother suck in a breath. "Just for tonight?"

He looked at Ellie again. "Maybe."

Their father nodded, and Sarah Lynne's heart swelled. "Does this mean you're coming back for *gut*?"

He didn't answer right away, just glanced at the ground, his hands going deeper into his pockets.

Ellie spoke. "Sarah Lynne, could you give me a ride home?"

Sarah Lynne was about to suggest that Chris do it, but then he looked at her and shook his head.

"*Ya.* I can take you home."

"*Danki.*"

Chris turned around and walked into the house, not saying good-bye to Ellie. Bewildered, Sarah Lynne looked to her mother, who shrugged and followed Chris inside. Her father went behind the house, presumably to check on the cows. The tension in the air was almost suffocating. She went to Ellie and put her hand on her shoulder. "Ready to *geh*?"

Ellie nodded, straightening her shoulders and her posture. "Where's the buggy?"

Sarah Lynne told her, and she walked to the driveway and climbed inside. Sarah Lynne joined her, and soon they were on the way to Ellie's house. She was determined to find out what was going on with her friend and her brother.

. . .

Ellie was miserable. She knew Chris wasn't going to give her a ride home once he heard her news. She doubted he'd ever want to see her again. The thought filled her with sadness.

"Ellie, what happened with you and Chris?" Sarah Lynne asked, sounding as perplexed as Ellie felt. "I thought everything was settled already. Now it looks like he's not sure he's going to stay."

Ellie wasn't sure how to answer. Maybe she should just tell her the truth, as she had told Chris. But she saw what Chris's reaction was. Who knew how Sarah Lynne would react, knowing her fiancé had been less than truthful to everyone? She brought her fingertip to her temple. How did this all get so complicated?

"Are you all right?" Sarah Lynne asked. "You've gone pale, Ellie. Is it your ankle?"

"*Nee.*" She tried to keep her voice steady, but she failed. "I'm . . . fine."

"You don't look or sound fine." The buggy slowed. "Ellie, you have to tell me what happened. Did Chris do something?"

She let out a bitter chuckle. "He didn't do anything wrong. He's done everything right." If only she could say the same thing for herself.

"Then why are you both upset? Chris looked like someone kicked him, and you're on the verge of tears." Sarah Lynne took her hand. "I care about you both so much. I can't stand to see you unhappy like this."

"I'll be okay, and so will Chris." She remembered telling Chris how God worked out everything for good. She held on to those words, now more than ever before.

. . .

Chris stumbled into the dark bedroom, not bothering to turn on the small lamp on the nightstand. Instead he walked into the hallway and made his way to the kitchen, turning on the gas lamp in there. He glanced at the battery-operated clock on the wall. Two thirty in the morning. He had hoped it would be at least closer to dawn. He hadn't slept a minute the entire night. How could he, when all he could think about was Ellie?

He sat down at the kitchen table, slumping in the chair. Stark silence enveloped him. It had been so long since he'd spent the night in an Amish home, and the quiet unnerved him. But he'd get used to it again.

Hard to believe more than a few hours ago everything had been so simple, and coming back to the church had seemed so clear, so God-ordained, that he had felt better about himself than he had in years. But Ellie's news had been like a punch in the mouth. The accident had been her fault as much as Isaiah's? Her fault that Caroline was dead? And the man he had resented for the past five years, whom he had tried to put in jail, had been protecting Ellie all this time. How was he supposed to make sense of that?

Isaiah had been behind the wheel . . . but if Ellie hadn't panicked and distracted him, the wreck might not have happened at all. And she had lived with this secret for five years. Even when he returned, she had said nothing to him about it. What had made her change her mind? A part of him wished she had stayed quiet. It was easier to resent Isaiah than her.

And what of his feelings for her? He cared about her, had wanted to court her after he set things right with God and the church. Had those feelings changed? He couldn't tell, not when they were competing with the confusion in his heart and soul.

"Christopher?"

He looked over his shoulder to see his father walking

into the room, wearing his broadfall pants and a white T-shirt. Chris looked down at his own T-shirt and boxer shorts. He'd been so preoccupied that he hadn't thought not to wear shorts in the house. That would have to change too.

"Everything okay?" His father sat down next to him.

It was the most his *daed* had said to him since he'd come back to Paradise. Even during supper he had been quiet, excusing himself right after he finished eating to go outside and check on the animals. Chris had thought to go with him, but he didn't want to push it. He was lucky his father was allowing him to stay here, because technically he was still in the *bann*.

But his father had come to him on his own volition, concern shining in his dark brown eyes. Chris looked at him for a moment. Like his mother, his father had more gray in his hair and beard, more creases at the corners of his eyes and mouth. But the man was still built like a small bull, his thick chest and muscular arms a testament to his profession as a blacksmith and farrier. His hair was mussed from sleep, and his eyes looked tired.

"Sorry I woke you up," Chris said.

"It's all right. I saw the light come on from the bedroom and thought you might be up. How about some coffee?"

Chris nodded, marveling at how his father's demeanor had changed in such a short time. It was as if the past five years had never happened. He rose from the chair. "I'll make it."

His father gestured for him to sit down. "I got it. Still like it strong enough to paint the side of the barn?"

With a chuckle Chris said, "*Ya*. I do."

His father filled the percolator with water from the sink, put a couple of scoops coffee in the basket, then set it on the gas stove, putting the lid on top of the pot. He turned the stove on, and the hiss of gas filled the room. Then he came back and sat down.

"Your *mamm* says you're coming back to the church."

Chris frowned. He hadn't said anything for sure about it to anyone other than Ellie and Bishop Ebersol. "What makes her say that?"

He shrugged. "She said she just knew. Knew the day you showed up here that God had brought you home. You've been fighting Him the whole time, apparently."

"*Ya*. Been doing a lot of that lately."

"So is she right? Are you rejoining the church?"

Chris ran his thumb along the edge of the oak table. "It looks that way."

"Well, that doesn't sound exactly definite." His *daed* scooted his chair back and rose. As he got two mugs down from the cupboard, the percolator started bubbling. He poured them each a cup and carried them to the table.

Wrapping his hands around the warm mug, Chris sighed. "I'm pretty confused right now."

"I can tell. That's what happens when you've been away from the Lord. The devil takes hold and mixes everything up." *Daed* took a sip of his coffee and made a face. "*Ya*. You should like this."

But Chris pushed the mug away. "But that's just it, *Daed*. I haven't been straying from the Lord. Even when I was in Apple Creek I went to church. I prayed. Read my Bible. And when I came back here, I knew it was God's leading, so *Mamm* was right about that. Then I found out about Sarah Lynne and Isaiah—"

"And there went your best-laid plans."

"*Ya*. Still, I had come to a place where I could finally let the past lie." *Thanks to Ellie.* "And I was ready to come back. I even talked to Bishop Ebersol and stopped by the used-car dealership in Paradise to talk to them about selling my car."

"That's *gut* to hear, Chris. Sounds like you are where God wants you to be. So what's the problem?"

"I found out something today. Something I didn't know." He toyed with the idea of confiding in his father, but he couldn't bring himself to spill Ellie's secret.

"And it's affecting your decision to come back to the community?"

"*Nee*, not that." He looked at his father.

"Does this have something to do with Ellie Chupp? I saw her here earlier."

"You could say that."

"You have feelings for her, don't you?"

Was he that transparent? "*Ya*. I do. After Caroline died, I never even looked at another woman. I wasn't interested in dating. Then I spend a couple days with Ellie and everything's changed."

"That's the way it was for me and your mother. We grew up together, but one day when I was seventeen I saw her at a singing, and it was like I'd seen her for the first time. I was gone after that. But she wasn't as easy to convince."

"Ellie isn't either. And then she told me something today . . ." He looked at his *daed*. "I can't betray her confidence."

"I wouldn't want you to." He took another drink of coffee and set down the mug. "But let me tell you this— you can't come back to the church because of Ellie or anyone else. There has to be a change in your heart and a willingness to forget the past, as God calls us to do."

Now he sounded like Bishop Ebersol.

"Believe me, I know."

His father stood up and yawned. "Can't believe I'm still sleepy after drinking that stuff, but I'm heading back to bed. Pray about your confusion, Chris. And know that God is not the author of it. Follow His leading. Not anyone else's."

"*Danki, Daed.*"

After his father left for bed, Chris thought about his advice. He had been praying all along, but had he been praying for the right thing? He'd asked God to help him forgive, but not to change his heart. Would that be the answer? He didn't know, but there was one way to find out. He got out of his chair and knelt on the hardwood floor, praying harder than he'd ever prayed before.

CHAPTER FOURTEEN

On Sunday morning Ellie arrived thirty minutes early at the home of the Keims, who were hosting church. She hadn't had a choice about the early arrival, as her mother always liked to be punctual. She greeted everyone, then took her seat on the outside bench and folded her cane.

The Keims didn't have enough room in their house to hold church inside, so they held it in their barn, the benches lined up in neat rows in the center. Ellie listened to the commotion around her, the low sounds of murmuring as people said hello and found their seats. She breathed in the scent of fresh hay and horses, knowing the Keim family would have spent hours making sure the barn was in pristine condition to hold church.

Normally Ellie was serene at the beginning of services, but this morning she was far from it. She couldn't stop twisting the hem of her apron. She hadn't spoken to Chris or Sarah Lynne since Friday. Which wasn't a surprise, since she'd kept to herself all day yesterday, not leaving the house under the ruse that her ankle still ached.

Her mother was pleased. "It's about time you listened to me about that ankle."

But Ellie didn't reveal the real reason she didn't want to leave the comfort of home, or why she was so quiet her father asked her what was wrong at least three times. Each time Ellie had told him everything was fine. How she wished that was so.

She fiddled with her hem some more, then stopped before her mother sat next to her and admonished her. Instead she clasped her hands tightly together, wondering if Chris would come to church today. She had thought about him all day yesterday, when her guilt over keeping her secret kept her mind in turmoil. She prayed that revealing her secret hadn't made him change his mind about the church. But then again, if he had, he wasn't coming back for the right reasons. Regardless of her feelings for him, she wanted him to reconcile with God and find peace on his own terms, not because of anything she said or did.

Her mother came and sat down beside her. It was her habit right before the service to spend the last few minutes in prayer, preparing her heart and mind. Ellie would do well to follow her example. She closed her eyes.

Heavenly Father, whatever happens today, please be with Chris. Show him the only true way to peace is to follow You, to surrender to You completely.

Before long the service began, and Ellie tried not to think about Chris, keeping her mind focused on Christ. After the congregation spent twenty minutes singing hymns, one of the ministers gave a short sermon on forgiveness, mentioning James 5:16. *"Confess your faults to one another, and pray one for another, that ye may be healed."* God's words spoke to Ellie's heart, causing a tiny spark to light within.

When the sermon ended, the congregation remained quiet, save a few murmurs from young children who were fidgeting in their seats. Ellie felt more relaxed than she had in days. She waited for the next part of the service to start. She recognized the familiar sound of Bishop Ebersol clearing his throat.

"Christopher Miller. Are you ready to confess your sin to God and the church?"

Ellie sucked in a breath as she heard Chris answer from the opposite side of the room.

"Ya."

He sounded penitent yet confident. The bishop asked him a few more questions, with Chris answering them all, including apologizing to Isaiah for trying to have him thrown in jail.

"Christopher, the past is in the past. It is forgotten, never to be brought up again."

Tears welled up in Ellie's eyes. He had come back to church. It had taken a great deal of courage to do what he had done. More courage than she had. Because while Chris had opened up his heart to forgiveness, she still kept her secret. Yet she wasn't sure if she could keep it any longer.

. . .

The first hour after the service was a whirlwind for Chris. He had gone from being ignored by almost everyone to being welcomed back to the community with open arms, literally. Friends he hadn't seen or talked to for five years told him how glad they were to see him and how they'd have to get together soon. His uncle even offered him a job at his blacksmith shop, and he'd been invited to two singings during the next couple of weeks. It amazed him how the words Bishop Ebersol had said after Chris's confession were so true. They would never bring up the past again.

But he had some unfinished business to take care of before he could settle the matter completely. Once he had a break from talking with everyone, he left the barn and headed for the Keim house, where he expected to find Ellie helping the women get lunch prepared. He searched for her in almost every room. He even approached her mother, who was suddenly as friendly as a golden retriever.

"She was in the living room last time I saw her." *Frau* Chupp put a plate of sandwiches out on the kitchen table. "She wanted to help in here, but I had to tell her *nee*." She lowered her voice. "Look how tiny this kitchen is. I didn't want her to trip or fall over anything. One injury a week is enough." She suddenly rubbed her hands together. "Let me know when you find her. I don't approve when she takes off on her own like this."

Chris held in his irritation. Ellie could take care of herself, and hopefully one day her mother would realize it. He smiled politely, leaving *Frau* Chupp to bustle around the "tiny kitchen," which to him seemed a good size. He went outside to the backyard but didn't see her right away. Where could she be? Had she left? He hoped not, but she had seemed so unnerved when he saw her during the service, maybe she had decided to go home.

A crisp breeze kicked up, slicing through his white dress shirt and pressing against the brim of his black hat. He glanced down at the black pants and vest he wore. His Sunday best. He'd found the clothes hanging in his closet, just as he'd left them five years ago. The trousers were a little loose at the waist, but between his mother's cooking and plenty of Ellie's homemade jelly, they would soon fit right.

He continued to look for her and had just about given up when he saw her walking along the pasture fence on the other side of the Keims' barn. He jogged to her, stopping short a few steps behind so as not to startle her. But she must have heard him anyway, because she halted her steps and turned around.

"Congratulations," she said, facing him but not looking directly at him. For some reason he thought that was on purpose. A smile formed on her face, but it was halfhearted. Even he could tell that.

"Can we talk, Ellie?"

She paused for a moment, then nodded.

He glanced around. They were pretty secluded behind the barn, although he could hear the sound of some of the kids playing a game of tag in the back-yard. "I wanted to thank you again. If it weren't for you, Ellie, I wouldn't be standing here, welcomed back by my *familye* and friends."

She shook her head, her smile disappearing. "Please," she said, her voice sounding thick. "Don't say that."

. . .

Ellie gripped her white cane, trying to keep a tight rein on her emotions, but failing. Her fingers went numb and she relaxed them, but only a little. She couldn't believe he was standing here thanking her. He should be angry with her for holding back the truth. Just as she was angry with herself.

"Ellie, it's true." She heard him move closer to her, as he tended to do when he talked to her. "You showed me how I could move on—"

"I lied to you." She couldn't keep the words inside any longer. "I lied to you and everyone else. I let Isaiah suffer for what I did."

"*Nee*, listen to me—"

"Don't try to make me feel better. It won't work." She released the cane and wiped her finger under her eye. "I still have nightmares sometimes. They're so vivid and clear, it's like I'm reliving the accident. Over and over." She hung her head. "I suppose that's what I deserve."

His hands suddenly covered her shoulders, and she jerked. "Are you done?"

She sniffed, nodding.

"*Gut*, because I see I need to set you straight on a few things. For one, you didn't lie to me."

"I did—"

His fingertip covered her mouth, sending a shiver through her spine. She froze. "If I have to," he said, his voice husky, "I'll make you stay quiet."

She didn't say anything else. How could she? He had taken not only her voice away but also her breath and heartbeat with just one simple gesture.

He removed his finger. "Ellie, I understand why Isaiah did what he did. I probably would have done the same thing to protect you. You admitting your secret finally showed me that I'd been unfair to him all along. But I should have realized that when I came back. My *schwester* wouldn't have picked a lesser *mann* to marry. She tried to tell me that. You did too. I was too thick-headed to accept it, not to mention I needed him to take the brunt of my anger. Because I couldn't blame the person I was really angry with."

"Who?"

"Caroline." He took a step back. "I'll admit, I was shocked when you told me the real story of what happened. I'd been told Isaiah had begged you all to ride with him, and that you and Caroline hadn't actually wanted to. But when I learned that Caroline was the one to suggest it . . . I didn't want to believe it at first. Then I had to, because she would do something like that. She was free-spirited, always willing to walk on the edge of danger."

Ellie nodded, remembering her friend's penchant for excitement. "Like the time she tried to get me to skate with her on the thin ice in the middle of her cousin's pond."

"Or when we were *kinner* and she dared me to jump off the roof of her *haus* onto the trampoline underneath it."

"I hope you had the *gut* sense to tell her *nee!*"

"Um, not exactly. What self-respecting ten-year-old would refuse a dare from a *maedel*?"

Ellie laughed, the tension draining out of her. She hadn't remi-nisced about Caroline this way for a long time. "Since you put it that way, you're right."

He chuckled, but it quickly faded. "When you told me about the accident, everything changed. I couldn't go on being angry at Isaiah. And I couldn't be angry at you." His fingertips skimmed across her cheek. "God showed me that."

She flinched at his unexpected gesture. His touch had been fleeting, and blissful. "I deserve your anger, Chris."

"*Nee.* The last thing you deserve is that. But even knowing the truth, I still had this pain inside me— there was something I couldn't let *geh*. I realized I was angry with Caroline."

"And now?"

"Did you hear what Bishop Ebersol said? The past is in the past. And for me, finally, it truly is."

Ellie smiled, her heart swelling with joy. There was a peace in Chris's tone, one she had never heard before. Yet despite her happiness for him, there was a sliver of guilt still burrowing its way through her.

"I know what you're thinking," he suddenly said.

"So now *you* have a sixth sense?"

"When it comes to you, *ya*, I do. You want to confess your part in the accident."

She nodded. "Isn't that the right thing to do?"

He took her hand and squeezed it. "It is. But you don't have to do it alone."

Ellie couldn't keep the tears from falling. She always thought she'd be alone. She had accepted it. Even fought for it at times. But now she didn't have to be.

. . .

"Are you ready to *geh* home?"

Sarah Lynne looked at Isaiah and smiled. Church had ended awhile ago, and she was still happy from seeing her brother reconciled with the community. Once the service was over, a burden had seemed to lift from Isaiah too. He was grinning as he led her to the buggy, and all she could think about was how happy she was that things finally were the way they should be. Their wedding was in less than two weeks, and her brother would be there. Her family was finally intact. *Thank You, Lord.*

But as she started to get into the buggy, she heard Ellie call out her name. She turned around to see Ellie and Chris approaching from behind the barn. She couldn't help but smile as she saw how her brother led her friend to the buggy. He'd not only come back to the church but possibly found love again. She couldn't think of anyone better for Chris than Ellie.

Yet as they neared, she could see something was wrong. Redness rimmed Ellie's eyes, and Chris's mouth was set in a grim, straight line. She stepped away from the buggy and walked toward them. "Ellie? Is something wrong?"

Isaiah appeared at Sarah Lynne's side. The two couples stood across from each other. She glanced at

Isaiah, whose happy expression had melted into wariness. But instead of directing his gaze to Chris, he was looking at Ellie.

"I need to talk to you, Sarah Lynne," Ellie said. She moved a little closer to Chris. "There's something you need to know."

"Ellie, don't." Isaiah stepped toward her.

Ellie's brows lifted as she turned to Isaiah, as if she were surprised he was here. "*Nee*, Isaiah. We can't keep this a secret anymore. Chris already knows."

Isaiah looked at Chris, who nodded.

"What secret?" Sarah Lynne's gaze darted from Isaiah to her brother.

"Ellie, you don't have to do this."

She stepped toward him. "Isaiah, I do. I should have told everyone a long time ago. You know that."

"But you don't have to tell everyone."

"Tell everyone what?" Frustration bubbled to the surface. "Will someone tell me what's going on?"

Ellie turned to Sarah Lynne. "The accident wasn't just Isaiah's fault. I'm to blame too."

Sarah Lynne listened as Ellie revealed how she caused the car crash. When Ellie finished, Sarah Lynne looked at Isaiah. He cast his gaze downward, and she knew Ellie was telling the truth. "Why didn't you say anything about this before?" she asked him.

"Don't be angry with Isaiah." Ellie groped for Sarah Lynne's arm. When she found it, she squeezed. "He was only protecting me."

"I'm not . . . angry." Hurt welled in her chest. "I don't understand. Why didn't you tell me?" She looked at

Isaiah. "Why didn't either of you trust me enough to tell me the truth?"

"We didn't tell anyone."

"But I'm going to be your wife!" She faced Christopher. "When did you find out?"

"The other day. When I came to the *haus* to stay." He moved closer to Ellie. "You and Isaiah need to talk."

"I'm sorry," Ellie said, her eyes shining with tears. "I really am."

When Chris and Ellie left, Sarah Lynne turned her back on Isaiah. He had lied to her, to everyone. And so had Ellie. She felt Isaiah touch her shoulder, but she stepped away. "Take me home, Isaiah."

They climbed into the buggy and didn't say anything for a long while as he drove to her house. Finally Isaiah spoke. "Don't blame Ellie for this. She was just doing what I asked her to."

She glanced at him. "So the accident wasn't her fault?"

He gripped the reins with both hands. "I was driving the car."

"But she distracted you."

"Not on purpose." He let out a long breath. "I did what I thought was right at the time. But now . . ." His shoulders slumped. "I don't know anymore."

Sarah Lynne moved closer to Isaiah and touched his arm. "I understand."

He looked at her. "You do?"

She nodded. "But I'm glad Ellie said something. I don't want any secrets between us, Isaiah."

He grinned. "There won't be. That was the only one."

Returning his smile, she leaned back in the seat. Now everything was truly right.

. . .

Two weeks later Ellie sat in the swing on Christopher's porch, breathing out a sigh of contentment. Isaiah and Sarah Lynne were married, and the gathering afterward was winding down. Her desserts had been a success, especially the cream cheese brownies. Her father had been right about bringing them.

"Mind if I join you?"

She smiled at the sound of Chris's voice and nodded. He sat down, making the swing propel forward.

"Great wedding," Chris said.

The swing continued to move back and forth.

"*Ya.*"

"You know what I'm going to ask you next."

Her shoulders tensed. "I do."

"And you know I'll keep asking until you say yes."

She turned toward him. He had been asking her to go out with him since that Sunday he had made his confession, and she had put him off. They were close friends, there was no denying that, just as there was no denying she wanted more. But she couldn't let it happen.

"Chris, there are plenty of other *maed* that are more—"

"Suitable, I know." He scooted a little closer to her. "What I don't understand is why you refuse to realize that you're the one suited for me."

She shook her head. "It's complicated."

"*Nee*, it's not. Ellie, I get it. You're worried I'm going to leave you like John did. I'm not like him."

And he wasn't. He had proved that over and over.

"But what if you find out you can't handle my being blind?"

"If you can handle it, which you do, then I can handle it too." He touched her chin, turning it toward him. "I care for you, Ellie Chupp. More than I ever cared for anyone in my life. I want us to go together, and not just on one or two dates. I'm talking about a lot of dates. But I don't want you to feel you have to compete with Caroline's memory."

"I don't feel that way."

"And I don't want to compete with John's. You once told me I'd have to let *geh* of Caroline to move on." He dropped his hand. "Can you let *geh* of John and move on with me?"

His question made her pause. She had gotten over John a long time ago. That wasn't what she had to release.

"I'm afraid," she said in a small voice.

"It's okay, Ellie." He kissed her cheek. "Whatever you're afraid of, I promise, we'll face it together. As long as you promise me one thing."

"What?"

"That someday, maybe even when we're old and gray, you'll make me some kumquat jelly."

She laughed and leaned against him, suddenly knowing that Chris meant everything he said. God had changed his heart . . . and through him, God was healing hers.

HEALING HEARTS

BETH WISEMAN

CHAPTER ONE

Levina Lapp peered through her kitchen window, past the red begonias on the sill, across the plush green grass that tickled her toes earlier in the day, to the end of her driveway. Her husband of thirty-one years stepped out of a yellow taxi, closed the door, and headed up the driveway toward his home. A home he hadn't stepped foot in for almost a year.

As Naaman approached, toting the same dingy red suitcase he'd left with last summer, he walked with a limp. Levina knew from his last letter that he'd injured himself during a barn raising while he was visiting cousins in Ohio. He'd downplayed his ten-foot fall, but Levina knew her husband well enough to recognize the pain in his expression as he eased his way up the concrete drive, taking each step slowly and deliberately.

"I'm going to visit Levi," he'd said eleven months ago. But they both knew that his trip was more than a visit. It was a re-evaluation of their lives. At least for Naaman it was. Levina was an unwilling participant in his venture, with little more than a brief consultation before he abandoned their marriage in pursuit of . . . what? She had no idea.

When the youngest of their five children married, she and Naaman were left alone. "Empty nesters," as the *Englisch* called it. It took a grand total of nine weeks before the silent life they led lured Naaman out the door and away from Lancaster County—away from their home and everything they'd ever known.

Now he was back, heading up the driveway, after asking if he could come home and work to heal their marriage.

Lavina smoothed the wrinkles from her dark blue dress and tried to calm her rapid heartbeat as Naaman struggled up the porch steps. She pulled the door open just as he was about to knock, which seemed strange yet respectful.

"Hello, Naaman." Levina held the door wide so he could enter. He was barely over the threshold when he set his suitcase down and pulled her into a hug.

"I've missed you." Naaman clung to her tightly, but Levina eased away and forced a smile.

Her husband looked exactly the same as he always had. Levina wondered how that could be, since she'd examined herself in the mirror just this morning and studied the tiny lines that feathered from the corners of her eyes—evidence that she'd recently celebrated her forty-ninth birthday. Her brown hair had more streaks of gray these days as well.

Naaman's beard was longer than it used to be, but he didn't have a speck of gray in his dark hair or in his beard. His face was weathered by sun and hard work, but the tiny age lines about his mouth and eyes seemed the same as when he'd left.

"I made lunch. Nothing fancy. I'm afraid I haven't cooked much lately." She stepped away from him. "I've been eating at Yoder's Pantry, since cooking for one just—" She shrugged, hearing self-pity in her comment. "Anyway, I made some chicken salad, and everything is on the table." Levina motioned toward the bowl of chicken salad, bread, pickled red beets, and snitz pie in the middle of the table.

"It looks *gut*, Levina." Naaman smiled as he eyed the offerings, and Levina took time to inspect him further.

His shoes looked new, but the clothes he wore could have been the same ones he'd left in—black trousers, a dark blue shirt, suspenders, straw hat. Of course, he still towered over her, but his shoulders looked broader. Or maybe they just seemed that way.

"Sit down. I'll pour you some meadow tea." Levina moved toward the refrigerator as Naaman took his seat at the head of the wooden table. She glanced over her shoulder to see him wipe sweat from his forehead. It was unseasonably hot for May.

"*Danki,*" he said when she placed the glass of iced tea in front of him.

She slid onto one of the backless benches to Naaman's right. They bowed their heads in silent prayer, then she waited until he made his sandwich before she scooped chicken salad onto a slice of bread.

"You've lost weight," he said after swallowing his first bite.

"Maybe a little." She took a bite of her sandwich and thought about all the laborious tasks she'd done around the farm since Naaman had left. Even with the children coming over to help, she had done much more physical labor than she was used to. It was no wonder she'd lost weight.

"Things will be easier on you now."

Naaman spoke without looking at her, but Levina heard the regret in his tone.

"Your trip from Ohio was *gut*, no?" Levina picked at her red beets with her fork and hoped the small-talk phase of Naaman's return wouldn't last long.

"*Ya*. It was a long bus ride, but uneventful." He looked up and smiled. "I'm just glad to be home." Naaman made himself another sandwich. "Mary couldn't make chicken salad like you do."

Levina forced another smile. He obviously intended the comment as a compliment. She fought the urge to scream, *Well, you wouldn't have been eating Levi's* frau's *cooking if you hadn't deserted your family here!*

Naaman ate a hearty helping of everything on the table, including two large slices of snitz pie. When he was done, he stood from the table and picked up his suitcase. "Guess I'll go unpack?" He waited, brows raised.

Levina nodded an acknowledgment and watched him walk across the den toward their bedroom. She started picking up the plates from the table and turned on the water in the sink. She ran her hand under the cool flow, waiting for it to get hot, then changed her mind and turned the faucet off. She made her way across the den.

When she reached the bedroom, Naaman had already opened his suitcase and was putting his clothes in the dresser. She stiffened as a strange sense of intrusion engulfed her.

He pressed his undergarments into the second drawer, where they'd always been, and turned to face her. "Everything looks different in here." He glanced around the room, clearly noticing the new quilt on the bed, rug on the floor, and a vase full of freshly cut flowers. She'd never put flowers in their bedroom before.

"*Ya.* I spruced it up a bit." Levina bit her bottom lip and wondered if she should tell Naaman about the other things that had changed while he was gone. She should probably warn him before tomorrow when the children would arrive for a visit, but his presence at home and in their bedroom—was enough to conquer for today. Tomorrow's problems would arrive soon enough.

· · ·

Levina headed back to the kitchen, and Naaman finished unpacking his suitcase. He planned to spend the rest of his life making things up to his wife. *What kind of man abandons his family for almost a year?*

He sat down on the bed and ran his hand along the green ivy tendrils that connected tiny blue and yellow flowers. Naaman wondered how long ago Levina had swapped the old quilt for the new one. Did the new quilt represent a new beginning for his homecoming, or had she replaced it the minute he left, representing a new beginning for herself?

Not a fair thought, he knew. Levina was never included in the decision-making when he left for Ohio.

He pulled off his hat and ran a hand through his hair, then gave a heavy sigh. Faith and prayer had taught him not to shoulder the burdens of the past, but his choice to leave his wife and home had been a mistake. Once he'd been gone for a while and realized the bad choice he'd made, he hadn't known how to get back home where he belonged.

Yet here he was. In his home, in his bedroom, with his wife cleaning the dinner dishes on the other side of the house as if nothing had changed.

But Naaman knew that everything had changed, and despite Levina's politeness, he could see resentment in her eyes, feel it in her touch, even hear it in her voice. He was here in person, but the road back to his wife had yet to be traveled.

Tomorrow he would see his children for the first time in eleven months. He'd written all five of them, and he knew which ones were less than accepting about his return—his two oldest children, Rosemary and Adam. Rosemary's third child was born while Naaman was away, and she'd let him know how she felt about that. And Adam had actually said he thought Naaman should be shunned for what he'd done.

He and Levina had raised their children in accordance with the *Ordnung*, so Adam was right to have that opinion, but even the bishop, who had written Naaman several times, had held out hope that Naaman would come home prior to such a drastic action.

Somehow he would find a way to make things right again.

. . .

Levina dressed for bed in the bathroom. Naaman had bathed first, after working in the barn all afternoon, and he was lying in their bed reading the Bible. Levina ran a brush through her hair. Although it was streaked with gray, she was pleased that it was still full and silky like it was in her youth.

She recalled the first time Naaman saw her with her hair to her waist and without her *kapp* on—their wedding night. Tonight some of those same anxious feelings swept through her, a combination of longing and fear. It was different, though. Thirty-one years ago she was an eighteen-year-old girl who feared the unknown and hoped to please her husband. Now her fear was that she would never trust him the way she once had.

"Levina, are you all right in there?"

She stopped brushing and sighed. "*Ya*, I'm fine." She began applying lotion to her hands, eyed her toothbrush, and realized that she didn't need to brush her teeth a second time. There was nothing left to do except go to bed. She couldn't stall forever.

Naaman closed the Bible when she walked in. He sat taller in the bed, already tucked beneath the covers. Only the lantern on his bedside table was illuminated, but she could see his features clearly. His extraordinary blue eyes brimmed with tenderness and passion as they roamed the length of her body, a muscle quivering at his jaw.

Levina thought about all the times she'd dreamed of this moment, when Naaman would come home and love her the way a husband loves his wife. She ran her hands down the sides of her white gown, then she looked toward the wooden floor. She took a deep breath and looked back up at him.

"*Mei lieb* . . . you look as beautiful as the day I married you."

Levina wanted to run to him, but her lack of trust and confusion melded together and she just stood there. How could he come back into her life after all this time and act as if nothing had changed? She'd slept alone for almost a year, wondering if she would spend the rest of her life without her husband by her side. Now here he was, all tucked in and waiting for her to resume their life together as husband and wife.

She took a slow pensive step backward, then two more, as the hopeful light in Naaman's eyes began to fade.

CHAPTER TWO

Levina blinked her eyes a few times before she realized that she was in Tillie's old room. She rolled onto her side and pulled the pink and white quilt up around her neck. Day was breaking, and tiny rays of sunlight shone through the window and onto the foot of the bed. Outside, the rooster crowed good morning and the far-off moo of a cow reminded her that she needed to get up and milk. Then she remembered that Naaman was home to handle that chore.

She threw back the covers, then sat on the edge of the bed and rubbed the sleep from her eyes as she recalled how long she'd lain in bed last night before sleep finally won out. Today would be a hard day for all of them, but Levina quickly set to praying that it would be a blessed day filled with forgiveness.

Please, Lord, help the children to see their father for the truly wonderful man he is and not just for his actions this past year. Help them to remember that all things are of Your will, even if we don't always understand Your plan for us at the time. May You bless this day with Your grace and be with us during these trying times.

Levina knew that she needed to heed this prayer as

well, to remember the many years Naaman had been a wonderful husband and doting father to their children. She stood up and walked to the closed door of Tillie's room, then slowly pulled it open. She was surprised to smell bacon. Thirty-one years of marriage, and she'd never known Naaman to cook breakfast. She wasn't even sure he knew how.

She scurried across the hall and eased the door open. The room was empty, the bed made. Levina breathed a sigh of relief as she walked to the row of pegs on the wall. She pulled down a dark green dress and quickly slipped out of her nightgown, glancing twice over her shoulder as she did so. It wasn't until she turned back around that she saw a piece of paper on the middle of the bed.

Slowly she eased toward the note and picked it up, then she squinted as she tried to focus. After finding her reading glasses on the nightstand, she read:

Mei dearest Levina,

I love you more today than I did yesterday, and less than I will tomorrow.

Your loving husband,
Naaman

Levina pushed her glasses up on her nose and read the note again, recalling how Naaman always used to tell her that. She pressed the note to her chest and tried to remember the last time he had said those words.

Her pulse quickened as she crept across the den and into the kitchen, expecting to find him preparing breakfast—or trying to—but the room was empty. However, the table was set and a serving plate of bacon, scrambled eggs, and toast awaited her. He'd set the rhubarb jelly right next to her plate, knowing it was her favorite. In the middle of the table was a glass vase filled with tiger lilies from their flower bed.

She walked to the window and saw Naaman walking into the barn, then she turned back to face the table. She sat down and filled her plate with bacon that was burnt to a crisp, overcooked eggs, and toast that was blackened on both sides. She'd sneak the leftovers to their Irish setter, Hitch, when she was done.

She picked up a piece of bacon with her fingers. As she bit into it, most of it crumbled in her hand, but she thought about what a lovely gesture this breakfast was. She took a few more bites, just to get her through until lunch, then scraped the rest onto a paper plate for Hitch.

After the dog enjoyed the leftovers and the kitchen was clean, Levina headed to the barn. Orange met with the green fields in the distance as the sun climbed upward, and fresh dew slipped between her toes as she strolled across the grass. She pulled the door open and saw that Naaman had just finished milking the cows. Her garden clogs were just inside the barn door, so she eased her feet into the shoes and took a couple of slow steps toward him.

"Where's Lou-Lou?" He looked up at her as he wiped his hands on his breeches.

Levina walked closer then sighed. "She died last month. I reckon I don't know what happened." Levina recalled the day she found the old cow on her side. "Maybe old age?"

"Remember when we named her?"

Levina smiled. "*Ya*. It was Tillie who called her that when she was young, and it just stuck."

They were quiet for a few moments, then Naaman walked to his workbench and ran a hand gingerly along the top. "I've missed building furniture."

"*Danki* for breakfast, Naaman. And for the flowers—and the note." She bit her lip for a moment, not wanting to hurt his feelings. "But you didn't have to make breakfast. You know I've always done that."

Naaman hung his head, then looked back up. "It was terrible."

"*Nee, nee* . . . it's not that. I just always—"

He chuckled. "No, Levina. It was awful. I ate as much as I could, and I reckon I hated to even set the table for you, but I thought you might eat a little."

Levina brought her hand to her mouth.

"I see you laughing." He pointed a playful finger at her.

"You never could cook, Naaman." She looked away. "But it was a very nice thing to do."

Naaman walked closer, until he was right in front of her. "I'm going to make things up to you, Levina, if it's the last thing I do."

"If you cook for us, it might *be* the last thing you do." She folded her arms across her chest but grinned.

Naaman got a look in his eye that she remembered from times past, a twinkle that always came before he said something very sweet. "I *will* make it up to you."

She inched one eyebrow upward. "See to it that you do." Then she spun around and walked out of the barn.

. . .

Naaman watched her walk to the house. If he didn't know better, he'd think she was the same spunky, playful woman he'd married over three decades ago. He couldn't recall the last time they'd joked like that, or done much of anything that didn't revolve around hard work and the children. Even though their lives had always included prayer, strong faith, and fellowship, the intimacy between husband and wife had eluded them for a long time.

Naaman thought about his time in Ohio. There'd been no pressure to do much of anything. He'd helped his cousin Levi with chores around the farm, but there was no worry about pleasing anyone else, and he had lots of time to himself.

Levi and Mary had two sons still living at home, both in their *rumschpringe*. The couple were going through some of the same things Naaman and Levina had experienced when their children were going through their running-around period. Levi was particularly perturbed when sixteen-year-old Ben sneaked into the house late one night, smelling of beer.

Naaman recalled a night like that with Adam. But once all of their *kinner* were out of the house, there was no one to focus on. Only Levina. And he didn't know her anymore.

He spent the rest of the morning working in the

barn, clearing the cobwebs from his workbench and reorganizing his tools and supplies. Not much was out of order, but it felt good to shuffle around among his own things. Levina brought a ham and cheese sandwich out to the barn when he didn't come in for dinner, but she didn't stay. In the afternoon, he repaired a section of fence between the house and the west field.

It was midafternoon when he crossed the yard and headed toward the house. He noticed that there was a fresh coat of white paint on the hundred-year-old structure. He wondered which one of his sons had painted the house while he was away—or had they worked together? There were also two new rocking chairs on the front porch and a variety of potted plants that weren't there when he left last summer. He eased his way up the porch steps then into the house. He could hear Levina humming in the kitchen, something he never remembered hearing her do before.

She jumped when he walked into the kitchen. "*Ach*, I didn't hear you come in." She went back to chopping potatoes.

Naaman ran his hand the length of his beard and watched her, although the humming had stopped. "I missed you in our bed last night."

Levina stopped chopping, but she kept her back to him as she spoke. "Did you miss me in your bed for the past eleven months?"

Ouch. "*Ya*, I did." It was the truth. He hadn't slept well while he was away. Nearly every night he'd reached across the bed to drape an arm across Levina, but always awoke to an empty bed to match his empty heart.

Neither of them spoke for a few minutes.

Naaman sat down at the kitchen table. "When will all the *kinner* be here?"

"Around five. In time for supper."

He glanced at the clock on the kitchen wall. Three thirty. "I reckon I'll go bathe before they arrive." He paused when she didn't say anything. "I'm really lookin' forward to seeing everyone, especially Rosemary's new little one." His heart hurt as he thought about his grandchild being born in his absence. He mentally calculated—Adam had four children, Jonathan had three, and Rosemary had given birth to . . . his tenth grandchild—a baby girl they'd named Leah. Soon his two youngest daughters, Freda and Tillie, would be adding to that number, he reckoned. "It will be *gut* for us all to be together," he added as he stood up from the table.

"I laid out some fresh towels for you, ones that came off the line today." Levina poured the chopped potatoes from the cutting board into a pot on the stove.

"*Danki.*"

Levina knew how much he liked towels fresh from the line. It was a nice gesture for her to put some out for him. But not un-common, he realized, wondering if he'd made a point to thank her in the past.

. . .

Levina added water to the pot of potatoes, lit the gas burner, then checked on the pot roast in the oven.

She turned around, leaned against the counter, and

sighed. Perhaps she should have told Naaman that they wouldn't *all* be together today. Levina had pleaded with Adam, but he wouldn't budge.

"He is not *mei daed*," Adam had said firmly.

When Levina tried to remind her son about forgiveness, Adam said his father should have thought about his actions before he abandoned his family. "I have shunned him."

"You can't make that decision, Adam," she'd told him. "That is for the bishop and elders to decide."

But Adam had refused to listen.

CHAPTER THREE

Rosemary waited for Glenn to bring the buggy to a stop in front of her brother's house.

"I just want to try one more time to talk Adam into coming." She glanced over her shoulder to check on Leah in the infant carrier and Sarah and Marie on either side of the baby. "I'll be right back."

Adam met her on the front porch. "Save your breath, Rosemary." He folded his arms across his chest and scowled. "I'm not going."

"Adam, are you sure?"

Her brother dropped his hands to his sides. "I don't want to be around him." He paused, then refolded his arms. "What about you? I thought you weren't going to speak to *Daed*. What happened to that?"

Rosemary sighed. "I know, I know." She pressed her lips together for a moment. "I'm still angry at him, Adam. But he's our father, and—and I guess I am also doing this for *Mamm*." She pointed a finger at him. "And for our *kinner*. They have a right to have a relationship with their *daadi*."

"My *kinner* will be just fine without him in their

lives. He should've thought about everything he could lose when he abandoned his family."

"What does Hannah think about this?"

"*Mei frau* will support my decision." Adam gave a taut jerk of his head.

"What about forgiveness, Adam?"

Adams's eyes widened. "Have *you* forgiven him, Rosemary?"

She tucked her chin. "I'm trying."

"He wasn't even here for little Leah's birth."

Rosemary faced off with her brother. "Okay, Adam. I can see this is going nowhere. I just wanted to try one more time." She turned her back and headed down the porch steps.

"Rosemary?"

She spun around. "*Ya?*"

"Tell *Mamm* I'm sorry."

Rosemary stared at her brother for a moment. "I will."

As she headed back to her family, Rosemary's heart was filled with conflicting emotions. Naaman Lapp was their father, and he'd always been a good one until a year ago. She'd always respected him more than any other man in the world—now she struggled to understand him and hoped she could hold her tongue today.

. . .

Naaman walked into the kitchen wearing his black Sunday vest over a burgundy-colored shirt Levina had never seen before. Levina didn't think he'd ever looked more handsome, but she could tell by the way the muscle in his jaw was working that he was nervous.

"You look very nice." She placed a tray of pickles on the table. "The *kinner* should be here any minute." She took a deep breath then sighed. "Naaman . . ."

He walked closer, raised a brow.

"Adam won't be here today." She bit her bottom lip. "Nor will Hannah and the children." She held her breath and waited for his response.

Naaman swallowed hard. "I guess it will take time for Adam to forgive me."

"I think so." Levina forced a smile, then turned to stir her green beans on the stove.

"What about you, Levina? Have you forgiven me?"

She turned to face him, and for a brief instant she almost went to him. His forlorn expression begged for a hug. "*Ya*, Naaman. I forgave you a long time ago."

"Because our faith requires it?" He hung his head slightly for a moment, then fearfully looked up at her.

Levina thought about easing his suffering, but she didn't want to lie. "*Ya*," she said softly. She took a deep breath, then went back to setting the table. A few moments later she heard the clippity-clop of hooves coming up the driveway.

Naaman walked to the window. "It looks like Freda and Jake." He paused, leaning his face closer to the glass. "And I think that's Tillie and Rufus behind them."

"You will be surprised when you see Tillie. Since she's been married, she's lost a lot of weight." Levina put a pitcher of iced tea in the middle of the table, then she brushed back a loose strand of hair that had fallen forward. "Tillie always loved to garden, and now that she has her own garden to tend to, along with her own house to take care of, she has trimmed up."

"I always thought she was perfect the way she was." Naaman turned briefly toward Levina and smiled.

"Tillie has always been a beautiful girl, but that extra weight she was carrying wasn't good for her. She'll have an easier pregnancy when the time comes, and that has nothing to do with vanity or pride."

Their youngest daughter had been the only one of their children to struggle with extra pounds, and Levina could tell that Tillie felt better about herself since she'd lost some weight. She walked toward the door when she heard footsteps on the porch. Naaman was quickly at her side, and her husband took a deep breath before he pulled the door open.

"Hello, *Daed*." Freda leaned forward and gave her father a hug.

Levina breathed a sigh of relief. To her surprise, Naaman eased away from Freda and embraced Jake in a hug as well.

Tillie came bouncing in behind her sister and brother-in-law and practically jumped into Naaman's arms. *"Daed!"* Her eyes filled with tears. "I missed you." She squeezed Naaman even tighter around the neck.

For Tillie, forgiveness had always come easily.

"You're squeezing him to death." Tillie's husband, Rufus, tapped his wife on the shoulder, and Tillie let go of her father so Rufus could shake his hand—but Naaman also pulled Rufus into a hug.

Levina tried to rest easier, knowing that two of her five children were accepting of and grateful for their father's return. She could see through the opened screen door that Rosemary was coming across the yard toting baby Leah. Glenn trailed behind her with their eight-year-old twins, Sarah and Marie.

"Hello, *Daed.*" Rosemary's smile was bleak and tight-lipped. Her arms were full, carrying Leah and the diaper bag, and Levina instantly wondered if she had planned it that way. Her husband's hands were free.

"So this is little Leah." Naaman leaned down and eyed his newest granddaughter. "Four months old, no?"

Rosemary cut her eyes toward Levina, then looked back at Naaman. "*Ya.*" She moved away from her father, even though he was still leaning down and looking at Leah, and kissed Levina on the cheek. "Where's Jonathan?"

"He's not here yet." Levina nudged Rosemary toward the den, out of earshot of the others. "Did you stop by Adam's?"

"*Ya.*" Rosemary sighed. "He's not coming, *Mamm.* He said he's sorry."

Levina let out a heavy sigh as she searched Rosemary's eyes. Rosemary had just turned thirty last month, and she and her husband recently celebrated their tenth wedding anniversary. Levina loved her children equally, but she was closest to Rosemary. She would continue to pray that Rosemary would soften where her father was concerned.

"Well, I'm glad you're here." Levina smiled as she reached for Leah. "Let me hold that precious bundle."

"She spit up on the way here." Rosemary handed the baby to her mother. "I reckon because Glenn was driving so fast." She rolled her eyes but smiled.

"Well, she won't spit up on her *mammi*, will you, Leah?" Levina touched the tip of her finger to Leah's nose, then realized how quiet it was in the other room. She carried Leah back into the kitchen and took a peek out the window. "The meal is ready, if you want to sit down at the table. I see Jonathan and Becky pulling into the driveway."

Levina watched Naaman walk to the door, still limping. She knew that Jonathan was glad his father had returned, and she expected a warm reunion between the two, but as he embraced his father in a hug, she let out another sigh of relief. Becky and their three young children all greeted Naaman with a hug as well.

"Rosemary, there's a fold-up table in the den for your girls and Jonathan's three." Levina pointed toward the other room as everyone began to take their seats at her table in the kitchen, which would hold all ten adults. "And the playpen is folded against the wall in there, if you want to lay Leah in it while you eat."

Naaman took a seat at the head of the table, and Levina recalled the many meals she'd shared with her children while he was away. Yet he just took his seat as if not a day had passed . . . She closed her eyes for a moment. *Please, Lord. I don't want to hold a grudge.*

Levina was the last to sit, and everyone bowed their heads in prayer.

She opened her eyes and saw Jonathan scooping

mashed potatoes on his plate. She narrowed her eyes in his direction.

"What?" His brows lifted beneath his sun-streaked bangs. "I said my blessings *fast*." He grinned. "I'm starving, *Mamm*."

As they all filled their plates, light conversation ensued. Jonathan talked about how much he enjoyed his new responsibilities at the furniture store where he'd worked for nearly six months. Naaman couldn't comment, since he didn't know what Jonathan had done before his promotion. Freda reported that her friend Rebecca, who was new to the area, was finally out of the hospital after surgery to remove a tumor in her stomach. Everyone at the table offered thanks and praise about the news. Naaman nodded, although he'd never met Freda's friend.

Tillie patiently waited to talk about her job at Yoder's Pantry, where she'd worked part-time for the past few months. Levina was glad to see Tillie directing her comments to Naaman.

"*Daed*, you and *Mamm* will have to come eat lunch together there. *Mamm* comes sometimes. They have the best pretzels in the world! And my friend Abby goes there a lot, too, for lunch. Remember Abby Kauffman, *Daed*? She married Joseph Lambert, right after he came home and was baptized."

Tillie's round little cheeks lifted above dimples that Levina was sure God made special just for Tillie. Her smile had always been contagious, and when she started talking, her hands became animated and her bubbly zest for life could lift anyone's spirits.

"*Mamm* and I helped teach Abby to cook. Abby's *mamm* passed a long time ago, so she'd never really learned how."

Levina was glad to see Naaman smiling.

"Anyway, I also love to talk to all the *Englisch* people when they come in." Tillie giggled. "They ask so many questions about our way of life, and I like telling them about our faith." She sat up taller. "*Mamm*, guess who came in yesterday?"

Levina swallowed a bite of beans. "Who?"

Tillie brought both hands to her chest and took a deep breath. "Bishop Ebersol." She paused, pressing her lips together. "And guess what he said?"

"Just tell us, Tillie." Jonathan chuckled, shaking his head. "I reckon everything is such a big deal to you."

"He said that my bread pudding was the best he'd ever eaten. What about that?" A smile filled Tillie's face. Then she almost bounced in her seat. "And Mr. Princeton came into Yoder's last week too!"

Naaman cleared his throat. "And who is Mr. Princeton?"

"He's the *Englisch* man who owns the Pantry along with Martha and John Yoder. That's why we can have electricity, since an *Englisch* person is part owner." Tillie reached across her husband for the salt.

Levina stifled a grin. Tillie's husband, Rufus, was the quietest fellow she'd ever met. But his eyes lit up every time Tillie spoke.

Tillie went on for at least another ten minutes, filling her father in about every new family who had moved in, those who had left, and who was courting whom.

With sadness in her eyes, she told him about the old widow who lived around the corner. "Sarah Dienner passed, too, *Daed*. Went in her sleep, they say. Her son is comin' to put the place up for sale, and—"

"Why don't you let *Daed* talk?" Rosemary interrupted. "I'm sure we'd all like to hear what he did in Ohio."

Levina drew in a deep breath as she watched Rosemary fold her arms across her chest.

"Well, *Daed*?" Rosemary arched her brows. "Tell us. Tell us all about Middlefield."

"Rosemary . . ." Levina said in a warning tone. No matter what, Naaman was still Rosemary's father.

"What, *Mamm*?" Rosemary shrugged. "So, *Daed* . . . tell us. What was so wonderful about Middlefield, Ohio, that it would cause you to abandon your family for almost a year?"

CHAPTER FOUR

Naaman glanced at Levina, whose cheeks were fiery red at their daughter's persistence. They didn't raise their children to be so outspoken, but Naaman knew he owed his family some answers. He had just been hoping it wouldn't have to be tonight.

"Rosemary, let's don't do this right now."

Levina's voice was firm, but Naaman saw the raw hurt in Rosemary's eyes. It was hard for him to believe that his eldest daughter was thirty years old. He didn't recall a gray hair on her head when he left; now he saw a thread of silver that had escaped the confines of her *kapp*.

Where had the time gone? He knew his family thought a year of that time had gone to waste. *Had it?*

"It's all right, Levina." He smiled slightly at his wife, then faced off with Rosemary. "I left here to find myself." It was a lame answer, and Naaman regretted it instantly.

"When did you get *lost*?" Rosemary's bottom lip was trembling as she spoke.

Naaman had never heard his daughter use that tone with him.

"Rosemary, I don't think this is the time . . ." Levina stood from the table and began to clear the dishes.

"No, *Mamm*. We'd all like to know. Wouldn't we?" Rosemary glanced around the table.

No one spoke or even gave a nod. Jonathan stared at his plate. Freda and Tillie looked across the table at each other and didn't move.

"I guess I got lost a long time ago, Rosemary," Naaman said with a forced calmness in his voice. He wondered if they could hear the sadness, mixed with anger . . . mostly at himself.

"And now you're found?" Rosemary's eyes filled with tears as she spoke. "Do you know how hard it was for *Mamm* while you were away? All the chores here, the way people talk, and—"

"Stop it." Levina stomped her foot.

In all his years, Naaman had never seen her do that.

"This is your father's *haus*, Rosemary. I will not have you disrespect him in this way." She nodded her head toward the den and lowered her voice. "And not in front of the children either."

One thing Naaman didn't need was Levina defending him. He felt like a stranger at his own table. He was still the head of the family, the decision maker, the one they'd all counted on for most of their lives. But he didn't have one logical thought that could make them understand the choice he'd made eleven months ago. He didn't understand it himself.

A heaviness settled around his heart as he stood from the table and watched Rosemary dab at a tear. Her husband placed his hand on top of hers and gave her a gentle pat. Glenn was a good man. A good husband and father. Naaman used to think of himself that way.

He looked around the table at his family, then swallowed hard. "I am sorry to *mei* family. I don't have a *gut* reason for being away." He turned to Levina. "Your *mamm* is a wonderful *frau*." Naaman looked at each one of his children around the table. "And the Lord blessed me far more than I deserve with each of you." He paused and took a breath. "Excuse me, please."

. . .

Levina waited until Naaman had closed the screen door behind him and was down the porch steps before she addressed their children.

"Your father is a *gut* man, and he is still the head of this household." She held up one finger when Rosemary opened her mouth to speak. "And it wonders me how you can speak to him with disrespect, Rosemary." Levina shook her head. "I won't have it."

Rosemary dabbed at her eyes with her napkin and sniffled. "I'm sorry, *Mamm*. It's just that we all watched how you suffered while he was gone, and now he's back as if nothing happened. I just don't understand it."

Levina wanted to blurt out that she didn't understand it either, but as much as she wanted to kick Naaman in the shins for what he'd done, her desire to shelter him from hurt far outweighed her own anger. *He is still my husband, and I love him.*

"But he's back." Tillie's eyes twinkled as she spoke

softly to her sister. "Let's just be happy and thankful about that."

Rosemary stood up. "*Mamm*, supper was *gut*, but I think we should go." She walked to the den, and Levina could hear her telling Sarah and Marie to finish their milk.

Freda started helping Levina clear the table. "Give her time, *Mamm*. Rosemary will come around. So will Adam." At twenty-three, Freda had always possessed a maturity beyond her years.

Levina smiled. "I hope you're right."

Her three sons-in-law and Jonathan all headed outside. Levina hoped they would join Naaman in the barn, where he often went after a meal. Rosemary was gathering up her children, and Levina suspected she would be rounding up her husband as well.

Levina washed dishes as Tillie dried, and Freda gathered up jams, jellies, and other items to be stored in the refrigerator. Rosemary entered the kitchen holding Leah in one arm and the infant carrier in the other. The twins were right behind her.

"*Mamm*, can we go out to the barn?" Sarah looked up at Rosemary with her big brown eyes, and Levina smiled to herself, remembering how Rosemary used to give Levina the same look when she wanted something.

"I guess so. But we'll be leaving soon."

Rosemary waited until her girls were halfway across the yard before she spoke. "It's just hard for me to watch *Daed* sitting at the head of the table." She put the carrier in the middle of the table, then carefully laid her sleeping baby in it. "I'm trying to forgive him.

I really am." She grabbed an empty pot from the stove and leaned around Levina to put it into the dishwater. "I just don't understand. Glenn would never do anything like that."

Levina felt her muscles tense as she turned to face her oldest daughter. "You don't know what anyone will do, Rosemary."

Tillie placed a dry plate in the cabinet then shrugged. "I read in a magazine that when people get old, they go through a midlife crisis." She paused, tilting her head to one side. "Maybe that's what happened to *Daed*."

"Tillie, where do you read such things?" Levina shook her head. *Old?*

"At the doctor's office. They have all kinds of magazines." Tillie raised her brows and grinned.

"What were you at the doctor for?" Levina stopped washing and turned to face her youngest daughter.

Tillie let out a heavy sigh. "I thought I might be in the family way." She frowned as she reached for another plate. "But I'm not."

"It'll happen, Tillie," Freda said. "I'm older than you and still waiting."

"The Lord will bless you both with *kinner* soon enough, I reckon." Levina drained the water from the sink, wiped the counter with the dishrag, then dried her hands. She walked to little Leah. "Such a blessing." She leaned down and kissed her newest grandchild on the head, then sat down at the kitchen table. She waited for all her girls to sit down.

"I know this is *hatt* for all of you, but we must try not to question God's will." Levina spoke the words her daughters expected, words they all knew were in accordance with the *Ordnung* by which they'd all been raised. But in her heart Levina knew that she'd been questioning God's will from the moment Naaman walked out the door last year. "You all know that your father is a *gut* man."

"I know that, *Mamm*." Rosemary brought both hands to her forehead. "I'm just so disappointed in him."

Leah started to fuss, so Freda picked her up. "I'm disappointed in him, too, Rosemary. But I love him, no matter what."

"So do I," Rosemary huffed. "I'm not saying I don't love him."

"*Mamm?*" Tillie propped her elbows on the table and held her chin with her hands. "Why do you think *Daed* left in the first place?"

Levina took a deep breath. "*Mei dochders*, your father only came home yesterday. We haven't had much time to talk." She focused on Rosemary. "But I reckon sometimes people grow apart, for reasons we aren't quite sure of. Now your *daed* and I have to find our way back to each other."

Rosemary grunted, then stood from the table. "*Daed* got lost, got found, and now you both have to find your way back to each other. That's a lot of lost and found."

"Stop it, Rosemary," Freda said sharply.

Tillie just smiled. "For *all* have sinned, and come short of the glory of God."

"I know, Tillie," Rosemary said with a heavy sigh. "Just give me some time." Then she looked at Levina and shook her head. "I don't know about Adam though, *Mamm*. He doesn't even like to talk about *Daed*. He gets really angry."

Levina nodded, but her mother's instinct told Levina that something else was bothering Adam. Yes, he was angry at his father . . . but Levina had noticed some things about Adam that perhaps the other children had not.

CHAPTER FIVE

Adam took a bite of his meat loaf and wondered if his mother had prepared a pot roast for supper. He loved Hannah's cooking, and the meat loaf was wonderful, but there was nothing quite like his mother's pot roast. He pictured Rosemary, Jonathan, Freda, and Tillie sitting around his parents' kitchen table, with their spouses and children, and regret pierced his heart. Then he envisioned his father sitting at the head of the table, and he scowled.

"Is something wrong with the meat loaf?" Hannah wiped mashed potatoes from Anna Mae's chin.

"No. It's *gut*. Like always." Adam smiled, then glanced around at his own family. Seven-year-old Ben and six-year-old Abner sat side by side, and four-year-old Katherine was in a booster chair across from them. Two-year-old Anna Mae was in a high chair next to Hannah. *I have a beautiful family. I would never leave them.*

"Can we be excused?" Ben set his fork on his plate, then rubbed his eyes.

Adam knew he'd worked his young boys hard today. While Adam plowed the fields, he'd left a long list of chores for Ben and Abner—clean the horse stalls, wash the buggy, and ready up the barn in preparation for worship service this Sunday. It was a tall order for such young lads, but Adam believed in hard work—something instilled in him by his own father. He grimaced again.

"*Ya.* You can both be excused following prayer."

They all bowed their heads, except for Anna Mae. When they were done, Adam took a bite of mashed potatoes and watched his boys get up from the table and head toward the den. "Boys?"

Ben and Abner turned around.

"*Ya, Daed?*" Ben said.

"You are *hatt* workers. You did a *gut* job today."

Both boys' faces lit up before they scooted off to take baths.

"That was nice, Adam. I'm glad you recognize the boys' hard work." Hannah helped Katherine from the booster chair and gently wiped her chin. Then she lifted Anna Mae from the high chair after also dabbing her face with a napkin. "Katherine, take Anna Mae's hand, and the two of you go into the den and look at your picture books while I clean the kitchen."

Adam wiped his own mouth and watched Hannah start to clear the dishes. He thought about his mother, and again he pictured the scene unfolding at his childhood home. Everyone there but him, he supposed. He wondered if his father headed to the barn after the meal, the way he'd always done. Did Jonathan and his brothers-in-law go? Did they tell jokes or talk about the day's events? Was everything back to normal, as if their father hadn't forsaken his family for almost a year?

"Your head is full with thoughts," Hannah said as she reached in front of him to take his plate. "Do you wish that we had gone to your father's homecoming supper?"

"No." Adam leaned back in his chair and looped his thumbs beneath his suspenders. "I don't have a father anymore."

Hannah let out a heavy sigh. "You don't mean that, Adam." She turned to put the plate in the sink.

"*Ya.* I do. What kind of a man leaves his family like that?"

Hannah turned around as the sink filled with water. "Why don't you ask him and find out?"

Adam stared long and hard at his wife of ten years. When did she start using such a tone with him? "I will not."

Hannah shrugged. "I reckon it will be your loss. Your *daed* is a *gut* man, and without talking to him, you don't know why he left." She spun around and began washing the dishes.

"Why are you defending him?" Adam heard the anger in his voice as he spoke. "What if it had been me? What if I had left you and the *kinner* and just taken off?"

Hannah spun around, clamped her jaw tight, and stared him down with brown eyes flecked with gold in the light of the propane lamp nearby. As the sun descended, a hazy orange glow filled the room. But even in the dim light, Adam saw the distinct hardening of his wife's eyes.

"I hope that will never happen," she finally said.

"Of course it will never happen." Adam looked away from her, shoved his chair back from the table, and stood up. "I'm going to go close up the barn for the night."

Hannah shrugged, then turned back around and started washing dishes again.

"Why do you do that?"

"Do what?" She didn't turn around.

"Shrug. You always do that. You shrug your shoulders at me when you don't agree with something." Adam folded his arms across his chest and waited for her to answer, but instead . . . she shrugged. He could feel his face turning red as he turned and headed out the door.

Lucky Daed. *He got a break from all this.*

• • •

Levina and Naaman said good-bye to their children and grandchildren, then sat down in the rocking chairs on the front porch.

"I missed these sunsets." Naaman didn't look at her, but instead seemed far away as they watched gray clouds pushing the sun toward freshly planted fields in the distance—crops planted by her sons and sons-in-law only a few weeks earlier.

Levina kicked her rocker into motion. "There's a storm coming. We'll need to close all the windows soon."

Naaman didn't say anything but continued to stare into the twilight.

"I'm sorry about Rosemary, Naaman. She will need

time to make room in her heart for you again." Levina decided not to mention anything about Adam.

"Don't apologize for Rosemary, Levina. I reckon all the *kinner* have a right to be angry with me." He shifted his weight to face her, then stirred uneasily in his chair. "Have you made room in your heart for me, Levina?"

They'd been avoiding the conversation that Levina knew they had to have. She took a deep breath and let it out slowly. "I reckon you've always been in my heart, Naaman. But . . ."

Naaman's blue eyes searched her face. "But what?"

"I–I don't understand." Levina swallowed hard and sat up taller, determined to stay strong as she asked the next question. "Was there someone else? Another woman in Middlefield?"

Naaman's mouth dropped open briefly, then he clamped it shut as his eyes darkened with emotion. He twisted in his chair to face her. "Levina . . ." He spoke in a broken whisper. "Never. There has never been anyone but you." He hung his head. "I'm sorry you have to ask that."

"Then why? Why, Naaman?" Levina's voice rose an octave as she spoke, and she suddenly wished she could take back the question. Fear and anxiety knotted inside her, and she wasn't sure she was prepared to hear his answer. She tucked her chin and held her breath.

"I guess I needed to find—"

"Don't you dare say that you needed to find yourself!" She interrupted him with reckless anger. "You can give that answer to your children, but I am your *frau*, Naaman. What did I do to cause you to leave our home, our life?" She covered her face with her hands and prayed she wouldn't cry, but even though she bit her lip until it throbbed like her pulse, a tear still spilled.

When she pulled her hands away, Naaman was in front of her on one knee, just as he had been when he proposed to her thirty-one years ago. He reached for her hand, pulled it to his mouth, and kissed it gently. His touch was more tender than Levina could recall. "I'm sorry, Levina."

She eased her hand from his. "Then explain to me, Naaman. I need to understand if we are going to move forward, because right now I–I don't trust you."

"I don't blame you for not trusting me, Levina." He spoke softly, but his voice was filled with steadfast determination. "But I promise you that I will spend the rest of my life making it up to you."

Levina drew in a deep breath, then let it out slowly. "Then tell me why you left."

He gazed into her eyes. "I think you know why I left, and to be honest—I'm not sure it pained you as much as you are letting on."

"How can you say that?" Levina bolted from the chair and scooted around him to stand on the edge of the porch. She stared into the gray skies. The crescent moon was suspended in the sky—off balance, the way Naaman's comment had left her feeling. She turned to face him and asked again, "How can you say that?"

Naaman opened his mouth to speak, but Levina held up one finger, something she often did with her children when she didn't want to hear what they had to say. "While you were away, do you have any idea what I went through? Not just the chores and hardships of running this farm, but the people . . ." She paused. "Even in our community, the people still talk. I was humiliated."

Naaman walked closer to her, his eyes filled with sorrow. "I will not deny that what I did was wrong." He tilted his head to one side and stared at her in a way she didn't recognize, a far-off, burning gaze that seemed to drill a hole all the way to her soul. "But let me ask you something . . ." He stroked his dark beard, not taking his eyes from her. "Didn't you ever think about it? Just once? Didn't you ever wonder what else was out there? Weren't you ever tempted to get away, to get to know the woman you are, to experience more than we've ever known here?" He latched onto her shoulders. "Levina, be honest. Tell me that you have never fantasized about just going out on your own to—"

She jerked from his grasp. "Never! Not once, Naaman. I would never dream of leaving our children or grandchildren. I'd have never left you to experience some late-in-life *rumschpringe*!"

"Really?" His doubtful blue eyes bored into hers.

Levina stepped away from him. "Don't do this, Naaman. Don't you try to justify your selfish actions by accusing me of having the same deceitful thoughts."

He held his palms up. "Okay. I'm sorry."

"I don't even know you!"

The truth filled the space around them, and Levina felt suffocated by the honesty that hung in the air. Such things shouldn't be discussed, and yet she knew that she and Naaman were crossing over into undiscovered territory—foreign terrain that left her unsteady on her feet.

Naaman eased closer, his eyes probing hers as if his intensity could unlock the secret place in her heart where all thoughts—good and bad—were stored. Slowly he reached up and brushed away a strand of hair that had fallen from beneath her *kapp*. His eyes never left hers as he leaned closer and brushed his lips to hers, sending a wave of emotion and excitement pulsing through her body as if she were a teenage girl once more.

"Then let's get to know each other again," he said softly before he kissed her again.

Levina couldn't remember the last time his kiss had left her weak in the knees.

CHAPTER SIX

Naaman woke up when a thunderclap shook the windows of the farmhouse. As he'd done for the past year, he reached over to drape an arm across Levina, only to find that he was alone in the bed.

He rolled from his side to his back, then locked his hands behind his head and watched the flashes of lightning brightening the room, only to have it go dark again. He closed his eyes and thought about his kiss with Levina last night. He couldn't remember the last time he'd felt such passion, such desire. But she'd quickly halted his efforts and made a firm commitment to sleep in Tillie's room. "For now," she'd said.

Another bolt of lightning shook the rafters. Naaman thought about all the storms Levina must have weathered alone in the house—thunderstorms had always frightened her. *What was I thinking to leave her?*

He crossed his ankles beneath the quilt, and the intimate moment between him and his wife replayed over and over in his mind. He'd offered to sleep in Tillie's room or one of the other bedrooms, but Levina insisted that he sleep in their bed since it was the largest bed in the house.

He uncrossed his ankles and straightened his left leg, then bent it at the knee, then put it down again and decided that there was no good position to stop the throbbing in his hip caused by his recent fall. The doctor said the hip was badly bruised and that only time would heal it, but the nagging pain only reminded him of Middlefield, which ultimately led to another self-lashing about what he'd done.

Dear heavenly Father, he prayed, *I may never understand what drove me to leave my family, but I pray that I am back on the right course and that my* frau *and* kinner *will accept me back into their hearts and forgive me for my selfishness.*

Another boom halted his prayer midway. It sounded like lightning hit a tree. He eased his legs over the side of the bed, then put on his black pants. The boards creaked beneath his bare feet as he tiptoed out of the bedroom and across the hallway. He could see a light coming from Tillie's room, and he slowly pushed the door open.

Levina was sitting up in the bed in her white nightgown, with her legs pulled to her chest. The lantern on her bedside table glowed, and stark fear glittered in her eyes.

"Levina, are you all right?" He took a hesitant step into Tillie's room, and a flash of light illuminated Levina's beautiful face as she smiled and her fear seemed to fade.

"*Ya.*" She crinkled her nose and frowned. "You know how I get scared when it's stormy outside." Another roar of thunder sent Levina's hands to her ears as she clamped her eyes closed.

Naaman walked to the side of the bed and hesitated, and instead walked to the rocking chair in the corner. He sat down and stared at his wife. He didn't think he'd ever wanted anything so badly in his life—just to hold her in his arms.

"Naaman, what are you doing?" She sat taller and narrowed her brows.

"Sleep, Levina." He spoke in a whisper. "I will stay here with you."

Levina pushed back long waves of hair from her face and shook her head. "That's silly. You don't have to do that. Go back to your bed, Naaman."

She spoke with authority, as if she were speaking to one of the children, but when another flash of lightning lit up the room, she was instantly transformed into a small child herself, scrunching her face up as she waited for the roar.

Naaman stood up and walked to the edge of the bed. "Levina, let me sit with you until you fall asleep."

"Go to your room, Naaman." She lowered her chin and looked up at him playfully. "Now."

Naaman winked at her. "You sure?"

"*Ya*. Now go." She shooed him with her hand.

He couldn't take his eyes from her, though. "You're so beautiful, Levina." He felt like a schoolboy with a crush on the prettiest girl in the eighth grade. Levina Beiler—she'd been his crush before he made her his wife.

They shared a smile, but Naaman saw the tremble in her lips. Fear of the storm? Fear of him? He wasn't sure. "Good night."

A few hours later Naaman awoke to the smell of bacon. Once he'd fallen back asleep, sometime after midnight, he'd slept uninterrupted. He sat up in bed, stretched his arms high, and then thanked the Lord for bringing him home where he belonged. He rubbed his eyes, stood up, and turned to make the bed. As he pulled the white cotton sheet taut on his side of the bed, he noticed the sheet tossed back on the other side, along with the quilt. Had he strayed that far over in the king-size bed? He never did that.

After running his hand the length of his beard a few times, he walked around to the other side of the bed. He picked up Levina's pillow and brought it to his face, then breathed in the smell of his wife, and again . . . he thanked God for the blessings of this new day.

· · ·

Levina felt giddy as a schoolgirl as she pulled the last piece of bacon from the skillet. It was an emotion that terrified and exhilarated her at the same time.

"*Guder mariye*, Levina."

Something about Naaman's suave tone made her think he knew she'd crawled into bed with him last night. She'd been ever so careful to stay far on her side, and she'd been quiet as she could be. Today would be a busy day, and she wanted to be fresh and alert. Curling up in the bed with Naaman provided a sense of familiarity and safety that she'd gone without for so long, and she'd slept peacefully the rest of the night. When morning came she'd sneaked downstairs before he ever knew she was there—or so she'd thought.

"*Guder mariye*," she said without turning around. She held her breath, waiting to see if he would say anything.

He sat down in his chair at the kitchen table. "Sleep well?"

Levina twisted her mouth to one side as she tried to decipher his tone of voice—still suave and a little too smug. "*Ya*, I slept very well, *danki*." She carried the plate of bacon and a bowl of eggs to the table. "And you? How did you sleep?"

Naaman folded his arms across a dark green shirt, a silly grin on his face. "Soundly. I don't think I woke up once."

Levina placed a basket of biscuits in the middle of the table and eased into her chair. She nodded, avoiding his eyes. "*Gut, gut*. Glad you slept well."

They both bowed their heads in prayer.

"What are your plans for today?" Naaman buttered a biscuit as he spoke.

"I go to market on Friday mornings, and then I have lunch at Yoder's Pantry."

Naaman's brow shot upward. "Where Tillie works?"

"*Ya*." Levina kept her head down as she scooped scrambled eggs onto her plate. She knew Naaman was waiting for an invitation, but she wasn't sure she wanted him to go with her to market—in public—until after he had his meeting with Bishop Ebersol. She thanked God every day that the bishop had not urged that Naaman be shunned.

She looked up to find him staring at her.

"Everything all right with breakfast?" Levina took a bite of her eggs.

"*Ya*. Much better than what I cooked for you." He kept staring at her, so she finally gave in.

"Do you—um—do you want to go to market with me, then to eat at Yoder's Pantry?"

"Sure."

Levina forced a smile, not sure of anything these days.

They ate quietly, and when they were done, she decided to broach two subjects that she wasn't looking forward to.

"You do remember that Bishop Ebersol will be here tomorrow at two o'clock, no?"

Naaman nodded. "*Ya*, I remember." His face clouded.

"And do you remember that worship service is at Adam's house on Sunday?"

Naaman's mouth took on an unpleasant twist as he chewed. After he swallowed, he rubbed his forehead with one hand. "I'm not sure I'm welcome there."

"It is worship service for our community, and you are in our community. Of course you're welcome." Levina gave a sharp nod.

"We will see."

"Are you thinking about not going?"

Naaman leaned back against the back of his chair. "Adam needs time, and I don't want to force myself on him."

Levina tapped her finger to her chin for a moment. "Naaman, you'll just need to trust me about this, but I think you need to force yourself on Adam. Something is going on with our oldest son."

CHAPTER SEVEN

Naaman parked the buggy outside of Yoder's Pantry as Levina scanned the parking lot. There were four other buggies tethered nearby, but it was impossible to distinguish between them. She dreaded walking in with Naaman, not knowing who she might bump into. Equally alarming was that Naaman latched onto her hand as they walked through the entrance. He knew that members of their community frowned upon public affection. She wiggled free of his grasp and frowned at him before they walked in, but he just shrugged—and with that childish grin on his face again.

"*Mamm! Daed!*" Tillie rushed to the front door right away. "Give me one minute, and I'll put you in our best seat by the window that faces away from the highway." Tillie bounced once on her toes and lifted her shoulders. "I'm so glad you're here!"

"That's *mei maedel*," Naaman said with a smile after Tillie skipped away.

"I hope she always keeps her childlike qualities." Levina folded her hands in front of her—just in case Naaman got any ideas—and scanned the restaurant. "Oh no," she whispered.

"What?" Naaman leaned closer.

"Eve Fisher is here, and she's a busybody."

"I know that I did not hear *mei gut frau* call some-one a busybody." Naaman grinned.

"Shh. Keep your voice down, Naaman." Levina held her head high as she scanned the rows of jams and jellies on the shelf to her right. She picked up a jar of rhubarb jam. "You know, Ellie Chupp makes a lot of these jams and jellies. She's dating Chris Miller—did I tell you he came back to the church? Tillie expects they'll get married this November."

She put the jar of jam back on the shelf and thumbed through various cookbooks, sundries, and of course, the large pretzels that Yoder's Pantry was famous for, each individually wrapped and tempting those who were on their way in or out.

Naaman was spinning a rack of books by the door. "Look at all these books with Amish women on the cover."

His puzzled expression caused Levina to giggle for a moment. Then she shrugged. "Lots of women in our community read these books. Who doesn't enjoy a good love story?" She blushed and grabbed the books from Naaman. After she placed them back on the rack, she turned her attention to those dining.

She hoped to avoid Eve Fisher . . . although she reckoned she should probably get used to the stares and the questions. Everyone would eventually wel-come Naaman back into the community, but folks were human, and Levina knew there would be some uncomfortable moments.

"I have your table all ready!" Tillie was carting two menus, and her contagious smile warmed Levina's heart.

She hoped and prayed that Tillie would be in the family way soon. Levina wished that for both her daughters. Freda and her husband had been trying a bit longer to have a baby, but it was starting to feel like a race between the two sisters. Levina hoped that neither of them was disappointed. She recalled how easily she had become pregnant with Rosemary, Adam, and Jonathan, but it took a little longer to become pregnant with Freda. And Tillie was somewhat of a surprise. Levina had been doubtful that she could have more children, due to complications during Freda's birth. She would remind both Freda and Tillie that all things happen on God's time frame.

Once they were seated, Levina knew there was no way to avoid Eve, who was sitting only one table over. Tillie brought them each a glass of sweet tea and promised to return shortly. Seconds later Eve rose from her chair and headed their way.

"Hello, Levina." She smiled warmly at Levina, then turned to Naaman. "And welcome back, Naaman."

Eve, like Levina, was nearing the age of fifty—but for reasons Levina couldn't grasp, the woman didn't look a day over thirty. She reminded herself that physical appearance didn't matter, while also realizing that she should have given some thought about how she was going to respond to comments about Naaman's return. "Hello, Eve."

Naaman tipped his head in Eve's direction, and Levina saw the muscle in his jaw tense.

"Is this your first time here, Naaman?" Eve smiled. "I've seen Levina in here many times, but I don't reckon many men come in for lunch. They are mostly working in the fields."

Levina could feel her blood starting to boil. Naaman could run circles around most men in this community when it came to hard work, and she wasn't about to let Eve Fisher suggest that he wasn't a hard worker.

"Our fields are planted, and Naaman didn't get much sleep last night, so I'm treating him to lunch out." She raised her chin a bit and smiled at Eve, but when Eve's eyes widened, Levina figured she'd better clarify her statement. "When it makes wet and thunders so much, I get nervous and can't sleep. Naaman was tending to me, making sure I wasn't afraid."

"I see." Eve bit her lip and raised her brow. "Well, I best be goin' back to my table. Nice to see you both. I suppose we'll see you on Sunday for worship at Adam's *haus*."

"*Ya*. See you then." Levina gave a quick wave as Eve left.

"You don't like her much, no?" Naaman took a sip of his tea but kept his eyes on Levina.

"Naaman, why would you say such a thing? I have no bad feelings for Eve." Levina pressed her lips together, then took a deep breath. *I will pray hard tonight.*

Tillie came bouncing back to the table with her friend Abby. "*Daed*, remember Abby Kauffman? Only she's Abby Lambert now!"

Naaman extended his hand to Abby. "*Ya*, I do. Solomon's girl. Nice to see you."

Abby shook Naaman's hand, then turned to Levina. "*Danki* for letting me spend so much time at your *haus*."

"We're always glad to have you, Abigail. I enjoy it when Tillie brings you over and we all cook together."

Abby turned to Tillie. "I guess I better get back to Anna." She pointed toward a nearby table where she was dining with a friend.

Levina nodded, then she and Naaman each ordered the special—chicken and dumplings with a side of corn.

"Great choice!" Tillie waved to another patron across the room. "I'll be back soon."

After a few moments, Naaman leaned his head to one side and gazed long and hard at Levina. She thought she knew what was on his mind, but he surprised her.

"You mentioned that something is goin' on with Adam. What do you mean?"

Levina wasn't sure where to start. "I think there might be problems with him and Hannah. He won't talk to me when I ask him if everything is all right, and Rosemary tried to talk to him too. He insists nothing is wrong, but, Naaman . . ." She paused. "Something *is* wrong, whether it has to do with Hannah or not."

Naaman didn't seem interested in looking Levina square in the eye anymore. He seemed to be looking everywhere but at her. "It saddens me to hear that." He looked up when he heard someone scooting toward them. Tillie placed large platters in front of them. "Healthy portions."

"*Ya*, the servings are always generous here." Levina smiled at her daughter. "*Danki*, Tillie."

Her baby girl folded her hands together as her eyes brightened. "I'm so glad the two of you are here—together."

Then Naaman did the unexpected. He reached across the table and latched onto Levina's hand, then spoke with touching sincerity. "I'm glad to be home."

Levina's eyes drifted to her left. Eve was straining her neck in their direction. It shouldn't matter, but she wanted Eve—and the world—to know that everything was going to be all right with her and Naaman. It was wrong, and Levina knew that her choices were judged only by God, but when she looked up and saw a tear roll down Tillie's face, she swallowed back her own emotions.

"I'm glad you're home, too, *Daed.*" Tillie leaned over and kissed her father on the cheek before she turned to leave.

Levina watched him struggling to keep his own emotions from becoming a public display. She gave his hand a squeeze. Her heart was filled with love for her husband and hope for the future, but she couldn't seem to conquer the distrust that threatened to destroy the moment and the future.

Would she always worry that he would leave again? How was she going to get past her own insecurities and move forward with the one man she'd always loved . . . but who had betrayed their union?

She started to pull her hand away but Naaman recaptured it.

"I will earn your trust, Levina. And I will never leave you again. Not ever."

Dear Lord, help me to believe him. And trust him.

CHAPTER EIGHT

Larry Dozier pulled his rental car into Beiler's Bed-and-Breakfast and wished he'd had time to change out of his sheriff's uniform before leaving Middlefield. Cops made people nervous, and the last thing he wanted to do was draw attention to himself. As he walked to the small office on the side of the B & B, he heard the sound of a buggy coming up the drive that ran parallel to the large brick establishment.

Buggies and Amish folks were nothing new to him since he lived right outside of Middlefield, one of the largest Amish settlements in Ohio. He'd noticed during his drive from the airport that Amish folks in these parts drove gray buggies instead of black, and he found it downright frightening that signs lined the main highway stating *Watch for Aggressive Drivers*. And where were the speed limit signs? He scratched his chin and wondered if he was the only one who noticed this. He'd never been to Paradise, Pennsylvania, before.

He walked from the back parking area, rounded the corner, and saw a sign on the door—*Office and Dining Area*. He entered the room and found an Amish woman tidying up behind a counter that boasted a large coffeepot, cups, sugar, creamer, and a tray of cookies. There were several small tables in the room covered with white tablecloths, each with two chairs tucked close. He breathed in the aroma of freshly baked goods that permeated the space around him. This is where he would be having breakfast for the next few mornings, or however long it took to find Naaman Lapp.

"Good afternoon." Larry walked to the counter and set his suitcase down. "I have a reservation for Larry Dozier."

"*Ya, ya.* I have your key right here." The young woman reached into her apron pocket and handed Larry a key. "You're in the Rose Room. It's on the third floor."

Larry took the key and noticed that the white covering on her head was different from those worn by the Amish women in Middlefield. "Thank you." He picked up his suitcase. "Did you say the third floor?"

"*Ya.* It was the only room we had left when you called yesterday to make a reservation."

Larry nodded and wondered if his knee would hold out up three flights of stairs.

"And, Mr. Dozier, breakfast is served between seven o'clock and nine o'clock. It's buffet-style, so just come when you're ready."

He was heading for the stairs when the woman called his name again. He twisted to face her. "Yes?"

"When you called yesterday, you weren't sure how long you would be staying. Do you know yet?"

Larry saw her eyeing him up and down. She was probably wondering what he was doing in town, although he didn't owe her any explanation. It was Friday afternoon, and Larry figured he would be in town at least until Monday or Tuesday. Tomorrow he had to find a quilt for Patsy and pick up a few other touristy items his wife had requested. Sunday, he wouldn't bother Naaman and his family. He had enough respect for the Amish folks not to intrude on a Sunday. "Plan on my staying through Monday night. If that changes, I'll let you know."

"That sounds fine. I just wanted to make sure you wouldn't be needing the room into the following weekend. We usually book up on the weekends."

"I imagine my business here will be taken care of by then."

. . .

After his trip with Levina to market and lunch at Yoder's Pantry, Naaman spent the rest of the day doing a list of odd jobs. He replaced the loose doorknob in the bathroom with one they'd bought that morning, carried a heavy box of books downstairs that Tillie wanted, and replaced a broken pane of glass in Jonathan's old room. Levina had told her older grandchildren not to play baseball so close to the house. She smiled to herself as she recalled the first time that Adam put a baseball through one of the windows. It wasn't the last time either.

For supper, she heated up some cream of carrot soup she had in the freezer and served it to Naaman with warmed butter bread. She and Naaman shared devotional time, followed by a small slice of German apple cake she had made earlier in the day. It all seemed very normal and familiar. Until bedtime.

Levina tried to focus on the gardening magazine she'd picked up in town, but her eyes were heavy and she kept having to adjust the lantern brighter and brighter to see. She pushed up her reading glasses on her nose and stifled a yawn.

"Levina, why don't you go to bed?" Naaman removed his own reading glasses and closed the book he was reading. "And let me sleep in Tillie's room tonight."

She yawned, then looked at her husband. "No, I will sleep in Tillie's room. It's no bother." She pulled her gaze from him and recalled the way she'd curled up in the bed with him the night before, quiet as she could be and careful not to get too close. She'd longed for the protectiveness of his arms around her, but until she was sure that she could trust him, she wouldn't slip back into her wifely role . . . even though her heart danced with excitement at the thought of Naaman loving her in that way.

Levina buried her head back in the magazine, but the words on the page blurred as she tried to recall the last time that she and Naaman were intimate. She couldn't remember. Were they too busy? Too tired? Or just uninterested? Levina could feel Naaman watching her intently, and even though she feared it would weaken her resolve, she looked up at him. The tenderness of his kiss lingered in her mind, and her desire to be held by her husband almost overrode her anxiety about trusting him again. But she forced herself to look away from his gaze, his eyes filled with tenderness and passion that she longed to share with him.

Such silliness. These were not proper thoughts for a middle-aged woman. *I'm a grandma, for goodness' sake.*

"Levina?"

"*Ya?*" Her heart raced. She recognized the suggestive tone of his voice, even though it had been a mighty long time since she'd heard it.

Naaman's brow furrowed. He opened his mouth to say something, clamped it shut, then opened and shut it again. Finally he drew in a deep breath and blew it out slowly. "I reckon I will bathe and go to bed."

"Good night." *And thank the Lord.*

Sharing a bed with Naaman was not a decision she could make casually, even though he was her husband. He betrayed their marriage vows the day he left for Middlefield, and she wasn't ready to let down her guard just yet. What if he decided that he didn't want to be here? Chose to leave again? Could her heart withstand another blow? For now, she wanted to keep a safe distance from him. But as she watched him walk across the den and down the hallway, there was nothing she wanted more than to follow him to their bedroom and fall into his arms.

. . .

After his bath, Naaman climbed into bed, again feeling guilty that Levina was across the hall in Tillie's old bed. It seemed wrong for her not to be in her own bed, but Naaman knew it would take time for his wife to trust him again. For the thousandth time he pondered why he'd ever left Lancaster County in the first place.

When he stretched his memory to that time in his life, he could recall the tightness in his chest, the sense of suffocation, doubt about everything in his life, and the pressure to flee all he'd ever known. He pulled the covers to his waist and watched rays of light from the lantern flickering on the ceiling above.

Naaman thought about Paul Zook. He remembered when his friend left his wife and family to go live among the *Englisch* over twenty years ago. Paul never came back, and Naaman didn't think he would ever understand Paul's decision. For Naaman, it had never been about living in the *Englisch* world. That didn't interest him. When he left for Ohio, it was supposed to be for a few weeks, just to clear his head, though he didn't tell Levina that. He just said he was going to visit his cousins, and he didn't elaborate much. He was pretty sure Levina knew it would be an extended stay.

What kind of man am I? Being back with Levina and around the children made him question his actions even more. With each day he was consumed with trying to forgive himself and yet make it up to his family. His burdens seemed heavier than before he left. It had been a selfish move, and he knew it. He'd spent his entire life doing everything he was supposed to do— provided for his family, raised his children according to the *Ordnung*, been an upstanding member of the community. And he'd been a good husband to Levina. *So why?*

His chest tightened when he thought about his visit

with Bishop Ebersol tomorrow. It was a meeting he
couldn't avoid, but shame filled him. It would be hard
to look the bishop in the eyes and explain his choices
when Naaman didn't even understand them himself.
He reached for the bottle of aspirin on his bedside table
and popped two pills into his mouth, followed by a
swig of water, and wondered if his hip was ever going
to feel normal again. Then he let out a heavy sigh and
settled into his pillow.

Dear Lord, help me to be a better man.

Naaman went through a long list of prayers, thanking God for all he'd been blessed with, but in the end,
he repeated what consumed him the most. *Please,
Lord, help me to be a better man.*

When the door to the bedroom suddenly swung
wide, Naaman didn't think he'd ever seen such beauty.
Levina stood in the doorway, her silky hair to her waist,
wearing a long white gown that reached almost to the
floor. In her bare feet she edged forward slowly into the
room. Naaman sat up in the bed.

"Levina, are you all right?" He turned the lantern
on his nightstand up a bit to see her better, which illuminated her face enough for Naaman to study her
expression. Her brown eyes were flat and unreadable
as stone, but Naaman could still see the unspoken pain
she'd been burdened with since he arrived. He swung
his legs over the side of the bed, grimacing as his hip
popped with the movement. "What is it?"

She was a few feet from the bed when Naaman stood
up. Her eyes shone brighter as she stepped into the
pale light from the lantern, and a twinkle of moonlight

spilled into the room. Had she come back to their marital bed, deciding to resume her role as his wife? Naaman tried to decipher the faraway look in her eyes. Was she longing for him the way he desired to be with her?

He took a step toward her, and with a slow and steady hand he reached up and ran a hand through her hair. "You look beautiful, Levina."

She didn't move as Naaman cupped her cheek. He leaned closer to kiss her, but she backed away, and there was undeniable pain in her eyes. Naaman braced himself for whatever she was about to say.

"Naaman?" She bit her bottom lip as tears filled her eyes.

"What is it, *mei leib*?" He stepped toward her, but she moved back farther, so he stood and waited, watching her eyes shift from remote and mysterious to sharp and assessing.

"I know I asked you this before, but I–I need to be sure that there wasn't someone else." She paused. "In Ohio. Are you telling me the truth, Naaman? If there was another woman, you must tell me."

Naaman's stomach sank as he ran a hand through his hair.

CHAPTER NINE

Levina held her breath as she watched his expression. Before he said a word, she already knew the answer.

"No, Levina."

It was the first time she had ever seen her husband's eyes fill with tears.

"I'm sorry that you didn't believe me the first time you asked."

Levina let out a slow sigh. "I'm sorry, too, but I just needed to ask again."

Naaman wrapped his arms around her, and she returned the hug. But as his embrace grew more intense, she pulled slowly away.

"I've missed you, Levina." He pushed back a strand of hair that had fallen forward across her cheek.

"I've missed you, too, Naaman, but..." She hung her head, but it was only a few seconds later when Naaman cupped her chin and gently raised her eyes back to his.

"But you don't trust me, no? You're worried I will leave again."

Levina nodded. "I'm sorry, Naaman. I need time." She paused and took another deep breath. His blue eyes pierced the short distance between them. "In some ways, Naaman, I know you better than any other human being in the world." She smiled. "I know that your jaw quivers when you're nervous. I know that strawberries make you sick to your stomach. Your feet are more ticklish than anyone I've ever known, even the children. You listen to more than just the weather on your radio in the barn . . . mostly country and western music. Your favorite color is yellow."

She paused again when she felt his hands on her arms. "You're a *gut* father to our children. You're smart about things many men in our community are not. Math, for example. And you never tire of a *gut* joke." Levina lowered her head for a moment as Naaman rubbed her arms, then she looked back up and watched the play of emotions on his face, seemingly unaware of where she was going with all this. "But, Naaman . . ."

"What is it, Levina?"

She stepped away from him, walked to the window, and gazed into the moonlit yard. "In some ways, Naaman . . . I feel like I don't know you at all." She turned slowly around. "And I don't know when that happened." Her heart sank as she spoke aloud the words that had previously been private thoughts.

Naaman walked around to the other side of the bed and sat down. Levina sat beside him. They were quiet for several moments, then Naaman spoke.

"Then let's get to know each other again."

Levina felt a combination of relief and sadness as she realized that Naaman felt the same way she did. She shrugged. "I don't know how to move forward,

Naaman, when I felt such betrayal." She twisted to face him. "How can I trust that you won't tire of your life here again and just leave?"

"I didn't tire of my life, Levina."

"Then please try to explain it to me."

Naaman rolled his head around on his neck, and Levina suspected it was the same knot above his shoulder blades that flared up from time to time. In the past she would work the soreness out by rubbing his neck in the evenings. But on this night she sat still and waited.

"I don't have an explanation, other than what I've already told you."

Levina stood up and turned to face him. "Well, I hope you have some sort of explanation for Bishop Ebersol tomorrow. Maybe there is something you can tell him that you can't tell me, no?"

Naaman stood up. "When I figure out why I acted the way I did, Levina, you will be the first to know."

Levina folded her arms across her chest, blew out a huff of exasperation, then turned to leave. She wasn't to the door yet when Naaman called her name. She spun around, frustration in her voice. "*Ya?*"

"Would you like to go on a picnic with me down by the creek, after my visit with Bishop Ebersol tomorrow? Then we could drive to Bird-in-Hand and eat ice cream at that place you like."

Levina scrunched her brows. "Naaman, we haven't done that since we were kids, and—"

He walked closer to her. "*Ya*, I know." He smiled. "Our *kinner* are grown. It's just the two of us. Let's be kids together again."

Levina recalled times long since past, the picnics, trips to get ice cream, swims in the creek. "You're not going to prepare the meal, are you?" Her features became more animated as she spoke.

"If you want me to, I will."

She chuckled. "I think not." She tapped her foot a few times. "Hmm. All right, Naaman. I will make us a light early supper to eat. We will have a—a date tomorrow after your visit with Bishop Ebersol."

"I'll look forward to it."

"Fine." Levina left the room, but as she made her way across the hall, a smile filled her face. She was looking forward to her date with Naaman too.

· · ·

Naaman busied himself all the next day, following a heavy breakfast to hold him over until their picnic later in the afternoon. He made repairs to the barn that were long overdue and even managed to get a new coat of white paint on one side. But as two o'clock approached, his stomach began to churn with anxiety. Bishop Ebersol was the toughest bishop their community had ever had, and Naaman was expecting harsh words. At least he had his date with Levina to look forward to.

It seemed odd to call it a date. But it was exciting to think of it that way. Naaman was going to court his wife, make her see him for the man he'd always been, the man she fell in love with—and, he hoped, make her forget and forgive the man he'd been the past year . . . a man who had fallen into selfish temptation. God was all-forgiving, but Naaman needed Levina to forgive him too. And Naaman needed to forgive himself.

Then there was the issue of Adam. He would see his son tomorrow at church service. If he thought too much about that, his stomach roiled with worry. So, one worry at a time. He walked into the den in time to hear a buggy coming up the drive.

"Naaman, I'm going to go visit Freda for a little bit while you visit with Bishop Ebersol. I'll excuse myself after saying hello to him, then I'll be back around three."

Naaman grinned. "Sure you don't want to stay?"

She chuckled. "*Ach*, no. You are on your own, *mei lieb*."

Naaman couldn't remember the last time Levina had referred to him with such affection. It sounded nice, and for a brief moment the soothing tone of her voice calmed his nerves.

They both waited for Bishop Ebersol to ease his way up the porch steps, holding steady to the railing. He was a tall man in his seventies with a gray beard that ran the length of his chest. His brows were always slanted inward, giving him the appearance of always being angry. But despite his intimidating looks and strict rulings within the district, Naaman had always thought him to be fair. In Naaman's case, he'd probably been more than fair, since he hadn't recommended a shunning.

"Hello, Bishop Ebersol." Levina opened the screen door for the bishop and stepped to the side. "I will let you and Naaman visit." She turned to Naaman. "There's a pitcher of iced sweet tea on the table, Naaman, and I've laid out some gingersnaps."

"*Danki*, Levina." Bishop Ebersol removed his hat to reveal a sparse supply of gray locks underneath. "This won't take long."

Naaman's chest tightened as he wondered if the expected length of the visit was good or bad for him. He motioned for the bishop to take a seat on the couch.

"Can I get you some tea and gingersnaps?"

Bishop Ebersol sat down. "No. Emma made me a snack before I came."

No stalling. He was going to get right to the point. Naaman sat down in the rocker across from the bishop.

"Don't look so nervous, Naaman." Bishop Ebersol narrowed his eyes even further, so his words did little to calm Naaman's nerves. "Is there anything that you would like to tell me about your—your visit with your cousins?"

"It was a bad decision." Naaman pressed his lips together. "And it won't happen again."

Bishop Ebersol chuckled, something Naaman didn't think he'd ever heard from the man. "You sound like my grandchildren when you say that. You didn't just break a curfew or tell a tiny lie, Naaman." Bishop Ebersol raised his big bushy brows. "You took off on a late-in-life *rumschpringe* of sorts, even if it wasn't to live among the *Englisch*. Am I correct?"

Naaman sighed. "I reckon so. And I regret it."

"Why?"

"Why do I regret it?" Naaman scowled. Wasn't it obvious? "It—it was wrong. I hurt my family."

Bishop Ebersol stroked his gray beard. "And what did you learn while you were gone, my friend?"

Naaman was surprised by the bishop's compassionate tone. He'd expected far worse, and it could still be forthcoming, but for now Naaman pondered exactly what he did learn while he was away. *Lord, please tell me there was a lesson in my actions.*

"Bishop, I reckon I learned that we can't run from our problems." He held his head in his hands for a moment, then looked back up to see the bishop waiting. "I was just as lonely in Middlefield as I was here in Lancaster County, and all the same things still plagued me. And added to that, I missed Levina and my children."

The bishop's eyes narrowed suspiciously. "Why did you stay gone so long?"

"The longer I was gone, the harder it became to return." Naaman sighed. "I don't know."

Bishop Ebersol actually grinned. "I hope you gave Levina better reasons than you are giving me."

Naaman forced a smile. "I don't think I have given her *gut* reasons at all, Bishop. I just don't understand myself, or why I did what I did."

"You might not understand the purpose of your trip for a long time, Naaman. Maybe not ever, or until you go before God in heaven. But we must remember—everything is God's will. It was His will for you to take that journey, and you must stop questioning it and move forth with your life, learning and growing in His glory."

"Why didn't you seek a shunning, Bishop Ebersol?"

The bishop let out a heavy sigh. "I think back to your wedding day, Naaman. I was a deacon back then. But I still remember the way you looked at Levina when you said your vows. And you've continued to look at her that same way. You've been a *gut* father to your children and an upstanding member of our community." He smiled slightly. "I had faith in you, that you would come back." He frowned a bit. "Although I didn't think it would take you almost a year."

Naaman nodded. "I've prayed about this every day since I left and every day since I've returned. It was so many things, Bishop Ebersol." Naaman paused, unsure whether to go on. "But it just seemed like Levina and me raised our *kinner*, worked hard, prayed, and tried to be *gut* members of the community, but I reckon somewhere along the way we just stopped talking. I mean, *really* talking. I didn't notice it as much until all the *kinner* were moved out. Then it just seemed—lonely." Naaman shook his head. "I didn't know *mei frau* anymore."

"And we know that all things work together for good to them that love God, to them who are the called according to his purpose."

Naaman thought for a moment about the Scripture reading. "Bishop Ebersol, I do know that all things are of God's will, but I don't know how there can be any purpose for my leaving my family."

"As I said, Naaman . . . the Lord always has a plan." Bishop Ebersol raised his hat to the top of his head. "So, what is your plan, Naaman?"

Naaman stroked his beard. "I reckon it will sound

strange, but Levina and I are going on a date later. In a way, I guess we are getting to know each other all over again."

Bishop Ebersol stood up, and Naaman did so also. "I think that is a *gut* idea, Naaman." He extended his hand to Naaman. "Welcome home."

"*Danki* for coming by." Naaman walked the bishop to the door, and the elderly man was almost to the end of the porch when he turned around, a twinkle in his eye and a grin on his face.

"I've been married fifty-seven years, Naaman. I'm not sure we ever completely know or understand the womenfolk. Keep that in mind as you move forward." He headed down the steps, holding tightly to the rail for support.

Naaman waved as the bishop steered his buggy away, and he wondered why he'd feared the man all these years. He could think more about their conversation later. Right now, he wanted to clean up a bit before his date with his wife.

CHAPTER TEN

Levina finished hemming a dress for Freda while Freda sewed buttons on a shirt she'd made for Jake. She glanced at the clock.

"Here you go." She handed the finished product to Freda. "I guess I best be on my way."

Freda set her own project down on the kitchen table where she and Levina were working and sipping iced tea. "It just seems weird for you and *Daed* to date. I mean, he is your husband, and you live together, and . . ." Freda shrugged. "That's not normal, *Mamm*."

Levina smiled. "Define 'normal' for me, *dochder*."

"Well, I reckon it's not being courted by your own husband." Freda crinkled her nose and scowled. "I can't imagine you and *Daed* out on a date. I mean, what will you do?" Freda waved her hand in the air frantically. "Never mind. I don't want to know."

"Freda!" Levina stood up. "You're talking nonsense. It will be nice to spend some time with your father away from work, our *haus*, and"—she grinned at her daughter—"all of our *kinner*."

"Is *Daed* going to worship service at Adam's house tomorrow?"

"*Ya*. We will both be there. And if you speak with your *bruder*, you remind him that I expect him to be respectful of his father no matter his personal feelings."

Freda nodded then frowned. "You're so forgiving, *Mamm*. I just don't know if I could be that way if Jake had done what *Daed* did."

"Of course you could. That's the way you were raised, Freda. And especially where your family is concerned, it shouldn't even be an issue." Levina raised her chin, driven to live by her own words. "Besides, you will understand more as you grow in your marriage. Now I need to go." She gave Freda a quick hug.

Freda sighed. "Have fun on your *date*."

"I plan to." Levina winked at her daughter, which produced a slight roll of the eyes from Freda. Levina didn't care. She had a date to go home and get ready for.

• • •

Naaman pulled out some aftershave he'd bought years ago. He couldn't even remember why he'd bought it. It certainly went against his ways, but he slathered some on his cheeks and neck just the same.

He'd just tucked a clean blue shirt into his black pants and pulled up his suspenders when he heard Levina pulling into the driveway. He headed down the stairs feeling a bit giddy.

"I just want to freshen up a little," Levina said as he met her at the bottom of the stairs. Then she grinned. "Naaman Lapp, is that cologne you're wearing?"

"Just for you, *mei lieb*." He tried to play it off casually, even though he could feel his face reddening. But when Levina smiled, he was glad he'd chosen to splash on the spicy fragrance.

"I'll be down in a minute." She brushed past him on the stairs. "I've already prepared our picnic lunch," she said from the top of the stairs. "You can grab it from the refrigerator."

Naaman walked to the kitchen, opened the refrigerator, and pulled out a wicker basket with a flat lid that opened in opposite directions. It barely fit on the bottom shelf. He closed the door, then set the basket on the kitchen table and took a peek inside. Two sandwiches, a container that looked like it might be potato salad, a jar of pickles, two slices of pie, a thermos, and . . .

Naaman reached around the food and pulled out a piece of pink paper that was tucked between the pie and the jar of pickles. Warmth filled his heart as he read the familiar note that was over thirty years old.

My Dearest Naaman,

You are the man I want to spend the rest of my life with. Our wedding is only two weeks away, and I can't wait to be your *frau*! Our love is blessed by God, and I know that a lifetime of happiness awaits us! We will have lots of *kinner* to fill our home. And we will grow old together! I love you so much. You are my everything. My Naaman. Forever.

Your Loving Bride to Be,
Levina

Naaman swallowed hard as his eyes dropped to the bottom of the page where Levina had written a more recent note.

> You are still my Naaman. The man I fell in love with. The man I want to spend the rest of my life with and grow old with. You have always been, and always will be . . . my Naaman.
>
> Lovingly Yours,
> Levina

Naaman gritted his teeth in frustration with himself. "I will make everything up to you, Levina. *Everything.*"

"I know you will."

Naaman jumped as he spun around to see Levina standing in the den, dressed in a dark green dress, black apron, and perfectly ironed *kapp*. In his mind's eye, she looked exactly the same as the day he proposed, on a picnic down by the creek.

"You look beautiful." He let out a sigh and wondered how he could have ever left her for so long.

"And you smell *gut*." She walked into the kitchen grinning, then stopped when she saw him holding the note. "*Ach*, you found it. I was going to give it to you later." She dropped her gaze and bit her bottom lip, and a blush filled her cheeks.

Naaman waited until she looked back up at him. "I remember finding this on the seat of my courting buggy. Where did you find it?"

"It's been in the hope chest."

"The cedar chest I made you for our one-year anniversary, the one at the foot of our bed?"

"*Ya.*"

Naaman grinned. "What else have you got in that chest?"

"All kinds of things. If you redeem yourself, perhaps I will show you."

Levina was full of playfulness and smiles, and Naaman didn't think he'd ever wanted to please anyone more than he wanted to please her on this blessed day.

He picked up the picnic basket and held his arm out. Levina latched on above his elbow, and together they headed out the door.

. . .

Larry carefully stuffed the quilt into the back of the rental car alongside some other trinkets Patsy had requested. He sure hoped she liked it. It was the closest thing to the picture she'd sent with him that he could find, a mixture of blues, yellows, and light greens—which Patsy said would accent their blue carpet nicely.

There were plenty of quilts handmade by the Amish in Middlefield, but Patsy had to have one from Lancaster County. So now she did, and Larry had paid a pretty penny for it—almost eight hundred dollars. But his girl was worth it. He smiled as he pictured the way her green eyes would light up when she saw it.

He started the car and headed back to the B & B. He really could have saved this trip until early on Monday, but Patsy's folks were coming to town and that seemed as good a reason as any to start his trip early. It gave him time to shop for his wife and have a little downtime before he caught up with Naaman Lapp. Tomorrow he planned to sleep in, catch the late Mass at the Catholic church he saw down the road, and then take in the ball game on television. Maybe just lie around in his socks and boxers, munching on popcorn and drinking a beer. He didn't usually drink, but something about a man in his socks and boxers, snacking on popcorn—it seemed to call for a brew in one hand. A special occasion of sorts. That was how he planned to spend his Sunday.

Larry parked in the back of Beiler's Bed-and-Breakfast in the designated parking area. He eyed the three flights of stairs going to his room. The Rose Room. He shook his head. It was a frilly room for ladies, but it would serve his purpose while he was here. As long as it had a television, which it did, he was in good shape. Now if he could just manage the stairs with these bad knees.

As he gathered up his purchases, he recalled the breakfast he'd had that morning. Best breakfast he'd ever had, though he'd never tell Patsy that. After thirty-five years of marriage, probably best to let her believe hers was the best breakfast on the planet. But the owner, a woman named Barbie, laid out a fine meal—French toast, bacon, fresh fruit, sausage patties, homemade bread, and the best raspberry yogurt that had ever crossed his lips. Amazing stuff. Larry had followed the woman's suggestion and poured fresh granola on top. He made a mental note to see if he could purchase some of that to take to Patsy.

The owner, Barbie, wasn't an Amish woman, like the woman who had checked him in. But that morning, when Larry heard Barbie talking to four couples at a nearby table, he couldn't help but ask her how she knew so much about the Amish. She seemed to know things the average Joe wouldn't. Turned out she had grown up Amish—Beachy Amish, she called it. Evidently it was a less conservative form of Amish, similar to the Mennonites.

It hadn't seemed the right time to ask her about Naaman Lapp. Since the Amish didn't have phones and didn't drive cars, it was a little difficult to get an address. He could have done it before he left Middlefield if he'd taken the time, but he was in a hurry to avoid the in-laws. Another thing he wouldn't mention to his wife.

He hobbled up the stairs with Patsy's gifts, hoping they would all fit in his suitcase for the trip home. By the time he reached the third floor, he was as winded as a ninety-year-old man, not the fifty-five-year-old he was.

Need more exercise.

Larry knew he needed to get back to the gym, but the closer he got to retirement, the more he seemed to forego exercise and enjoy foods that should probably be forbidden at his age. Patsy kept him on a fairly strict diet, low in carbohydrates and cholesterol. He'd never cheated on his wife except when it came to food, indulging in his favorites behind her back.

This was his last road trip prior to his retirement. Once he found Naaman Lapp, he was done. And this thing with Naaman was different. It was personal.

CHAPTER ELEVEN

Levina waited for Naaman to spread the blanket by the water's edge.

"How's this?" He placed the picnic basket in the middle of the red-and-blue-checked quilt and motioned for her to sit down.

"It's perfect." She was almost certain that this was the exact spot where he'd proposed to her over thirty-one years ago. Coincidence? She didn't think so.

She pulled her black sweater around her. There was a nip in the air, but the sun shone brightly, and it truly was the perfect day.

"Are you cold?" he asked, sitting down beside her.

"*Nee*. I'm fine. This is a lovely spot. Is it . . ."

Naaman smiled. "*Ya*, it is."

Levina pulled out two paper plates and two napkins, then she retrieved all the lunch goodies she'd brought. "That was a long time ago," she said softly. "I was an eighteen-year-old girl." She smiled. "You proposed the day after your twentieth birthday."

"*Ya*." Naaman watched her spoon some potato salad onto his plate.

Levina thought about how he had missed their

thirty-first anniversary this past December, along with all the holidays, then pushed the thought aside. This was a fresh start, a new beginning for them, and she was going to trust Naaman completely. She had to. Faith, hope, love—and trust—were the foundations for a good marriage.

They ate their lunch in relative silence, commenting on two squirrels chasing each other nearby and how much the creek was up from the recent rains. When they were done, Levina packed everything except their plastic tea glasses back into the basket.

"That was wonderful, Levina." Naaman lay back on the blanket and rested on his elbows, then he crossed his ankles, cringing as he did so.

"Your hip still bothering you?" Levina had noticed him still limping a little.

"Not as much as it was. The doc in Middlefield said it would just take awhile to heal. I hope it doesn't take too much longer; there's much to be done around the farm, and I don't want this holding me back."

Levina glanced around. Not a soul anywhere. She lay down on her side, propped her head in her hand, and faced her husband.

"We've had a *gut* life, haven't we?" Naaman reached over and grabbed her hand.

Levina grinned. "You make it sound like our life is over. I choose to believe that it's just beginning."

Naaman intertwined his fingers with hers and gave her a gentle squeeze. "Today can be the first day of the rest of our lives."

Levina giggled. "Naaman! I've heard that before. It's

a popular catchphrase the *Englisch* use." She pulled her hand from his and pointed a finger in his direction. "You're going to have to do better than that."

He twisted around and lay on his side, facing her, but groaned as he did so. He chuckled. "I sound like an old man." He reached for her hand again. "Do you remember the day Rosemary was born? The way it was storming, and we worried how we would get to the hospital? That was back before phones were allowed in the barn." Naaman shook his head. "I reckon that's the most scared I've ever been in my life. Scared me to death that you might have that baby at home."

"Women do it all the time, but with midwives—not a husband who is in a complete state of panic." Levina laughed at the recollection of Naaman's actions that day. "Remember how you flagged down that car on the highway? Those two *Englisch* teenagers didn't know what to think."

"But they helped us. That boy helped me get you into the car, and the *Englisch* girl was wise enough to ask if you'd packed a bag."

"Which I had. She went and got it for me."

They were quiet for a few moments, the gentle breeze rustling the leaves overhead as the sun continued to shine brightly.

"We've been *gut* parents, haven't we?" Naaman squeezed her hand again and smiled.

"*Ya*, I think so. And we are blessed that all five of our *kinner* chose to be baptized into the faith and stayed in this community."

They were quiet again, and Levina was sure she could

read Naaman's mind. Raising children had been something that they'd partnered on in every area, making
sure the children had complete understanding of the
Ordnung. They'd worried together when each one ventured into their *rumschpringe* and held steady to their
faith through the challenging teenage years. All of their
children loved the land and worked hard, even the girls,
who Levina believed had turned out to be better cooks
than she was. Yes, she and Naaman had been the best
parents they could be.

Naaman avoided her eyes, tucked his chin. "I am so
sorry, Levina. I am so sorry that I left."

She squeezed his hand. "I know you are, Naaman.
And I've thought a lot about it, even more so now that
you're back." She paused in recollection, intertwining
her fingers with his. "I think that once we'd done our
job as parents, we didn't know what to do with each
other. It's been so long since we focused on just us."

"That's what I want to do now. Focus on us. Tell me
what would make you happy."

Levina filled with warmth as she thought about
some of the things she'd dreamed of doing with
Naaman. She let go of his hand and tapped her finger
to her chin. "Let's see. Do you really want to know?
Because you might be very surprised."

His eyes swept over her face as he smiled. "Surprise me."

"Okay." She bit her bottom lip and thought for a
minute. "It would make me happy to eat at Yoder's
Pantry once a week, since we don't have *kinner* to feed."

Naaman nodded for her to go on.

"I would like to fly a kite."

Naaman chuckled, and Levina playfully held up a finger. "*Ya*, I know it is something *kinner* usually do, but I have never flown a kite. I want to shirk work one afternoon and run barefoot through the grass in the far pasture on a sunny summer day when the winds are high . . . and fly a kite."

"Do we own a kite?" Naaman lifted his brows.

"Not yet."

Naaman smiled. "Go on."

"I would like to go to Florida. So many folks in our community vacation in Florida. I would like to see the ocean in Florida."

"Then we will." Naaman shifted his weight a bit. "And?"

"And I would like to paint a picture. A landscape painting that Bishop Ebersol would approve of. I'd like to do it on real canvas with real paints." Levina felt her face turning red. She shook her head. "I know that sounds so whimsical, but I've always wondered what it would be like to—"

Naaman reached over and pulled her into his arms and kissed her on the neck.

"Naaman! Someone might see." She tried to push him away. But she didn't try very hard.

"Who?" He glanced around them. "The trees?" He chuckled, then went on. "You are going to do all of those things, *mei lieb*. And much more. I'm going to make sure that you are happy always."

Levina forced herself out of his embrace, then sat up and crossed her legs beneath her. She gazed into his eyes. "Now, Naaman . . . you tell me what you would like to do during this second half of our lives."

Naaman took a deep breath. "Levina, I don't feel worthy. I already did something I wanted, without ever even consulting you. Let me spend the rest of my life making you happy."

Levina smiled and shook her head. "We are partners, Naaman. We always have been. It's just that in the past we focused all our efforts on the children and everything else but ourselves. In this second half of our life, we'll still be a partnership. What is something you would like to do?"

Naaman sat up and faced her, looping his thumbs beneath his suspenders. "I would like to make furniture and sell it to the local shops. I've made things here and there for pleasure, for the children and for friends, but I'd like to spend more time doing that."

Levina nodded. "I think you should, then. What else?"

"I would like never to have to eat shoofly pie again the rest of my life."

Levina widened her eyes in shock. "What?" She slapped her palms on her legs. "What in the world are you talkin' about?"

Naaman shrugged. "I don't care for it."

Levina crossed her arms across her chest. "Naaman, everyone likes shoofly pie."

"Not me."

"Then why have you been eating it all these years?" Levina narrowed her eyes at him.

"Because everyone says yours is the best in the

county, and . . ." He shrugged. "What kind of Amish man doesn't like shoofly pie?" He grimaced. "I reckon I don't really care for molasses at all."

Levina couldn't speak or close her mouth. Finally she shook her head. "Now, Naaman, how could I have not known that?"

"That's what this is about, no? Getting to know each other better."

Levina threw her head back and laughed until Naaman was laughing so hard with her that both of them struggled to catch their breath.

"I reckon so, Naaman. I reckon so." She struggled to compose herself. "So, what else? What else would you like to do?"

"I'd like to play that guitar in the basement, the one Freda brought into the house while she was in her *rumschpringe*."

Levina arched one eyebrow. "It's against the rules, Naaman. You know that the *Ordnung* says that musical instruments invoke unnecessary emotion. That's why we stored it in the basement."

"In the big picture of rules to be broken, Levina, I reckon I just don't see the Lord minding if I strum that guitar from time to time when no one is around."

Levina smiled. "All right, Naaman. What else?"

Naaman leaned slowly forward and kissed her on the lips. "I want to love you for the rest of my life."

Levina kissed him back, again and again . . .

CHAPTER TWELVE

Larry enjoyed his third helping of raspberry yogurt with a generous amount of fresh granola on top. Two other couples were just leaving when he sat down at eight forty-five. This seemed like a good time to inquire about Naaman Lapp.

"I just can't seem to get enough of this yogurt. I sure would like to take some back to my wife, if I can stuff one more thing in my suitcase." Larry smiled at Barbie Beiler as she placed a few fresh pancakes in the warming tray on the counter.

"I have a friend who makes and sells it. If you're not traveling too far, I bet it would keep until you get home. I'll call her if you're interested in purchasing some."

"Thanks. That'd be great." Larry stood up, then helped himself to all the pancakes she'd laid out. "I'm looking for an Amish fellow by the name of Naaman Lapp. Do you know him?"

Barbie stopped wiping the counter behind the food trays. "I'm sorry. I'll be right back. I need to check my pie in the oven."

She stepped through the door to the kitchen and closed it behind her.

After about ten minutes Larry figured she wasn't coming back. Maybe Barbie was avoiding his question because she'd heard he was a sheriff. He'd been sure to wear his street clothes after the first evening, but the woman who checked him in might have told her.

He opened the newspaper on the table, knowing he had some time to kill before church. He'd ask again about Naaman after he attended Mass and before he got settled in for his ball game on television. He looked down at his protruding belly, then he slathered butter all over his stack of pancakes before soaking them with maple syrup.

Patsy would have a fit.

Levina opened her eyes Sunday morning, and Naaman was propped up on his elbow staring at her.

"*Guder mariye, mei lieb.*" Naaman draped an arm across her. "How did you sleep?"

"Better than I have in . . ." She paused, not wanting to bring up the past. "In a long time."

"I love you so much, Levina." Naaman leaned down and snuggled close to her.

Levina chuckled.

"What?" Naaman sounded alarmed.

"I was just thinking . . . what kind of a girl does this . . . you know . . . on her first *date*?" Levina smiled. She didn't think she'd ever been happier than at this moment. Last night there was an honesty between them that seemed new, fresh, and alive.

"*Ya.* Shame on you, *mei lieb,*" he teased as he pulled her closer.

They lay quietly for a while, and Levina was wishing

they could lie there all day, but today was worship service—at Adam's house.

"We have to get up and get ready, Naaman." She eased away from him.

Naaman rolled on his back. "*Ya*. I know."

"I'm sure everything will go fine with Adam. I'm hoping you get to talk to him alone. Maybe you can find out what is going on with him."

"Levina, Adam doesn't even want to be around me, so I reckon I don't know why you think he'll open up to me."

Levina pulled her robe closed and lifted her chin. "Because you are his father. That's why."

Naaman scowled. "Can't we just stay in bed all day and play sick?" He grinned as he folded his hands behind his head.

"We cannot. Now get up and get ready, Naaman Lapp." Levina arched her brow. "Before I go bake you a shoofly pie and serve it to you for breakfast."

Naaman let out an exaggerated moan as he climbed out of bed. "If I have to."

"Up! Up!" She snapped her fingers and walked to the bathroom, humming.

Today was going to be a good day. The best day. She could feel it.

. . .

Adam set the last of the chairs in the barn. Four rows of ten for the women, four rows of ten facing those for the men, and six chairs in the middle for the bishop and deacons. He dreaded having to face his father, but it was a day of worship, and he would be respectful of the day and the situation at hand.

"I wish we had a bigger *haus* so we didn't have to have worship in the barn."

Adam turned when he heard Hannah. "Our *haus* is fine. We only hold worship once every nine or ten months anyway."

Hannah shrugged, and Adam fought the urge to say something. He started straightening the chairs in the rows.

"Adam, I hope things go *gut* with your *daed* today."

He looked up at her as he moved one chair in line with the others. "I won't be disrespectful, if that's what you're worried about."

Hannah didn't say anything. She just stood watching him work, twisting the string on her *kapp* with her finger.

He put the last chair in line, then put his hands on his hips. "What is it, Hannah?"

She shrugged again, and Adam took a deep breath and glared at her. "I have work to do out here."

"I was just checking on you, Adam. I just wanted to tell you that I hoped things went *gut* with your *daed*. That's all."

"*Danki.*" He got the broom and started sweeping around the chairs, but Hannah just stood there. "Anything else?"

"Adam, what is wrong with you? Why are you acting like this?" Hannah's voice cracked as she spoke.

Adam felt like a *dummkopf*. But he didn't have time

to get into this now. "Nothing, Hannah. Nothing is wrong."

"Something is wrong, Adam. Something has been wrong for a while, and I don't understand." She wiped a tear from her cheek. "It wonders me what is going on with you. Please talk to me."

"Hannah . . ." Adam stopped sweeping and closed his eyes for a moment. When he opened them, he caught her brushing away another tear. He couldn't stand to see her cry, but now was not the time to have a serious talk about anything. He leaned the broom against one of the chairs and went to her. "Hannah, can we talk about our problems later?"

"I didn't realize we had any, Adam. We're so blessed, in so many ways."

Adam hung his head. "I don't want to talk about it right now."

Hannah spun around and ran back to the house, crying. Adam wanted to go to her, to comfort her, tell her how much he loved her. But his feet were rooted to the wooden floor in the barn.

Lord, why am I so confused? What is wrong with me?

Naaman entered his son's house with Levina. All of his children, their spouses, and his grandchildren were already there when they arrived, and each greeted them when they walked in the door. Even Adam.

Adam's greeting was forced, barely a nod and a hello, but it was better than total avoidance. But Naaman was confident that Adam would be respectful, no matter his ill will. He'd have his mother to answer to otherwise.

Naaman turned to Levina, feeling more in love

with her than ever before. They were going to spend the rest of their lives living out their dreams. Going to Florida, flying kites, and—he smiled—no more shoofly pie.

Following the three-hour service, they all shared a meal on tables set up outside the barn. Then, as was customary, the men began to gather together on the far side of the barn to talk and tell jokes while the women finished cleaning up.

Naaman had heard enough jokes in his day. He didn't want to leave Levina for one second. "Let's just stay on the porch together," he said.

Levina grinned. "And do what?"

Naaman grabbed her hand and brought it to his lips. "I just want to be with you."

Levina giggled like a schoolgirl as she playfully pulled her hand away. "Naaman, people are watching, and I need to go help the others make things tidy."

. . .

"What are they *doing*?" Rosemary grabbed Freda by her sleeve and pulled her to the window. "Look. Just look at them!" She shook her head. "It's embarrassing, them acting like this."

"Let go of me." Freda shook loose of Rosemary's hold. "They're just standing there."

"Well, you should have seen them a minute ago. *Daed* picked up her hand and kissed it, right there on the front porch. No tellin' who saw. They are acting like teenagers."

"*Ach*, Rosemary, I'm sure it wasn't as troubling as you're making it out to be."

"Oh no?" Rosemary grabbed Freda again and turned her toward the window. "Look at that!"

"Keep your voice down. Others will hear." Freda parked her gaze on their parents, and Rosemary watched as Freda's jaw dropped. "They're kissing. In public!"

"I'm going to go out there and tell them that they are acting inappropriately, and that it's embarrassing."

"I think it's sweet."

Rosemary and Freda turned to see Tillie standing behind them, looking over their shoulders, a grin on her face.

"Sweet?" Rosemary folded her arms across her chest. "It's not proper for two middle-aged people to act like that, especially in light of *Daed's* absence the past year."

"Maybe they have found their way back to each other and fallen in love all over again." Tillie's eyes glowed with romantic illusions, and Rosemary rolled her own eyes.

"I've said it before, and I'll say it again . . . all this lost-and-found business is *dumm*."

Freda gasped. "Look! He kissed her again. On the mouth!"

"I think it is beautiful to see our parents like this, and shame on both of you for not being happy for them." Tillie scowled and walked toward the other room.

Rosemary tried to organize her thoughts. "Freda, you agree, no? They are behaving badly."

Freda kept her eyes on her parents, who were now

just gazing into each other's eyes. "I don't know. I want them to be happy, but maybe we should go and talk to them nicely about these public displays."

"*Ya*. Let's do that." Rosemary moved toward the door and Freda followed.

"Hello, girls," their mother said as Rosemary and Freda approached them on the porch. "Lovely service today, no?"

"And a lovely day," their father added with a strange, dreamy tone to his voice. Rosemary looked at Freda briefly, then she lifted her chin and faced her parents.

"We—we just wanted to talk to you for a minute."

"Of course, dear." *Mamm* pushed back a strand of hair that had fallen from beneath her *kapp* and smiled. "What is it?"

Before Rosemary could answer, *Mamm* had already turned back toward their father.

Is she batting her eyes at him?

Rosemary searched the area to make sure no one was in earshot, then she leaned closer to her parents. "What are the two of you *doing* out here?"

Mamm narrowed her eyebrows. "What do you mean?"

Rosemary let out a big gasp. "All this nonsense." She raised her arms in frustration and waved them in the air. "This . . . kissing." She glanced around again. "Someone is going to see, and it's—it's just not right."

"Hmm. I see." *Mamm* grinned at *Daed*.

"I'm not sure you do," Rosemary said, folding her arms across her chest.

"Levina, I think the girls are right." *Daed* latched

onto *Mamm's* hand. "Let's go where we can be alone." Then he winked at their mother.

"Where are you going?" Freda asked.

"Home." *Daed* put his arm around *Mamm.*

Rosemary squeezed her eyes closed for a moment. *Please, Freda . . . don't ask any more questions.*

"To do what? It's still early. No one leaves so soon after worship service." Freda glanced at Rosemary, who was too fearful of her parents' answer to move.

Mamm glanced toward the sky. "Hmm. It's windy."

"*Ya*. It is."

"Should we? What do you think?"

Rosemary and Freda watched the private conversation unfolding between their parents.

Then *Mamm* whispered in *Daed's* ear.

"*Ya*. I reckon you're right," *Daed* said to *Mamm.* "We will be staying awhile longer."

Rosemary looked back and forth between them and wondered if Freda was half as perplexed as she was. "*Gut*. Now try to behave yourselves, for goodness' sake."

Rosemary nodded, then she and Freda turned to walk back into the house. She'd almost cleared the distance between her and her parents when she heard her mother say, "Kiss me again, Naaman."

Rosemary slammed the door behind her. *Silly, silly parents.*

CHAPTER THIRTEEN

Naaman chuckled after Rosemary and Freda were back in the house. "You sure played that up, Levina."

"It was great fun to watch their expressions." Levina smiled. "Shame on us." She sighed. "I hope our children will always be as happy with their spouses as we are at this very moment."

"I pray for that too."

"When are you going to talk to Adam? It looks like the last of the guests are leaving, except for our immediate family."

"I'd rather go home and snuggle up with you."

"I thought we were going to fly a kite."

Naaman dabbed his tongue to his first finger, then held it up. "Wind is dying down. I think snuggling sounds better."

"Talk to Adam. Make things right, and see if you can find out what is going on with him." Levina grinned. "Then home to snuggle."

Naaman couldn't remember the last time he felt this content, but the situation with Adam lingered like a dark cloud above them. Naaman needed to talk to him, but he had little hope that Adam would give him the time of day just yet. Pushing him might be the wrong thing to do. But Levina sure did seem worried about him, for reasons that seemed to have nothing to do with Naaman.

Naaman crossed the yard and met Adam and Hannah. "It was a *gut* service today."

Adam nodded but didn't make eye contact with his father.

"So glad you're here, Naaman." Hannah gave Naaman a hug, and over her shoulder Naaman could see Adam scowl.

"*Danki*, Hannah." He eased out of the hug. "Would you mind if I talk to Adam for a few minutes?"

"Of course not." Hannah smiled, but before she even walked away, Adam spoke up.

"We don't have anything to talk about." He folded his arms across his chest.

"Maybe no, maybe yes." Naaman held his position as he looped his thumbs beneath his suspenders.

Hannah stepped toward Adam, and Naaman saw tears in her eyes. "Talk to your father, Adam."

"This is not your business, Hannah."

Naaman was shocked by the way Adam spoke to his wife, and as Hannah's cheeks turned a rosy shade of pink, Naaman was wishing Adam was still of the age to be taken behind the woodshed for a good spanking.

"Please, Adam." Hannah dabbed at her eyes. "Your father is a wise man. Whatever is bothering you, or if you're angry at him—or me—or . . . I just don't know, but maybe you should talk to him."

"It's all right, Hannah. I'm sure Adam will come to me when he's ready."

A tear rolled down her cheek. "It might be too late by then," she said as she turned and ran back toward the house.

"Adam?" Naaman took a few steps closer, but Adam clenched his jaw tight and stared at the ground. "I know you are angry with me, and I don't blame you. I also know that there is something else going on with you. Your mother senses this, and I can see it now too." Naaman paused with a sigh. "I am here for you if you want to talk to me."

When Adam didn't move, Naaman reluctantly turned to go find Levina, but the sound of his son's voice caused him to turn back around.

"Must be nice to leave all responsibility for a year-long vacation, no?"

Naaman walked back to his son. "Is that what you think it was—a vacation?"

"*Ya.* That's exactly what it was."

"I should not have left, Adam. I regret it."

"But you did it, just the same."

"*Ya.* I did."

They stood quietly for a few moments. Naaman could see his son's bottom lip trembling.

"Don't you think we'd all like to do what you did? Just leave?" Adam glared at his father with such loathing that Naaman was tempted to walk away, but now he saw the deeper issue.

Beneath the outpouring of anger, Naaman could see the pain his son was in. Now how was he going to explain to Adam that his feelings are normal but that they should not be acted on as Naaman had done? He chose his words carefully.

"Is that what you want to do, Adam? Leave your family?"

"Of course not. I would never abandon Hannah and the *kinner*."

Naaman studied him for a moment. "Let's go for a walk, Adam."

Adam grunted. "I'm not going on a walk with you."

Naaman looped his thumbs beneath his suspenders. "*Ya*, you are. Let's go." He hoped the firmness of his tone would coax his son to remember that Naaman was still his father.

Naaman set off, and slowly Adam joined his side. Neither of them spoke until they reached the barbed-wire fence separating the cows from the yard. Adam put a foot on the bottom wire and pushed it back and forth as he stared at the ground. Naaman rested an elbow atop a fence post and waited.

"I–I would never leave my family."

Adam's words stung Naaman, even though he was glad Adam repeated his earlier comment.

"But—I think about what it would be like, to go into the world, to see things, and not have responsibilities. Like you did." He narrowed his eyes at Naaman.

"I regret what I did, Adam." Naaman sighed. "I ask the Lord's forgiveness every day, and I try not to question how my leaving could have been His will." Naaman paused. He knew he must speak candidly. "Your mother and I spent most of our years raising you *kinner*, and once you were all gone, it felt—lonely. I didn't really know your mother anymore. We were just two people sharing meals. That's how it seemed anyway. But, Adam . . . leaving was not the answer. And I didn't leave to go see the world." He raised his brows. "I had an active *rumschpringe*, and I saw all I needed to. If that were what I'd been seeking, I wouldn't have gone to Levi's home in Ohio. I just felt like I needed to be alone."

"You weren't alone there, *Daed*. Levi and his family were there."

"No, I wasn't alone. There were people around me, but a man can be alone in his heart if he chooses. And for reasons I didn't even understand, I chose to be alone."

"Why did you come back?"

"I missed your mother and all of you." Naaman shrugged. "No amount of distance was going to cure the mixed-up feelings I had. I knew I needed to come back and face my fears."

Adam stopped popping the barbed wire back and forth with his foot, and for the first time he looked directly at his father. "What kind of fears?"

Naaman wished he didn't have to have this awkward conversation with his son, but if it helped Adam not to make the same mistake, it would be worth it.

Please, Lord, help me to help Adam through my mistakes and experiences.

At that moment Naaman speculated whether or not his leaving could have been part of a larger plan, God's plan. Could the choices he'd made ultimately affect Adam's future decisions?

Naaman took a deep breath and released it slowly.

"I was afraid that your mother and I would never reconnect with each other—that we'd been wonderful parents but lost the love we once shared."

Adam looked at the ground and kicked at the grass. "That's how I feel sometimes. I work all day, and Hannah works hard too. By the time we tend to the *kinner*, there ain't much time left for—for us."

"Adam, I've made mistakes. All I can do is tell you what I've learned. A marriage has to be nurtured the same way you nurture your *kinner*. Your *mamm* and I stopped doing that somewhere along the way and woke up one day to realize we didn't really know each other anymore . . . that is, we didn't know each other the way we once did, when we were young and in love."

Adam gazed out toward the pasture.

"Do you love Hannah?" Naaman moved closer to his son.

"*Ya*." Adam turned to Naaman. "But she gets on my nerves sometimes."

Naaman chuckled. "And I'm sure you get on hers. That's just part of a relationship." He rubbed his forehead. "In some ways I don't feel like I have the right to talk with you about this, after what I did. But, Adam, if it helps you not to make the same mistakes I did, then perhaps this was God's plan."

Adam continued to gaze into the pasture.

"When is the last time you and Hannah had a date? Just the two of you? Maybe a night out to dinner or a picnic?"

Adam grunted. "*Daed*, I don't remember us doing that since before the *kinner* were here."

Naaman ran his hand the length of his beard. "I wish your *mamm* and I had made more time to spend with each other while you children were growing up."

Adam nodded, then looked Naaman square in the eyes. "I love Hannah, *Daed*."

"I know you do, *sohn*." Naaman took a chance and put a hand on Adam's shoulder. "Don't make the same mistake I did. I never stopped loving your mother. Distance might make the heart grow fonder, but it also puts a wedge in something beautiful that's not meant to be separated." He pulled his hand back slowly. "Why don't you and Hannah plan a night out soon, or even a whole day together? Let your *mamm* and me keep the *kinner*."

"A whole day? What would we do?" A grin tipped at the corner of Adam's mouth.

Naaman raised his brows. "Anything you want. You said you wanted to get out and see things, go places . . . Take Hannah somewhere with you."

Adam ran a hand down his beard. "Hannah and I used to like to go to Pequea Creek, have a picnic, and go fishing. I don't even remember the last time . . ." He shook his head as his voice trailed off. Then he scowled. "But I reckon the *kinner* would like to go to the creek too."

"And you should take them sometime. But there is nothing wrong with you and Hannah having some . . . some romance, by yourselves."

Adam's face turned a tad red, but Naaman continued. "Your *mamm* and I just had a picnic at Pequea Creek."

"I still don't understand how you could just leave *Mamm* . . . and us."

Naaman resisted the urge to hang his head in shame and instead looked his son in the eyes. "I don't understand either. But I'm home. In time, I hope you can forgive me."

"You know that it's our way."

"And I also know that forgiveness does not always come easily—for any of us. I'm sorry for the hurt I caused you, your brother and sisters, and mostly *Mamm*."

"I think I'd like to go talk to Hannah."

Naaman nodded, then he watched as Adam walked away.

Adam took about ten steps before he turned around. *"Danki, Daed."*

Naaman smiled, then followed Adam toward the house to find Levina.

CHAPTER FOURTEEN

Larry rolled over and pried one eye open to look at the clock. How in the world had he slept until nine thirty? Worst part was, he'd missed breakfast downstairs. No homemade yogurt with granola on top today. He rubbed his eyes, then forced himself to sit on the side of the bed.

He had planned to pin down the owner this morning and get an address for Naaman Lapp. His stomach growled as he headed to the shower, past an empty pizza box and two beer bottles. It had been a great ball game, but he probably should have foregone the late-night movie—and the beer.

Once he was shaved and in his street clothes, he flipped through a binder that listed the recommended eateries nearby. After reading brief descriptions of each, he decided on Yoder's Pantry. *Authentic Amish food— breakfast, lunch, and supper.*

Maybe the folks there would know where to find Naaman Lapp. And maybe they would have that yogurt he'd missed out on this morning. Surely Patsy couldn't fault him for the yogurt. He was pretty sure it was good for him.

His knees popped on every single stair on his way down to the car, but once he pulled out, it was only a five-minute drive to Yoder's Pantry.

When he walked into the restaurant, a young Amish woman was placing jars of jams and jellies on a rack by the door.

"Hello." He waited for her to put the last jar on the shelf. "I need a table for one. Also, I was wondering if you know where I can find Naaman Lapp. I'm an old friend of his."

The girl looked up at him with stunning blue eyes that seemed to see right through him. "I don't work here. The hostess should be out in a minute."

"I'm sorry. I saw you putting the jellies on the shelf, so I just assumed you worked here."

"That's all right." She fumbled with the jars, using both hands to line them up side by side on the shelf

"So do you happen to know Naaman Lapp?"

"*Ya*, I know him." The girl looked up at him, but again she seemed to be staring through him.

"So . . . can you tell me where I can find him?" Larry saw her face muscles tense.

"I'm not sure."

"Maybe an address?" Larry saw two other Amish women in the distance, but they were scurrying to deliver food.

"I don't know the address."

Larry raked a hand through his hair and sighed. Most Amish folks he knew back in Ohio had a phone in the barn, even though phones weren't allowed in their homes, but he doubted this woman was going to share any information. "Well, could you give me directions?"

"I don't think so."

Larry pulled a card from his pocket. "Can you ask him to call this number, if you see him?"

"If I *see* him, I will."

When she didn't reach for the card, Larry placed it on the shelf near the jams. "Thank you."

A moment later a much more chipper Amish woman hurried across the floor toward him.

"Hello!"

She jumped up a bit on her toes, which caused Larry to grin.

"How many? Would you like a window seat or a booth?"

"Uh, just me." Larry started to follow her, but the other woman started speaking loudly to her in Pennsylvania *Deitsch*. He recognized the dialect from back home.

His hostess stopped, turned, and glared at him. It was a look of obvious displeasure, and Larry raised his brows and waited. Then she pointed to a booth right inside the entrance. "This okay?"

Before he could answer, she'd scooted back to the other woman.

"Sure," he whispered to himself as he sat down.

• • •

Tillie hurried back to Ellie. "What do you mean he's a sheriff looking for *mei daed*?"

"Irma, who works for Barbie Beiler, said that a man came into the bed-and-breakfast on Friday, dressed as a sheriff. The next day that same man asked Barbie where he could find your father. When this man started asking questions, I couldn't help but worry it's the sheriff Irma was talking about."

"What did you tell him?" Tillie twisted to look briefly at the man, then turned back to Ellie.

"He asked if I knew the address, which I really don't. Then he asked if I could give him directions. And I really can't, because we go a different way from home than going from here."

"Then what happened?"

"He asked if I saw your *daed*, would I tell him to call him." Ellie grinned. "I told him that if I *see* him, I will."

Tillie smiled. Ellie had been blind for the past several years, due to optic nerve damage. Most people couldn't tell because her eyes looked fine—although after a short while you noticed that her line of vision was always a little off.

"I don't think he and *Mamm* are coming in today, but you did *gut*, Ellie," Tillie said. "*Ach!* I need to go tell the other girls to avoid his questions. I don't want anyone to lie—just avoid him."

"Why do you think he's looking for your *daed*?"

"I don't know. But things are going so *gut* with him and *mei mamm*, I don't want to stir up trouble. Besides, I know *Daed* couldn't have done anything bad."

"He left a card." Ellie felt around the shelf, and Tillie saw a white business card next to a jar of jam.

"I got it." Tillie picked up the card and read *Larry*

Dozier. And there was a phone number. She tucked it into the pocket of her apron. "I'm going to go warn the other girls."

. . .

Larry had never seen such a speedy group of waitresses in his entire life. They bustled about like there was a fire in the building.

"Here you go, sir." An Amish woman he hadn't seen yet placed a small bowl of cheese spread and another bowl that looked like peanut butter spread alongside a basket of pretzels. Larry had noticed the sign outside proclaiming the "best pretzels in the county."

"Thank you. I'm ready to—"

But she was gone. Scooted right off before he had time to order. He glanced around at the four servers waiting on other customers. In between taking orders and delivering food, they would gather in a circle, then look in his direction. He wasn't imagining it.

Everyone buzzed about, but they didn't seem in any hurry to take his order. Finally the bubbly girl who had met him at the door showed up. "And what would you like, sir?"

"I'll have the meat loaf with mashed potatoes." Patsy hated meat loaf, so this was his opportunity to splurge on something he didn't get at home. "And ranch dressing on my salad."

"Sure." She spun on her heel.

"Miss?" Larry made sure he said it loud enough that she couldn't ignore him.

When she turned around, her face dropped into the saddest frown he'd ever seen. *"Ya?"*

"I just wanted to ask you if you knew where I could find Naaman Lapp? I'm a friend of his, and—"

The girl bit her bottom lip so hard it hurt Larry to watch.

"I have to turn in your order. We're very busy, and if I don't, it could take forever to get your food!" She spun around and was gone.

Larry sat motionless, watching her. "Okay," he said again to himself.

He dipped a warm pretzel into the cheese sauce and brought it to his mouth, dripping a tiny bit on the white table. Closing his eyes, he savored the salty taste against his tongue before biting into the moist bread. This was comfort food at its best, and Larry knew he agreed with the sign outside. This was the best pretzel in the county. Perhaps in the world, he thought, as he dipped the remainder into the peanut spread. Equally delicious. Right up there with the homemade yogurt.

The doctor, along with Patsy, had said to cut back on carbs, but today was not the day for it. He reached for another pretzel and decided to double-dip—first into the cheese sauce, then the peanut butter spread. *Pure heaven.*

He was appreciating the last little bit of the pretzel when every waitress in the joint suddenly darted toward the front door. Larry strained to see what they were doing, but they rounded the corner and were out of sight. He shoved the last bite into his mouth, hoping his salad would arrive soon. Or that more pretzels would be forthcoming.

. . .

Tillie made it to her father ahead of the other girls and pushed him back toward the front door of Yoder's Pantry.

"*Daed*, what are you doing here?"

Her father scowled as he stumbled backward. "Your *mamm* asked me to drop off this casserole dish you left at Adam's yesterday. And she has some raisin puffs for you and Rufus." He narrowed his eyes at her. "What is wrong with you?"

Tillie motioned with her hand for the other girls to go back around the corner, then she whispered to Annie. "Go make sure that man doesn't get up or try to go to the bathroom or anything."

"How will I stop him?" Annie's eyes rounded with surprise, but she nodded and left.

"Stop *who* from going to the bathroom?" *Daed* took a step forward and leaned his head around the corner, but Tillie grabbed his arm and coaxed him back toward the entrance.

"We're just very busy, *Daed*. Tell *Mamm danki*, and I'll see you later." She opened the door of the restaurant for him to leave.

"*Mei maedel*, it wonders me what is wrong with you." *Daed* shook his head but he did back out the door, and Tillie breathed a sigh of relief.

What had her *daed* done to make a sheriff come to town looking for him?

CHAPTER FIFTEEN

After her shift at Yoder's Pantry was over, Tillie stopped by Freda's house on the way home. She was tethering her horse when Freda met her in the yard.

"Hi, Tillie." Freda took a bite of a banana as she glided across the yard barefoot.

Tillie put her hands on her hips. "We have a problem."

Freda swallowed, "What kind of problem?"

"Our father, that's what!"

Freda's expression grew concerned. "Did something happen? Is he sick? What is it, Tillie?"

Tillie turned her head from one side to the other, scanning the area. With no one in sight, she still felt the need to whisper. "Our *daed* is a wanted man!"

"Tillie, what are you talking about?" Freda folded her hands across her chest, the hint of a smile on her face.

"It's not funny, Freda. There is a sheriff in town looking for *Daed*. He must have gotten in trouble while he was away."

"What kind of trouble?"

Tillie lifted her shoulders, then dropped them. "How should I know? The kind that makes a lawman come lookin' for ya. A tall man with beady eyes and a big belly came into Yoder's Pantry. He was asking where to find *Daed*." Tillie took a deep breath. "This sheriff man is staying at Beiler's, and he asked Barbie too."

"Tillie, are you sure about all this?" Freda thrust her hands onto her hips. "Because you make such a big deal outta every little thing."

"Well, I reckon a sheriff looking for *Daed* is a big deal, no?"

"What could he have done?"

Tillie paced the yard for a few moments. "I don't know, but things are going so *gut* between him and *Mamm*. And he's home. I just don't want him to have to leave again. For prison! *Ach*, Freda, what are we going to do?"

"Tillie, that man will find *Daed*. You can't stop him. *Daed* ain't that hard to find."

"Hmm . . ." Tillie tapped her finger to her chin. "I wonder how long he's planning to stay. Maybe he'll get tired of looking and go back home."

"Probably depends on how bad a thing *Daed* did."

"What do you think it could be?"

Freda shrugged. "I don't know. It's hard to imagine *Daed* in trouble, enough to make a lawman come lookin' for him."

"The girls at Yoder's Pantry are helping me spread the word not to tell that beady-eyed man anything about *Daed*."

"Tillie, are you asking folks to lie?"

"Of course not." Tillie lowered her chin, then raised her eyes to Freda. "Just to avoid the truth. I have to go. But make sure that Jonathan knows. And . . ." Tillie twisted her mouth from side to side as she thought. "Might be best not to mention this to Rosemary or Adam just yet. Adam might haul *Daed* straight to the man, happy to have *Daed* spend the rest of his days in a jail cell!"

"Tillie, stop being so dramatic. Besides, *Mamm* said that Adam and *Daed* talked yesterday after worship service, and things are on the mend between them."

"Just the same, I reckon we don't say anything just yet. Maybe just to Jonathan."

"Whatever you say, Tillie. But I think maybe you should at least talk to Rosemary. She'll know what to do."

Tillie shook her head. "No, no. Rosemary tells *Mamm* everything. You know that. I'm going to go spread the word to everyone I can think of. *Mamm* and *Daed* need time to work on their relationship, alone and with no troubles." She gave a taut nod of her head.

Freda chuckled. "Tillie, you read too many of those magazines at the doctor's office."

"This is not funny, Freda. Not funny at all! Make sure you tell Jake to let everyone know not to tell."

"Tillie, *Daed* is not above the law for whatever he did. Just like the *Englisch*, we're responsible for our actions. It's just a matter of time—"

"Don't say that." Tillie pointed a finger at her sister, then she turned to leave, still wondering what law their father could have broken.

• • •

By late afternoon Larry knew he would be staying at least one more day in Lancaster County, since Naaman Lapp was proving to be the most elusive man he'd ever pursued. Every person Larry had come in contact with today had avoided him like he was . . . a sheriff in pursuit of a criminal. Larry shook his head and smiled as he walked into the small breakfast area at the B & B.

"I'm going to need to stay at least one more night," he told the same Amish girl who'd been there when he arrived.

"Sure. That's fine. But the rest of the week is already booked up." She smiled as if this was the best news on the planet. "I'm sorry."

"What? I thought you said I wouldn't have to worry about it until the weekend. This is only Monday."

Still smiling, the woman shrugged. "Big group of ladies called to book four rooms, starting tomorrow."

"Couldn't you have checked with me?"

Her smile fell. "I'm sorry, Mr. Dozier. We have to accept those who are a for-sure thing. You didn't think you'd be staying past today. I'm sorry for the inconvenience."

Larry sighed. "So I need to check out tomorrow morning?"

The woman smiled again. "Yes, sir. By noon, please."

Larry eyed some sticky buns on a plate near the woman. "May I?"

"Sure." She pushed the platter toward him.

Patsy would have my behind for this. He took a bite

as he walked out the door. He hoped he could find Naaman in the morning, then be on his way back home by tomorrow afternoon, instead of having to find another place to stay.

. . .

Levina wasn't sure exactly what her two youngest daughters were trying to pull, but Rosemary had gotten wind of their antics first thing this sunny Tuesday morning and had come straight to tell Levina about it.

"I heard it from Rebecca, who heard from Sarah, that *Daed* is on the run from the law. Sarah heard from her husband, who heard it at the market in Bird-in-Hand. And Paul Dienner said that Big John at the hardware store said *Daed* is going to prison for a very long time. And Tillie and Freda are running around town telling everyone not to tell where you and *Daed* live. Evidently the sheriff man went into Yoder's Pantry looking for him."

Levina turned off the water in the sink, dried her hands on her apron, then spun to face her daughter. "What for? What did he supposedly do?" She wasn't sure what was more upsetting—Naaman's crime or the fact that the entire community was talking about it and bordering on breaking the law themselves by hiding Naaman. Just when she thought they could put embarrassment behind them, this happens.

"I don't know, *Mamm*." Rosemary sat down at the table.

"Where are my grandchildren?"

"Glenn is with them." Rosemary reached for a left-over biscuit. "He thought I should come right over here and tell you."

"Did he, now?" Levina opened the refrigerator and pulled out a jar of rhubarb jam. She pulled a spoon from the drawer and placed the spoon and jam in front of Rosemary.

Rosemary piled the jam on one half of the biscuit, then she began talking with her mouth still full. "What are you going to do?"

Levina sat down. "What do you mean?"

Rosemary swallowed. "Are you going to ask *Daed*?"

"I am not going to disrespect your father by asking him about petty rumors." Levina's stomach churned, though she was doing her best not to let Rosemary know.

"But, *Mamm* . . . there is a lawman lookin' for *Daed*. He did something."

Levina put her head in her hands, then looked back up at Rosemary. "The good Lord will provide the answers when He's ready. And so will your father."

Rosemary stuffed the other half of the biscuit into her mouth. "I can't believe you're not gonna ask him about this."

I can't believe it either.

Things were better between her and Naaman than they'd ever been. Levina recalled the past couple of days. Sunday night after worship at Adam's, they cuddled together on the couch, holding hands and reading the Bible. Monday they'd each worked hard all day, but after supper they'd taken a walk, then gone to bed early. Levina smiled. Things were perfect. If her world was getting ready to fall apart again, she wanted to enjoy these special moments while they lasted.

. . .

Naaman put the last coat of varnish on the oak dresser, then he stood back to inspect his work. It was small, perfect for a baby's room—for whichever of his youngest daughters needed it first.

"Very nice," Levina said as she strolled in holding two glasses. "I brought you some sweet tea."

"Danki." He accepted the tea, took a large gulp, then set it down on his workbench. "I reckon this will be for either Tillie's or Freda's *kinner.*"

"It seems to be a race between those two." Levina grinned. "What are you going to do if they both get pregnant at the same time?"

Naaman pointed to his right, to a stack of wood he planned to use for his next project. "I'm prepared."

It was only midmorning, so Naaman pushed back thoughts of a nap with Levina. All he could think about these days was holding her in his arms. He was like a teenager in love, and he wanted to spend every waking minute with her.

She edged closer and smiled, the type of expression that made Naaman think perhaps a nap was in order after all. "What's your plan for the day?"

Naaman smiled and lifted his eyebrows up and down. "Depends. What are your plans?"

"Stop that, Naaman." Levina waved him to shush, but with a grin on her face. "With the *kinner* gone, I reckon our days aren't as full, but there is still much to be done around here. I'm planning to finish the wash this morning before lunch and get it out to dry."

"When did wash day change from Monday to Tuesday?"

Levina crossed her arms across her chest. "When you returned and we started taking naps all the time." She lifted her chin, still grinning.

"*Ach*, I see." He took a swig of his tea. "What did Rosemary want this morning?"

"Just to chat." Levina shrugged.

"That reminds me. Tillie acted mighty strange yesterday when I went to drop off the things you sent. It was like she couldn't get me out of Yoder's Pantry fast enough." He scratched his chin. "That girl was hiding something, but I reckon I haven't a clue what. You know anything?"

Levina shrugged again. "You know Tillie. She always has something going on, and if she doesn't she creates something to keep herself entertained."

"Hmm . . ." Naaman eyed Levina and tried to figure out if she was being completely truthful. His wife always knew what the *kinner* were up to.

"Hannah stopped by while you were tending to the cows in the pasture yesterday afternoon. She was glad that you and Adam talked. Whatever you said to him, she said he seems like a much happier person. I was so glad to hear that."

Naaman nodded. "They are young, but I think they will be fine."

"What about you and Adam?"

Naaman pulled his straw hat from his head and wiped his forehead. "I think things will be all right. Just gonna take Adam a little time to understand why . . ." Naaman trailed off, not wanting to bring up the past.

"I'm going to get the wringer going and start on those clothes. I've got some beef stew simmering on the stove."

"Sounds *gut*. I'm going to put the knobs on this dresser, and then it will be ready for whichever *dochder* needs it first."

"It's a beautiful piece of furniture, Naaman."

He smiled, not sure if life could be any more perfect.

CHAPTER SIXTEEN

Tuesday morning Larry checked out of Beiler's B & B and into a small hotel at the edge of town after not being able to find a room at any of the other bed-and-breakfasts in the area. The first two Amish-owned establishments told him they were full, but not until after he mentioned his name. He ventured into two more B & Bs in Gordonville, and although the places weren't Amish-owned, he'd spotted some Amish women outside in the yard. These inns were full, too . . . after they asked for his name.

It didn't take a brain surgeon to figure out that the community was protecting Naaman Lapp from the big bad sheriff. Larry smiled as he settled onto the bed in the small room, then he picked up the phone.

"Bill, I need you to get an address for an Amish man named Naaman Lapp. He lives in Lancaster County, Pennsylvania, in the town of Paradise."

"You mean to tell me that you can't track down one Amish fellow in that small town?" His partner chuckled.

"Yeah, I know. I think folks around here are hiding him, so to speak. It's a pretty close-knit community."

"Let me get you an address, and I'll call you back."

Larry hung up, propped the pillows behind him, then flipped on the television. He couldn't believe he was still here after four days. But there were worse places to be when one was avoiding the in-laws. Besides, Patsy would be thrilled with the quilt and all the trinkets he'd picked up for her. And he was enjoying some mighty good food.

He crossed his ankles and starting switching the channels. It wouldn't take long for Bill to get him an address, and Larry planned to head to Naaman's place right after lunch. Maybe lunch at Yoder's Pantry again. More of those warm pretzels dipped in cheese sauce and peanut butter spread. Just thinking about it made his mouth water.

. . .

Levina pinned the sheets to the line while Naaman cleaned the stalls in the barn. Hard as she tried, she couldn't shake her conversation with Rosemary. She'd prayed hard about it all morning, asking God to guide her to do the right thing, and she knew she needed to confront Naaman about what Rosemary said. She didn't want there to be anything between them. They were in a good, honest place, and she'd never been happier. This new information made her uneasy, and she couldn't stop wondering what it was that Naaman had done to bring a sheriff to town. Her healing heart was still fragile, but she would have to know the truth.

She trembled as fear overtook her like a winter's

wind slapping against her bare skin. *Please, God, whatever Naaman did, I pray it wasn't too bad. Please don't take him from me again.* Naaman was a good man, and even if he'd done something he shouldn't have, he wasn't the type of man to run away.

Levina froze as she realized that he was *exactly* the type to run away. He'd proven that. Then it hit her—hard. Maybe that was the reason her husband had come home—because he was in trouble with the law. Her head began to spin. Would Naaman have ever come home if there hadn't been trouble in Middlefield? Maybe he didn't have a choice. Maybe home was the only place he had to go. *Did I get him back by default?*

She took a deep breath, then blew it out slowly as she pinned the corner of the last sheet.

By the time Naaman came in for lunch, Levina had dreamed up every possible scenario as to why a sheriff would be looking for him. Did he leave Ohio owing someone money? Did he drive a car while he was there and get a violation of some sort? Maybe he'd had an accident? The "maybes" kept going through her head, but logically she couldn't wrap her mind around the idea of Naaman doing anything illegal, much less not fessing up to it. She was just going to have to ask him.

"Something smells *gut* in here." Naaman walked into the kitchen, put his hat on the rack, and wasted no time wrapping his arms around her waist as she stirred the stew. Just the feel of his arms around her sent a shiver of longing through her. They were on their second honeymoon, and Levina wished it could go on like this forever. Maybe she'd wait to ask him about the sheriff.

When they'd finished eating, Naaman kissed her on the cheek while she washed the dishes. Then he did something he'd never done. He began to dry the dishes and put them away.

"Why are you doing that?" She asked the question with a sharper tone than she intended as she turned to face him.

His jaw dropped slightly. "Just trying to help you."

She forced a smile, but her thoughts returned to a bad place. *Maybe you are just trying to solidify your place in our household so that I will stand by you when the lawman comes. Maybe the only reason you came back is because you have nowhere else to go.*

"That's not where that goes." She dried her hands on her apron, then pulled the large spoon from the drawer where Naaman had put it. She hung it on the rack near the stove.

"Levina, is everything all right?" Hesitantly, Naaman picked up another plate and started to dry it.

"*Ya.*" She walked back to the sink and resumed washing, but didn't look at him. "I–I have some errands to run this afternoon."

"I can finish up in the shop and go with you." He smiled as he put away a plate in the cabinet.

"No." She shook her head. "You would be bored. I have to go by Rebecca Deinner's house to pick up some cookbooks to take to Yoder's Pantry, and I have to stop by Barbie Beiler's Bed-and-Breakfast." She quickly looked at Naaman to see if the mention of Beiler's B & B generated any kind of reaction. Nothing.

"Well, okay. I'll take the spring buggy to pick up

some parts I need to fix one of the generators." He kissed her on the cheek again. "But I hope to meet back here before too long." He winked at her as he put the last dish up. Then he pulled his hat from the rack and headed out the door.

Levina dried her hands and took a deep breath. She couldn't take this anymore. She'd just go find the sheriff at Barbie's B & B and find out exactly what he wanted. Waiting around for him to just show up was going to make her crazy.

• • •

Larry scribbled down Naaman's address on a piece of hotel stationery, thanked Bill, and hung up the phone. No time like the present, he figured. Once he found Naaman Lapp, he could head back home to Patsy. He was missing her more than ever by now, and she'd said during their phone conversation earlier that morning that her parents were leaving. Patsy's parents were good people, but they rode him even more than Patsy about his diet, the occasional beer, and his lack of exercise. And it wasn't just that. Patsy's mother had a high-pitched voice that sounded sweet the first few minutes you were around her, but after about an hour it turned into an annoying, almost yappy little squeak. Fortunately Patsy hadn't inherited that trait.

An hour later he was pulling into the driveway off Black Horse Road. He was impressed by the way folks around here kept their property. Nothing out of place, and yards that would make any homeowners' association proud. Naaman's homestead consisted of a freshly painted white clapboard house surrounded by a white picket fence, and a large barn on either side. He didn't see any buggies, though.

He waited an ample amount of time at the door, but when no one answered, he headed back to the car, stopping to pet an Irish setter on the way out. "Where's your owner, buddy?"

No problem. He'd catch some overdue lunch, then try again later. No shortage of good food in these parts, that was for sure.

. . .

Levina whisked into the breakfast area of Beiler's Bed-and-Breakfast. Empty. She knocked on the kitchen door, then she pushed it open a few inches. All dark. Her friend was probably cleaning one of the guest rooms. She went around the corner just in time to see Irma walking out of a first-floor guest room, toting a cleaning bucket filled with supplies.

"Levina, what brings you here?" Irma smiled as she approached her.

"I–I know you're probably not supposed to do this, Irma, but I'm looking for a lawman that I think was staying here. I need to talk to him." Levina scrunched her face up and bit her lip, not sure if Irma would help her or not.

"You mean the big man who is looking for Naaman?" Irma looked like she was holding her breath.

So much for the embarrassment of this whole thing.

"*Ya.* I really need to talk with him. Can you tell me what room he's in?"

"He checked out. I mean, he wanted to stay, but he only had the room until Tuesday noon, and we had a last-minute group of ladies call for the only four rooms we had left." Irma leaned closer and whispered, "Is Naaman in trouble?"

Levina grinned and waved her hand at Irma. "No, no. It's nothing. Do you know where he went?"

Irma shook her head. "No. But Tillie and Freda made it a point to tell everyone around here not to tell the lawman where Naaman lived. So I reckon some folks might not rent to him either."

My girls should know better than this. "Irma, I'm sure that Naaman didn't do anything, but we can't have the community trying to hide him. It isn't right. Do you know if this policeman is from Ohio?"

"I reckon I don't know. He didn't say. He's a sheriff, though. He had on a sheriff's uniform when he checked in."

"Hmm . . . All right. *Danki.*" Levina waved as she turned to leave.

"Hope everything is all right, Levina!"

So do I. Levina nodded.

. . .

Paradiso was right down the block, an Italian restaurant Larry hadn't tried since he arrived. Another place probably filled with forbidden foods. He smiled as he walked in.

The smell of garlic and oregano filled his nostrils, and a hostess seated him right away. He scanned the menu, not even allowing his eyes to peruse the healthy section. Patsy always wanted to eat heart healthy. *Gotta love her.*

"Would you like to try our special?" The waitress pointed to a large chalkboard on her right. Larry squinted to have a look. Baked lasagna, salad, and garlic bread.

"That looks good." He handed the woman his menu. "I'll have the special. Ranch dressing, please, ma'am."

After his salad, Larry savored the rich taste of the lasagna and cleaned his plate. Truly some of the best Italian food he'd ever had.

Then he got the strangest pain in his chest.

CHAPTER SEVENTEEN

Levina tried to find the sheriff at four more bed-and-breakfasts, but she decided there were just too many places to check. Next stop—Yoder's Pantry. Tillie was probably almost through with her shift, and Levina had a few questions for her.

"*Mamm!* I'm just getting ready to clock out for the day. What brings you here?"

Levina put her hands on her hips. "Tillie Mae, is it true that you and Freda have been running round town telling people not to tell a certain sheriff where your father lives?"

Tillie lowered her chin and twisted her mouth from side to side. "Hmm. You found out about that, no? How?"

"Rosemary heard from Rebecca, who heard from someone else, who heard from someone else."

"Figures that she would tell you right away."

"You should have told me, Tillie. I heard that he came here." Levina glanced over Tillie's shoulder to make sure no one could hear, but lowered her voice anyway. "Did he say why he is looking for your father?"

"I didn't talk to him. Ellie did. But I saw him.

He's a big, scary-looking man with a big stomach."
Tillie clasped her hands in front of her, looked down,
and shook her head. "What do you think *Daed* did,
Mamm?"

"We don't know that he did anything, Tillie, but you
can't involve the entire community by asking them to
hide your father." Levina let out a heavy sigh. "It could
be a misunderstanding or any number of things."

"Like what?"

"I don't know, Tillie. But let's not presume the worst.
Maybe your *daed* drove a car without a license or some
other thing of little worry. The man, the sheriff, has
already checked out of Beiler's B & B, but—"

"*Gut!* Maybe he's gone."

"No. He wanted the room for another night, but
Beiler's was full. He's around here somewhere." Levina
shrugged. "No use lookin' for him, I guess. I'm sure he's
going to find us, so we'll just wait."

Tillie stood quietly for a while, which wasn't like
her. Then she gazed into her mother's eyes. "Don't let
him leave again, *Mamm*. Whatever you do."

Tillie's eyes were brimming, and Levina swallowed
back her own tears.

"I don't want your *daed* to go anywhere, but if he
did something wrong, Tillie . . ." She stopped when
Tillie dabbed at her eyes. "Try not to worry, and I'll
let you know when I find out what's goin' on." Levina
pulled Tillie into a quick hug, then she decided there
was nothing to do but go home.

As she left Yoder's Pantry, her heart was heavy. *Please,
Lord, give me strength.* She couldn't help but fear that

Naaman was only home because of whatever trouble he'd gotten into in Middlefield. Yet she'd allowed him back into her heart, further than he'd been in many, many years. She swiped at a tear as she flicked the reins, unsure whether to say anything to Naaman or just wait for the sheriff to show up.

. . .

Levina seemed nervous as a cat. Naaman asked her several times throughout the course of the evening what was wrong, but she said her stomach was just a little upset. It was more than that, he knew, but whatever it was, she wasn't talking.

He looked over the rim of his reading glasses. Levina had her head buried in the Bible, but he didn't think she'd turned a page since they sat down on the couch an hour ago.

"Levina, are you sure you're all right?" He pulled his glasses off and closed his own Bible, then twisted slightly on the couch to face her. "I see you lookin' out the window from time to time. You expecting someone?"

She pushed her reading glasses up her nose and kept her head in the book. "No. Are you?" She looked up at him, raised her brows.

Naaman grimaced. "No. I'm not expecting anyone. Should I be?"

Levina let out a heavy sigh. "I reckon not."

"Do you want to go to bed?"

She glowered in his direction. "It's too early for bed, Naaman. It's not even dark yet."

Her sharp tone of voice didn't leave room for discussion, so he stayed quiet. They'd been going to bed early all week. But something had changed, and Naaman was desperate to find out what.

Two hours later nothing had improved, and Naaman was tired. "Do you mind if I go on to bed?"

She didn't look up. "No, that's fine. I'll be there shortly."

He took two steps and turned around. "Levina?"

This time she looked up and raised her eyes above her glasses. *"Ya?"*

"I love you with all my heart. I'm glad to be home. And I'm sorry, still, for everything."

Levina swallowed hard. "I know, Naaman. I love you too."

He kept his eyes locked with hers for a few moments, trying to figure out what was on her mind, but there were no clues in her staid expresssion. When she lowered her head, he eased up the flight of stairs to their bedroom, longing for his wife to join him and wondering what had changed between them.

. . .

Larry sat down on his bed at the hotel and put his arm across his full belly. This was surely the worst case of indigestion he'd ever had. Bad enough to keep him from going back to Naaman's house, and he'd been anxious to take care of things with Naaman so he could get home to Patsy. He popped two more Tums in his mouth, then he decided to take a shower before he called his wife.

He'd barely wrapped a towel around himself when he heard his cell phone ringing—a zingy little ringtone that Patsy had assigned herself.

"Hello, dear. Miss me?" Larry smiled as he spoke, hoping to forget about the heartburn that had settled in the middle of his chest.

"Have you not found that man yet, Larry? Good grief. You're an officer of the law, for goodness' sake."

"Well, you know . . . the first day, there was shopping to do for my lovely wife. Then I didn't want to bother the Amish folks on a Sunday, and yesterday I struck out. Not a soul around here would tell me where that man lives."

"Why didn't you just ask Bill to get the address?"

"I finally did, and I went there earlier today, but no one was home. I was planning to go back this evening, but I'm telling you, Patsy, I have the worst case of indigestion I've ever had in my life." Larry cringed, wishing he could take back the statement.

"Larry Dozier, what have you been eating? You haven't been sticking to our diet, have you? What have I told you about eating fat-filled, cholesterol-soaked foods that aren't good for you—"

Larry held the phone a few inches from his ear as she went on. *Good to be loved.*

"Yes, dear. Yes, dear." He just kept agreeing with her. Always best.

"You know I only tell you these things because I love you."

"I love you, too, dear. And tomorrow morning, first thing, I'm going to Naaman Lapp's house. I'll catch the first flight out after that."

"I can't wait to see my quilt!"

Larry smiled. He loved to hear Patsy happy, and he couldn't wait to see the look on her face when she saw the quilt. "I'll call you tomorrow when I have my business wrapped up."

"I love you. I'll talk to you tomorrow."

"Love you, too, dear."

Larry changed into his pajamas, took two more Tums, then folded himself onto the bed. He flipped the channels on the television, but he couldn't concentrate. The tightness in his chest was getting worse, not better, and he was having trouble catching his breath.

Oh no. As the possibility of having a heart attack hit him, he reached over to grab his cell phone, but he quickly fell back against the pillows. He was being crushed, something so heavy on his chest, he couldn't breathe.

Why am I not breathing? He wanted to breathe but nothing was happening, and the weight on his chest was unbearable.

Dear Lord, am I dying?

Yes.

Larry heard the voice loud and clear, and he knew who it was.

I'm afraid, God.

Patsy's face flashed in front of him, then each of his three children's faces, then his entire life began to play in his mind like a slide show. He thought about how he had only recently turned his life over to God, after years of doubts as a nonbeliever. Six months ago he'd even been baptized. Patsy, who'd always been strong in her faith, said it was the happiest day of her life. Larry agreed with her. Getting to know God and His Son, Jesus, had changed his life.

My life. It's over, isn't it?

He heard the soft voice again. *Yes. Don't be afraid.*

His body wasn't moving. There was no air coming out of his lungs. But a white light filled the room and gave him an immediate sense of comfort.

And he was no longer afraid.

CHAPTER EIGHTEEN

Two days later Levina was still on edge, watching the window and waiting for the sheriff to break whatever bad news was forthcoming. *But why is he waiting?*

Maybe there was another Naaman Lapp somewhere else, outside of their town of Paradise. Or maybe he just changed his mind.

She thought about how happy she and Naaman had been since his return.

"Guder mariye, mei lieb." Naaman walked in full of smiles and kissed her on the cheek.

Levina took a deep breath and tried to fend off her worry. *"Guder mariye."*

She stared at her saucepan on the burner and waited for the water, brown sugar, and butter to come to a boil. Then she poured it into a casserole dish and set it aside. Naaman loved the syrupy pancake bake she'd learned from her mother years ago. Both her parents had passed away, and Levina always thought of her mother when she made this favorite of Naaman's.

Levina wondered if things would have been different if Naaman's parents were still alive. Would he have confided in his father about his problems? Like Levina, Naaman had been an only child—something uncommon in their community. She'd always wondered if that was one of the many reasons they'd taken to each other so easily.

Naaman sat down at the table and started reading the *Intelligencer Journal* while Levina combined the rest of the ingredients to put on top of the first layer of their breakfast—an egg, milk, salt, sugar, butter, flour, and some baking powder. The pancake bake was a little too sweet for her taste, but it had been a favorite of the children's as well as Naaman's.

"Is that pancake bake I smell?" Naaman raised his eyes above his reading glasses.

"It is. Just for you." Levina placed the casserole dish in the oven. "But it will be about thirty minutes." She closed the oven and turned to face him. "The girls are coming for lunch today. Will you be here?"

"No." Naaman pulled his glasses off and smiled. "When Jonathan was here last time, I showed him the dresser I'd made. He told the folks at the furniture store where he works, so I am supposed to go meet with them about doing some special-order projects."

"Naaman, that's great. I know how much you're enjoying that." Levina sat down at the kitchen table. "And it would be nice to supplement our income, since we don't do as much farming as some of the folks around here."

"I won't let this take away from my chores around here, though."

"*Ach*, I know. But it's nice to have something on the

side. I enjoy taking jams, jellies, and crafts to Yoder's Pantry."

Naaman reached across the table and latched onto Levina's hand. "Life is good. God is good. We have so much to look forward to." He grinned. "And we will fly a kite, and we will go to Florida."

Levina thought again about the sheriff, but she pushed her doubts about Naaman's return to the back of her mind. If he had done something all that bad and was on the run, the sheriff would have found them by now.

After they chatted about various home repairs they hoped to do, they enjoyed Levina's casserole. Naaman helped himself to seconds . . . and thirds. As sunlight crept above the horizon, the kitchen began to fill with natural light. Levina turned off the two gas lanterns; then she began to clean the kitchen. She busied herself, even humming, as Naaman finished reading the newspaper.

The *Intelligencer Journal* was the most-viewed newspaper in the county—by both the *Englisch* and Amish. Most of those in their district subscribed to it, in addition to *The Budget* and *Die Botschaft*, both of which served Amish communities throughout the country.

The more she hummed, the more it quieted the worry in her heart. She was looking forward to Rosemary, Tillie, and Freda coming for lunch. Tillie had the day off, and they'd made the plans days ago. She hoped that the conversation wouldn't focus on the sheriff, or the past. Levina wanted to simply enjoy what the future held for them.

She'd just put the last of the clean dishes in the cabinet when she heard Naaman stand up. She turned to see him pulling his hat from the nearby rack. As he placed the hat on his head, his mouth was pulled into a frown, and his eyes were glassy with emotion.

"Naaman, what's wrong?" Levina dried her hands on the dish towel and moved toward him. "What is it?"

Naaman tried to smile, but Levina could see the muscle in his jaw quiver as he blinked his eyes. "Uh . . . nothing. Just lots on *mei* mind. I need to go." He hurriedly kissed her on the mouth, then he was out the door before Levina could say anything else.

She needed to dust and then run the floor sweeper over the downstairs before the girls came at noon, but there was plenty of time for that. She pulled out a chair at the kitchen table and sat down, then pulled the *Intelligencer* toward her. The headline that caught her eye caused her heart to skip a beat.

Middlefield Sheriff Found Dead at Junction Inn.

Levina brought her hand to her chest and tried to calm her rapid heartbeat. She leaned closer to the paper, but all the lines blurred. She reached across the table and grabbed Naaman's reading glasses, which he'd hastily left behind.

After adjusting the glasses, she began to read beneath the picture of a man with balding brown hair and solemn expression, wearing a sheriff's uniform.

Larry Dozier, 58, a sheriff from Middlefield, Ohio, was found dead in his room at the Junction Inn in Paradise on Wednesday. Authorities say that Dozier was in

town on business when he apparently had a massive
heart attack in his room on the second floor. Dozier's
body was found in his bed the next morning when an
employee at the inn entered to clean his room.

Dozier was a 30-year veteran of the Geauge County
Sheriff's Department. He is survived by his wife, Patsy,
two sons and a daughter.

Levina reread the article two more times, but her
heartbeat didn't slow down. She said a quick prayer for
Larry Dozier's family before she stood up and began to
pace in her kitchen.

Is that why Naaman ran out the door? Did he realize
that he'd been found out for whatever it was that he'd
done? Would he run again? Levina breathed deeply
and tried to keep her thoughts clear. When that didn't
work, she decided to start on her housework. Cleaning
had become a stress reliever over the past year. She
probably had the cleanest house in the district, and it
really didn't need dusting, but she gathered her dusting
rag and set out to work, hoping and praying her nerves
would settle before her daughters arrived.

. . .

Naaman steered his buggy across Lincoln Highway and
headed to the furniture store where Jonathan worked, a
place filled with various handcrafted fixtures and furniture, much of it made by Amish men in the area. He
was excited about the prospect of adding his furniture to
the inventory. But he couldn't stop thinking about Larry

Dozier and the family he'd left behind. As he wondered why the Middlefield sheriff was in Lancaster County, Naaman suspected that it had something to do with him.

He parked his topless spring buggy outside of Lyman's Furniture, then he tethered his horse. Jonathan met him as he walked in the entrance.

"Mr. Lyman is waiting to talk to you, *Daed*."

Naaman nodded and tried to clear his mind so that he could make a good business presentation to Doug Lyman, but his thoughts kept veering back to the sheriff.

. . .

Levina gave the kitchen floor another once-over, which it certainly didn't need, but staying busy was all that was keeping her sane this morning. She looked at the clock and realized her daughters would be here any minute. She poured herself into a chair in the kitchen, then she read the article about Larry Dozier one more time and tried to decide whether or not to show it to the girls.

Rosemary would likely push her to question Naaman about it. Tillie would try to persuade her not to say anything, for fear it would push Naaman away. Levina didn't know what Freda would think. Freda was less predictable than her other two daughters.

It was five minutes later when they all trailed up the driveway. Rosemary had baby Leah and the twins with her. Levina put the newspaper on top of the refrigerator, then met all of them in the yard.

"It's so nice out here, I thought maybe we could eat

lunch outside." Levina pointed to the picnic table in the yard covered with a red-checked tablecloth she'd picked up at the savings store in town.

"I love this time of year!" Tillie skipped across the yard, then she wrapped her arms around Levina. "Beautiful day to eat outside."

Freda also greeted her with a hug, but Levina knew right away that Rosemary was unhappy about something. She set the baby carrier on the ground, barely hugged Levina, then urged the twins to go play in the sandbox that Naaman had built for them last spring.

"I saw the article in the newspaper about the sheriff from Middlefield. Did you see it, *Mamm*?"

"What article?" Freda leaned down to pick up Leah from her carrier, then stood up and faced her mother.

Tillie looked at Rosemary, then at her mother. "*Ya*, what article?"

"A sheriff from Middlefield, Ohio, died at the Junction Inn Tuesday night." Rosemary put her hand on her hip. "Sure would be a coincidence if it wasn't the same sheriff lookin' for *Daed*."

As much as Levina wanted to avoid the conversation, she knew there was only one way to find out for sure. "I'll be right back."

Levina came back toting the newspaper, still opened to the article, and she pushed it toward Tillie. "Is this the man you saw at Yoder's Pantry, the one asking about *Daed*?"

Tillie gasped as she brought her hand to her mouth. "That's him all right. Isn't he scary-looking?" She pulled her hand down and grimaced.

"Tillie. Don't speak that way about the dead." Levina folded her arms across her chest and waited for Tillie to read the article, then Freda.

"Guess we'll never know what *Daed* did, huh?" Freda handed the *Intelligencer* back to Levina.

"*Ach*, I'm sure they'll send someone else," Rosemary said.

Ignoring Rosemary's smart tone, Levina chose to answer Freda's comment. "I have told all of you, we don't know that *Daed* did anything. Did any of you mention this to Adam or Jonathan?"

"Not about the man dying. But Adam and Jonathan both know someone was looking for *Daed*," Tillie said. "They said they wouldn't say anything to *Daed* until you had a chance to talk to him. So, did ya?" Tillie's eyes widened.

"No. Not yet."

"Why not, *Mamm*? You're going to have to ask him about it." Rosemary stuffed her hands in the pockets of her apron.

"No, she doesn't, Rosemary! *Mamm* does not have to ever mention this." Tillie's eyes pleaded with her mother's. "Don't do anything to make *Daed* leave again. He's home. That sheriff man is—is dead. This whole thing will just go away."

Levina narrowed her eyes at Tillie. "I didn't realize I did something to make *Daed* leave in the first place."

"That's not what I meant." Tillie hung her head.

Levina turned to Freda and waited for her to voice her opinion.

Freda looked at Tillie, then at Rosemary, and finally

back at Levina. "I think you need to ask him about it, *Mamm*. Otherwise it is going to bother you—the not knowing."

Levina was quiet for a moment. "Since all of you know . . ." She glared at Tillie. "As well as most of the town—I don't see how I can avoid talking to your father about this. No tellin' what sort of rumors are already spreading."

Freda let out a heavy sigh. "Well, I-I hate to say it, but there is already a nasty rumor floating around the district."

Levina's stomach dropped. *What now?*

CHAPTER NINETEEN

Levina paced the floor in the den for a long while after her daughters left. She'd been fighting back tears from the minute Freda informed them that folks not only thought Namman was on the run for a crime he'd committed in Ohio but also suspected he had another woman there. Levina had never felt so humiliated in her life . . . and she couldn't help but share some of their suspicions.

She thought about how things had been since Naaman's return. So loving, so passionate. Levina hadn't felt so alive and in love in years. To have a glimpse of what the rest of her life could be like, only to have it threatened by her own lack of trust, was not an option. She had to clear the air. Naaman had never told a lie in his life, that she knew about, so she tried to prepare herself for the truth—whatever that might be.

When he walked in about ten minutes later, Levina knew right away that something was wrong by the look on his face.

Naaman took off his hat and set it down on the coffee table, then he sat down on the couch. He put his head in his hands for a moment, then looked up at her and shook his head. "I don't understand it. Last week Mr. Lyman was all excited about carrying some of my furniture in his store. Today when we sat down to talk, he couldn't seem to look me in the eye, and then he told me that he already had too much inventory. I asked him about special orders, but he wasn't interested." Naaman rubbed his forehead. "He excused himself after our brief visit and said he had another appointment."

Levina sat down beside him. Despite all her worries, her heart hurt for Naaman. "I'm sorry, Naaman. I know you were hopeful about working with Mr. Lyman. But our income is fine, and—"

"It's not that. I know we're all right financially. But that represented part of our new beginning, and . . ." He paused. "I had the strangest feeling that Jonathan knew Mr. Lyman's reasons, but he wouldn't share them."

Levina couldn't decide if this was the worst possible time or the best to have the much needed conversation with Naaman. She wanted to wrap her arms around him, but darkness hung between them. For there to be peace, she knew, there had to be honesty.

"Naaman . . ."

He looked into her eyes, and Levina didn't think she had ever dreaded having a conversation with her husband this much. She took a deep breath. "People are talking around town. Lots of people."

Naaman furrowed his brow and sat up taller. "What people? What are they saying?"

Levina felt her heart beating way too fast. "They . . . they are saying you might have had a woman in Middlefield."

Naaman latched onto her shoulders. "Levina, no. Levina, no, no, no." He hung his head for a moment, then he looked back in her eyes, which were starting to tear up. "Never. I have no explanation for what I did, but I would never, ever betray our wedding vows. I've told you all this."

Levina knew she needed to bring up the sheriff, but one crisis at a time was all she could handle. "But you did betray our wedding vows when you left, Naaman." She pulled away from him and stood up. "And it's hard for me to trust you."

"Levina," he pleaded as he stood up. "I thought we were past all this. And folks will stop with these silly rumors. Surely you don't think I would—"

"I don't know anything anymore, Naaman!" She stomped her foot and let the tears pour down her face. "I don't know! I don't understand! I'm confused about everything!"

"Levina," he said tenderly as he tried to pull her to him. "Things have been so wonderful between us. This is the happiest I've ever been in my life. And I meant what I said. I will spend the rest of my life making it up to you. Please don't let this set us back. I love you so much."

She stepped back away from him and swiped at her eyes. "I love you, too, Naaman. And I've been happier than I can ever remember being."

"Then, Levina, let's don't worry about anyone else. It's just you and me, and I love you."

She sniffled and held her chin up slightly. "There's more, Naaman."

"More what? What are you talking about?"

"There's been a sheriff in town looking for you."

Naaman hung his head. "I figured that out when I saw an article in the newspaper about his death."

"What did you do, Naaman? Did you only come home because you were in trouble?"

"No! No, Levina."

They heard a car coming and turned toward the window. The timing couldn't have been worse.

Levina wiped her eyes on the sleeve of her dress and tried to gather herself. "Are you expecting anyone?"

"No."

Naaman looked like a broken man, and part of her wanted to comfort him, but she just stood there. Then she shuffled to the door, feeling more than a little broken herself. She looked through the screen and watched a woman getting out of a white four-door car. As the woman shuffled through the grass, she kept her head down, and Levina couldn't see her face. But when the woman reached up and dabbed at her eyes, Levina felt weak in the knees.

Now what? Why is an Englisch *woman here crying?*

When the woman reached the porch, Levina talked to her through the screen. "Can I help you?"

The woman was short and plump, with graying brown hair, and her eyes were heavy with sadness. "I'm looking for Naaman Lapp."

Before Levina could answer, Naaman was at the door. He eased Levina out of the way, pulled the screen door open, and embraced the woman. "Patsy, I'm so sorry. I'm so very sorry."

The woman cried harder as Naaman held her in his arms.

Levina didn't move, didn't speak. She felt like a stranger to her own husband at this moment.

Finally he pulled from the hug and motioned the woman inside. "Please sit down, Patsy." Then he turned to Levina. "Levina, this is Patsy."

As the woman sat down on the couch, Naaman continued. "And, Patsy, this is my wife, Levina."

Patsy raised her hand to Levina as she sniffled. "I've heard so much about you, dear. So many wonderful things."

Levina smiled and shook her hand, knowing she couldn't return the sentiment. She had no clue who this woman was.

Naaman sat down on the couch beside Patsy, and Levina slowly backed into a rocker in the corner and watched the scene unfold.

"Larry was a *gut* man, Patsy. He will be greatly missed."

Levina held her breath for a moment. *Larry?*

"He was indebted to you, Naaman." Patsy dabbed her eyes with a wrinkled tissue she had in her left hand. "He might not have known how to say it, but he loved you like a brother."

Naaman hung his head, then Patsy put her hand on his cheek.

"You are a good man, too, Naaman." She looked across the room at Levina. "I can't tell you how grateful we are that Naaman showed up in Middlefield." She shook her head.

Levina could barely force a smile as she struggled to put the pieces of this strange puzzle together.

"Of course he belonged here with you, Levina," the woman added. "And I knew the Lord would guide him back to his home." She smiled a bit. "But I'm so glad we met him first. Naaman introduced Larry to the Lord. I'd tried for our entire married life, but he had so many doubts." She turned back to Naaman. "I don't know what you said to him, Naaman, to make him turn his life over to God, but it gives me great peace to know that when Larry left this world he went to be with God."

Levina swallowed hard and thought about all the times she'd questioned God's plan.

Naaman's head was down as he spoke. "And we know that all things work together for good to them who love God, to them who are the called according to his purpose." Naaman looked up, smiling slightly. "It's not our way to minister, but from the time I met Larry, I felt the Lord guiding me to share my faith with him."

Patsy turned to Levina and eased into a smile. "We've been friends with Levi and Mary for years, and we were at their house having supper the evening that Naaman arrived. He and my Larry hit it off right away." Her expression grew somber. "They were both lost souls, each with his own problems. But I believe that sometimes the good Lord introduces people who can guide each other onto the path God has planned for them." Her face brightened a bit as she continued. "In the months that followed, Larry would drop by their house, and he and Naaman would talk for hours out in the barn while doing various projects. I don't know what those men talked about, but I do know this . . . Naaman is home where he belongs. And my Larry is with our Lord in heaven."

She took a deep breath, then she reached into the small black purse in her lap. "This is why Larry was looking for you." She pushed a small box in Naaman's direction. "You left before Larry had a chance to tell you good-bye, and it was important to him for you to have this."

Naaman eyed the small container, not bigger than a pillbox, and Levina watched him remove the small lid. His eyes watered almost instantly as he pulled out a man's gold ring.

Patsy put her hand on Namaan's. "I know you folks don't wear jewelry, but I believe you know why Larry got this ring?"

Levina watched her husband blink back tears. "*Ya*. His police department gave it to him because he saved a life."

Patsy patted Namaan's hand. "And Larry said you saved *his* life. He wanted you to have this as a remembrance." She pulled her hand back and placed it in her lap. "And I think, Naaman, that Larry just wanted to thank you in person. You left so quickly and all."

Naaman glanced at Levina, then back at Patsy. "When I knew it was right in my heart to come home, I just wanted to leave right then."

"I understand." Patsy stood up. "I need to go now."

Naaman and Levina both walked her to the door. Levina wondered how different life would have been for everyone if Naaman hadn't left. For starters, she and Naaman might have spent the rest of their lives the way they were before, instead of falling in love all over again and sharing a new honesty and intimacy that they'd never had. Would their oldest son have made a terrible mistake by leaving his own family at some point, if not for Naaman sharing his experience? And what about Larry Dozier? What if Mr. Dozier had never met Naaman Lapp?

"*A man's heart deviseth his way; but the Lord directeth his steps.*"

Levina smiled as the Scripture came into her head. The Lord always had a plan, and Levina felt more grounded in her faith than she had been in a long time. She'd been raised not to question the will of God, yet she had recently. But as the door closed behind Patsy, Levina felt a sense of calm that she hadn't felt the past few days.

She and Naaman waved as Patsy got into her car and pulled out of the driveway.

"I love you, Naaman." Levina touched her husband's cheek. "And Patsy is right. You are a *gut* man."

Naaman put his hand on top of hers and pressed her palm closer to his face. "I should have never left you."

Levina smiled. "It wonders me how differently things might have turned out if you hadn't." She pulled her hand from his face, intertwined her fingers with his. "I'm sorry I doubted you, Naaman."

He gave her hand a squeeze as he smiled back at her. "I don't blame you, Levina. My actions—"

"No, Naaman." She put a silencing finger to his lips. "My doubts drove a wedge between us." She cupped his cheek in her hand. "There must always be trust. From now on."

Naaman nodded as she pulled her hand away, then he gently kissed her on the lips.

After he slowly eased out of the kiss, Levina gently led him across the den, toward the stairs. "I think it's time for a nap." She winked at him as they headed upstairs.

CHAPTER TWENTY

Levina floated around her kitchen with the energy of a woman half her age and the heart of a giddy teenager in love. It had been almost a month since Patsy's visit, and since then, she and Naaman had resumed their role as newlyweds. They'd even flown a kite, but instead of doing it alone, they'd shared the experience with Adam and Hannah's children one afternoon while their son and his wife enjoyed some time alone together.

Levina and Naaman had agreed that there is no greater joy than to see happiness in the eyes of children at play. And it was refreshing to see Adam and Hannah's relationship taking on a new closeness that Levina could identify with. She was glad Adam and Naaman had patched things up and that Adam and Hannah had come for Saturday supper today along with the rest of her children, their spouses, and all her grandchildren.

Two weeks earlier Mr. Lyman had come to the house to talk to Naaman about stocking furniture at his store, and he apologized for listening to nasty rumors. The men shook on a deal, and Naaman was on top of the world. Their fields were filled with the promise of a bountiful harvest, and Levina wasn't sure life could be any grander. Today as her family gathered together for Saturday supper, festivity and fellowship were in the air.

After the meal the older children were playing a game of tag while the adults sat around the picnic tables outside. Levina was holding Leah. Sunshine mixed with a cool breeze to make for a perfect day.

"I have some news," Tillie announced as she grinned at Rufus.

Levina smiled as she readjusted Leah in her arms. She'd noticed all afternoon a certain "glow" about her youngest daughter. "What's that, Tillie?"

Tillie stood up from the picnic table and bounced on her toes, as she was known to do. A smile filled her face as she blurted, "We're in the family way!"

"*Ach*, Tillie! That's wonderful news!" Levina handed Leah to Rosemary, then she walked to Tillie and gave her a hug. "I suspected as much," she whispered to Tillie, who just giggled.

"So, *Daed*. I was wondering about that beautiful chest you just made, the one in the barn." Tillie giggled. "The one perfect for a baby's room!"

Naaman grinned. "Well, Tillie, I reckon—"

"Wait a minute!" Freda stood up. "I have news too."

Levina brought her hand to her chest and wondered how she could have missed it. She'd known every time that Rosemary was pregnant as well as both her daughters-in-law. Could it be . . . ?

"I am also in the family way!" And to everyone's surprise, Freda began to jump up and down.

"Oh my!" Levina ran to her other daughter. "*Two* new grandbabies for me to love!" She threw her arms around Freda. "I'm so happy for you, Freda."

Freda eased out of the hug and turned to Naaman. "And I'm the oldest. I think I should have the chest."

Naaman's face split into a wide grin, and Levina wasn't sure if it was because both his young daughters were with child or because they both wanted the chest he'd worked so hard on.

"No, no." Tillie wagged a finger at Freda playfully. "I asked first."

Freda thrust her hands on her hips. "I say whoever's baby comes first should have the chest. When are you due, Tillie?"

"March the second. When are you due?"

Freda frowned. "That's the same day I'm due!"

But instead of bickering, Tillie and Freda hugged each other.

"How exciting for us," Tillie said. "This will be so fun."

"*Ya, ya,*" Freda said, smiling.

Naaman stood up and looped his thumbs under his suspenders. "Well, this will give me plenty of time to make a second chest. Then both my girls will have a new chest of drawers for these new additions to our family." He glanced around at his family. "And I'll start on the new piece of furniture as soon as I get back from my trip."

Levina couldn't breathe. She couldn't move. *What trip?* She reminded herself that she trusted her husband, and she refused to allow herself to take a step backward, but as she waited for him to go on, her heart thudded against her chest. No one spoke, and Levina kept her eyes locked with Naaman's as she spoke in a whisper. "What trip?"

Naaman glanced around at their children and grandchildren. "I'm afraid that all of you will have to do without me for two weeks."

He walked closer to Levina, and she was relieved to hear him say he would only be gone for two weeks. *But where?*

Naaman put his arm around her and stood taller. "And you're all going to have to do without your *mamm* for two weeks too." He reached into his pocket and held up a small envelope, then waved it in the air as he grinned. "Because we will be traveling by bus to Florida." He smiled at Levina, gazing into her eyes as he spoke. "Your mother wants to see the ocean."

Levina gasped as she threw her arms around his neck. "*Ach*, Naaman!"

He gently eased her away, then kissed her on the lips.

"*Ach*, stop! Your *kinner* are watching!" Tillie giggled, and Levina heard the rest of her loved ones snickering and poking playful fun.

She didn't care. She kissed her husband again. "I love you, Naaman."

He held her tight. "I love you, too, *mei leib*."

ACKNOWLEDGMENTS

KELLY LONG:

I'd like to acknowledge my editor, Natalie Hanemann, that encourager of words! Thank you for listening . . . Beth Wiseman and Kathy Fuller, two delicious word users . . . LB Norton, my line editor . . . Dan Miller, my Amish consultant and good ear . . . Brenda Lott, my critique partner and encourager . . . my family, both near and far . . . and, most importantly, the living God who has given me the opportunity to write for Him.

KATHY FULLER:

There are so many people to thank for helping me tell Ellie and Christopher's story. Thank you to my wonderful and insightful editors, Natalie Hanemann and LB Norton, for their advice, encouragement, and direction. To my agent, Tamela, who is always just a phone call away. To Cecelia Dowdy for reviewing the story and for answering my questions about living with someone who is visually impaired. To my former student, Hannah Bowser, who for four years allowed me a glimpse of the world through her eyes. A big thank-you to Beth Wiseman and especially Barbie Beiler for reading over the manuscript and helping me with the details. And to my wonderful friend and critique partner, Jill Eileen Smith. Thank you for making sure I kept the story on track and for your invaluable feedback.

BETH WISEMAN:

To my husband and best friend, Patrick. You rock, baby! And I couldn't write these books without the support of my family and friends—or without my mother-in-law, who cooks for us twice a week. Love you all! Heartfelt thanks to Barbie Beiler, the folks at Thomas Nelson, and particularly to my editor, Natalie Hanemann, who holds a special place in my heart. Kathy and Kelly, such an honor to work with both of you on this collaboration. And LB Norton, it is always a pleasure to work with you! Special thanks to my mom, who continues to inspire and encourage me. I love you, Mother, and I think Daddy is smiling from heaven. To my agent, Mary Sue Seymour—thanks for all you do, my friend. Blessed be to God, who continues to put the stories in my head that He wants me to share.

OTHER NOVELS BY THE AUTHORS

ABOUT THE AUTHORS

KELLY LONG is the author of *Sarah's Garden*, the first novel in the Patch of Heaven series. She was born and raised in the mountains of Northern Pennsylvania. She's been married for nearly twenty-five years and has five children.

. . .

KATHLEEN FULLER is the author of the best—selling novels *A Man of His Word* and *An Honest Love*. When she's not writing, she enjoys traveling and spending time with her family and farm pets.

. . .

BETH WISEMAN is hailed as a top voice in Amish fiction. She is the author of numerous bestsellers including the Daughters of the Promise series and the Land of Canaan series. She and her family live in Texas.